ALSO BY ALLEN DRURY

The Advise and Consent Series

ADVISE AND CONSENT
A SHADE OF DIFFERENCE
CAPABLE OF HONOR
PRESERVE AND PROTECT
COME NINEVEH, COME TYRE
THE PROMISE OF JOY

Other Washington Novels

ANNA HASTINGS
MARK COFFIN, U.S.S.
THE HILL OF SUMMER
THE ROADS OF EARTH
DECISION
PENTAGON

Novels of Ancient Egypt

A GOD AGAINST THE GODS
RETURN TO THEBES

The University Novels

TOWARD WHAT BRIGHT GLORY?
INTO WHAT FAR HARBOR?

Other Novels

THAT SUMMER: A CALIFORNIA NOVEL
THE THRONE OF SATURN: A NOVEL OF SPACE AND POLITICS

Nonfiction

A SENATE JOURNAL
THREE KIDS IN A CART
"A VERY STRANGE SOCIETY"
COURAGE AND HESITATION (WITH FRED MAROON)
EGYPT: THE ETERNAL SMILE (WITH ALEX GOTFRYD)

ALLEN DRURY

A THING OF STATE

A NOVEL

A LISA DREW BOOK

SCRIBNER

NEW YORK   LONDON   TORONTO   SYDNEY   TOKYO   SINGAPORE

SCRIBNER
1230 Avenue of the Americas
New York, NY 10020

DESIGNED BY ERICH HOBBING

Manufactured in the United States of America

1   3   5   7   9   10   8   6   4   2

Library of Congress Cataloging-in-Publication Data
Drury, Allen.
A thing of State : a novel / Allen Drury.
p.   cm.
"A Lisa Drew book."
I. Title.
PS3554.R8T45 1995
813'.54—dc20   95-8857
CIP

ISBN 0-684-80702-5

To my sister Anne
Number One fan and lifelong best friend

"Not . . . Any Actual Nation, Living or Dead"

The standard disclaimer appears in many novels, including this one: No character is based upon any actual person, living or dead. Some might suggest the addition here: Greater Lolómé and Lesser Lolómé are not based upon any actual nation, living or dead.

And yet, why bother?

It isn't that the living examples are so few that any particular one can justifiably be singled out as inspiration for this novel.

It is that there are so many that it is impossible to say which contributed most to the composites that became my fictitious Greater and Lesser Lolómés.

How many Greater Lolómés do we have, for instance? Iraq, Iran, Somalia, North Korea, Serbia, Russia, India, and China, just to get the ball rolling. And Lesser Lolómés? Kuwait, South Korea, Bosnia, Chechnya, Kashmir, and Tibet, for starters.

No doubt the news will bring us several more of each by morning.

And of American administrations—caught in the middle, lost and blundering in a world of such furious animosities and reviving imperialisms, always in recent years tentative and uncertain, hesitant and unsure, in search of an elusive peace that can only be achieved by facing up to, not sliding out from under, its harsh and rigorous demands.

This manuscript was delivered to the publisher in September 1994, but time is relatively unimportant here. Spin the wheel on any of three recent American Presidents, two Democratic, one Republican, and the story is the same.

Stop at almost any day—it will be a day of noisy American threat, empty American bluster, futile American bluff and bombastic statements of high, but quickly abandoned, American principle.

Stop at almost any day—it will be a day of American ducking, dodging, weaseling, double-talk, retreat, and evasion of great-power responsibility—anything to avoid biting the bullet—or grasping the nettle—or whatever metaphor you want to use for having the simple guts to exercise American power, as a great power must exercise it if it wishes to remain a great power.

Such is the state of affairs as the old millennium ends and the new begins. The wheel spins, the cycle repeats. Yesterday's history is today's and tomorrow's. The more it changes, to quote the ever-cynical but frequently accurate French, the more it is the same thing.

Therein—not in any one day or any one nation but in most days and many nations of this unhappy era—lies the inspiration to sit upon the ground and tell sad stories of the death of kings and the decline of great states. The pattern, unchanging, grinds on. Only genuine courage, foresight, and unflinching firmness in the just and judicious use of power can reverse it.

In these days when the men who hold power in Washington are afraid to use it, either from fundamental lack of character or an overweening desire to win votes—or both—courage, foresight, and unflinching firmness are far from being in control of the foreign policies of the United States of America.

No one nation, no one act of equivocation, provided the inspiration here.

Nowadays, it is everywhere.

ALLEN DRURY

PRINCIPAL CHARACTERS IN THE NOVEL

IN WASHINGTON

At the State Department

Raymond Cass Stanley, Secretary of State

Mary, his wife, former ambassador to Egypt

Elizabeth ("Bets"), their daughter

Samir Hashimi, her husband

Basil Rifkin, Counselor

Hugo Mallerbie, Undersecretary for International Security Affairs

Brad Temple, Undersecretary for Political Affairs

Gage McGregor, director, policy planning

Joan Cohn-Bourassa, Assistant Secretary for Near Eastern Affairs

Achmed ("Boo") Bourassa, her husband

Reginald Pennebaker ("Penny") Sims, former Secretary of State

At the White House

The President

The First Lady

The Vice President

Jaime Serrano, National Security Adviser

At the Pentagon

Arlie McGregor, Secretary of Defense

Gen. Wilson Rathbun, chairman, Joint Chiefs

On the Hill

Senator Richard Emmett ("Willie") Wilson, of California, chairman, Senate Foreign Relations Committee

Rep. John Jones of Alabama, chairman, House Appropriations Subcommittee on the State Department

In the Media

James Van Rensselaer Burden, columnist and pundit: "As I See It"

Kelly Able Montague, anchorman and creator of "Washington Wrangle" and "WorldView"

Sally Holliwell, network congressional correspondent: "Capitol Perspective"

Timothy Bates, columnist and pundit: "It Seems to Me"

In the Diplomatic Corps

Li Peng Liu, ambassador, People's Republic of China

Vladimir Novotny, ambassador, Second Soviet Republic

Georges Marranne, ambassador of France

Sir Anthony Marsden, ambassador of Great Britain

Kwazze Kumbatta ("KWA-zee Koom-BAH-tah"), Secretary-General, United Nations

In Georgetown

Dolly Munson, a hostess

IN GREATER LOLÓMÉ

In the "Pink House"

Sidi bin Sidi bin Sidi, The Wearer of the Two Hats, Light of the Horizon, Supreme Commander and President for Life of All the Peoples of Lolómé; "Seedy Sidi"

Sidi bin Sidi bin Sidi bin Sidi, his son; "Young Sidi"; "Jerk, Junior"

In the American Embassy

William ("Big Bill") Bullock, ambassador and contributor

Creed Moncrief, CIA, "assistant to the ambassador"

IN LESSER LOLÓMÉ

In the Palace

Sheikh Mustafa bin Muhammed, Descendant of the Prophet, Eternal Ruler; "The Mouse"

In the American Embassy

Arthur Reeves Burton, ambassador

ONE

P ointe Sinistre lies at the southern end of the Bay of Lolómé, a two-mile-long succession of gradually diminishing stone escarpments that look from a distance as though a school of giant dolphins had piled one atop another and decided to go to sleep there. The highest and largest abuts the stark scrub-clad Mountains of Lolómé that separate the barren coast from the desert interior. The smallest, at the foot of the mountains, plunges into the perpetually boiling sea.

It is a setting made for drama. Many have taken place there over the centuries. On this day in spring when the calendar is racing toward the year 2000, the newest and perhaps most ominous will presently engage the attentions of the entire world and particularly those of the President and State Department of the United States of America.

For America, for Greater (and Lesser) Lolómé, and indeed for everyone on the face of the planet, it is the worst of times.

There is no "best" to counterbalance. The best is in hiding, under fire, trying to escape, suffering agonies, dying under torture, being "ethnically cleansed" from homes and cities, starving, succumbing to shotgun wounds on battlefields, in streets and schoolyards, being exploded by bombs, subjected to mental and physical abuse, rape, battery, incest, expiring by the hundreds and thousands every day as a result of crimes occasionally understandable but far more often capricious, wayward, and, in a curiously weird sense, carefree.

Hypocrisy, Greed, Corruption, and Cruelty ride the globe. In every land, on every sea, the good and the well intentioned struggle endlessly against the forces of dissolution and chaos that attack their societies. Nowhere in all the vast expanse of humanity's desperate strivings is there any really convincing evidence for hope.

Hope, like God, exists because humanity cannot endure the ghastly closing years of the terrible twentieth century without it. But even a partial roll call of humanity's agonies discloses how flimsy are the foundations upon which it rests.

In such a world there are, of course, those who profit and survive quite happily.

They are people like The Wearer of the Two Hats, Light of the Horizon, Supreme Commander and President for Life of All the Peoples of Lolómé, Sidi bin Sidi bin Sidi, who sits on the highest peak of Pointe Sinistre in his heavily fortified pink concrete fortress and thumbs his nose at the United States and its annoying President, at the United Nations, and at everyone else, including many, desperate but defeated, in his own land.

His domain is not, to the casual glance, all that important. It is only geography—and, more recently, his newfound, evil friends—who have made Greater Lolómé important to the world; that, and Sidi's long-standing ambition to conquer and absorb annoying Lesser Lolómé, which sits like an angry boil atop the misshapen "head" that the fanciful can see in the map of Greater Lolómé.

Greater Lolómé is actually a rather small part of the earth's surface; it is "Greater" by definition of its President, which he has persuaded the world to accept. It certainly does have many more square miles of desolate emptiness than Lesser Lolómé. Unfortunately, however, it is Lesser Lolómé that has the oil.

Greater Lolómé has almost none. Greater Lolómé has strategic position, but this, if truth were ever told in international affairs, is about all there is to Greater Lolómé and its approximately ten million illiterate, poverty-stricken, barely subsisting tribal peoples.

But due to the devious shrewdness and grimly unrelenting tenacity of The Wearer of the Two Hats, Light of the Horizon, Supreme Commander and President for Life of All the Peoples of Lolómé, Sidi bin Sidi bin Sidi, Greater Lolómé now looms much larger on the world scene than many a nation ten times its size and ten times higher up the ladder of civilization.

"Civilization," indeed, is not a word to be applied lightly to any nation in these final years of the twentieth century, let alone one so backward and so supremely touchy as Greater Lolómé. The very word is suspect. It is unfair, unjust, prejudicial, subtly and insidiously Eurocentric. "Civilization" by whose definition? "Civilization" on whose terms?

The word, when used to subtly but definitely derogate Greater Lolómé, does not take into account the major achievements of its peoples—their overwhelming and unstoppable urge to breed and breed and breed, regardless of the fact that if the population were one-third its present size it still would not have enough to live on . . . its peoples' deep love of the land and their deep respect for nature, as shown by the haphazard and indiscriminate grazing and hunting that over the centuries have resulted in the destruction of most of its major wildlife, virtually all of its major vegetation, and nine-tenths of its arable topsoil . . . and the reverence for human life—and the tourist dollar—that have preserved the ancient but still officially sanctioned rituals that periodically destroy several hundred of its most promising and most rebellious youths . . . all of those things, in fact, which prompt the secret, and sometimes not-so-secret, admiration with which Greater Lolómé's admirers compare its simple, instinctively-at-one-with-nature ways with the crippled commercialism of their own "civilization" in the West.

It is no wonder, then, that Sidi bin Sidi bin Sidi sits in his bristling pink concrete compound—"the Pink House," a reference as instantly recognizable throughout the world as "the White House"—and thumbs his nose at the United States and at all who agree with its critical official approach to his country and particularly to himself. He knows he has the sneaking, if not always openly expressed, admiration of his part of the world, and of many in the West too.

It is a time for the thumbing of noses, a time for the collapse of "civilizations," a time for the schemes of Sidi bin Sidi bin Sidi and all like him, everywhere.

"When you look around the world," as Sidi's fellow President, he of the United States, often says, "what do you see? One hell of a mess, one hell of an unrelieved, ghastly, fucking mess. How the hell are we ever going to get out of it?"

In the case of this President, the use of the pronoun *we* has a much wider application than it does when used by President Sidi bin Sidi bin Sidi. The President of the United States, or POTUS, as he is referred to in the language of his own Secret Service, of necessity takes a broader view than the President of Greater Lolómé, or POGL. But not even the POTUS, at this juncture, can contribute as much to the world's growing disarray and ever-growing chaos as the POGL (whom the POTUS refers to, in moments of real exasperation, as "Old Three Esses," or "Seedy Sidi").

It is not surprising, perhaps, that the chaos of the world, creeping across every border, challenging the stability of every nation, eroding the safety and the stability of every society and every people, should have brought to power such a man as The Wearer of the Two Hats, Light of the Horizon, Supreme Commander and President for Life of All the Peoples of Lolómé, Sidi bin Sidi bin Sidi.

For thirty-eight of his forty-seven years he was known in his desert tribe, and in the army which he joined at eighteen, simply as Sidi Muhammed Bakki. It is only in the last nine that he has proclaimed himself to be Sidi bin Sidi bin Sidi, which in Arabic means Sidi son of Sidi son of Sidi. His proclamation establishing this name was ostensibly to honor his father and grandfather, ignorant wanderers of the desert. Sophisticated and skeptical observers, of whom there are many among the media covering the area, are sure that this was only a preliminary to declaring himself king or emperor, probably under the title Sidi III, which would give him a ready-made dynasty and further his obvious intention that his son, Sidi bin Sidi bin Sidi bin Sidi, should succeed him.

"Young Sidi," as he is known (or "Jerk, Junior," to POTUS), has come home from a happy four years as a drunken womanizer at Harvard University to become general and commander of his father's Special Guard. He has already made it clear that his talents in the fields of corruption, torture, rapine, and general mayhem are equal to, if not greater than, his father's. So the instant dynasty idea is logical. Monarch and heir are already in place, and all seems set for many more years of cruel and ruthless tyranny over Greater Lolómé.

Except, of course, for the evil Americans, whose constant fulminations against him give Sidi bin Sidi bin Sidi his only real uneasiness. Agents of the Great Satan have tried to unseat him before, without success, but they are not giving up. It is only the unexpected assistance just offered him by one (or is it more?) of the region's major monsters that give him the renewed energy and greatly expanded military muscle to meet the Great Satan's continuing onslaught.

So far, this is secret to the world; but unknown at the moment to Sidi, the technological devils of the West have struck again. The word has already reached Washington, and busy minds are at work trying to devise a response.

It will be an interesting battle of wills in which only Sidi's iron nerve and desert shrewdness will once again sustain him in a contest of whose successful outcome he will be quite sure . . . although not, of course, *entirely* sure. There is always the chance that Washington may outsmart him. On the basis of past performance in the area, this is not likely; but it cannot be ruled out. It will almost surely feature another attempt by America to use the ruler of Lesser Lolómé in its sinister games—a weak reed, Sidi thinks contemptuously, if ever there was one.

Sheikh Mustafa bin Muhammed, Descendant of the Prophet and Eternal Ruler of Lesser Lolómé (known to POTUS and world media as "The Mouse"), is one more in the string of mad old men in camel-hair caftans who have so greatly disrupted the region and the world in recent years. He is a tiny, shrunken, seemingly somnolent eighty-five-year-old, a weird fanatic whose whispery old voice has a hypnotic effect upon his own peoples and many others in the area. His principal achievement recently has been to father his 107th child, a daughter, at age eighty-three.

In Washington they will soon be debating whether his preservation in power is worth having the ambassador to Greater Lolómé, William "Big Bill" Bullock, "campaign contributor supremo," as he is referred to dryly in the professional Foreign Service, approach Sidi and threaten him with dire consequences if he attempts any attack on The Mouse.

Such a mission, if ordered, will be one of the things the President will mean at a Rose Garden photo opportunity when he responds solemnly to his clamorous questioners of the media that he is "considering several different options . . . but will definitely rule out any use of American troops. . . ."

The Mouse has served American interests before, and now, as he sits in his palace—not quite so grand, but equally as fortified, as Sidi's pink excrescence—he is thinking in his shrewd little mind that he will, if the occasion arises again, be equally compliant, but, this time, will exact a greater price for it than he has before.

There have been times, particularly on the occasion four years ago when Sidi attempted to take a page from the book of his secret patron and launch an outright assault on Lesser Lolómé, when The Mouse was so grateful for American aid that he asked from America only the gift of continued independence for himself, his extended family, and the patch of enormously oil-rich desert Allah has seen fit to give them. To his secret bafflement, this was all that America wanted—just that Lesser Lolómé continue to produce relatively low-priced oil and to act, as its geographic position has given it the ability to do, as a barrier against onslaughts by Greater Lolómé upon oil producers farther north who are even more wealthy and even more destructive of "human rights" than he is.

"Human rights" form a concept that not only The Mouse and his family, but also Sidi and the great majority of their fellow rulers of sand and palm find hard to understand. *They* all have *their* rights, and that seems sufficient to them. The proposition that their subjects might have some too seems the most outrageous affront to common sense that they could possibly imagine. Mustafa bin Muhammed takes care of his people in every material way, giving each of them out of his own oil-rich pockets an annual stipend enormous by their standards, providing those who wish to leave the desert with free public housing, building major highways (one north-south and one east-west), airports, and monumental buildings each adorned with his own mammoth statue, dispensing the bounties of the desert with a firm and evenhanded generosity. If this means that they must submit also to the most rigorous control of their thoughts and actions, if it means that they must dutifully bow down and worship the autocratic decrees (and sometimes rather odd sexual preferences) of Mustafa bin Muhammed, Sidi bin Sidi bin Sidi, and all the rest of their autocratic fellow rulers, well, that seems to The Mouse and his likes a modest price for their peoples to pay.

"Human rights" form a nice concept for the self-righteous Americans to rant on about, but The Mouse often wonders why they do it. Their own record is not always that great, and why they think they have a right to impose their own special version of "human rights" upon everyone else he cannot understand. It only makes him, and all who must bear the brunt of the constant flood of pious preachings from Washington, restive and contemptuous—particularly when America's own interests are involved.

On the occasion when America's show of force saved The Mouse from being swallowed by the President of Greater Lolómé, the United States could have used the opportunity to enforce some genuine rights upon Lesser Lolómé—to insist on the establishment of a genuinely representative, democratic legislature, for instance—to require Mustafa and the hundreds of what the present President of the United States refers to privately as "his Rolls-Royce relatives" to abandon some of their selfishly profligate habits and adopt a more circumspect way of life—to establish a genuine system of justice, doing away with the harsh and lethal punishments which are meted out automatically for the most minor infractions of Mustafa's laws and proclamations—in short, to generally loosen up and lighten up one of the area's most oppressive tyrannies.

But America did not do this. Its then President, greatly enamored of the cousinship of kings and always desperately seeking "the stability thing" in any international crisis, did not wish to be too harsh with his fellow head of state, Sheikh Mustafa. Also he was too busy nurturing the myth of "joint United Nations action" as a shield behind which to hide (as The Mouse, Sidi, and their fellow tyrants construed it) American hesitations and cowardice. And so the moment for change—and for courage—passed. And in the minds of The Mouse, Sidi, and all their fellow rulers, America went down still another notch in the subtle ranking of fear and respect by which men and events in their area (and, indeed, throughout the world) have been judged, and responded to, as far back as history runs.

Next time, Sheikh Mustafa tells himself as he studies with great unease the reports his spies have brought back this day from Greater Lolómé, he will demand of America that it assist him not only in turning back any renewed assault from his southern neighbor but also that it will get rid of Sidi once and for all. The Mouse also has an heir—twenty or thirty of them, actually, all fine, well-educated, shrewd young men with glib British accents and three-thousand-dollar tailor-made British suits, skilled in evasion, deceit, and the ruthless, insidious ways of their region's ancient diplomacy. From their ranks he is ready to choose a ruler for Greater Lolómé.

When Sidi bin Sidi bin Sidi and Jerk, Junior, have been staked out in the desert for the buzzards to pick out their eyes and entrails and ants to eat the rest, The Mouse will be ready to name a favorite son to assume the throne of Greater Lolómé, and in due course, upon his own demise, reunite the two countries into that truly Great Lolómé from which they were originally carved by the ignorant pens of the impatient British, back in the days before an ironic Allah—too late for Western recapture—revealed exactly what lay beneath the endless, empty wastes.

No one in the region except Sidi and The Mouse knows at this moment the potentials for new troubles that have suddenly developed. But even so, there is a sudden ominous tension that seems to be occurring throughout the region. No one outside the two Lolómés (and the nasty powers responsible for it) has anything solid upon which to base apprehension, but in every capital the instinct, subtle as a fleeting desert wind at twilight, is beginning to alert them all. Most do not know where the threat will come from, when it will burst into the open, but many are becoming convinced that it is there. In that chaotic part of the world anything can happen at any time. It has, from time immemorial, and it will, into time unforeseeable.

In Washington, too, the tension is rising. Everything, these days, comes back to Washington, where men and women, burdened with the constantly demanding problems of their own troubled land, would give anything if they could to be left alone to take care of their own national housekeeping without having to worry about everyone else's. But at this point in history, they seem to have no choice.

"Somebody has to do it," the incumbent President of the United States says with a weary irony, aware that the way America does it is not always, by any means, the wisest, the soundest, the most constructive— "But," as he adds with a troubled sigh, "there doesn't seem to be anybody else."

This attitude, which is often articulated publicly in the White House, the Congress, the media, and by the average citizenry of the great Republic, often draws scathing rejoinders from other peoples resentful of what seems to be complacent, egotistical, unasked-for burden-carrying.

They do not see the fears and uncertainties that underlie it.

America at heart is no more confident than anyone else.

But somebody has to do it.

And nobody can do it better.

Or so America's leaders manage to persuade themselves.

---

1 Not, of course, that all of them felt that way.

Certainly he did not, Secretary of State Raymond Cass Stanley reminded himself as he stood on the terrace outside his seventh-floor office atop the department's Main Building at 2201 C Street, N.W., in Foggy Bottom.

Across the Potomac he could see, on this spring-bright day, the equally enormous domain of his principal domestic antagonist, Secretary of Defense Arlie McGregor.

Arlie and the Pentagon, though bitterly upset, greatly alarmed, and considerably diminished by the headlong, unilateral American disarmament of the Clinton years, still thought they ran the world. Ray Stanley knew *he* didn't. In fact, despite his forty years of steady advancement up the ladder of the Foreign Service, the world's incorrigible intransigence continued to surprise him every day. No sensible man could afford to be arrogant in the face of its myriad insane uncertainties.

If Arlie and his sidekick, Gen. Wilson Rathbun, chairman of the Joint Chiefs of Staff, had an ounce of humility, Ray Stanley thought tartly now, they would be as startled, dismayed, and flabbergasted as he was by the news just conveyed to him by the Deputy Secretary of State, Eula Lee Montgomery.

Eula Lee ("Eulie," as she was universally known throughout the beehive of busy offices beneath his feet, and "Lulie" to him after four decades together in the Foreign Service) was not one to be overly taken aback by events. Yet even she, six feet two and 235 pounds of outwardly monumental black calm, had been a little perturbed when she brought him the just-decoded message from the embassy in Greater Lolómé, fifteen minutes ago.

"That bastard," she said, not bothering to identify which of the many bastards the United States had to face these days—nor did she need to, there was one who for years had indisputably been first among equals—"is doing it again. When are we going to kick that smug ape's butt once and for all?"

The question hung in the air, almost visibly dripping with the icicles of her contempt. People in Washington—people everywhere—had been asking the question for years. Each new administration took office secretly determined to do it. Each found endless reasons why it could not be done.

Eulie, who talked like a trooper in the privacy of top-level offices no matter how much she sounded like a Baptist preacher on the public platform, repeated her exasperated query:

"When are we going to kick that smug ape's butt once and for all?"

Raymond Cass Stanley sighed and resorted to his standard gesture in moments of stress, removing his glasses from their usual perch atop his leonine head and cleaning them on the underside of his tie.

"Now, Lulie," he said mildly, "you know very well we can't do anything without the support of our friends across the river"—he nodded toward the Pentagon—"and *his* support"—his nod swung back in the general direction of the White House, hidden from them by the trees and buildings of Pennsylvania Avenue—"and we haven't got either. Furthermore, I don't think, myself, that we should move too hastily to—"

"Ray," she interrupted with the familiarity born of three joint posts in the Middle East and many years together in the department, "you wouldn't touch a fly in Arabia if you had your druthers, let alone that murderous thug, and you know it. He knows it, everybody in the Middle East knows it, everybody in this town knows it. Why else do they think they can push State around the way they do? It's a disgrace."

"Sometimes," he said, still mildly, though as always with Eulie, tempted to respond as bluntly as she, "State does the pushing and sometimes we get pushed. I think it balances out pretty well in the long run."

She uttered the famous disgusted "Tsssk!" through her teeth which encompassed everything from mild annoyance to all-out expletive, depending on her tone, and shook her head angrily.

"Don't be a pantywaist, Ray," she advised. "Stand up to 'em. Stand up to 'em! I suppose there'll be a National Security Council meeting about it. I want you to take me with you."

"That will upset Arlie and Bill Rathbun," he said with a smile. "And maybe the President as well. Are you sure you want to barge in?"

"Will they kick me out?" she demanded.

"I doubt it," he said, smile broadening. "They know you."

"All right," she said with satisfaction. "Let me know as soon as you get the word."

"I will," he promised. "How's Herbie?"

At this reference to her quiet little husband, retired after many years as a leading lawyer in the office of the counsel of the department and now suffering from pancreatic cancer in their beautiful Federal-era home in Georgetown, her stern expression suddenly crumpled.

"Not good, Ray," she said soberly. "Pray for him."

"I do, Lulie," he said softly. "I do."

"Thank you," she said, turning away, but not before he caught the glint of tears. "You're a good man, Ray. Now," she said, suddenly brisk again as she sailed grandly out the door, "let's see some action on Lolómé."

But action on Lolómé, he reflected now as he turned away from the terrace and returned to his desk, was easier said than done. And Eulie symbolized exactly why. So did many others who, on this day as on almost every other day in the calendar as the twentieth century hurtled toward its close, carried the possibility of disaster for the world and the certainty of confusion—political, diplomatic, ethical, and moral—for the great Republic.

Not in Jaime Serrano's mind, however, Ray Stanley told himself with some annoyance as he waited for the national security adviser's call from the White House. This sort of thing was tailor-made for Jaime, who loved nothing so much as a crisis he could manage—or at least stage-manage, the Secretary of State thought scornfully.

Jaime Serrano was a naturalized Cuban American who had come over in the first wave of Castro escapees and, aided by his wife's fortune, had promptly made a killing in Florida real estate by bilking his fellow countrymen in ways that by now were buried deep, or lost, in the records and legends of Dade County. Out of it he had emerged as owner of a sizable section of the city of Miami, half a dozen suburban throwaway advertising newspapers, and a great desire, hitherto undisclosed, to be a mover and shaker in international affairs. The ultimate objective, never expressed and always denied, was of course to return to Cuba as President.

How he had progressed from Dade County to the powerful post of national security adviser was one of those Washington stories that rarely made any sense in any context outside Washington but could easily be understood there. It began with a $200,000 campaign contribution and wound up with Jaime as Assistant Secretary of State for Latin American Affairs.

Jaime's small, dark, bustling figure and the considerably larger figure of his wife, the former Maria Christina Delgado, scion of a wealthy family whose members had also fled Cuba in the first wave on the eve of the downfall of Fulgencio Batista, soon became fixtures on the Washington social scene. Jaime also emerged as one of the most articulate witnesses before the Senate and House committees dealing with the development, oversight, and funding of international policies and actions.

And, much to the not-always-concealed surprise of his friends and supporters, one of the most intelligent and farsighted, too.

"You see?" he had once whispered to Raymond Cass Stanley when they were appearing together before the Senate Foreign Affairs Committee to testify on the foreign aid bill, "It ees not jus' Maria's money! I make sense for me, too!"

"That's right, Jaime," Ray Stanley conceded with a smile. "That you do."

And that he did, until suddenly one day the previous national security adviser ran afoul of the First Lady in some still unclear fashion and, for reasons known only to the frequently unknowable gentleman who sat in the Oval Office, a finger reached down as in a Michelangelo painting and touched the finger of Assistant Secretary Serrano and suddenly, presto-chango, he was national security adviser.

He had now been in office almost a year, and his record, Ray Stanley had to concede, was really quite good. As a personality he was inclined to be interfering, aggressive, sometimes explosive, and more often than not inclined to be dictatorial toward State—"a real pain in the you-know-what," as Eulie sometimes remarked, although his basic good nature usually came to his rescue. Like most people, she too had to concede that he did his job with competence and some really genuine insights into the complex international situations that confronted his employer.

As such, he was apparently set to remain in office as long as the President did; which, according to whatever poll you read over morning coffee, might or might not be another four years.

The only thing he really found a little annoying about Jaime, Ray Stanley often thought, was the fact that he had risen to his present eminence without the sort of profoundly valuable preparation which he, Ray Stanley, felt he himself had gone through. Not that he would have willingly given up the office of SecState, of course, that was the cap all Foreign Service regulars dreamed of for their outwardly glamorous but often rather bleak and boring careers; he did not envy the national security adviser's headaches, though he sometimes envied him the power that was able to give Ray Stanley headaches. But it did seem that sometimes people who didn't deserve influence in foreign affairs acquired it by means far from the patient service and diligent loyalty to U.S. interests that had characterized his and Mary's careers, Eulie's, and that of many thousands in the Foreign Service and in the civil service categories that worked with, and for, the F.S.

When he had emerged from the University of Michigan, which he had attended as a very young World War II veteran under the G.I. Bill of Rights, Raymond Cass Stanley had at first thought he would go into law, at that time still a well-thought-of profession not yet sullied by the burst of wildly irresponsible, lawyer-encouraged litigation that would come later. Quite by accident—he was to learn later that many and many a career in the Foreign Service had begun "quite by accident"—he had been "dragged," as he put it humorously in many of his public speeches over the years—to a lecture by the then Secretary of State. Since the dragging was done by the girl he hoped to marry, Ray Stanley went along.

Mary Porter was very pretty, very bright, and very determined; and long, lean, lanky Ray soon realized that he was going to have to pay considerable attention to her ambitions if he wanted to blend them with his own. He had never been particularly interested in foreign affairs except as everyone was involved in them in those days simply by the sheer overwhelming impact of the war, but that was Mary's field of study, and that was what she wanted him to go into. It was what she intended to do herself, and if he wanted to come along and be a part of her life, he had better get moving. She was leaving for Washington within a week after graduation to apply for the Foreign Service.

That precipitated everything. A hitherto shy Ray proposed, Mary accepted instantly, they wired her parents in Chicago and his in Indiana, appeared before a judge three days later, and as the week expired, were on a train en route to D.C. Today, Mary was still very pretty, very bright, and very determined; and Ray, still long and lanky, if no longer quite so lean, was Secretary of State, after the recent three-year period, so well publicized in the media, during which they had simultaneously been ambassadors, she to Egypt and he to Greece. After that, she had retired but was still credited in Washington gossip with "running the department"; and he was sometimes dismissed patronizingly by the media as a "nice, mild, rather dull, and not very forceful Secretary"—except for two things.

The first was that, more successfully than anyone since Dean Acheson had managed to do, he looked the part.

The second was that he possessed a flintlike honesty and integrity that some found "unyielding and difficult" but others, more perceptive, valued in a capital city where these qualities were not always found in public servants.

Standing six feet four, holding himself always erect and commanding, kindly and courtly of manner, possessed of almost fluorescently white hair, deep-set dark eyes, high cheekbones, a generous, almost-always-smiling mouth, and a charm that could turn suddenly and disconcertingly into a forbiddingly reserved disapproval when crossed, he was to many a formidable but heartening father figure on the international scene.

"He just *looks* like a Secretary of State," one of his most persistent critics, the columnist James Van Rensselaer Burden ("As I See It," 323 newspapers, TV talk shows, books, lectures, etc.) put it.

"If Jimmy Van says so," Ray Stanley remarked with a chuckle when the remark was passed along to him by the inevitable Georgetown gossip, "it must be true."

And it was; and the disturbing and sometimes rather sad thing about it was that looking the part was even more important, in this television age, than it had been back in Acheson's heyday in the late 1940s.

The quality of secretaries of state had fluctuated a good deal in recent decades, and so had the sometimes wildly skewed perceptions of them in other countries. It did help, as another of his media critics, Able Montague (anchorman and creator of the popular shows "Washington Wrangle" and "WorldView"), had remarked recently, to "look like God on a Sunday afternoon."

(Again, Ray Stanley had responded with amusement, "Able really does run on, doesn't he?")

But it was true. When he embarked, as secretaries of state had become expected to do these days on every possible image-making pretext for the President, on "shuttle diplomacy," it did help when the plane door opened and out stepped "dignified, white-haired, commanding," etc., etc. Raymond Cass Stanley.

("Don't let it go to your head," Mary often prompted. "It's the substance that counts.")

Well, he thought now as his secretary entered to inform him that what they referred to humorously between themselves as "the usual suspects" were waiting in the outer office to see him, he did have the substance and it did count. Harassed at times by Jaime, thwarted at times by the Pentagon, annoyed at times by the pontifical pinpricks of media types such as Jimmy Van and Able Montague, frustrated and impatient at times with the committees on the Hill, he nonetheless managed to maintain a basically unruffled approach to his demanding and tiring job. Substance was what he had, and substance was what he brought to the task. If some didn't like it, they had the chance to overrule him. He was determined it wouldn't happen this time.

Perhaps he *was* "an Arabist," as they were called in the department; perhaps he did tend to favor the desert peoples, now so wealthy and arrogant, whose modest beginnings he could associate with his own in their desert capitals so long ago; perhaps the department's "Israelites" did consider him too pro-Arab. The great schism between Arabists and Israelites had dominated policy toward the Middle East in the department for many decades.

He supposed his position in the unceasing and sometimes exceedingly bitter push-and-shove had been inevitable ever since he, Mary, and a tall, dramatic (and then almost hawk-thin) black girl named Eula Lee had been assigned together to the embassy in Riyadh, Saudi Arabia, thirty-five years ago. From that point on, their careers had roughly paralleled one another. It was some considerable tribute, Ray thought, to the present occupant of the White House that he had turned to the ranks of the professional Foreign Service when he chose both his Secretary and Deputy Secretary of State.

Brilliant minds—or not so brilliant, depending on the issues they had to face and the particular periods of unrest in which they had to face them—had filled the offices before, but not often were either drawn from the professional ranks. Academic laurels—business achievements—campaign contributions—the he-feels-comfortable-with-him syndrome—there were many standards for picking a Secretary of State and his immediate subordinates. Some secretaries had been adequate, a few outstanding, a tiny handful brilliant; many bore out the dry French aphorism, "There are no great men, only great occasions and the men who happen to be there at the time."

Without being immodest, Ray Stanley thought he might well qualify in the "outstanding" category. Not the best of the best but certainly very far from the worst; a good, moderate, toward-the-top-of-the-rankings Secretary, determined to serve his country and his President as the times might dictate, fully equipped by age and experience to do so.

On the floors below, the life of the department flowed on, sometimes, he thought, almost irrespective of who sat in the impressive office on the seventh floor. He looked around now at its many antiques, carefully collected over recent decades in the great rehabilitation that had gone on under the prodding of department officials and others who felt that the Secretary's office should look as portentous and important as many in the department felt the department to be.

The office exuded, he had to admit, a most impressive atmosphere, rich, luxurious, hushed, deliberately overwhelming. He hoped, as he had before on the eve of such interdepartmental conferences as the one about to begin, that it would impose some restraints of order and comity on the participants; but he knew this was probably a vain hope. His office might cow heads of state, intimidate kings and princes and lords of the desert, but it did not often slow down the usual suspects; not when, as on this lovely spring day about to heat up into another crisis, each had his or her ax to grind in the labyrinthine, Machiavellian, and often exquisitely bloody battles over foreign policy that went on all the time in Foggy Bottom.

*　　　*　　　*

Elsewhere in Washington, and in many places far from Washington, various people as convinced as Sidi bin Sidi bin Sidi and Sheikh Mustafa of the righteousness of their causes and the importance of their countries' interests, were also about to become part of what the President of the United States would refer to later as "the ungluing of Lolómé." That it came close to ungluing the rest of the world was something the President preferred not to dwell upon; or upon his own part in an episode which, he also remarked, "was either a watershed in international affairs . . . or just more of the same."

That he could dismiss it so lightly in view of his own performance was typical of the curiously detached spirit in which he approached his great responsibilities; an apparent lightheartedness that infuriated his critics and made even his most partisan supporters uneasy.

"I can't understand him," Ray Stanley often confided to Mary. "He just doesn't seem to care."

They marveled that a mind "so ironic and so removed," as Mary put it, should have achieved the apex of the American political system with such a seemingly almost frivolous attitude; yet there he was. Among the Secretary of State's many other problems was that of having to deal with this rather strange individual who had, after all, crowned Ray's career with the high office he now held, and presumably depended upon him in many areas of foreign policy that he himself sometimes seemed too remote to care about.

All Presidents, Ray Stanley had concluded after many years of observing politics and serving in the government, were "rather strange" people; it took a certain larger-than-life ego and ambition, an unusual and ruthless ability to balance ethics with necessity, a personality that in the last analysis defied analysis, to achieve residency at 1600 Pennsylvania Avenue. All this, plus an aptitude for public performance which, in the television age, was perhaps the most important single ingredient. "The camera doesn't lie"—but it did; it did. It was no more capable of penetrating the bland and exterior shell of Presidents than any other medium. It only transmitted an impression. If the impression was skillfully enough devised and shrewdly enough presented, there were only superficial clues to what lay beneath.

So it was with the present incumbent, risen to power, first through the governorship of his native Minnesota, and then through the Senate, where he served a single, rather perfunctory term before seeking the White House. But even in that collegial body, where members were usually appraised accurately by their fellow members, he had remained something of an enigma, essentially withdrawn and unknowable, so bent upon his own ultimate purposes that he often gave the impression of just making a pit stop on his way to more important matters. The quick smile was there, the easy grin, the joke, the backslap, the hearty guffaw, the seemingly complete candor of mind and emotion, the carefully managed public image; but always, as Jaime Serrano had confided to Ray not long ago in a moment of candid frustration, "sometheeng ees held back." With it, the President performed such domestic and foreign miracles as he deigned to involve himself in. The last go-round with the two Lolómés had also been the last time he had really exerted himself; and that, the Secretary felt, was not a particularly good omen for the new crisis now brewing in the desert sands.

On that occasion Seedy Sidi, as the chief executive soon took to calling him in the privacy of the Oval Office, had launched an impulsive, but for a couple of weeks overwhelming, attack on the ill-trained and virtually helpless "army" of Lesser Lolómé. The President had reacted like a prior outwardly involved and inwardly curiously detached occupant of the White House: he had slapped together a hasty international "coalition" and gone to war.

His coalition was much flimsier, much shakier, much more reluctant; but given the flimsy nature of Sidi's forces, equally effective in restoring the status quo.

Interestingly—but equally ominous for the future, Ray Stanley thought—"the second Gulf war" had ended in the same undecided fashion as the first—"the half-assed conclusion of a half-assed concept," as the President's principal critic on the Hill, Senator "Willie" Wilson, chairman of the Senate Foreign Relations Committee, acidly described it. "The second Gulf war" had turned out to be essentially "nothing more than a skirmish in the sand," to quote the chairman again—except that, facing a crisis, a President of the United States had once again deliberately taken refuge behind the United Nations to flaunt his courage and conceal his hesitations. In what had increasingly become the pattern since the first Gulf War, a President had again made his country hostage to the 110—or 120—or was it 250, so fast was the world disintegrating into impossible political bits—ancient states, new states, city-states, island states, and tiny-dot-of-land states that comprised the international organization.

The United States, its options for decisive leadership increasingly tied like Gulliver by the thousand silken threads of UN weakness and obfuscation, was by deliberate choice of its Presidents crippled down even further in the exercise of that leadership which its position as "the world's sole remaining superpower" (for the time being—China, Japan, Germany, and the increasingly insistent Second Soviet Republic were coming up fast on the turn) imposed upon it.

In recent years, as Ray Stanley saw it, America's chief executives had deliberately ducked this responsibility and, in so doing, had thrown away their ability to lead the world. They had done so, Ray thought, *because they had no real idea what else to do. They did not want to lead, because that would expose to the world their lack of ideas and their inability to formulate fundamental policy.* It was no wonder the United Nations was such an eagerly sought shield for them. It made their weaknesses easy to hide, respectable, politically quite safe. The convenient myth of "United Nations unity" made life simple for them. If they got it, fine; if they didn't, well, what was a poor President to do? Be a real leader? Perish the thought!

"I'll be damned," the chairman had also said, "if putting the American horse *behind* the United Nations cart, instead of in front of it where it ought to be, is any way to climb the mountain."

But that was how it was being done in the final years of the topsy-turvy twentieth century.

At the same time, with the most bland inconsistency, American Presidents, through their Secretaries of State, were always lecturing the world from a stance of high moral righteousness about the ills of this government here, that government there, a frowned-upon internal development in some country, a defiant refusal to live up to American standards in some other.

"You have set yourself up," the Russian ambassador had remarked bitterly to Ray Stanley not long ago, "as the moral preachers to the world. You're as bad as the Pope, but at least he has almost two thousand years of history behind him. What gives the United States this right, we all wonder?"

To which, the Secretary had to admit, he had found only the lamest and most inadequate of answers. His reply, in fact, had deteriorated into an almost inaudible mumble, to which the Russian had listened with his characteristic, beady-bright, skeptical look. It had not been, Ray reflected uncomfortably later, one of his own better moments.

But, he thought with a long-suffering sigh as the usual suspects came in, life had to go on. What, in their combined wisdom, should State suggest at the NSC meeting to avoid another slide into the international La Brea tar pit of "United Nations unity"? He watched them enter—all, as usual, prepared to do battle for their particular point of view.

First came the most aggressive and, as always, probably the best informed and best prepared: Joan Cohn-Bourassa, Assistant Secretary for Near Eastern Affairs; chosen by the President for her job because, as a Jew married to "Boo" Bourassa from Syria, she was a famous and highly touted "fair-minded" expert on her particular area of interest, "the Arab-Jewish Dilemma," on which she had been teaching and holding graduate seminars for the past two decades at Yale University. It was at Yale that she had met Boo, then a graduate student in atomic physics, and after defying her parents and his, had virtually demanded that he marry her. Boo was an amiable soul whose ultimate purposes, whatever they might be, were successfully concealed by his easygoing nature and silly nickname, which he had acquired in undergraduate days when his fraternity brothers had started calling him "Abu ben Adam" instead of his real name, which was Achmed. Soon shortened to "Abu" and then to "Boo," the nickname had stuck and would be with him for life. He didn't mind. Boo Bourassa—that plump, amiable, always smiling, everybody's friend—had his own agenda and didn't mind playing the gentle buffoon if that would conceal it. Not even Joan, steel-trap mind, severe hairdo, and combative manner notwithstanding, suspected what it was. Hers was so obvious and vocal that she quite overshadowed him. Which was fine with him.

"I'm the Bourassa of Cohn-Bourassa," he always told new acquaintances with a grin. "My wife is that dramatic lady over there."

And so she was, Ray Stanley thought with a rather tired amusement, small, dark, driving, and intense, intense, *intense*. And so famous, because Joan Cohn-Bourassa was a highly publicized Arabist; and mighty, therefore, were her words in the land.

After her came Eulie Montgomery, again holding in her hand the decoded dispatch from the American embassy in Greater Lolómé. She winked at Ray as she took her seat along the big oval table at which he held top department conferences. Eulie always enjoyed these tussles, in which she quite often crossed swords with Joanie Bourassa. Honors were usually pretty well divided when the smoke of battle cleared.

"I like the Ay-rabs," Eulie often said with a humorously exaggerated pronunciation, "but I can't say I'm really partisan toward either side. I'm in the middle of the muddled Middle East."

This attitude did not please Joanie, who wanted everybody, as she said, "to stand up and be counted," which meant that she wanted them to fit themselves into the neat little boxes where she put people in her mind. Eulie didn't fit, nor did Gage McGregor, director of the policy planning staff, who now came "swanning in," as the British ambassador to Washington, no friend, described him: tall, thin, slick, and trim, giving an impression of being somewhat willowy but with a whim of iron underneath, as the ambassador had discovered on more than one occasion; sometimes an Arabist, sometimes an Israelite, more often off on some tangent entirely and uniquely his own.

Basil Rifkin, counsel of the department, was also tall, thin, not at all willowy, but rather an iron rail with little flexibility and a legal brilliance that had put him at the top of his class at Harvard Law School. In due time he became attorney general of New York. Now he was one of Washington's shrewdest operators, stopping through, Ray Stanley always felt, on his way somewhere else, presumably the Supreme Court. He and his equally shrewd little wife, Effie, were close friends of the President and First Lady, which, Ray supposed, was one of the better ways to go about it. There was no doubt where Basil stood. He made no bones about being adamantly pro-Israel. "And why shouldn't I be?" he demanded bluntly. Nobody had a good counter for that one.

Brad Temple and Hugo Mallerbie came in together, completing the usual suspects the Secretary wanted for this particular brainstorming session. Brad, Undersecretary for Political Affairs, was a former congressman from California and former member of the House International Affairs Committee who had done a yeoman job of helping the

President carry his difficult state in the last election. He was generally considered in the department to be an excellent choice for dealing with what most department employees regarded as the major bane of their existence, namely, the Congress of the United States—"those windy bastards . . . those interfering bastards . . . *those bastards."*

Brad was short, dumpy, gone to fat, given to loud, boisterous, and seemingly quite open and direct approaches to people and events. Behind the tousled and rumpled outward appearance lurked, as Basil Rifkin often remarked, a mind as devious as Machiavelli's and a purpose as tenacious as a cat's. He had the departmental reputation of "knowing where all the bodies are buried on the Hill." He didn't, but he knew about enough of them to give him considerable clout when it came to the formulation and successful conduct of policy.

Hugo Mallerbie, Undersecretary for International Security Affairs, was an almost complete contrast: small, quiet, deliberately inconspicuous, faceless, and gray, fading as much as possible into the background, from which position he sopped up information like a sponge and processed it back out again in a close-to-the-vest operation that missed few things that threatened the U.S. position around the world or his own position in the department. A veteran of both the FBI and the CIA, in which he had served consecutively for approximately a decade each before coming to the State Department, he really did know where a lot of the bodies were buried, just as he knew now what the Deputy Secretary of State was about to announce, having learned of it through his own channels within ten minutes after she did. That his own channels included a secretary in her office was something she didn't know about and he wasn't going to tell her; the girl was only one of many lower-ranking employees in the department who reported interesting things from time to time to Hugo Mallerbie. They, along with many similar contacts in U.S. ambassadorial and consular offices overseas, gave Hugo, as he often reflected with considerable satisfaction, "quite a handle" on what was going on.

"Lulie," the Secretary suggested when they were all seated and looking at him expectantly from around the table, "why don't you tell us what you have?"

"Yes, I will," she said, putting on her glasses and peering down her nose at the papers she held. "This comes in from two sources. One is

Creed Moncrief, who is officially 'assistant to the ambassador' in Greater Lolómé, off-record CIA, and the other is Regina Gates, officially deputy chief of mission in the embassy in Lesser Lolómé, also CIA. The messages were received by the Agency via satellite an hour ago within five minutes of each other. The substance is the same. Creed reports that Sidi has received four or five atomic bombs over the course of the last five months. He says Sidi has also received a total of ten long-range missiles in the past year, sneaked in piecemeal and assembled in the underground chambers beneath the Pink House on Point Sinistre, where secret launching facilities have also been constructed." She paused and shook her head in amazement. "How this could all go on without anybody catching it sooner is beyond me, but then, Hugo, a lot of things in the intelligence community, including its frequent stupidity, are beyond me. Anyway," she went on firmly as Hugo Mallerbie shifted in his seat, obviously prepared to do battle, "there it is. Regina reports this same information has been received by what she refers to as Sheikh Mustafa's 'desert intelligence network,' as she calls it, which, like all these countries, is pretty damned good even though it exists without visible means of communication and seems to run on camel dung. Regina says The Mouse is terrified of an immediate attack by Sidi, and Israel is also highly alarmed, as they are afraid they may be next, or maybe even head the list of Sidi's priorities. That may have been the real reason for his being given the weapons. We don't know yet." She paused, peered over her glasses.

"That's it," she concluded crisply. "There'll probably be a National Security Council meeting on it soon, maybe as early as this afternoon. What's State's position?"

The signals, as the Secretary expected, were mixed, but the final decision—as much as any decision was ever "final" at State, policy was constantly shifting on all fronts—was exactly what he foresaw. After the usual suspects had their say and dispersed to their offices below, Eulie told him with some asperity that it was exactly what she had foreseen, too. He liked it. She didn't.

"Too much like State," she said. "The same old story. Confusion, confliction, caution. Endless, endless caution. One more clear, uncomplicated shining beacon of resolve from Foggy Bottom."

"We need more like that," he responded, unruffled.

"God help us!" she exclaimed with a snort. "Isn't *he*"—that universal *he* of the bureaucracy which only meant one man—"indecisive enough without us encouraging him?"

"He's doing very comfortably in the polls," Ray Stanley pointed out.

She snorted again. "'Polls!' That's government?"

"It passes for it, in our times."

"Yes," she conceded. "Well. Not for me, Ray. Not for me."

"Well, Lulie," he said with his charming smile, "everybody knows you're the toughest man on the payroll. There has to be room for a little give and take."

"We'll give," she said bluntly, "and Sidi and his friend will take. They've all got our number, overseas."

Nonetheless, he had felt, as Joanie Bourassa fired the first salvo, that it was going to be a good discussion, "getting our ducks in a row," as Brad Temple was wont to say on almost every occasion, for the much tougher discussion they all anticipated in the NSC.

"I must say," Joan said, looking even more intense than she usually did, which was saying a lot, "that I think we definitely need more detailed information before we can recommend that this government take any stand that might lead to renewed military involvement in the Middle East. You know how opposed the media are to it. To say nothing of the Hill."

"That's getting your priorities straight," Basil Rifkin said dryly. "Particularly with this President."

"We can't ignore them," she said sharply. "Either of them."

"And we can't ignore the threat of another marauder's expedition over there, either," Basil retorted.

"Do you want us to threaten military action?" Joan demanded. "That's your solution to everything, Basil."

"No, it's not," he said with equal sharpness. "That's nonsense. You're so involved with your precious Arabs that you don't want us to say anything remotely harsh to anybody, including your precious Sidi."

"He isn't my precious Sidi," she said. "And anyway, he has considerable justification on his side. The Lolómés didn't ask the British to split them in two, you know. He has a right to want to reunify the country."

"Oh, *that's* the excuse," Basil Rifkin said, again in the tone of slightly amused disbelief that could always provoke an annoyed response from the naturally indignant, which Joan Cohn-Bourassa was. "Sixty years ago or such a matter, and it's still the excuse."

"Israel uses the excuse of thousands of years for everything," she said.

"You really don't like the Jews, do you?" Basil inquired blandly. "What soured you on your heritage, Joanie?"

"Oh, stop it," she said angrily. "Just *stop it!* I can get along without your smart-aleck type of argument very well, thank you! I'm just as— just as—"

"This really isn't getting us anywhere, you know," the Secretary remarked in the mild tone that Brad Temple referred to as "velvet-clad iron." "If you want to put this on a personal level, Basil, we won't make such progress. I take it, Joanie, that you are opposed to warning Sidi against attacking Lesser Lolómé or doing anything else that might upset the equilibrium over there."

"I certainly don't think a public warning is necessary," she said. "Get old Big Balls Bullock to get on his horse and go riding up to the Pink House door with all guns blazing. He can do it off the record, if it has to be done. I don't think this department needs to go out on a limb."

"And if Sidi doesn't behave?" Hugo Mallerbie interjected quietly. "Then what?"

"Then we make it a little more public," Gage McGregor said with his disconcerting little giggle that often undercut serious discussion.

"And too late," Basil Rifkin said.

"Too late," Gage agreed, giggling again. "We've got to be tougher with him than that."

"We ought to get at the source," Eula Lee Montgomery said flatly. "We ought to use this as the final excuse to go after the bastard who is probably the principal one behind all this and *get him.*"

"Maybe that can be arranged, too," Brad Temple suggested. "Get 'em both with one fell swoop."

"A clichéd expression and a clichéd idea," Joan Cohn-Bourassa snapped. "That's typical of your profound thinking, Brad. We can tell you've been around the Hill a long time."

"I hear," Hugo Mallerbie said in the same soft, quiet tone, "that you have a few malcontents in the Near East division who might want us to take a really strong stand this time. Any signs of revolt in the ranks, Joanie?"

"Not that I know of," she said calmly. "Anyway, what difference does it make? The final decision is mine."

"Not with the media around," Eulie said. "Don't get too big for your britches, girl."

"Don't 'girl' me, Eulie!" Joan Bourassa snapped.

"Why, no, ma'am," Eulie said with a big smile. "I know how touchy you folks are about being patronized."

"Oh—!" Joanie exclaimed, exasperated, as they all laughed. "Can't we please have a serious discussion of this? It is, after all, a serious matter."

"It is," the Deputy Secretary agreed, more soberly. "So far, Joanie's obviously against a strong public reaction at this time. Basil's for it, Gage is having his usual giggle, Brad's skittering over the surface of things as befits a good ex-congressman, and Hugo, as always, is being a mystery man. Can we get a little nearer to a clarification on this? Ray?"

"I hear you," the Secretary said with a smile. "Shall I poll the precincts?"

Brad held up his hand.

"More discussion first, if you please," he said. "We've got a tough situation on the Hill, as you know."

"All right," the Secretary said. "Give us the Hill in ten well-chosen words."

"The Hill, as always, is full of many voices," Brad said. "The key players, as always these days, are Willie Wilson in the Senate and Johnny Jones in the House. You know Willie; he's pushing eighty and into his dotage—"

"That will be the day," the Secretary interrupted. "Willie pushing eighty is ten times men half his age."

"You are right," Brad conceded with a cheerful grin. "He is still one smart cookie. But he *is* chairman of Senate Foreign Relations Committee, and that makes him a problem. He's always been a hawk."

"Or always so characterized by the media," Eulie suggested. "That doesn't mean it's so."

"It ain't necessarily so!" Gage sang out. It startled them all.

"All *right,*" Brad Temple said sternly. "Be serious for once, please, Gage. As for that son of a bitch Johnny Jones in the House—"

"Chairman of the House Appropriations Subcommittee on the State Department," Joan Cohn-Bourassa said, "and my principal cross. An absolutely charming fellow. I'm still getting reports on the way he terrorized the natives on his last trip to Asia. Not only all the sexual skulduggery we've come to expect from him, but things like buying up antiques against local law, smuggling them in his official luggage, cheating customs, and then reselling them through an antiques shop in his district operated by a cousin. To say nothing of all the privileges of housing and transportation and temporary girlfriends he demands as chairman from our embassy and consular people. Oh, he's a first-rate citizen, is Johnny Jones of Alabama."

"Leak it to the *Post* and the *Times*," Basil Rifkin suggested. "They'll get him."

"We tried," Joan said, "but there's something there, we don't know what. We didn't get very far. Up to this moment, he's led a charmed life."

"He's a dove on the Middle East just like you are," Basil pointed out dryly. "Maybe that protects him with folks who agree. You, for instance. You ought to get along like a house afire."

"He'll support me on this, I'm sure," Joan said calmly. "Willie Wilson, I'm not so sure."

"How about the House International Affairs Committee?"

"As long as Henry Slattery is chairman," Joan said with the scorn most observers reserved for that amicable and virtually senile gentleman from Wyoming, "Johnny Jones will continue to be the key House player on foreign affairs. That's just the way it is."

"You're so right," Brad Temple agreed. "I would think," he added thoughtfully, "that it might be better, as you say, to refrain from recommending any official position on this latest business with Sidi, at least until we get more information."

"How much information do we want?" Basil Rifkin demanded. "The CIA is pretty sure of its facts, isn't it, Eulie?"

She nodded.

"I called the director as soon as I received the report, and he thinks the information is probably essentially correct. They're pursuing it further, however. You may have a point, Brad."

"I think, before we do anything else," Gage said, "that it's about time for another general statement warning against further nuclear proliferation among nontreaty states."

"That'll shrivel 'em," Basil said. "That would be, what, the three thousandth—or is it the four thousandth—time that we have viewed with alarm on that subject?"

"Nonetheless," Gage said, getting the stubborn tone they all knew, "we on the policy planning staff would much prefer to keep this as vague and general as possible, for the time being. If we have to do anything at all, that is. Why do we have to do anything at all?"

"Maybe we won't," Ray Stanley said. "Maybe the NSC will prefer to put a damper on the whole thing. For the moment, at least."

"And what will you recommend, as a member of the NSC?" Basil inquired.

"How do you all vote?" the Secretary responded.

"I'm for a strong warning," Basil said flatly.

"I'm against it," Joan Cohn-Bourassa said.

"I'm against it, I think, at the moment," Brad Temple said.

"I'm against it," Hugo Mallerbie said.

"So am I," Gage McGregor said.

"I'm for it," Eula Lee Montgomery said bluntly. "This is one more chance for State to muck up. We're always wishy-washying. We're always dilly-dallying. I would like us just for once to say flat-out *no.*"

"Do you think that will really stop Sidi?" Gage inquired.

"Or his friend?" Joan agreed. "Or friends? I think not. We have to give diplomacy a chance."

"Four against a warning," the Secretary said, "two for." He smiled, removing any sting of arrogance. "The head of the table doesn't need your votes to prevail, but he thanks you for them. Sorry, Lulie, and sorry, Basil, but I'm going to NSC with State's recommendation that we sit tight for the moment and do nothing."

"So typical," the Deputy Secretary said vehemently. "So damned typical. I don't think we can possibly gain any respect in the world by this sort of—"

The Secretary held up a hand and stopped her.

"You and I have already agreed that you're going with me, Lulie, so you'll have plenty of chance to take your views right to headquarters, OK?"

"Well," she said, not entirely mollified, "OK. In the meantime, I'd suggest that we play this thing damned close to our vests. I don't want to hear it on the evening news, so watch yourself with staff, please."

"Tight as a drum," Gage said with another giggle.

"That's Washington," Eulie said, "for sure. Tight as a drum. I don't think."

"Eulie is of course entirely right," the Secretary said as they stood and prepared to leave. "Mum's the word, right down the line. OK?"

And, agreeing solemnly, they all bade him farewell and went off to their respective offices below. He turned to the Deputy Secretary.

"Want to bet, Lulie?" he inquired with a wry smile.

"No," she said in a tired tone, "I don't want to bet. I just wish some-body in this town had the sense to keep his—or her—damned mouth shut about anything, that's all. But I'm not putting any money on it."

"Me neither," he agreed ruefully. "Somebody always spills the beans."

But as they were to find out later, the news, when it finally came, was not revealed by anyone at State, NSC, the White House, the Hill, or any other home of those industrious blabbers-to-the-media who had become such a standard feature of Washington life in recent years.

Nor was it the typical indirect, semi-anonymous, designed-to-be-denied-if-the-rumpus-is-too-great trial balloon at which recent admin-istrations had become so adept.

It could not even be classified as a leak. It was an announcement.

The arrogance with which it was presented to the world—"the sheer, bold effrontery of it," to quote Willie Wilson—indicated that it was a far more serious matter than they had all anticipated, and accelerated it at once into a major confrontation that would soon test everyone involved to the limit of their abilities for diplomacy, forcefulness, effectiveness, and skill.

2　First, however, the customary minuet had to be performed.

The pattern established in recent years was too sacred, now, to be broken.

First the State Department conference, already held . . .

Then the National Security Council meeting, about to be held . . .

Then the secret conferrings with the people in the field, getting their advice, considering it, usually ignoring it because, after all, they were only on the scene and what did they know about it—"the process of getting our ducks in a row," as Brad Temple said. "Throwing it all in the pot," as the President put it . . .

Informing "the necessary people" on the Hill . . .

"Preparing the media," which involved a sort of pre-leakage in which one had to be sure that the information went to people who could be really helpful, not just to malcontents who might begin raising hell too soon and upset the schedule; a process to be handled with care in private telephone calls because everybody was tapped these days, even the President; and with thoughtful discretion in murmured conversations at White House state dinners, or at Georgetown functions such as those at the homes of social leaders like the widowed Dolly Munson, still going strong at eighty-three . . .

Then the first public leakages, to such can-be-counted-on outlets as the *Times*, the *Post*, Larry King, MacNeil-Lehrer, leading columnists such as Jimmy Van Rensselaer Burden and Tim Bates . . .

Then the loud public backlash from the Hill, carefully invited, carefully planned, to stir up public opinion and test how far an administration dared go . . .

Then the sudden things-getting-out-of-hand when the wrong people in the media and on the Hill began to clamor . . .

Then the President, questioned sternly by the White House press corps (that righteous soul and conscience of the nation), backing away, obfuscating, covering his tracks, "keeping his options open" in the deft game, all moves anticipated, all bases covered, no surprises, that he and the media played with each other all the time . . .

Then the demands from the Hill for "clear-cut, decisive leadership from the White House" . . .

Then the agitations from the United Nations, discreetly invited, calmly parried, the shield of "UN action" brought smoothly to the fore . . .

Then the vigorous public statements from the President and his Secretary of State: they will—they won't—they're thinking—they're planning—they're ducking—they're dodging—they're about to become the scourge of the universe—or fly away like the gentlest puff of smoke in the desert wind . . .

And *then*—

But *then,* in this particular instance, the challenge issued, the gauntlet flung down—all the carefully coordinated steps thrown out of kilter, brought to naught, because the best-laid plans of mice and men are not enough, these days, when many men are self-interested and a lot of mice have their own agendas. . . .

"Ray!" Jaime Serrano exclaimed from the White House about five P.M. on that first afternoon. "You have heard the news from Lolómé! We mus' talk. We mus' talk. Can you be here at seven P.M. for an NSC meeting?"

"I could," the Secretary said, "but Mary and I are supposed to be at Dolly Munson's for dinner at eight. Won't it cause a lot of unnecessary preliminary stir if I suddenly cancel?"

"Don't cancel," Jaime suggested. "Arrive late."

"In this town?" Ray Stanley said. "That's even worse. They'd all be on me like a flash. 'What's up, Mr. Secretary? What can you tell us, Ray?' Not with that crowd, thanks. She always has a lot of media. I couldn't carry it off."

"You could carry anything off," Jaime Serrano said. "The President wants you. Be here."

"Yes, *sir!*" Ray Stanley said. "I can always have a sudden virus. Mary can always represent us. Dolly will understand."

"Dolly understands everything," Jaime said with a chuckle. "She's been around this town so long."

"That's what I'm afraid of," the Secretary said. "However. As a matter of fact, we already have State's recommendation ready for you."

"You have polled the whole depar'men'," Jaime said with wry surprise. "We are impressed."

"As much of it as necessary to give the Secretary adequate cover," Ray said with a chuckle of his own. "You know the department, the most amorphous institution in Washington. Some Secretaries, such as George Shultz, have liked to work through and with the bureaucracy, some, like Kissinger and Jim Baker, have run it all out of their hip pockets with a tiny handful of close advisers and to hell with the bureaucracy. It's wide open to any method a Secretary chooses. My method—"

"We know your method," Jaime said.

The Secretary chuckled again. "Saves time, wear, and tear," he observed. "Eulie will be coming with me."

"At leas' we'll know there's some division in the depar'men'," Jaime said. "It won't be all jus' your say-so. Good!"

Basically, the Secretary reflected as the national security adviser hung up, it *was* pretty much his say-so. He had received a clear reporting of where his subordinates stood. It was not, as Basil Rifkin had remarked on a previous occasion, "as though we need a lot of charts and statistics to understand one another. We're all predictable."

And so they were, Ray thought, particularly with regard to the Middle East. He and his top aides all had very definite ideas as to where they wanted State to go in that area. They had expressed them so many times to one another that prolonged discussion was not often necessary. And, as he had reminded them gently, the head of the table had the final vote, the forcefulness of it depending almost entirely on his own character and view of the world.

If he was himself a Secretary in the Kissinger-Baker mode, and he supposed he was in spite of his usual careful appearance of attention to conflicting views among his subordinates, it was because the department really was amorphous and that method was, in his mind, the only really efficient way to run it.

Along with Treasury, it was one of the two oldest departments of the federal government, created in 1789 to succeed the original Department of Foreign Affairs created in 1781, when the Articles of Confederation were succeeded by the Constitution of the United States. Its employees had always felt themselves a cut above the rest of the government because they, after all, were continuing custodians of the foreign policy of the United States. "Presidents come, Presidents go," as Willie Wilson had once remarked, not sounding too happy about it, "but the State Department goes on forever."

In recent times this self-importance had led to such bland assertions, published in the department's official brochure, that it (and apparently it alone) "leads the United States toward the global challenges of the 21st century." It wasn't that the department ignored the fact that others might also be involved in the creation of foreign policy; it was just that it sounded as though it wasn't aware that they even existed.

The unconscious arrogance of this statement, its critics thought, was a very accurate indication of the way the department and its employees regarded themselves.

"And after all," Basil Rifkin liked to say with a sardonic smile, "it's true, isn't it?"

Too many thought so, the Secretary felt, for the department to coexist in entire comfort with other departments of the government that had, over the years, been able to encroach upon much of State's territory. Nearly every embassy, for instance, had its military attaché from the Department of Defense, its agricultural attaché from the Department of Agriculture, its commercial attaché from the Department of Commerce, its never officially acknowledged but always there representative of the CIA. Wherever there was a pretext, the other departments and agencies moved in, each with its own special channels to the media. He had felt from his earliest days in the Middle East that this diluted and weakened State's position and diluted and weakened the formulation of American foreign policy. But there it was, and they had to live with it, even though it made almost inevitable the confrontation he knew was going to occur when he and Eulie, riding beside him now in the Secretary's official limousine, reached the White House.

The Pentagon: Public Enemy No. 1 in State's eyes, as Secretary after Secretary had concluded when engaging in the endless tussles over policy that went back and forth across the Potomac. Arlie McGregor, Secretary of Defense, would be with him in general on the policy he was already encapsulating as "Go slow on Sidi," but there would be some Pentagon twist put on it, some way of moving in and trying to appropriate the issue, even if it was only the constantly reiterated assertion that "sound military policy" had to take precedence in all crises.

He reflected with satisfaction as the limousine swung in under the East Portico of the White House that at least for the time being the media were not swarming all over them with their own characteristic confrontational arrogance. Most of them had gone home, some to collapse after a day spent chasing the President from pillar to post on one of his busier schedules, some to change to tux and formal dress for official Washington's magic socializing hours of eight to eleven P.M. Use of the East Portico was designed to thwart any last lingering bright-eyes who might be keeping watch on the main entrance or the west entrance. He was pleased to note that they were greeted only by the familiar, pleasant presence of the chief usher, backed by a couple of lounging Secret Service men behind the glass doors.

"Evening, Mr. Secretary—Madame Secretary," the chief usher, a black as statuesque as Eulie, greeted them cordially.

"Roman," the Secretary said warmly, "how are you?"

"Fine, thanks," the chief usher said.

"How's the extended family?" Eulie inquired.

"Very good, ma'am," he said with a pleased smile. "Everybody doing well." His expression sobered. "And Mr. Montgomery?"

She sighed.

"Poorly. But we keep hoping."

"All you can do," he said with a sympathetic cluck. "Such a pleasant gentleman."

"Yes," she said, voice breaking a little in the only topic on which the Secretary had ever known the Deputy Secretary to reveal her inner tension. "Thank you."

"Come on in, Mr. Secretary, Madame Secretary," Roman said. "The President's waiting."

"Anybody else here?" Eulie asked.

The chief usher grinned. "You know Secretary McGregor and General Rathbun," he said. His tone became a little dry. "They're always the early birds who catch the worm."

"Or hope to catch it," Ray Stanley said with a chuckle. "We at State always hope to get there first."

"Have to move fast to catch that Pentagon," Roman remarked with an answering chuckle. "Those military men move mighty fast sometimes."

"Well," the Secretary said. "We shall see. Right, Lulie?"

"You tell me," she said with a smile as they went on in, to nod to the Secret Service and head along the hall to the West Wing. "I'm just along for the ride."

"That'll be the day," the Secretary said, and the chief usher laughed.

"Not the way we hear it, is it, Mr. Secretary? Go right along, now. He'll be down in a minute."

Walking the familiar corridors that he had walked so often down the years, at meetings, official functions, in the last decade formal state dinners as he rose steadily toward the top of the Foreign Service, the Secretary was struck, as always, by the simple, overpowering dignity of this house. Its occupant might be enormously popular, abysmally unpopular, or, in the fluctuations of Presidents, somewhere in between, sliding up and down with each new poll claiming to show what the American people and the world were thinking at any given moment—but the White House remained simply and overwhelmingly the White House. Like Everest, it was there, always present, unique, unchanging in the American mind. There was nothing like it, so much history, so much of human living, power, ambition, dreams—so much of America; lovely to look at from the outside at any time of day or any season; lighted up on a soft spring night, white and gleaming in the winter snow, stately, always stately, aloof yet intimate, carrying the hopes of a still hopeful people, a still glowing vision dimmed somewhat by the social and political erosion of the past years but still symbolizing something unique and precious for its own people, and for the world.

It lent dignity and purpose to all who passed within its doors. Some might not appreciate it fully, but very few were unimpressed. It appeared to be, and in its ultimate place in the American scheme of things it was, shining, perfect and pure, a symbol along with the Capitol and the Supreme Court building, the supreme physical expression of the great dream brought forth upon this continent and now so challenged, in so many ways, by so many vindictive enemies and so many almost insoluble domestic problems.

We won't let you destroy it, the Secretary told these swarming attackers silently in his mind. *The dream is ours and we won't let you destroy it.*

It was probably a useless and rather silly thing to say, but he felt better for having expressed it.

As they entered the small, intimate Roosevelt Room, named for the ebullient Teddy, where the President liked to hold his private conferences, Ray could tell that Arlie and Gen. Wilson Rathbun, chairman of the Joint Chiefs of Staff, were loaded for bear. They might not always know exactly what bear, he thought dryly, but they were always loaded for it.

"Ray—" the Secretary of Defense said. "Eulie—you two look loaded for bear."

"Funny," Ray Stanley said with quick amusement, "I was thinking the same thing about you and Bill. Don't we agree on Sidi?"

"Maybe," Arlie McGregor said warily. "Maybe you and I and Bill do. I'm not sure about Eulie."

"I'll sign onto anything that takes a forceful stand on things," she said. "Anything with a little backbone in it. Does that make me a radical?"

"The worst one in Washington," General Rathbun said with a grin as a door opened and the President stepped in with his quick, authoritative gait—somewhat slowed today, Ray thought; perhaps some worry was penetrating the armor? But the voice was cheerful, the mood upbeat.

"If we don't watch Eulie," the President said, "she'll have us in a third Gulf war, stringing up Sidi on Pointe Sinistre one day and blasting his secret sponsors out of the sand on the next. Where," he demanded abruptly, "is the CIA? Where's the Vice President? Where's my national security adviser?"

"Here, Mr. President!" Jaime Serrano exclaimed, breathless from an obvious dash down the hall. "I am *here!*"

"About time," the President observed, smiling with that rather dangerous amicability that could change quite suddenly to sarcastic impatience and even, on occasion, explosive anger. He was not detached where his own ego and the dignity of his office were concerned. Challenges to those, as Mary said, "bring out the tiger. Too bad that doesn't apply to foreign policy."

But perhaps it was just as well, the Secretary thought now, as the tell-tale first flush of annoyance subsided on the presidential cheek and the surface good nature resumed control. Maybe it was just as well that the chief executive was very cautious about committing his country—and his own political and historical position—to any swift and decisive action that might threaten them. It might, perhaps, have saved himself and the country from much hasty and ill-advised action; although, in Eulie Montgomery's view, it only weakened further the strength—"the *consistent* strength," as she often emphasized—that she felt the United States and its executive should show.

"And the Vice President?" the President inquired as they all took seats around the table.

"He is coming," Jaime said. "He has been notified. He is on the way."

"I hope so," the President said, "even though"—his voice dropped to an intimate level and he grinned an intimate we-all-know-what-we-think grin—"even though we could probably get along very well with-out— Ah, Hank!" he exclaimed cordially, changing gears in an instant as they had often seen him do, as the Vice President hurried in, somewhat flustered. "*There* you are!"

"Sorry, Mr. President," the Vice President said, with the easy grin that had extricated him from difficult situations all his life. It was youthful and boyish. ("Because he *is* youthful and boyish," Eulie Montgomery often said. "God help us if anything happens to the President.") "I was trapped by some staffers with a report on our let's-cut-the-government-waste program."

"Not *another* one!" the President exclaimed in mock horror. "Well, that's all right," he added as they all laughed. "You were engaged in good work. We just didn't want to start without you."

"I should hope not!" the Vice President said cheerfully as Eulie winked at Ray across the table: *Little does he know,* she conveyed as clearly as though she had spoken. Everybody in Washington thought the Vice President was dumb, dumb, dumb; sadly and sometimes rather touchingly, he was secretly more hurt by this than he ever let on and was determined to prove them all wrong. His only problem was that the President, who had created him politically, never gave him a chance to do so.

"Now the CIA," the President said, "and we can begin."

"Right here, Mr. President," Eldridge Barnes said calmly, entering without haste and slipping into his seat at the table with the same air of smooth self-confidence he brought to everything. He was sixty, looked fifty, had affairs like forty, and all in all was one of the smartest men ever to head his ubiquitous agency.

"Let's begin with you," the President suggested. "Your people have everybody excited with these reports about old Sidi and his bombs. Do you believe it's true?"

"We have no reason to disbelieve it," Eldridge Barnes said. "Creed Moncrief—"

"That name!" the President exclaimed. "Every time I hear it I don't believe it."

"It isn't his fault," Eldridge Barnes observed. "Talk to Mr. and Mrs. Moncrief. Anyway, Creed and Regina Gates in Lesser Lolómé—"

"That's more like it," the President said. "A name after my own heart." Eldridge refused to let the President fluster him, which the President liked to do if he could; he usually couldn't.

"Creed and Regina," the director repeated calmly, "are two of our best people anywhere and both have these rumors going around. Both say they come from very reliable sources that have generally been proven correct at various significant times in the past. Both are checking further. Meanwhile, they've let us know so we can make up our minds what to do if the rumors prove out." He looked at the President with dispassionate interest. "What *are* we going to do, Mr. President?"

"What do you people advise?" the President retorted.

"That's the easy way," the director remarked.

The President looked quite annoyed for a second, but before he could respond, the Secretary of Defense did.

"We at the Pentagon," he began (in what Ray Stanley thought of as "his usual grand manner"), "would like to be very sure of all the facts before we commit ourselves to anything that might conceivably involve any military action—"

"Who's talking about military action?" the President inquired blandly.

"I am," Arlie said, flushing a little but standing his ground. "Surely the option has to be considered. If it's going to be, we just want to make our position very clear. Unless we can be very sure that our mission is limited and clearly defined, unless we can be very sure that the consequences of our action have been clearly understood and completely anticipated, unless we have an absolutely rigid timetable for ending the mission, and are absolutely sure of victory—"

The Deputy Secretary of State snorted.

"That sounds like the military, all right," she observed acidly. "After the first Gulf War somebody in this house went around crowing about how 'the Vietnam syndrome is dead.' He was absolutely wrong. It's alive and well and living in the Pentagon. When were all the aspects of a mission 'absolutely clear' at its inception? When were all the consequences known in advance or even halfway predictable? What timetable was ever made that wasn't changed, and often drastically, by events in the field? When was anyone 'absolutely sure' of victory? War sets its own rules. You know that as well as we do. And you folks over there are absolutely scared to death of it. *That's* the problem."

"It is *not* the problem!" Arlie McGregor snapped. "We're simply trying to impose some rational thinking on people like you who won't be happy unless we're sending troops and tanks and planes and ships and maybe even missiles and A-bombs into every tight situation on the face of the globe. We can't do it." His face set in stubborn lines. "We won't do it!"

"You will if I tell you to," the President observed cheerfully. There was a stunned silence.

"Surely—" Arlie said after a moment, voice a little unsteady but recovering. "Surely you don't contemplate—"

"No, of course not," the President said with one of his baffling changes of mood—or changes of what seemed to be his mood. "Not for a minute. I just wanted to keep things in perspective. Of course we have to have more facts before we do anything. How long will it be before Creed Moncrief—*love* that name!—and Miss Regina can get a final fix on it, El? Have they given you a timetable? Have you given them one?"

"Mutual pledges of urgency at both ends," Eldridge Barnes said. "They know we want it fast—they want us to have it fast. Meanwhile, though, as I said at the beginning, I think we should recognize that these two young people—young and *very* bright—were correct to suggest that we decide now what to do about it, should the rumors be correct." He gave the President a bland stare. "Is there some opposition here to doing some advance planning, Mr. President?"

"Not a bit," the President said amicably. "Ray, you've been very silent in the face of your deputy's little tirade—"

"Not tirade, Mr. President," Eula Lee Montgomery said firmly. "Just factual analysis. I resent that word."

"I'm sorry, Eulie," the President said, turning on the charm, which clearly did not impress her very much. "Of course you were right to put things in perspective. The Pentagon needs a little dressing down once in a while, right, Arlie and Bill? One learns from it. God knows I expect Eulie to tell *me* off at any moment. It will be good for me!"

"That's right, Mr. President," she agreed, unperturbed. "Indeed it would. So watch it!"

"Look, folks," the President said with a chuckle. "She isn't laughing, either. Boy, is my tail in a wringer!"

And at this, of course, they all laughed, some more easily than others, but all relieved that the increasing tension had, at least for the moment, been broken.

"You asked me, Mr. President," Ray Stanley said, "what I thought. Without repeating or joining all of Eulie's strictures, I do think she has some good points—even though, on balance, I do tend to agree, as my friends from Defense know, with their general feeling that caution and circumspection are almost always advisable in our response to international crises. I do wonder, in this instance, if this *is* a crisis. Surely you people have your own sources in the Lolómés, Bill?"

"You're being diplomatic, Ray," General Rathbun said, looking, as always, as plain as an old shoe and as trustworthy, which was why his popularity with the American people remained consistently high. "You know damned well we have military attachés in both places. After getting the Agency report this morning like you did, I talked to both of them. They don't seem as bothered as Moncrief and Gates. They say they haven't heard anything quite so definite. Could it be your people are being a little hysterical, El?"

"Better hysterical," Eldridge Barnes retorted, "than blinkered by preconceived notions about the Middle East. Both Creed and Regina are in their second tours of duty there. Neither of your people has been there before. What do they know?"

"Well," General Rathbun said, putting a little starch in his normally level tones, "I don't know that I'd put it quite like that. They're both veterans of several overseas assignments—"

"Where?" El Barnes demanded. "The Seychelles and the Maldives?"

"No," Bill Rathbun said patiently, his normally impassive face beginning to crinkle a bit with anger. "Germany and Poland, if you must know. Anyway, they say they don't see any reason to send up any flares, yet. Based on *my* sources, I'd say go slow."

"Which might only indicate that your sources aren't always the best," El Barnes suggested. "Mr. President," he said, turning directly to the chief executive, who was listening to all this with a deliberately exaggerated wonderment, "I would appreciate it if the work of the Agency could be given its proper rating in the scheme of things. We do, after all, have our carefully cultivated sources. We do, after all, keep a constant alert for changes which is not always duplicated in other departments and agencies of the government. We are, after all—"

"You are, after all," the President interrupted, "a very challenging and confrontational type of individual, always anxious to protect your turf. Which may or may not be a good thing."

"Doesn't everybody?" the director of the CIA inquired blandly. "I feel I have better turf than most to protect."

"Many opinions on that, El," Ray Stanley remarked. "Anyway, aren't we straying a bit? The essential here is a divergence of opinion and our task here, it seems to me, is to decide of our own judgments, which is the more valid. With all respects to the CIA—"

"For which you don't have many," the director observed.

"Turnabout's fair play," the Secretary said with a smile. "In—any—event, the CIA says eether and the Pentagon says eyether, so let's call the whole thing off. Or shall we? I'd say yes, basically. I'd say let's go slowly until we have more information one way or the other. And proceed from there."

"Which may be when?" his deputy inquired with some skepticism. "It seems to me that if there is something there, time is of the essence. If we intend to issue a warning to Sidi, better now before things get really established. And the Agency says they likely may be well established. With all respects to you, Bill, I think the reports from these two kids in the field are sufficiently detailed already so that we'd be perfectly justified to go ahead as though we had absolute proof."

"To what end?" General Rathbun inquired. "To what purpose? You criticize the military all the time, Eulie, and maybe to some extent your criticisms are justified. But just remember that we almost never get a clear-cut decision on policy out of you civilians. There's no direct and consistent line of policy on anything; everything's as shifting as the sands of Sidi's deserts. Give us a clear-cut, consistent directive for once in your lives, and we'll gladly follow it. But what do you want to do now, say 'Scat!' and hope the bombs, if Sidi has them, will go away, and the missile launchers disappear? And if it's to be something more than 'Scat!,' then what is it? That's what we in the Pentagon want to know. You can call it lingering Vietnam syndrome if you like, but we call it common sense. Where do we go, what do we do? Have you got an idea, except to make a noise and try to bluff him out of whatever his pals are putting him up to?"

"Boy!" Eulie Montgomery said. "I'll bet that's the longest speech I've ever heard you make, Bill Rathbun. OK, you challenge me, I'll tell you what I'd do. I'd announce that we have good reason to believe that Sidi has bombs and the means to launch them, and I'd warn him that if he doesn't prove the contrary to the satisfaction of the international community, then we'll put on the pressure, starting with economic sanctions, and go on from there."

"Go on to where?" General Rathbun inquired. "And with what? Now you want to get into the same old pattern that's been characteristic of American administrations for at least the last ten years. Bluff—threat—loud noises—sanctions that hurt only the people, not the leaders, who take care of themselves very well, thank you very much—and then a puff of dust as it all settles down again, with nothing to show for it but damaged people, scot-free leaders, and one more slide down the scale of world prestige for the United States of America. Haven't we had enough of that? Better to keep our mouths shut and say nothing until we're ready to back it up, it seems to me."

"You aren't arguing with *me*," Eula Lee Montgomery said. "You're looking at one high-ranking government official who is quite willing to back up what she advocates with force, if need be. I've been a longtime opponent of the bluff-and-puff school of American foreign policy, as Ray well knows. I think we have enough to go on with Sidi, right now. Let's do it. Let's not crawfish again. Let's rock 'em and shock 'em and be a *real* leader, for a change. It's been a long time."

"Of course," the President observed thoughtfully, "you aren't taking

56

into account world opinion and the United Nations, which might be opposed to even a hint of strong action on our part. They're so afraid it would turn out to be action conducted independently of them—"

"Oh, well," she said in a dismissive tone. "If we're going to worry about the United Nations—"

"I have to," the President said.

She looked at him with an exaggerated blankness. "Why?"

"Because it's a fundamental principle of American diplomacy that we must always act in accordance with UN decisions and policies," the President said calmly. "My recent predecessors established that, and it seems to me a good principle to follow."

"A good excuse to follow," she remarked dryly, and not for the first time but the first time today, the President looked quite annoyed with his Deputy Secretary of State.

"Are you accusing me of hiding behind the UN, Eulie?" he inquired with a dangerous mildness.

She stood her ground. "It's been done. Frequently. In the last two terms."

"Only when America's best interests were clearly served by it!" he snapped.

She shrugged and settled back in her chair. "Over to you, Mr. President," she said. "You're obviously going to do whatever you want to do, regardless of any advice you receive here."

"With all respects to you, Eulie," the Secretary of State said mildly, "I think the majority of the advice he's going to get here is going to be exactly what everybody but you seems to want him to follow. Namely, go slow. Don't put us out on a limb. Wait for further clarification. Be prudent."

"Be timorous," she murmured, and then said, "Oh, hell!" in a louder tone. "You do what you want to do, of course. I've said my say, I'm out of it. It's been nice knowing you all."

"You aren't going anywhere," the President said calmly. "I need somebody to say 'no' once in a while. You aren't leaving. Relax . . . So, then. Does anybody think we ought to do something drastic at this point?"

"One thing you might do," the Secretary of State suggested quietly, as the Deputy Secretary shifted her papers and stared down at the table, flushed and flustered but stubbornly unconvinced, "if you feel like it,

Mr. President, is talk directly to the ambassadors, right now, and get their input."

The President looked thoughtful.

"I could," he said. "Why not? Jaime, why don't you have the Signal Corps boys set it up and have the calls patched in here on my phone. How long would it take?"

"Oh—ten minutes, I suppose," Jaime Serrano said. "It's morning over there. Everybody's up. Or ought to be."

"Good," the President said. "And Hank"—the Vice President, earnestly silent, jumped as though he had been shot—"call the kitchen and tell them to get some coffee and pastries up here, pronto . . . You all know where the facilities are. We'll reconvene in twenty." He smiled. "Do you want me to call Dolly Munson and make your excuses, Ray? You may not make that dinner."

"Why don't you?" the Secretary agreed with an answering smile. "She'll keep the secret."

"She's a dear old thing," the President said. "I'll do that."

Twenty minutes later, coffee and pastries on the table, the Vice President again an earnest, silent presence, Dolly pleased and mollified, the voice of the Signal Corps commander came evenly over the intercom, which the President had turned up so they could all hear.

"The ambassadors to the Lolómés, Mr. President," he said. "On line to you and linked to each other. Conference call ready to go ahead."

"Thank you," the President said, leaning forward slightly to the transmitter. "Big Bill Bullock!" he exclaimed in a jocular tone, sliding instantly into his hail-fellow-well-met mode. "Stately, dignified Arthur Reeves Burton, ambassador plenipotentiary and extraordinary! How the hell are you both?"

"Fine, Mr. President," Bill Bullock answered in his heavy, gravelly voice from Greater Lolómé.

"Very well, thank you, Mr. President," said Arthur Reeves Burton from Lesser Lolómé, sounding as stately and dignified as the President described him: like Ray Stanley and Eulie Montgomery, he went back a long way in the Foreign Service.

Bill Bullock, self-made oil millionaire from Texas—"Not *another* one!" Senator Wilson exclaimed dryly when his nomination came up to the Senate Foreign Relations Committee—sounded as though he had just completed a big meal of barbecued spareribs. Well fed, well housed, and well satisfied was the sound of Big Bill Bullock; or, as Joan Cohn-Bourassa had acidly described him—

"Bill—" the President said, "Arthur—what's going on over there? You know what Moncrief and Gates sent us today. Anything to it?"

"Quite a lot, I think," Ambassador Bullock said. "The slimy bastards are on the loose again, Mr. President. I think we have a problem."

"I wouldn't put it quite that way," politely confirmed Ambassador Burton, sixty-two and another longtime Arabist. "But basically, I agree."

"Arthur likes these desert scorpions," Bill Bullock said with a jovial laugh. "They don't impress me."

"I daresay it's mutual," Arthur Burton remarked dryly. "You have a way of making friends wherever you go, Bill."

"Boys!" the President said, as jovial as Big Bill. "No temper, now! No tantrums. Everybody solemn here. If it *is* solemn. You both think so."

"I do," Bill Bullock said. "Arthur always cuts them plenty of slack."

"Not always," Arthur Reeves Burton protested with a small, exasperated sigh. "Come off it, Bill. The chief wants to know what's really going on here. I've said I agree with you. It's all in how we handle it."

"Isn't it always?" the President said with an exasperated sigh of his own. "So the reports are correct, then—you believe."

"Yes," they replied together.

"Details?" the President demanded.

"Essentially what Creed and Regina report," Ambassador Burton said. "Three bombs, maybe more, from sources we haven't quite identified yet. The principal possibilities are Russia—China—North Korea—"

"And don't forget the likeliest," Bill Bullock said. "Your friend the father of all chaos, sitting back and pulling the strings and putting Sidi up to all kinds of mischief. God, how I hate that guy. And how I despise Sidi. I hope they're both listening."

"Oh, I hope not," the President said. "It isn't supposed to be possible. Though it might be a good thing for them to hear how determined we are."

"You mean that?" the Deputy Secretary murmured. She saw the President's expression. "You mean that." She subsided.

"And the launching facilities?" the President inquired.

Ambassador Bullock snorted.

"Hell!" he said. "Do you know what old Sidi had the nerve to tell me when I asked about all those construction trucks going in and out of the Pink House gates? He said he was 'expanding my personal facilities.' He said he was adding to the palace because it seems the Sultan of Brunei has just finished adding forty new rooms to *his* monstrous little cabana on Borneo and Sidi doesn't want to be outdone. I said that seemed like a damned sight far away for him to get jealous, but he just shrugged and gave me that bearded Cheshire Cat smile of his."

"So what did you do then, Bill?" Eulie Montgomery inquired.

He uttered a startled little laugh.

"Eulie!" he said. "How many people are sitting in on this, Mr. President?"

"NSC meeting," the President said. "We think it's that important. So what did you do?"

"Let it pass," Bill Bullock said. "What was I supposed to do, go poking around? I wouldn't be allowed in. Anyway, Moncrief did that, and very efficiently, it seems to me. He has good sources, that kid. Anyway, I, for one, believe their report. What do you think about it, Arthur?"

"I'm convinced there's substantial cause for concern," Arthur Reeves Burton said carefully. "So does The Mouse, incidentally. He's terrified. Regina is equally competent. Whether we should go public with our concerns at this particular moment—?" His voice trailed away into an obvious question mark.

"That's what we're trying to decide," the President said. "Not getting very far, but maybe we will now that you two have put your official stamp on it. I take it you agree that it won't hurt to have some sort of general response worked out."

"A carefully planned response," Ambassador Burton said, and the President gave a pleased little chuckle.

"Sooner or later," he observed, "somebody comes up with the perfect phrase, not always deliberately. Deliberately from you, of course, Arthur," he added quickly, "you're always deliberate. Anyway, if and when this does become public—as it will sooner or later, no matter how hard we try— somebody on somebody's staff will spill the beans to the media—then we'll say we've decided on 'a carefully planned response' whose nature we won't divulge. But we'll emphasize that it's ready. That ought to make them stop and think."

"Stop and think. There's another sidestep from Washington," Eulie Montgomery said with a sniff. "That will really stop them in their tracks."

"Eulie, Eulie!" the President said. "You're always so *predictable*. I'll huff and I'll puff a bit and make it sound ominous. Trust me."

In far-off Greater Lolómé, Ambassador Bullock cleared his throat.

"I'm with Eulie, Mr. President," he remarked. "I think you really ought to bear down on these rattlesnakes. I really think there's a real danger here. We've got to be really tough this time."

"What do you think, Arthur?" the President inquired.

Like his colleague, the ambassador to Lesser Lolómé cleared his throat, but in a slower, more thoughtful way.

"I've already said I'm convinced there's a problem and a real threat to peace in the region. Mustafa called me in this morning and begged for help; terrified, as I said. But I think much more can be done with quiet, behind-the-scenes diplomacy than with any public confrontation. If Bill, for instance, were to talk to Sidi and make clear to him—"

"Why don't you talk to him yourself, Mr. President?" Ambassador Bullock suggested. "Man to man. Ruler to rule. King to king. Flatter him and threaten him simultaneously. Tell him what a great leader he is but tell him if he doesn't comply we'll cut his balls off—oops, sorry, Eulie!"

"I've heard the expression," the Deputy Secretary remarked dryly. "I'd dispense with the 'great leader' bit and go directly to the realities if I were you, Mr. President."

"Which, perhaps fortunately, you are not," the President said, and then softened it with the charming smile he could turn on when necessary. "Fortunately for *me*, that is; the country might be much better off. So, Bill, you think I ought to go straight to Old Three Esses himself right now, hm?"

"He's in the Pink House," Bill Bullock said. "It shouldn't be hard to get through to him. If he'll accept your call, that is."

"You mean that son of a bitch would *refuse* to speak to me?" the President demanded, blithely ignoring the fact that not only had the U.S. effectively blocked Sidi in the second Gulf war, but as recently as a press conference last week the President had referred to him as "one of the sleaziest scourges of the Middle East." These items did not deter the chief executive. "Jaime!" he ordered. "Get him on the line!"

"Perhaps, Mr. President," Ray Stanley said as the national security adviser picked up the phone to the Signal Corps and went to work, "you would prefer us to leave—"

"No, no, no," the President said. "Sit tight. I mean you all to hear this. Silently, though, Eulie, OK? Silence is golden. And officially requested."

They were all silent for several minutes while Jaime exhorted the Signal Corps to hurry it up. Presently he turned and gestured to the President with a smile and a wink.

"Mr. Secretary?" he inquired. "This is Jaime Serrano in Washington. Is His Excellency there?"

There was a slight scratch of static, swiftly cleared. The flutelike tones of Sidi's personal secretary, known to the international community, inaccurately, unfairly, but universally as "The Eunuch," came on the line.

"His Excellency the President for Life is not available at the moment," he said with a regretful sigh. "He is so sorry that he cannot—"

"The President of the United States wishes to speak to him," Jaime Serrano interrupted. "As soon as possible. The President of the United States does not like to be kept waiting."

"And the President of Greater Lolómé does not like to be addressed like a servant!" the Eunuch responded sharply, plummy tones noticeably less friendly. "If the President of the United States will wait for a moment," he added, more mildly, "I shall see whether or not it suits the convenience of the President of Greater Lolómé to talk with him."

"Please do," the national security adviser said in an unimpressed tone. "It is a matter of some urgency."

"We cannot recall any matter of urgency between our two countries at the moment," the Eunuch said. He could not resist a parting shot. "At least, not one that *we* recognize as such. Please be patient."

The President refrained from comment but did not look pleased. As the silence lengthened, a noticeable flush of annoyance began to spread across his face. Everyone became very silent. War might be declared in the next five minutes. No one really thought so, but such is the power of that office in that area that no one would have been truly surprised if it had happened.

"Mr. President," Sidi's voice, heavy and emphatic, boomed out with a startling loudness. As always in their conversations, a note of barely suppressed sarcasm underlay it; they had never liked one another, and events had not improved their relationship. As always, his carefully tutored English was fluent and expressive.

"To what do I owe the infinite honor of this call?" he asked.

"Your Excellency," the President said, "no honor I can confer upon you with my call can possibly equal the honor you confer upon me by accepting it." He winked at Eulie. "It is a small matter, Mr. President, of atomic bombs. And missiles. And missile launchers. How about it?"

There was a perceptible silence but no indication of surprise or agitation.

"How about it?" Sidi inquired.

"Is it true?"

A certain caution crept into Sidi's tone, but he still did not sound at all perturbed.

"And if it were?"

"Is it?"

"Who can say?"

"You can. Is it?"

"I really must know, Mr. President," Sidi said blandly, "what the purpose of this interrogatory is. If what you postulate were true, I suppose you would threaten me with dire punishments, such being the high moral ground of the United States in world affairs. If it were not, then you would simply make yourself ridiculous by resorting to such tactics. So, *you* must tell *me*."

"No, you must tell me, Excellency," the President said. His tone became dry. "Save me from making a fool of myself, Mr. President. Save me, save me!"

"Now," Sidi said, permitting himself a sudden show of indignation, "you mock me, Mr. President. It is not a nice game. Nor is it productive. I shall tell you nothing. How about *that*?"

For a moment the President was silent. Then he tried a different tack.

"You are not one of my favorite people in this world, Mr. President—"

Sidi laughed without rancor.

"It is mutual, Mr. President."

"—so it would be very easy for me to become angry with you and threaten some reprisal—"

"It is not threats of reprisals we respect, Mr. President," Sidi remarked. "Only orders for them. Are you ordering?"

"Not yet," the President said.

Sidi laughed again, quite comfortably.

"Good," he said. "I was greatly concerned. For a moment. So, then, Mr. President, what can I do for you? What is the purpose of this call?"

"The purpose," the President said, "is to verify the reports we have received relative to at least three, possibly five, atomic bombs now in your possession, plus ten missiles with which to deliver them, plus launching capabilities constructed beneath the surface of Pointe Sinistre, disguised, God help us, as 'expanding your personal facilities' to make the Sultan of Brunei jealous. What a delightful motive. If true."

"You doubt it," Sidi said with a heavy sadness. "Cannot an honorable man accept the word of an honorable man? What becomes of civilized discourse, if this be not the case?"

"Our sources are quite impeccable, Mr. President."

"Oh, yes," Sidi said thoughtfully. "Young Mr. Moncrief, known as special political assistant to the ambassador. Very special. I think I shall demand the recall of Mr. Moncrief. At once. Either that, or I shall expel him . . ." His tone trailed away, came back strong. "Unless, of course, he meets with some unfortunate accident."

"I would not recommend it, Mr. President," the President said calmly.

"You would not," Sidi said, "but I may have to. Accidents do happen sometimes, to meddlesome foreigners in this desert world. And who more meddlesome than young Mr. Moncrief?"

"Such an event would bring immediate and devastating punishment," the President said.

"Oh, Mr. President!" Sidi exclaimed. "Who could prove it? It would be an accident. It would be a very well-executed accident." He chuckled suddenly, the cruel, dispassionate sound so many terrified supplicants heard in the Pink House cellars just prior to oblivion. "'Executed,'" he repeated thoughtfully, "may be just the right word. But accidental, in his case. It is the least we could do out of respect for the ancient friendship between our two countries."

"Never any friendship, Excellency," the President said, "and never any trust. If you harm that boy, Greater Lolómé will suffer. If I can arrange it, you will suffer personally."

"Mr. President!" Sidi said, gently chiding. "You forget that the laws of your noble nation specifically prevent anything so crude as the assassination of foreign leaders. All of us foreign leaders have never understood why the United States was so noble, but since you are, we are all very grateful. Possibly it is because you people don't want anyone to assassinate *you*." He chuckled again, the same cold, dispassionate sound. "This does not necessarily follow."

"Are you threatening *me*, now, Excellency?" the President inquired. "This is getting tiresome. I repeat, harm that boy and a lot of things are going to happen very quickly."

"Oh, Mr. President," Sidi said. "You are always saying things like that, and who cares? You never do anything."

Jaime Serrano, hastily scribbling, tossed a note on the President's desk: *Remember the bombs.* The President nodded.

"We have once," he said, "and we will again. Which brings me back to the basic purpose of this call. You have bombs, you have missiles, you have launchers. You have them quite suddenly, from a source or sources we have not yet determined, though we have a pretty good idea. We do not like this. I want to warn you, privately but emphatically, that the United States and its allies are prepared to take whatever action may be necessary to destroy this threat to the peace of the region and the peace of the world."

"'Destroy'?" Sidi echoed, not sounding at all impressed. "Are you prepared to go that far, on your own? Without congressional support, without media support, without the support of the country? And what 'allies'? You mean they will follow you once again down the same old caravan route to nowhere? I doubt it, Mr. President. I doubt it very much."

"I am contacting them immediately," the President said. "I am confident they will respond, as they have before, to the peace-threatening moves of you and your sponsor."

"You may get them to say 'tut-tut,'" Sidi remarked. "You may even get them to say, 'Oh, my goodness.' But more than that? I wish you luck."

"So it is true," the President said.

Sidi's tone became flatly defiant.

"Suppose it were, still this seems to be the best you can do, Mr. President—one more threat. The world has grown accustomed to American threats in recent years, the record is long and pathetic. Bosnia—Somalia—North Korea—China—Haiti—Chechnya—wherever the White House has decided that loud noises are a substitute for strong action. It is an old story to the world. Why should it impress me now?"

"We took up arms before," the President reminded, "and we can do it again."

"I was not really prepared then," Sidi said. "It is a different story now. As always America has delayed too much, debated too much, taken counsel of its fears too much. It will take counsel of them again, and your so-called allies will fall obediently in behind, as craven as you are. They won't act without you—and you won't act. It is a formula the world has come to know very well in recent years. Is that all you can say to me, Mr. President? If so, I have better things to do while I arrange to destroy the peace of the world. It may not even be necessary. Mustafa is shitting green camel dung at this very moment. It will not take much to conquer him this time. He will go down in a day."

"Excellency," the President said, his tone finally beginning to show the exasperation he felt, "I must warn you that unless you adhere to your obligations under the nuclear proliferation treaty—"

"I am going to abrogate it."

"Then you must be prepared to face the most devastating consequences."

"I am prepared to take that risk."

"Mr. President. I must warn you that when we bring this matter to the United Nations—"

Sidi laughed aloud, a short, harsh bark.

"—when we bring this matter to the United Nations," the President repeated as firmly as he could, "I am sure we will have the unanimous support of the Security Council—"

Sidi laughed again.

"Which will be just as strong as you are. Which isn't much."

The President's tone became cold.

"I shall not talk to you again, Mr. President. We will now proceed along all the tracks open to us."

"It will do you no good," Sidi said, with an open contempt in his voice that chilled them all. "May Allah defeat all your efforts and confound all infidels."

"If you wish to talk more sensibly," the President said, "call me any time of day or night. There may still be a little time to work something out."

Sidi laughed again his short, harsh bark.

"First the threat and then the back-down," he said. "How American!" And went off the line.

For several moments no one spoke in the Roosevelt Room. Presently Eulie Montgomery inquired dryly, "And?"

"I think he'll come around," the President said with the comfortable, down-home confidence he often liked to display to the public. "It's a shock to him that we know. It will take him a little time to absorb it, and then he'll call me back and be reasonable."

"I'm glad you're so sure," she said.

The President smiled.

"They always do," he said. "There has to be some face saving, and perhaps a huff and puff or two from him, and then it will all die down and go away. He won't really dare to carry out any of his threats in the face of world opinion. It'll work out. You'll see."

"Mr. President," Ambassador Bullock said slowly, "with all respects, I am not so sure. He's been nursing his grudge ever since we forced him to retreat from Lesser Lolómé last time. Now he's been given the tools to do something about it. I'm not so sure he's just going to back off. When I saw him yesterday I seemed to detect a greatly increased arrogance there; from his tone today, I'd say it's doubled or even tripled. He's sounding suddenly like one tough cookie. It may have gone to his head, whether justified or not. If he thinks it is, he's going to be awfully hard to bluff."

"Who says I'm bluffing?" the President inquired sharply.

"Mr. President," Arlie McGregor demanded, sounding genuinely alarmed, "do you mean that? Are you actually going to expect us to launch an immediate—"

The President looked annoyed.

"For *heaven's* sake," he said, "it's Seedy Sidi I'm supposed to be scaring, not my own Secretary of Defense. Of course I'm not asking the Pentagon to launch an immediate attack on anybody. If we have to take armed action in this matter, it will only be after we've exhausted all other possible means of containment. I have a lot to do myself, first. I'm going to contact the major allies, I'm going to discuss it with the Secretary-General at the UN, we'll have to get the Hill and the media lined up, we're going to have to generate at least a reasonable percentage of support in the polls—"

"How long will all that take, Mr. President?" Ray Stanley inquired.

The President shrugged.

"A week? Two? It shouldn't take very long. You and Eulie and my national security adviser will all be involved in it. The one thing I must stress is that this is all completely off the record for the moment. I'm going to give Sidi sufficient time, without public pressure, to come around; and at the same time, I'm going to be building that 'carefully planned response' you advocate, Arthur. I think that with a combination of careful diplomacy and a little garden-variety psychology, I can persuade him to give up any wild ideas he has, without going to a public confrontation that might create a lot of headaches. Therefore this is all completely quiet for the moment."

"Our people at State are going to be wondering, Mr. President," Ray Stanley said.

The President nodded. "Tell your immediate people, sure, but keep it minimal. I don't want to hear about it on the evening news."

"I've heard that before," the Secretary said with a smile.

"I've said it before," his deputy observed. "A couple of dozen million times. It rarely does any good."

"This time it had better," the President said in a tone that was not amused. "Otherwise some heads will roll in the department—in any department that violates the ban. OK, Defense? CIA? NSC?"

They all nodded soberly.

"As for you boys on the spot," the President said, "we'll be in constant communication, so stay alert. I want you to see Sidi tomorrow, Bill, and tell him that we are taking immediate steps to isolate Greater Lolómé and organize the strongest possible international pressure—"

"Until he does what?" Ambassador Bullock inquired. "What's the requirement?"

"That he cooperate fully with an immediate inspection by the International Atomic Energy Agency and renounce any further territorial ambition in Lesser Lolómé."

"He won't like that," Bill Bullock said. "What if he refuses?"

"He won't refuse," the President said with calm and utter confidence. "And you, Arthur, tell The Mouse to keep calm. We aren't going to abandon him."

"He will be relieved to hear that," Arthur Reeves Burton said, so smoothly that no one could tell whether he was genuinely agreeing or being politely skeptical.

The President looked a little odd for a second but decided to avoid friction and accept his words as endorsement.

"Good," he said. "Thank you both for your input and support."

"Thank you, Mr. President," they said in unison, and went off the line.

"OK, Jaime," he said, "you stay with me for a bit and we'll do a little planning. The rest of you have a good evening and we'll be in touch first thing in the morning." His eye fell on the Vice President, trying hard to be a good sport but still looking somewhat crestfallen. "Oh, and Hank, of course, you stay too. You can tell me how to go about handling the Senate."

"Yes, sir!" the Vice President said, looking relieved and pleased.

"Give my love to Dolly, Ray," the President said. "You can still make her dinner, after all."

The Secretary of State smiled.

"With pleasure," he said. "And congratulations on your handling of Sidi. I think you have him analyzed correctly."

In the limousine which would drop Eulie off at her home in Georgetown before taking the Secretary along to Dolly's beautiful old house near Dumbarton Oaks, she turned squarely to him and said sternly, "Ray Stanley, you ought to be ashamed of yourself. You do *not!*"

"Do not what?" he inquired blandly.

"You know what. Think the President has Sidi analyzed correctly. Or handled him effectively. Why do you say things like that?"

He smiled.

"He's the President. And I'm his Secretary of State. I can't be too harsh."

"I almost told him myself," she said, "except he would have expected a sour note from me. You have enough prestige to disagree and make him pay attention."

69

"It's a matter of not expending one's capital too fast or too freely," he said. "I may need to tell him something later, if this doesn't work out."

"But I thought you were against putting too much pressure on Sidi," she said. "Why the reversal?"

"I'm not reversing," he protested mildly. "I'm just waiting to see what's going to happen."

"I might have known. What do I tell the others? They'll be calling me."

"Tell them basically what was decided," he said. "That we're organizing a 'carefully planned response' in the hope that it will defuse the situation before it ever becomes public and requires some more drastic action. That's good diplomacy, isn't it?"

3   Home from Dolly's, listening to Mary's even breathing beside
him in their big canopied four-poster bed in their spectacular Potomac-
view apartment in Washington Harbor, he again was not so sure, either
of his own ability to contribute to solutions of the world's problems, or
of the course the President seemed determined to follow with Sidi.

Like Bill Bullock, Ray Stanley felt that there had been an even more
arrogant intransigence in Sidi's tone, an even more adamant and hard-
line response, than in their previous encounters with him. For all the
President's confidence in his own powers to con, cajole, and ultimately
convince and/or coerce his opponents, the Secretary of State was not so
positive that they were going to work this time. Thanks to his sinister
friend or friends, Sidi apparently did have bombs now and—at least to
hear him talk—the restraints such an awesome responsibility ought to
impose upon leaders of nations were no longer of controlling importance to him. More important now seemed to be the fulfillment of his
own imperialistic ambitions toward Lesser Lolómé, with all the ramifi-
cations a successful conquest would have upon the world's oil trade, and
not least, the further deterioration of America's standing in the eyes of
other nations.

Domination of a key segment of the world's oil was obviously of vital
economic interest to the President of Greater Lolómé and so, too, the
Secretary could concede, was the sentimental ambition to reunite what
British map-drawers had put asunder so long ago. But underlying those
ambitions was an even more sinister and implacable motivation: to tear
down and if possible destroy the power, prestige, and ability to influence
world events, of the United States of America.

This was now, unhappily, a dominant motivation of many leaders of
the world's peoples, and the Secretary had to acknowledge, unhappily,

---

71

that what seemed sinister and implacable to him seemed only right and fitting to them. No matter the great triumphs of World War II, the contributions to saving civilization from the onslaughts of Hitler and subsequent tyrants, no matter the endless record of overwhelming generosity to nations and peoples in need, no matter the carrying high, however imperfectly, of the banners of human freedom and decency.

No nation in all of history, he firmly believed, had ever had a higher quotient of idealism or offered more unstintingly of hope and assistance to humankind. No nation had ever lived to see its motives so besmirched, its purposes so lied about, its efforts turned so glibly into mockery and hate. America had ventured great things and often failed them greatly. It was the failures that leaders like Sidi (and many ostensibly far less sinister and far more friendly) had used to instill in their peoples contempt and hatred for America, and used also as a springboard for their jealous and vindictive attempts to undercut, thwart, and ultimately bring down the bumbling if good-hearted giant of the West.

They simply did not admit the existence of the good heart, or the generosity or the decency. The hate was too much; by the end of the twentieth century it all had gone on too long. Vengeance upon America was too convenient a concealment for their own corruptions, too easy a means to achieve their own ruthless ambitions.

If they could bring America down, the Secretary thought gloomily now, there would be celebrations in many places, some expected but some quite surprising, around the globe; but what would be left of freedom and decency, and who would man the barricades, then? And what would happen to the world's helpless individuals in the great vacuum of power left behind?

He sighed heavily and rolled over, trying at three A.M. to lure elusive sleep. As always, he knew it would elude him until its own good time, which frequently of late was not until the first light of dawn began to creep over the uneasy capital of "the world's sole remaining superpower." What did it profit "the world's sole remaining superpower" if its enemies and even many of its professed friends were secretly jealous and resentful of its influence, and inclined to be rather happily gratified when it slipped and stumbled?

Nor were they all foreigners who felt that way, he reflected unhappily. His conversations at Dolly's had been quite typical.

Dolly herself was still, at eighty-three, a vivacious, charming white-haired patrician beauty after four decades as "one of Washington's leading political hostesses—if not *the* leading one," as the *Post*'s society editor put it. As the widow of a former Senate majority leader, Bob Munson of Michigan, she had always been at the center of political Washington's ever-churning social life. "Administrations come and administrations go," the society editor had written. "Dolly Munson, infinitely gracious, infinitely well informed—and infinitely in the thick of it—goes on forever."

And so she did, entertaining at her enormous house near Dumbarton Oaks in Georgetown at least once and sometimes, particularly when a new administration came in, as many as three and four times a week. Her parties were often an indication of the prevailing political winds in the capital, valued not only because being able to say "I'm going to Dolly's" was an instant indicator of where you stood on the constantly changing ladder of political preference, but also an infallible indicator of where the power centers might be shifting at any particular time. In recent months she had put an increasing emphasis on top leaders from the Hill and top figures in the media. Both were always in demand at political Washington's parties, but somehow Dolly's guest lists always seemed the most significant. Certainly to be on one was still one of the most avidly sought accolades in Washington. Tonight had been no exception.

When he had arrived, a little late after the limousine dropped Eulie off on nearby R Street and deposited him at Dolly's, he had found several of those he had expected. He was "out of uniform," he explained to Dolly, because he had not had time to change to the inevitable black tie.

"That's all right," she had said with her comfortable laugh. "Mary's already arrived alone, and that's one flag up to our friends of the media. Now you arrive in 'civilian clothes,' and that's another. Obviously you've been at some late meeting. And obviously an important meeting. What's up?"

"Dolly, dear," he said, kissing her on the cheek, "as always, you smell like a million dollars."

"I have several," she said with a chuckle. "Don't change the subject. What's up, I said."

"Just some routine matters in the department," he said blandly.

"Where I'm sure you keep a change of clothes," she said, linking her arm in his and drawing him into the crowded living room. "Which you didn't use. So you probably came from the White House. What's got the NSC excited at this late hour?"

"Dolly," he said, "you're too much. Be a good girl and someday I may tell you."

"Might as well tell me now," she said. "This foursome will have it out of you in no time."

She gestured to Senator Wilson, engaged in an obviously animated chat with James Van Rensselaer Burden, Able Montague, and that "demon newshen," as *Time* anachronistically referred to her, Sally Holliwell, TV congressional correspondent and doyenne of one of the less hectic weekly talk shows, "Capitol Perspective."

All four swung around to stare up at him with lively interest as he came down the three steps to the living room level and gently disengaged himself from Dolly's arm.

"All right for you, then," she said lightly. "It will just have to be a secret—for the moment. Meanwhile, I'll throw you to the tender mercies of these four sharpies. We'll eat in fifteen minutes."

"Thank you so much," he said with an easy laugh. "For not siccing them onto me. For being so discreet. For being so—Dolly."

"That's me," she said cheerfully as she moved off toward Boo and Joan Cohn-Bourassa, talking busily with the Iraqi ambassador and the deputy head of mission of the embassy of Iran.

"What's the secret, Ray?" Willie Wilson inquired. "Is it something we should know?"

"You," he said amicably. "Not these three vultures."

Able Montague immediately put on his you-can't-fool-me expression, Sally Holliwell looked suitably aggressive, and Jimmy Van, always conscious of his dignity, still managed to look down his patrician nose and permit a gleam of condescending curiosity to enter his studiously impersonal glance. Sally had come up through the ranks of the wire services, the *Post* and the *Times* before being lured away by television; Able was a little Irish bulldog grown grizzled in the capital's cutthroat media competition; Jimmy Van never let you forget that he was a descendant of a distinguished family and a product of Groton and Harvard, even though the world was now in a condition in which Groton and Harvard were rather low on the list of humanity's major concerns. They were not that low in Washington, where "*some* breeding still counts, thank God, though God knows how much longer," as Jimmy expressed it with a superior and rather delicate sigh to his colleagues.

"You obviously came here in a hurry, Mr. Secretary," Sally observed with a knowing air. "You sure you don't want to tell us something?"

"I'm sure I don't want to tell you anything," Ray Stanley said, still amicably.

"Maybe Joanie Bourassa knows," Able said, shrewd little eyes sparkling with the challenge of the chase. "She and Boo are usually pretty well informed."

"What's to know?" the Secretary inquired innocently. "I was working a little late at the department so I just came right over."

"Without changing?" Jimmy Van inquired in his customary languid, semi-British drawl, precious but concealing a shrewd mind. "That's not like our perfect model of a perfect Secretary. No, Ray, you can't fool us. Something is definitely Up."

"And who better to ferret it out than the media's finest, whom I see before me," the Secretary remarked. He made a split-second calculation: the administration did, after all, "have to get the media lined up," as the President put it, and these were powerful players. "Well, I'll tell you—" he began in a casual voice, having learned from many years of experience that one can say almost anything in a crowded room and get away with it, if the manner is conversational enough.

Senator Wilson held up a warning hand, handsome white head cocked quizzically to one side, expression warning. "Are you sure you want to do this, Ray? I thought you said it was just for my ears."

"Don't worry, Willie," the Secretary said with a chuckle. "I'll only tell them what I want them to know."

"He means that, gang," Able Montague said. "Is that a challenge, or is it a challenge?"

"It's a challenge," Sally Holliwell said.

"We shall pursue it with the utmost vigor to the ends of the earth," Jimmy Van promised with mock solemnity. His expression became serious. "What's the latest doom-and-gloom, then, Mr. Secretary? It must be something portentous, to make you arrive late and disheveled at Dolly's."

"Late," Ray Stanley said with a smile. "Never, I hope, disheveled. Our friend Sidi may be causing trouble again."

They were all suddenly serious and intent.

"Oh?" Able Montague inquired. "How so?"

"And how soon?" Sally Holliwell inquired, and added, not entirely in jest, "We have to tape the weekend show tomorrow afternoon. Will he do his damage in time for us to get it in?"

"I don't know about that," Ray Stanley said, "but he may oblige pretty soon, the way it looks."

"Tell him to speed it up," she said, half-wry, half-serious. "These things are all better if they happen a little before deadline."

"As most well-informed international brigands are aware, these days," Jimmy Van observed. "They usually cooperate, don't they?"

"Not always Sidi," she said. "He's a wild card."

"And about to get wilder, I take it," Senator Wilson said. "What's prompting this latest furor? I assume he's threatening The Mouse again?"

"Oh, yes," the Secretary said. "What else would he be doing?"

"Thereby threatening our oil supplies," Jimmy Van said in a spiteful tone. "The be-all and end-all of our foreign policy in the region."

"So why do you think this is any more serious than any other time?" Able inquired. "Why is it serious enough to warrant an NSC meeting?"

"I didn't say there was an NSC meeting," the Secretary objected.

Able looked knowing and followed the same deductive line Dolly had.

"Oh, come now. Late arrival in mufti—no time to stop at home or the department and change—must have come from somewhere important enough to disrupt normal schedule, namely, 1600 Pennsylvania—only excuse for 1600 Pennsylvania this time of night, NSC meeting. Right?"

"You said all that," Ray said with the chuckle he used to deflect importunate questioners. "I didn't. I knew all I'd have to give you would be the bare facts, and you'd take it from there."

"Yes," Jimmy Van said, languid drawl becoming more pronounced as he began to zero in on it. "But that doesn't tell us *why* the NSC meeting. Do you always react this strongly to Sidi's routine threats?"

"We always take him seriously," Ray Stanley said. He lowered his voice, but still with an easy air of casual conversation that misled both the Chief Justice, who passed by and nodded, and Joanie Bourassa, who, not having been informed of the NSC results, smiled and waved brightly from across the room.

"Confidentially," he said. "According to reports we get—"

"From whom?" Able interrupted.

"'Sources,'" Ray Stanley said blandly. "Isn't that what you people always quote? 'Sources' always have all the information. Anyway, we have been advised that Sidi has been acquiring substantial additions to his military force—"

"From whom?" Able repeated, and grinned. "You might as well tell us, Mr. Secretary. I've found my key question in all this. And intend to keep on asking it."

"You bulldogs of the media!" Ray exclaimed with a laugh. "We don't know from whom, and we don't really know for certain all the details. But we do know he's being much more belligerent all of a sudden, and we do know it may pose some threat to the peace of the region and possibly the peace of the world. Why don't you get your teeth into the possibilities, Able? Speculation, conjuration, admonition! They ought to keep both 'Washington Wrangle' and 'WorldView' going for a while."

"I'm sure it will move to the top of the agenda for both," Able said with the undisguised pride he always showed in his two highly rated television programs. "But you still haven't given us the other piece of the puzzle."

"Right," Jimmy Van agreed, scooping up a stuffed mushroom from a passing tray and consuming it in one smoothly practiced gulp. "What," he added, as he cleaned his fingers delicately, one by one, with a cocktail napkin, "is the U.S. going to do about it?"

"Well," Ray Stanley said soberly, turning his head to survey their happily gossiping fellow guests so that only Willie Wilson, for whom it was intended, caught his quick wink, "that is something you may seriously and genuinely speculate about. No decision has been reached except to monitor the situation closely and, if necessary, prepare a carefully planned response."

"Which would be?" Sally inquired, also disposing of a mushroom— how many tons of hors d'oeuvres did the average Washington party-goer consume in a year, the Secretary wondered. "Another military escapade?"

"I don't know at this time," the Secretary said. His tone of sober thoughtfulness turned deeply confidential, though his expression remained blandly uncommunicative for the benefit of those shrewd observers who might be watching them, of whom there were many at a party at Dolly's. "That's where your input would be very helpful to us. How strong a response do you think the country would stand for?"

"Oh, well," James Van Rensselaer Burden said in a haughtily dismissive tone, "if this is just a trial balloon because that wimpish soul in the White House doesn't trust his own judgment and wants us to do his thinking for him—"

"And stir up the country for him," Able Montague interjected.

"And put on the pressure for his benefit," Sally Holliwell said. "Well, I, for one, say the hell with it." Her sharp-featured face, sharp of mouth, sharp of nose, sharp of chin, sharp of eyes, able to smile but coldly, looked even sharper than usual. "Let him take a position on his own, for once! Why should we always play water boy?"

"Water person, darling," Able said with a chuckle, going for the smoked salmon and sour cream offered by one of Dolly's favorite catering staff. "Let's keep our genders straight. Yes, Ray, how about it? What does he want to do? Or does he know?"

"I repeat," Ray Stanley said calmly, "we're watching the situation very closely. We hope we don't have to take any action at all. If we do, it will, we hope, be appropriate and carefully planned." He shrugged with deliberate indifference. "Use it or not, as you like." He smiled. "You don't have to be reporters, you know. This is a happy social occasion at Dolly's. Nobody is supposed to have a care in the world. Enjoy!"

"We'll use it," Able promised with a rather grim smile.

"Oh, yes," Jimmy Van agreed, elevating his nose and looking down it through his deliberately out-of-fashion pince-nez, "you may be sure of that. With," he added with satisfaction as he mentioned the name of his 323-newspaper column, "considerable disapproval in the case of 'As I See It,' I can tell you."

"It certainly won't fly on 'Capitol Perspective,'" Sally Holliwell agreed, "if this is going to involve any kind of imperialistic, big-stick attempt to bludgeon a silly two-bit old opponent—to say nothing of the American people—into bowing to the administration's will." She turned to Willie Wilson with a very firm smile. "You'll come on my program and condemn it, won't you, Senator?"

"He'll have to consider all the aspects and weigh all the considerations before he can give you an answer to that one," Able remarked with a sly little grin.

"Don't we always?" Willie inquired blandly. "That's our job, on the Hill."

"I simply won't stand for another ridiculous and foredoomed use of American military force!" Sally said flatly. "I just won't have it!"

"And there," Willie said with a grin that did not, and was not intended to, rob it of sting, "speaks the chairman of the Joint Chiefs of Staff. Or the President. Take your pick. Which would you rather be, Sally?"

"I'm a member of the Washington media," Sally said with a tart conviction that was obviously absolutely sincere and not softened a bit by the rather strained smile with which she spoke, "and that's quite powerful enough for me, thank you."

"It does give one an enviable ability to attack without responsibility, doesn't it?" Senator Wilson said. "And without being exposed to the same public scrutiny you bestow so lovingly upon others. Who guards the guardians? A ridiculous question, in this day and age. The answer was established years ago: no one."

"Well," Ray Stanley remarked, as their media friends all looked starchily offended, and the conversation threatened to go further in obviously hostile and predictable directions he didn't really think they all wanted to go, "Dolly will be ringing the dinner bell any moment, and I must find my lovely wife and at least say hello before we go in. I think"—he pulled out the seating card he had been given at the door and gave it a quick glance—"that I'm going to have the great privilege and pleasure of being seated next to Mrs. Ambassador van der Heuft of the Netherlands."

"Lucky you!" Sally said, coming down from her imperious high with a rather shaky laugh, since she, like all of them, did not really want a major argument in public; and anyway, her program awaited.

"The loveliest rose in the garden," Able Montague said with a dry little chuckle. "Before we part, though, Mr. Secretary, I just wanted to say that I, too, shall be most strongly opposed to any use of force by the United States."

"Or even any belligerent and unnecessary rhetoric," James Van Rensselaer Burden agreed. "There is such a thing as being too crude, you know. Too, *too* crude."

"Willie," the Secretary said, "come along and say hello to Mary."

"I already h—" Willie started to say and caught himself. "By all means. Can't get too much of a good thing."

"Right," Ray said. "Take care, you all." He smiled pleasantly, took Willie's arm, and steered him into the crowd just as Dolly appeared at the door and began rounding up the guests in her pleasantly firm fashion.

"Now," Willie said quickly, "what is all this?"

"Three big ones," the Secretary murmured in his ear as they smiled their way to Mary across the room. "At least. And the long-range missiles to deliver them. Plus new launching facilities beneath Pointe Sinistre. Another move on Lesser Lolómé, and God knows what else."

"Bad," Willie said.

"Bad," the Secretary agreed.

"Come along," Dolly said, materializing between them and linking an arm with each. "You, too, Mary. Feed your faces and let those razor-sharp minds charged with the preservation of civilization rest for a while."

And so the Secretary did, chatting brightly and innocuously with apple-plump Mrs. Ambassador van der Heuft of the Netherlands on his right and mantis-thin Mrs. Ambassador Tri Van Duen of Vietnam on his left. Both tried to pump him on various subjects of interest to their husbands, seated elsewhere among the tables for eight with which Dolly always filled her dining room, but with lifelong skill he turned it all aside and kept the conversation on the straight and humdrum road. He was aware of their frustration and amused by it, but never indicated by so much as a twitch that he knew what they were attempting. It was all part of the Washington game.

There were no more confrontations such as he had enjoyed with the media, and he did enjoy them, particularly when he could shepherd the formulations of a news story as he had tonight. He was sure they would raise hell, but they would get the public debate going; and, as usual with many of the Washington press corps, their obvious bias would create a healthy skepticism of what they said in the minds of many readers and viewers, and a consequent healthy discounting of it.

For the remainder of the evening he let the tides of chatter sweep over him and didn't bother to think very much; kept his mouth going with all requisite politeness but, as Mary described it, "turned his mind off and gave it a rest." When Dolly at leave-taking expressed regret that Eulie had not been able to make it, he told her that he understood Eulie's long ordeal might soon be coming to an end. They paid regretful but admiring tribute to her strength of character and to the loving concern she had shown throughout for Herbie. "Small consolation at the moment you lose a life's companion," Dolly said with the sigh of one who knew. "But comforting, in time."

(At that moment on R Street, the Deputy Secretary of State had just been roused from uneasy sleep by her husband's voice calling weakly from the adjoining room. His doctors had telephoned that afternoon, just before she left to go to the White House for the NSC meeting, to tell her that they gave him perhaps another two weeks before the inevitable occurred. Always realistic, which usually meant pessimistic too, she gave him even less. With the instinct of thirty years of marriage, she knew he concurred. They were now equally dedicated to making his last days as comfortable as possible for one another. On his part this coupled a steadily weakening physical condition with a gentle, almost luminous determination to go gracefully and without fuss; and on hers, a determination to see it through as bravely and lovingly as she could.

(She thought now, for an instant and without regret, of Dolly's party; then dismissed it. Ray had been there, surrounded by media; and perhaps it was as well that there had been no hint to those high-priced, famous ferrets, that there was any friction within the department. Not that it was ever open friction: she and the Secretary had long ago agreed to disagree on some aspects of foreign policy. So far, none of their conflicts had ever surfaced outside the department. In any event, her place was here. There would be time tomorrow, and perhaps for days and weeks to come, if Sidi did not swiftly pull in his horns, when she would have more than enough opportunities to state her position.

(She dismissed all that and went dutifully and gladly to answer her dying husband's call; a tall, heavy, statuesque, and quite forbidding woman, moving with the lightness that often accompanies height and weight such as hers, carrying the burden of a breaking heart, along with all her other burdens, with grace.)

The Secretary was in bed by midnight, but as usual he was still awake at one A.M., restless, tense, his mind racing in chaotic disjunction ranging from the most innocuous to the most gravely portentous. He tried not to stir too much, tried to keep his breathing regular, diligently pretended sleep. As always, it didn't work.

"So what are our friends in the media going to do?" Mary inquired quietly at his side. "Eat you alive?"

"Probably," he said.

"What is it this time?" she asked, and after he told her, uttered a small, exasperated sound.

"He *is* annoying, that one," she said. "I wish we could wipe out these two-bit tyrants when we have the chance. Every time we leave one essentially untouched, he rises like the phoenix to plague us again. We never learn. We never have the guts to follow through. It's disheartening."

"It's symptomatic," he said. "Willie Wilson thinks there's a dry rot at the heart of our whole decision-making process in State, Pentagon, and White House. But I don't see how we can proceed much differently than we are."

"So you wind up with State and the Pentagon wanting to go slow and the President tempted to throw his weight around."

"He did throw it around," the Secretary said with a wry chuckle. "Sidi threw it right back at him. So now he's going to embark on an effort, momentarily secret but soon to become ostentatiously public, to get Sidi's attention and to get our allies and the UN to put on the pressure. Diplomatic, at first. Then sanctions. Then reestablishing the coalition as a form of public pressure. Plus continued efforts at behind-the-scenes pressure—"

"Which you've just told me have already failed."

"I'm inclined to agree with the President that they will succeed in the long run. When Sidi has time to think it over."

"Suppose he thinks it over and decides to go right ahead?"

"Now, Mary," he said patiently. "You're beginning to sound like Eulie."

"Eulie and I have been seeing eye to eye on things for forty years. I do hope your influence comes down on the side of being tough with him. It's the only language he respects."

"You two," he said. "You'd have us in a third Gulf war in a minute, if you had your way."

"That isn't fair, Ray Stanley. Just because we're more skeptical than you are about our friends in the Middle East—just because we're more realistic—" She laughed. "But, then, women *are* more realistic, right?"

"I'm trying to be more realistic," he said. "There are limits to what we can do in the world, given how numerous our interests are and how thinly spread our forces are."

"And how sympathetic you are to the Arabs versus the rest of the world. Eulie and I have had this argument with you ever since we first met her in Riyadh, and you haven't changed one bit. Thank goodness I've been able to maintain a little objectivity over the years. Thank goodness somebody in the family isn't besotted with the Arabs."

"I'm not 'besotted with the Arabs,'" he protested mildly. "Sympathetic to a good many of their aspirations, yes. Not so impressed with some of Israel's, yes. But not 'besotted' with either one, I hope. I like to think I'm a better Secretary of State than that."

"You're a very good Secretary of State," she conceded. "But I think you should be a little more decisive with Sidi."

"The President doesn't really want us to be more decisive with Sidi," he said, "despite the tough talk. He really does think Sidi will back down, with enough skillful pressure. But apply *real* pressure? Naked force? Not likely or possible, with so much else to worry about. And I certainly support him in that."

"We'll regret it," she predicted. "But let's go to sleep. I don't feel like an extended argument right now. I had a long and exhausting talk with Bets this afternoon and I'm worn out. In addition to which I had to sparkle for my dinner partner at Dolly's, the Chief Justice. That man is brilliant but dullsville. I hope Mesdames van der Heuft and Van Duen were livelier for you."

"Not noticeably," he said with a chuckle. "Neither is the smartest woman that ever came down the pike, though Madame van der Heuft has the edge, such as it is." He sighed, suddenly serious, and responded to the name of their daughter and only child, now in the throes of possible divorce. "What's new with Bets? More crisis?"

She sighed, too.

"Oh, yes. Samir has suddenly taken to staying out late until all hours—she doesn't know why—and the children are asking questions—and her girlfriends, particularly Joanie Bourassa, are commiserating and also asking questions—and life in general is just sheer hell—and she's about to give up."

"I thought she'd given up a couple of months ago," he said. "What's changed?"

"Well, she keeps hoping. And I keep telling her to hang in there—the same things we've said right along. I think Samir has been a good husband according to his lights."

"I think he's really gone a long way toward adapting to our Western ways," he agreed. "He's really been very considerate to her and the kids, I think. And very respectful to us. Couldn't ask for a more thoughtful son-in-law."

"I think it's the staying out late that's provoked this latest row," she said. "He's really never done that, even though he comes from a culture that's very male-oriented and night-oriented. If they were still living in Cairo, she'd be lucky to see him home more than one or two nights a week. As near as I can gather, he hasn't started going out much more than that. And it seems it's only in the last month or so."

"The fragile forties," he remarked, "when, if you're going to wander, it really begins."

"He hasn't been a wanderer. That's what's got her upset."

"Does she have any idea where he goes?"

"He tells her he's going to the mosque on Massachusetts Avenue, for one thing, and then he talks vaguely about some 'really nice new club in Georgetown where a lot of embassy people go.' She asked him to take her there tonight, as a matter of fact, but he brushed her off with some excuse that didn't ring true and apparently flung out of the house with an unusual vehemence, for him. He's usually such a mild soul."

"I think she ought to calm down," he said. "I doubt if he's going to leave her."

"Well, who ever knows? But I agree, it certainly wouldn't be like him as we've known him for twelve years. My only thought is . . ." Her voice trailed away for a moment, came back with a note of something being seriously considered. "My only thought is whether he's getting involved with some fundamentalist group that could be dangerous to him, to you, and to all the family."

"There are plenty around," he agreed thoughtfully. "But surely the deputy counselor of the Egyptian embassy isn't going to let himself get involved in anything like that. It would be all his job was worth—probably all his life was worth. Our son-in-law is no fool, after all."

"Of course that's at the heart of all Bets's worries. She got thoroughly scared of extremists during their years in Cairo. And so did I, you must remember. It's no fun being the American ambassador with a lot of kooks running around the streets indistinguishable from your average good-natured, easygoing fellahin, not knowing which of them may suddenly loom out of the crowd to throw a bomb at you."

"I know," he said. "You were a brave lady."

"It wasn't all that easy for you in Greece, either," she noted, and chuckled suddenly. "We really were a rather remarkable diplomatic couple, weren't we? Maybe we justified all that flattering publicity we got."

"Including *National Enquirer*'s GHOST OF PHARAOH HAUNTS U.S. AMBASSADOR'S BEDROOM," he suggested.

She laughed.

"Even that," she said. "As long as they spelled my name right."

"Those were the great days," he said with mock nostalgia. "Secretary of State is a relative backwater."

"Oh, sure," she said. "You love it, and you know it. Anyway, I told Bets to try to calm down and try not to let it get to her. I predicted he'd be back to his domesticated ways shortly."

"I hope so," he said thoughtfully. "I wonder if I should ask Hugo Mallerbie to see what he can find out about these nocturnal absences and this 'really nice new club in Georgetown where a lot of embassy people go.' He has his contacts."

"Only if he can do it without alerting the Egyptian embassy," she said, tone suddenly dead serious. "I wouldn't want them to get suspicious of him. That could be quite disastrous, if they were to get the wrong ideas about him."

"I know," he said. "I won't convey any suspicions to Hugo. It will all be a family matter designed to set my little girl's mind at ease."

"Hugo," she said dryly, "can start with nothing and end up with an entire scenario. He can be two jumps ahead of you before you know it. Please do be careful with him."

"I will," he promised. "I'm not even sure I'll do it. I'll talk to Bets myself tomorrow and see how she feels. It may all have blown over by then, like so many other things. . . . It *is* interesting, you know," he said, abruptly thoughtful, "that Joanie Bourassa is 'commiserating' with her. Is Joanie having the same trouble with Boo?"

"That was my word," she said. "But yes, I gather there's some bond of sympathy and similar experience."

"Also in recent weeks?"

"I gather."

"Hmph."

"Yes, that's what I think, too. Maybe Hugo can widen his inquiries a bit."

"Now, listen to us," he said. "Here we go, typical Washington, typical world-we-live-in. Not a scrap of evidence to go on, not a reason in the world to suspect two perfectly decent Arabs who are close to us and whom we've known for years, particularly the one who is married to our daughter and father of our grandchildren—and we're off and running like the most hysterical conspiracy buffs imagining the imminent wrath of Allah."

"Well—" she said slowly. "Not entirely, Ray. We *don't* live in a very pleasant world, and strange things really *do* happen. I'm not averse to finding out things, if only for our daughter's peace of mind. And mine, I might add."

"And mine," he agreed, "of course. Still, it's a commentary."

"Not on us," she said. "We didn't make it so."

"Didn't we?" he inquired gloomily. "America has a lot to answer for."

"I refuse to construct a balancing act between international morality and immorality at this ungodly hour of the night," she said firmly, turning on her side. "I'm going to sleep. Let me know what Hugo reports."

"In due course," he said, also turning on his side, adjusting the two pillows he used to keep the recurring flux of a long-standing hiatal hernia at bay. "In due course."

But he wondered, as he began to drift toward sleep, if he really would ask Hugo to do anything at all. Samir in all likelihood was telling the exact truth, it was all innocent and just a temporary urge to get away now and then from the sometimes rather stifling uxoriousness of American life, so different from his own male-controlled native society. The same thing undoubtedly applied to Boo. His last thought brought a wry

86

smile to his lips as he dropped off: if anybody needed a break from domesticity now and then it was Boo Bourassa from Syria, tied to a powerhouse like Joanie.

Only he wasn't tied, really: that was the problem.

And therein lay many a restless night for the State Department's brightest assistant secretary. Right now, Joan Cohn-Bourassa also was lying awake, in their rambling house overlooking the Potomac in Arlington, Virginia, wondering, as she had frequently in twenty years of marriage and even more so in these recent weeks, where Boo was now.

He had accompanied her dutifully, as he always did, to Dolly Munson's party; charmed, as he always did, their hostess and everyone else on the premises with his quick wit and shrewd appraisals of the day's events; come dutifully home, apparently to call it a night and go to rest as a good husband should; and then suddenly appeared out of his dressing room clad in the scruffy jeans and worn old leather jacket—not even Ralph Lauren or Gucci! she noted with automatic scorn—that he affected when he wanted to disappear into the anonymous Georgetown night. Where he went, God only knew. Maybe Allah did. Joan Cohn-Bourassa, in any event, did not.

His appearance, bright-eyed and bushy-tailed and obviously ready to go at almost midnight, had precipitated one of their increasingly frequent, increasingly bitter arguments as she had attempted, with her usual lack of finesse and success, to persuade him to abandon whatever he had in mind. At least, she was bitter. Boo smiled amicably and shrugged and let it all roll off his back.

"Where are you going?" she had demanded sharply, even as she told herself that the confrontational approach had never been the way to handle Boo. But they were getting on, entering their mid-forties, and at her recent birthday (forty-four) something had suddenly seemed to snap inside. She found that she was getting tired of domestic diplomacy and playing second fiddle and being subservient in a way her State Department colleagues, among whom her reputation for brusqueness was legendary, could never have imagined. It was time, she had abruptly decided, for Joanie Bourassa to be Joanie Bourassa. Increasingly in these recent weeks she had let him have it, verbally and once, about a week ago, even physically, with a flying shoe which he had caught gracefully and tossed back at her with an inimitable puckish smile.

"Now, Joanie," he said this time, easygoing grin coming with apparent spontaneity to his darkly handsome face, "you mustn't take that tone with me. I'm only going to the mosque to meet some friends of mine and pray a little and then we're going to a club in Georgetown which is a favorite Arab hangout and have some shish kebab and tea and talk awhile. It's only midnight, after all. The night is yet young."

"Take me with you," she demanded, as her friend the Secretary of State's daughter Bets had done in the identical situation a few hours before. Boo's response had not been to take umbrage, as Samir had. He was much more experienced. He just became more humorous, more amicable, more easygoing; and more infuriating.

"It's just men," he said. "It's just man-talk. You know us Arabs. We love to sit around for hours and just talk. No harm in it." His smile became quite disarming. "We never really settle anything, though we like to think we do. It just goes 'round and 'round and 'round."

"Then I don't see why you want to waste time on it," she snapped. "I just can't see the purpose in it."

"Well, you wouldn't," he said with an air of kindly tolerance that she found frustratingly patronizing. "It really isn't your nature. Joan Cohn-Bourassa gets results! She's famous for results! It isn't her cup of tea to just talk without a purpose. Capital P. I'm surprised you don't understand that about us after all these years. You're supposed to be such a friend of the Arabs, and yet you don't seem to understand us." He uttered a wistful sigh that was intended to infuriate further, and did. "It's sad, you know? The great Arabist and she gets impatient with us. That's no way to get anywhere, in the Middle East."

"Oh, come on!" she said angrily. "Don't be disingenuous. The Arabs don't have any better friend than I am and you know it. Anyway, we're not talking about the whole Arab world. I'm talking about my husband who wants to go out catting around after midnight by himself *in Georgetown,* for God's sake. That's what I'm talking about."

"Now, you know I'm not doing that," he protested mildly. "Look!" His expression took on the earnest, open air she was coming to dislike intensely. "Do you really think I'm being physically unfaithful to you? Really?"

She studied him for a long moment, shook her head impatiently.

"No, I don't. I truly don't. But then what *are* you doing? That's what I can't figure out."

"Just talking," he repeated. "Men like to talk. Arab men particularly like to talk. It's our culture. It's our nature. We can't help ourselves. It isn't as though this is the first time I've gone out to talk with my friends in twenty years of marriage."

"But not as often or as consistently as you have in the past several weeks," she said.

He shrugged.

"Sometime I will take you with me and you'll see. But I can't right now."

"Why not?"

"Because the others wouldn't like it," he said. "It would upset them. They're always kidding me about being married to the world's most famous Jewish Arabist, as it is. They'd never understand it if you actually dared to crash their male citadel."

"One of these days," she promised grimly, "I *will*. And then what will you say?"

"'Meet my wife Joanie,'" he said, "'whom I love and of whom I am very proud.' Don't wait up. I may be quite late."

And with a smile, a wave, and a last, quick-disappearing grin like some swarthy Cheshire Cat, he was out the door and gone before she could quite grasp the fact that he intended to go in spite of her. But she should have grasped it: it had happened often enough in the past month or so, far more often than it ever had before.

Now it was almost one o'clock, and in the big double bed they shared—except on his nights out, when she increasingly often found him in the morning curled up on one of the big overstuffed sofas in the living room—she was tossing and turning, tossing and turning. She was furious with him, furious with herself for letting him upset her, furious with her supercharged mind that kept spinning around and around and wasting precious minutes on absolute trivia. If she could only think of something constructive, she told herself angrily, she could stand it. But not the absolute time-consuming, sleep-defying junk that clogged her mind now.

Joan Cohn-Bourassa, to quote a recent "Style" section profile in the

Washington Post, "has perhaps the best mind and the shortest fuse of anyone in the State Department. Her ability to analyze swiftly, decide without hesitation and act immediately has already made her a force to be respected and feared in Foggy Bottom. By what appears to be an inborn ability to strip all issues to their essentials and apply her conclusions rapidly without fear or favor, she has already achieved the position of the department's most effective, and most attractive, dynamo."

Effective, she thought wryly now—sometimes. Attractive—well, the writer had her own feminist agenda to pursue, and every woman who performed with an ounce of decisiveness automatically became attractive—unless, of course, she was a member of the opposition party, in which case she became obstreperous, obstructive, and "not particularly distinguished" in appearance and personality. Joanie Bourassa did not think of herself as particularly attractive, but she did make a point of being well groomed. With her short, wiry stature, her slicked-back, slightly graying black hair held in place by her trademark barrette, and her challenging, no-nonsense air, she did indeed give the impression of being a dynamo—at the moment, she thought in wry frustration, producing sparks but no real directed energy. This was repugnant to her orderly mind and an increasing source of irritation with Boo, off somewhere with his fellow talkers in the soft spring night of the beautiful, murder-ridden capital, which was not, in these closing years of the twentieth century, the safest place to be.

With a great effort of will she forced herself to come back to the immediate problem before the department, particularly her own Near Eastern Affairs section of it. She knew there had been an NSC meeting at the White House concerning Sidi's latest démarche, and she knew the bare bones of the CIA report, as transmitted by Eulie, which formed the basis of that concern; but that was all. Had there been a decision at the White House? And if so, what was it?

She had hoped she might be able to corner the Secretary for a moment at Dolly's and get a quick briefing from him, but either by accident or design he had somehow always seemed to be drifting away to some other part of the room. She had noted his quick exchange with Senator Wilson and observed Willie's expression of quickly suppressed surprise and dismay, and had concluded accurately that Ray was passing along the gist of the CIA report. But whether he had informed Willie of any White House decision she couldn't tell; and later at table when it developed that she would be Willie's dinner partner, she had tried indirectly and unsuccessfully to elicit some indication from him. Willie, as always, was too old and shrewd a hand at the game to reveal anything; he had even pretended, with a twinkle in his eye, that he was trying to get information from her. When he had finally brought their brief and amicable sparring match to a conclusion, he had said with a chuckle, "Well, Joanie, I'm afraid that we're equally ignorant, right? Ray hasn't told either of us, yet. But I can guess what you want him to say."

"That's right," she retorted crisply. "I want him to tell me that the NSC decision was to proceed slowly and with great caution where Sidi is concerned. He's a megalomaniac, and too much pressure can only make him worse. I'm not worried, though. We had a meeting about it at State this morning. I know the Secretary feels as I do." She gave Willie a sharp, sidewise glance. "I suppose you don't. You want us to lay down an ultimatum and go in with all guns blazing."

"No," Willie said slowly. "Not really. But I do want us to determine a position and *stick with it*. If I know our man in the White House, he's like some of our other recent men in the White House. He'll be firm today and waffle tomorrow. This doesn't stop people like Sidi, and each time it happens it only confuses the country and our allies and convinces the world all over again that the U.S. is being weak and indecisive and we can't be trusted to stand firm on anything. All of which are bad."

"'A foolish consistency is the hobgoblin of little minds,'" she quoted with a smile.

"One of the most pernicious things Ralph Waldo Emerson ever said," Willie observed, but amicably. "Always quoted triumphantly, out of context, by people like you. Nobody ever accused you of being inconsistent, Joanie. And I challenge you on the word 'foolish' as it applies to me. I like to think my consistencies aren't foolish. Particularly in the realm of foreign affairs."

"So," she said, deciding to find out, "are you going to hold hearings on it?"

"Perhaps," he said. "It depends on how fast and how far this thing develops."

"Haven't we got enough troubles at State?" she inquired humorously. "Must you people always keep at us?"

***

"It's good for you," Willie said. "It keeps you on your toes. Wait until Johnny Jones decides to get into the act."

"That scum," she said, lowering her voice and glancing across the room to the table where the chairman of the House Appropriations Subcommittee on the State Department was holding forth. "I know Dolly likes to stir things up, but why invite *that* particular sleazebag?"

"If Secretary Bourassa is referring to my distinguished colleague from the other body," Willie said with mock solemnity, "I must ask her to be more respectful."

"Ha!" she said. "Respect! That'll be the day."

"Nonetheless," Willie said, "he may want to get into it. Then whatever we do to you on the Senate side will seem like patty-cakes."

"You can be pretty rough, too, Senator," she remarked. "In your kindly, grandfatherly way."

"I am a grandfather," he said. "And, I hope, kindly. We'll just have to see how things go. Let me know when you get something definite on the White House's attitude."

"I think you've already got it pretty well pegged," she said. "From your point of view. From mine, I think it makes sense. I agreed this morning to go on Sally Holliwell's 'Capitol Perspective' next week. By then it ought to be pretty well out in the open."

"So have I," he said. "What a coincidence. Had somebody told her already?"

"Not that I know of. But you know Washington and how things get around. Or maybe it's just some instinct for what's coming up in the news. We haven't had a good, rousing crisis in the Middle East for a while. Maybe the media's just concluded that it's time for one."

"Sidi obviously has," he observed, as the Secretary of Human Services on his left broke in to command his attention in her brusque, homespun way. He tossed Joanie a wry smile over his shoulder as he turned away. "Have fun."

And now at one A.M. she still didn't know what had been decided at the White House and would not, presumably, until she got to her office in Main Building this coming morning and Ray either called her in to tell her or telephoned. She could offer him the firm news that Willie Wilson and the Senate Foreign Relations Committee would probably want to get into things quite early in the game, probably before the administration had a chance to clarify or really firm up its position; and that close behind would come their favorite nemesis on the House side, Joltin' Johnny Jones, as Ray often referred to him. Followed by all sorts of annoying hoo-hah on the floors of both houses. Democracy in action, she thought with a tired, impatient sigh; necessary but damned annoying, sometimes.

And having by now given herself something concrete to think about, she finally dropped off to sleep; but not before one last exasperated thought for her wandering husband. Bets was having the identical trouble with Samir. What were they up to, for heaven's sake?

This was what you got, as her mother in Brooklyn often remarked, for marrying the enemy. They were just different, that's all; just plain different. And although Joanie often disputed this hotly with Mom, she admitted to herself that she never would really understand them as long as she lived, for all her great reputation as a student of Arab affairs and "an Arabist" in the incessant internal arguments of the State Department. The only saving grace of it was that the arguments were almost always over ideas, approaches, attitudes, philosophical and moral concepts. In that kind of combat, Joanie Bourassa knew from long experience that she could almost always more than hold her own.

In the gracious, narrow (sixteen feet wide, forty deep, three stories and basement) Federal house on Capitol Hill that he shared with two young members of the California delegation in the House, Senator Wilson had reached the same conclusion, one that always came to him after one of his sometimes cantankerous, usually good-natured skirmishes with the Assistant Secretary for Near Eastern Affairs. Joanie was a brilliant, aggressive, and skillful advocate and defender of the standard State Department approach to the world. Which could be summed up as:

Wait.

Go slow.

Be cautious.

Don't try to initiate and develop: new ideas are anathema and almost always virtually impossible to move through the bureaucracy, given the years of prior conditioning that many of the most powerful have undergone in their years in the Foreign Service.

So wait.

Go slow.

And above all, don't innovate. To do so would be to go out on a limb and risk your career if what you proposed proved disastrous.

So, don't. Be cautious. Be careful. Be safe.

State was as bad as the Pentagon, the Senator sometimes thought with a frustrated sigh, except that in the Pentagon you had perhaps even more reason for cautious inaction than you did at State, because there you had the rigid military hierarchy that could provide quite immediate punishment if you raised your head too far above water. State had somewhat more freedom, being a relatively amorphous conglomeration of independent principalities, all of them with immediate access, if they so chose, to the media and other means of influencing the public. But the dead weight of Don't Be Too Bright and Don't Challenge the Official Wisdom was almost equally repressive and deadly, in the long run.

Still, it always pained him to find someone as intellectually superior as Joan Bourassa falling in with the official line—indeed, from her pro-Arab perspective, giving it additional strength. His own view, stated in many committee hearings and an occasional speech on the floor, was more direct and, perhaps, more simplistic. But, he had found, the world was a simplistic place. Its leaders, many of them vicious, evil, and ruthless men, did not engage in the long, tortuous, tied-up-in-knots ratiocinations of the overly educated, overly sensitized, overly anguished Americans. In many places of power around the globe, leaders knew what they wanted and they acted; and more often than not, particularly in these recent years, their gut instincts were more than a match for the perpetually soul-searching, nitpicking, own-navel-examining leaders of "the world's sole remaining superpower."

Willie's own gut instinct, based on shrewd observation of humankind going back to university days, was to be prepared—be slow to threaten but be willing to respond when challenged—and having decided to respond, *respond.* Don't hesitate, don't waffle, don't back down; and above all, don't have second thoughts about the wisdom of it all in the middle of the contest.

That way, he was convinced from a lifetime's experience, lay loss of will, loss of courage, and ultimately, loss of the sound objectives of freedom and democracy which the leaders of the Sole Remaining Superpower

often enunciated but just as often lost along the way in a welter of hesitation, procrastination, and overly complicated second-guessing; sometimes encouraged by reluctant, timorous allies but essentially the result
of having great power and not having the guts to exercise it as strongly
and decisively as it must be exercised if it is not ultimately to be dissipated
beyond recovery and allowed to slip into the dustbin of history.

He had come home from Dolly's to spend a final hour reading the
text of two bills his young colleagues wanted his advice on before they
introduced them in the House. One was an amendment to the Defense
Department appropriations bill that would, in essence, direct the President to "provide all necessary means, equipment, and support to protect
U.S. troops in any and all United Nations peace-keeping or other efforts
. . . without reference to any arrangements made by any other non-
American participants in such peace-keeping or other efforts for the
protection, defense, and/or support of their own forces."

The other was a nonbinding sense-of-the-Congress resolution that
would specifically ban the President from providing U.S. "participation
in, or support for, any future United Nations peace-keeping or other
efforts . . . without two-thirds prior approval of Congress."

Both, he knew, didn't have a chance in their efforts to limit the President's prerogatives in foreign affairs—he would have to lead the fight
against them if they survived by some miracle and came over to the Senate—but he didn't want to discourage his youthful colleagues too early
in the game. Both were in their thirties, eager and idealistic, as he himself had been when he first came to the House more than forty years
before; no need to stomp on them too early, he thought with a sigh. But
how to explain to them the realities of Hill and White House, State and
Defense? Maybe it might be better to let them sail into it headlong: the
quicker the slap-down, the sooner the bounce-back. He was fond of
them both, both married, with children, both struggling to make ends
meet, both midweek bachelors who left their families at home on the
other side of the continent because they couldn't afford to support two
households on a congressman's salary; which was why they had wound
up sharing the comfortable quarters he offered two blocks away from
work—and even that not always a safe walk, even in broad daylight,
these days.

Their eagerness and idealism kept him on his toes, he reflected as he got ready for bed and thought once more of his little skirmish with Joan Bourassa. That was probably why he had taken to renting out rooms on a regular basis soon after Donna's death twenty years ago. His tenants admired and respected him personally, if not always his political positions, and even there, he found them stimulating. Many and many a lively debate had raged around the fireplace in the narrow old living room, when one or another of his roomers had invited some of their fellow congressmen in for "one of Willie's brainstormers."

"You keep an old man young," he told them when the guests departed, surfeited on something as simple as hot dogs and beer, replete to overflowing with lively arguments and, usually, good-natured controversy. Even on the rare occasions when someone got a little high and a little angry, it was stimulating; and most times it was friendly, intelligent, and constructive. He often congratulated himself when one of these sessions was over that, in his quiet way, he had quite a bit of influence in the House, as well as his long-established influence in the Senate.

"Sage of the Senate," his fraternity brother Tim Bates often called him with a mixture of joshing and affection when he telephoned or came up to the Senate for lunch, as he often did. Timmy, also eighty, was retired after a long and distinguished career as a nationally syndicated columnist for Anna Hastings's *Washington Inquirer.* He still wrote an occasional Sunday analytical piece—"thumb-suckers," as they were known in the trade—which was always faithfully sent out to some three hundred former clients, many of whom were still flatteringly glad to print his commentaries. Timmy, too, still had an influence, and the satisfaction that went with it.

"For two old geezers," he sometimes remarked fondly to Willie, "we're still doing all right."

"Better than most," Willie agreed.

"And you most of all," Timmy remarked, with an affectionate echo of the respect that had first been born when Willie was student-body president at the university, so long ago. And he had added with a smile: "As always."

It was true, of course. Willie was still one of the major players in politics and government; although he had secretly decided that this term would be it: two more years and out, gone with the millennium. He had always carefully refrained from public comment on seniors who had out-

lived their usefulness but lingered on in the Senate on the fund of con-
stituent sentimentality built up over the years, just enough to return
them to office against the challenge of far more youthful Senate
wannabes. He had seen many of them go down, finally, to humiliating
defeat when time and health became opponents just too tough to beat.
Not for him, though he had not told Timmy or his kids, all of whom
wanted him to "retire and take it easy," as they often said.

"You could die in harness, Dad," Latt had remarked as recently as a
couple of weeks ago. "But it wouldn't become you."

With this he had agreed, although he was inwardly quite tickled by
the turn events were apparently taking with Sidi. He had figured he was
good for about one more big battle before hanging up his shield, one
more contest of wills in the legislative cockpit he had known and loved
so well for so long; and very likely old Seedy Sidi was going to provide the
occasion for it.

Or maybe not. Maybe the man in the White House would be as firm,
decisive, and unyielding as Willie thought he should be; maybe there
wouldn't be any need for domestic battle, but only with the Middle
East's most dangerous provocateurs; and with them, if need be, he
could only hope it would be a battle short, sharp, and, for once, decisive.

He wasn't at all sanguine about this, though, he thought as he
entered the little elevator he had installed five years ago and ascended to
his third-floor suite of rooms.

From there he could see, through the new-growth leaves of spring
stirring in the mild breeze, the dome of the Capitol rising white and
pure against the late-night sky. Once more unto the breach, dear friends,
he thought wryly, or close the wall up with another hell of a wrangle
between a feisty group of colleagues, led by him, and the White House.

I'm ready for it, he told the tricky gentleman now presumably sleeping at the other end of Pennsylvania Avenue as he turned out the light.

Old Willie's waiting.

And so, too, was Joltin' Johnny Jones of Alabama, also still awake at this
late hour, engaged in his favorite activity with two compliant young
female secretaries from the staff of the House Appropriations Committee.

Johnny was always very much aware of "all that phony stuff 'bout sex-

ual harassment," as he described it, that had so agitated his female colleagues in House and Senate, and the females on their respective staffs,
and the females in the media, and ever' other God-damned female busy-
body in creation in the early nineties. Johnny knew a trick or two to get
around that.

"Here," he'd say, whipping out the big ole huntin' knife he used to
hunt coons in Alabama. "Wanna cut it off?"

This either provoked a stern and angry look and an immediate
farewell, or a spontaneous giggle. If the latter, he knew he was on safe
ground.

"Give me a buzz as soon as we adjourn," he'd say, slippin' 'em a piece
of paper with his private direct phone number on it; and at least 50 percent of the time, they did. Which wasn't a bad average, he thought with
satisfaction now as he returned to the fray with a barely suppressed
whoop and a holler, greeted with equally muffled but equally delighted
screams from his companions in the suburban motel room they were
occupying for the purpose. (He always had them do the rentin', and so
far that had proved a fine safeguard. In his twenty years of such activity
on the Hill, he had never been caught—yet.)

Johnny Jones hadn't heard about Sidi at the moment, and even if he
had, the worthless old bastard (slightly younger than Johnny) would
have been the farthest thing from his mind at this particular delicious
moment. His reaction toward the Middle East was automatic anyway:
"fuck 'em all," was his attitude; and, to Foggy Bottom's constant annoyance and his constant delight, that was his attitude toward the State
Department as well.

He didn't much care what the issue was with State, he just enjoyed
yankin' their lily-livered, pantywaist, nancy-fancy, airy-fairy chains. And
then turnin' right around and demandin' all sorts of special treatment
from them when he went on one of his "inspection trips." He made 'em
crawl on the witness stand and he made 'em crawl in Bangkok or Madrid
or you name it. He despised them and they despised him. He couldn't
say exactly why, it had always been that way ever since he first came to
the House. They made his skin crawl with their smug, superior ways and
their smug, condescending attitude toward a good Southern boy. He
and the department hated each other, and he made sure to take it out on
them every chance he got.

He didn't know what their next head-on collision would be, but he knew there would be one.

Dithering old farts like Willie Wilson in the Senate might try to protect 'em, but Johnny Jones in the House was always there to expose their infinite shortcomings. And make 'em take it, and swallow it, too.

Something of the same anticipation, perhaps not quite so personalized—perhaps more institutionalized, which was how the Secretary of State often described it to his colleagues in the department—was dominating the thoughts of three of the media's finest as they completed their notes on their conversations and observations at Dolly Munson's party.

Each of them always made a practice of doing this after an evening out on Washington's nonstop sociopolitical circuit. It was an absolutely necessary, indispensable way of assisting memory in the replay of quotations, impressions, hunches, guesses, inadvertent blurts and revelations—the hodgepodge of fleeting but invaluable bits and pieces that went into news coverage of the capital's constantly shifting tides and personalities. Somebody, under the prod of good food and good liquor, inadvertently said something—somebody deliberately leaked something, in the traditional, mutually understood Washington way—somebody looked funny at somebody else—somebody actually came right out with some concealed animosity or political ambition—it was all grist for the mill.

From such squibs and squiddities, as Tim Bates described them, came weighty columns, profound TV commentaries, eagerly informative Sunday newspaper articles and magazine pieces, to help educate an incorrigibly obtuse and backward public. It was necessary, it was duty, it was fun. News gathering *was* fun, and nowhere more so than in this self-consciously important summit of the Western world, where men and women walked mighty through their days, and where the course of the sun, the stars, and the planets were often rearranged and sometimes decided—or so they convinced themselves, on such occasions as a party at Dolly's . . . or Pamela's . . . or Kay's . . . or whoever was the most ubiquitous favorite party-giver on any given night.

In his exquisite, antique-filled bachelor house on P Street in Georgetown, James Van Rensselaer Burden was just closing up his John Quincy

Adams writing desk, his handwritten notes placed neatly beside the old-fashioned Remington upright on which he always delicately tapped out his somewhat precious, but always well-informed, column, "As I See It."

Jimmy Van, as he was always referred to in the Washington world of Anybody Who Was Anybody, had been married—once. It had not diverted him from old, familiar pastimes, and when these were discovered in due course by his stylish wife, divorced spouse of another rather fragile Georgetown gentleman, she had proved to be not as tolerant as many other wealthy ladies in similar situations. She had, in fact, left him flat, but she had also left him the house and a million-dollar settlement, a tribute to a lingering affection and the fact that Jimmy Van, among other things, was really quite a likable man. He need never have written another thing, Jimmy often told himself, and still he would have been able to live out his life in complete comfort; but he had been a highly successful, very well respected, self-supporting journalist before she came along, and in his mid-fifties he didn't see any reason to be any less successful, respected, or self-supporting. On his part, it had been an experiment that hadn't worked; what it had been on hers, he never quite figured out. But he was able to dismiss it quite lightheartedly because its termination permitted him to devote his creative energies fully once again to the reportorial life he loved to the exclusion, really, of almost everything else.

If he hadn't still been in the thick of it he would have missed it all terribly. It was, simply, great fun to cover the Hill; attend (quite frequently) White House state dinners and (less frequently but still often enough to boast about it) more informal family gatherings; and be a guest on a regular basis at such ego-uppers as those given by Dolly . . . and Pam . . . and Kay.

And he would have missed most of all the chance to skewer the targets of his sometimes waspishly vindictive but always well-rounded and well-reasoned dislikes. Nobody could ever accuse Jimmy Van of being a lightweight thinker; "Profundity sticks out all over him," Willie Wilson had once remarked dryly. He had his prejudices and he didn't hesitate to express them, but he backed them (usually) with thoroughly logical (as he saw it) argument. It made him a formidable (if somewhat old-fashioned and gradually becoming out-of-date) force in the Washington media.

"One of the last of the dinosaurs," he often described himself to young colleagues with a deprecating chuckle, in his clipped, Groton-Harvard-hello, Berkeley Square accent. But he didn't really believe it for one minute.

Now he had tomorrow's column well in mind. Obviously Sidi, whom he too regarded as "that old bastard," though Sidi was ten years younger, was about to make trouble again. In what form or in what manner or with what resources—or when—Ray Stanley had, as always, been too tricky to disclose. But there was enough for a typical Jimmy Van column: suavely derogatory, smoothly denunciatory, grandly but stingingly disapproving of State and particularly a President who, for all his frequent hospitality, Jimmy regarded as both too belligerent and too hesitant, depending on which he perceived to be more politically advantageous at any particular moment.

Jimmy would fax a copy of it off to the Oval Office in the morning as soon as he had finished it, he promised himself with satisfaction now. He expected the usual tart response, followed by the usual conciliatory invitation to "drop by and see me—call Jaime and have him set it up for next week sometime. We need to have a talk."

And possibly, either in the immediate response or in the talk later—which Jimmy fully intended to hold the President to—the wary chief executive would divulge the full story behind the Secretary's little cat-and-mouse game at Dolly's.

At the same moment, in her stylishly modern apartment in a stylishly modern building in Rosslyn, Virginia, just across Key Bridge from the District, which lay sparkling at her feet, Sally Holliwell was also turning in. She too had completed the same task as Jimmy Van and, in his comfortable old family house on Cathedral Avenue in northwest Washington, Able Montague.

Sally was forty-three, "a tough lady," as she was universally regarded in the world of Washington media, politics, and society, who had come up the hard way—"clawed her way up," Able put it privately at the Press Club bar, from which it inevitably got back to her with the speed of light. But that didn't bother her. She shook it off with the thick skin the successful develop in the fiercely competitive climate of television and the even fiercer climate of the Washington media as a whole. The customary response of the astute to insult or derogation—"It's just jealousy. And anyway, I may need him (her) later"—concealed a wealth of personal affronts, disparaging remarks, outright feuds, and almost-but-not-quite burned bridges. Life went on roughshod over feelings that could not afford to be sensitive if one were to achieve the one great prize they all desired—power. Power meant success. And with it fortune and the exhilarating knowledge that one was Really on the Inside, In the Know, One of the People Who Really Make Things Happen in Your Nation's Capital—and, by extension in this era of instant communication, the whole wide world. This was a satisfaction superior to none in many hundreds of shrewd, sharp, clever journalistic minds.

Among whom, as even her enemies, who were many, had to concede, Sally Holliwell was indisputably and unchallengeably one.

She had come to the capital a wide-eyed young reporter from the Los Angeles bureau of the *Washington Post*. In no time her quick news sense, dogged persistence, and slashing, biting style that fitted in so well with so many of the *Post*'s innumerable likes and dislikes, had moved her quickly to Washington and the national desk. From there it was a short hop (over several dead bodies, as wounded colleagues muttered later) to the congressional staff, and from there with the speed of light—"It's a bird, it's a plane, it's Super Sally!" as they also said—she had been offered a job by a major TV network, accepted, and in six months, developed, sold, and made as permanent as anything on TV could be, her lively, controversial, and justly famous show, "Capitol Perspective."

Now she appeared every Sunday before dazzled millions, surrounded by her corps of attendant news hawks, female and male—those of the former being those whose ambitions were either so well established that they were no real competition, or youngsters too new to Washington to be any threat to her. And always one or two guests, usually one from the Hill and one from "downtown," where resided secretaries, assistant secretaries, and others permanently-in-the-news-for-four-years because of their administrative offices.

By a stroke of what was known enviously as "Sally's luck," she had already lined up Joan Bourassa, thinking they might talk about the latest clashes in the ongoing Israeli-Palestinian adjustments, and Willie Wilson, quite by impulse, at Dolly Munson's. Their enigmatic sparring match with Ray Stanley had made her luck even better; when it became apparent that a new crisis might be brewing in the Middle East, her challenge to Willie had become suddenly an ideal situation. He had agreed to appear and she intended to confirm it with him first thing in the morning when he reached his office.

He and Joanie would make an ideal combination this coming Sunday, particularly if by then the media had been able to smoke out what was really going on, or if the White House had decided to release it either through official statement or in one of the carefully contrived "leaks" that in recent years had supplanted so much of legitimate news digging. She also might—what the hell—call Johnny Jones and invite him to be on, too. And she knew she could get Jimmy Van and Able Montague; they were always glad to go on her show for the exposure and also because, as Able had recently broken down and admitted, "You're always fun, Sally. You're hell on wheels."

She enjoyed this rather mixed reputation. It would be a good show, and it might just light a fire under an administration that she regarded as incorrigibly tricky, devious, and crafty. Also, it would enable her and Able and Jimmy Van to make very clear their insistence that the United States not stumble headlong into another disastrous no-win muddle in the Middle East. She was, as she had told the Secretary, adamantly opposed to this, and she knew nine-tenths of the media were too. As she had told Ray Stanley, she just wouldn't have it. She knew her colleagues wouldn't either.

Of course she realized her panel could be considered grossly one-sided, but she was comfortably aware from long experience with the American audience that very few of them were sophisticated and attentive enough to realize this. Anyway, it would, as usual, be concealed by the general liveliness of the conversation. And Joanie, though uncomfortable, would have to provide some semblance of balance by supporting the administration; and Willie would be somewhere in the middle; and Johnny Jones would be raving against the department, as always; and she and Jimmy Van and Able Montague would, by contrast, emerge as voices of sweet reason and cool objectivity.

She loved the feeling of power she got from her show; they all loved their power. Satisfied, righteous, and content, mutually and self-congratulatory, they sailed untouchable through their days, never really challenged, never really held to account. "Always the judges, never the judged," as Willie Wilson had once remarked. It was great and they adored it.

She turned out the lights and took one last look at the night-bright city stretching away on the other side of the Potomac, the Lincoln Memorial seemingly almost at her feet, the Jefferson Memorial off to the right beside the Tidal Basin, the Washington Monument stark and straight beyond the Lincoln, the Capitol completing the panorama at the far end of Pennsylvania Avenue atop the distant Hill. She, too, loved Washington, and unlike many of her fellow citizens, she did not despair of it. It was just a matter of keeping the government on the right track and giving it the infallible advice she and her colleagues were impelled, and superbly equipped, to provide. Like most of them, she took this responsibility very seriously. It was, after all, a great one.

She closed the curtains and snuggled into her frilly but essentially austere and usually lonely bed. Very few men dared attempt a sortie against Sally Holliwell's self-sufficient citadel. Virtually none, now, as the years advanced.

She didn't care.

She had the power, and that was enough.

It was impossible to overemphasize its comforts.

In much the same mood, a mile or so away across the river in his comfortable, big family home on Cathedral Avenue in the District, Kelly Able Montague was also completing notes, impressions, preliminary thoughts on what he would say in the morning when he taped another "Washington Wrangle" and "WorldView." The first appeared on television Sunday mornings, the latter on radio starting at six P.M. Saturday evenings and running at intermittent intervals on stations all over the country, all weekend. Both had large and faithful audiences, and both he enjoyed mightily.

"Washington Wrangle," in which he and a panel of four or five media colleagues shouted happily at one another for half an hour about major issues of the day, he described as "my version of throwing the overalls in Mrs. Murphy's chowder."

"WorldView"—its title always run together, never separated, never hyphenated—was "me and somebody famous playing Moses on the mountaintop," one-on-one interviews with Cabinet officials, congressional leaders, and even, on several occasions in recent years, the President himself.

It was about time to try for him again, Able thought now as he prepared to slip quietly in beside Claire, his placidly sleeping wife of thirty years. Particularly if Sidi was really about to go on the rampage again in the Middle East. This would make it extra hard to nail down the busy chief executive—or at least he claimed he was busy, Able thought skeptically. Like most of the media, he often wondered just how busy the President actually was. That they were never able to find out simply emphasized that the White House was still, for all the prying ways of today's media, an impregnable retreat for a man who wished to use it that way. This one, annoyingly, did.

Able had come to Washington in the zenith of the bright Kennedy sun whose dark side, turned away from the earth, concealed so many things. Subsequent unravelings of the myth had made him even more skeptical of those in political power than he had been before. In fact, his skepticism had a bitter edge because he had arrived in town a true believer. When that idol fell from its pedestal, it took the faith of a lot of innocents with it. None had been greater than that of Kelly Able Montague. None suffered a more devastating tumble.

Able he had actually been in all of his professional life, though in earlier years people called him Kelly. Soon after coming to Washington in the bureau of the *New York Times,* however, he had assiduously begun to cultivate the use of his middle name. The excuse was the need to fit his often front-paged byline into the *Times*'s typography. The letter count in three names cumulatively as long as his was just too much, his employers thought. When he looked mildly displeased with Kelly Montague and suggested innocently that maybe Able wasn't such a bad name for a *Times* correspondent, they had been amused and agreed. Very soon Able Montague, as he liked to recount with satisfaction to the journalism classes he occasionally taught at Georgetown University, became a moniker to reckon with.

Having started as combined reporter and editor of a little mining town weekly in the Rocky Mountain West, he had gone from there to the *Chicago Sun-Times,* and from there to *Newsday* on Long Island, and from there in due course to the *Times* Albany bureau and from there to

Washington. He was shrewd, sharp, tenacious, and, well—able. He had a round little figure and a round little face, always smiling, always friendly, "seemingly innocent as the day is long," Ray Stanley had remarked after his first encounter with Able's clever and often acrid tongue. "He's all sorts of good things, but you have to watch him. He bites."

And so he did, prodding his contentious colleagues into the escalations of volume and disputatiousness that made "Washington Wrangle" such a highly popular show, leading his guests on "WorldView" into verbal traps from which they could not extricate themselves without all sorts of embarrassing political and personal contortions. It made him a justly famous national figure and a rightly feared interviewer. Ray Stanley had even gone so far as to paraphrase the old saw about Napoleon.

"Able was I ere I saw Able," the Secretary said. "*En garde,* all ye who enter there!"

Able basked in this, as well he might. In addition to his own shows, he was a regular on several others; lectured from time to time at Georgetown to suitably awed and impressed young minds; maintained a profitable professional lecturing schedule ($12,000 a crack was his latest figure, and his agent promised even more next year); did an occasional op-ed piece for the *Times* or the *Post,* an occasional article for *Atlantic* or *Harper's,* or even occasionally (just for the hell of it) the *National Review.*

The pixieish smile and engaging wit that could slice a politician's pretexts in two before he knew what hit him translated in all Able's areas of endeavor into a most satisfying life. Everything was high-profile, high-profit, high-controversy—and fun.

He did enjoy it, fully as much as Jimmy Van or Sally Holliwell or any other of the mighty panjandrums of the media who had been elevated to such staggering prominence and power in the age of overcommunication and perpetual hype. Words carried instantaneously to the ends of the earth—a raised eyebrow in Washington that could be seen simultaneously in Tiblisi—a skeptical expression in New York that sent its message on delivery to Cape Town and Buenos Aires—it was a fearsome impact and, as the best of them recognized and honored, a fearsome responsibility.

Some took it as their birthright, earth's rightful tribute to minds superior and all-knowing. Able was not so egocentric or arrogant. He had come up the hard way and gone through the chairs, as he liked to say, and he appreciated every day how fortunate he was to be where he was, and how necessary it was for him to be right. Like most of his colleagues, he never doubted that he *was* right, but in return there was never, behind the engaging grin and disarming personality, anything frivolous or irresponsible.

"Able Montague is one of us," the Secretary had also commented on a famous occasion; and by that he meant that Able, like himself, was one of that small conscientious fraternity of the bright and the educated who in essence sat on top of the world and ran it for the generally uninformed and unsophisticated billions who toiled along below. That they often disagreed among themselves accounted for most of the world's ills and conflicts; but that was the price a not always grateful humanity paid for having their special minds and perceptions to guide it.

So it was now with "Sidi's latest fling," as Able thought of it. The Secretary had obviously not given them the full details at Dolly's, but Able expected they would come out soon. He intended to call the President and invite him to be his guest at the next taping of "WorldView." The President might refuse, it was awfully short notice, but Able didn't think he would.

The bright and the educated would have to handle the new Sidi crisis, if there was one; they would also have to tell the masses below what to think about it. And that was where Able and his colleagues could be of inestimable assistance to the world. The President, well aware of Able's audience, might well be pleased to take advantage of it.

As for the thing itself, whatever it was Sidi was huffing and puffing about, Able was not impressed, just on the face of it. They had all been around the track with Sidi before. He was all bluff, and a bluff from weakness, at that. This was probably just one more bluff. Able did not feel half so annoyed with Sidi for bluffing as he did with his own country as he anticipated what he knew he would refer to as "overreacting."

If there was any one thing that had exasperated Able Montague in recent years, it was the American tendency to rush in with all flags flying and all guns blazing, at least rhetorically.

It was true that the combined pressure of print and television influenced public opinion—and public opinion in turn influenced Congress—and various Presidents had in turn been influenced by Congress, in the long, winding chain of American responsibility and decision making. This had usually moderated the initial overreaction into something the media and "the sensible folks we hope to influence," as Able liked to put it modestly, "could live with." But it was sometimes nip and tuck, and on several occasions, the whole thing had gotten out of hand and the tensions had accelerated into unpleasant confrontations that could have meant real disaster if Presidents had not stepped back and thought better of it.

Thus the first Gulf War—and the second—and now, who knew, maybe this new annoyance from Sidi would turn out to be another wild adventure.

In spite of the media's sound advice, public opinion might still run wild and stampede Congress, and get the White House wavering and waffling and drifting into that dangerously panicky and erratic mode where anything could happen. *If they would just listen to us,* he thought rather despairingly now; if everybody would just *behave.*

He was as determined as Jimmy Van or Sally or anybody else he knew in the media that he would make sure that, this time, things did not get out of hand.

Suddenly he was wide awake again. He had another source and he didn't care if he woke him up. It would impress him with how gravely he, Able Montague, felt about any possible escalation of the situation. And he, Able, would make him realize that most of his colleagues felt the same way—so the White House had better pay attention.

He slipped out of bed as carefully and quietly as he had slipped in. Claire, the thirty-year reporter's wife, was so well trained that she didn't even wake up, just mumbled something incoherent, turned over, and started gently snoring again. He put on his robe and slippers, went quietly down to his study, closed the door, found in the top desk drawer his little book of top-secret private numbers. Almost everybody's top-secret private number in Washington was known to somebody in the media. Able's list was one of the best.

There was a startled oath in Spanish whose general import he understood, followed by a drowsy but rapidly clearing response; then, in impatient English, "Yess? What ees it?"

"Jaime," Able said quickly, "this is Able. Sorry to wake you up, but . . ."

"I was dreaming of Dolly's party," Jaime said, accent lessening as he came fully awake. "What a blast!"

"Very nice," Able said.

"I was thinking," the national security adviser said, "what if an atomic bomb had fallen on us all. How would America continue? How would the world function without us? How would—"

"That's very interesting, Jaime," Able Montague interrupted, "but I'm calling about a serious matter—"

"That would not be serious?" Jaime Serrano inquired blandly. "Quite much so, I would say."

"—about which you may be able to give me some clarification," Able continued, refusing to be diverted. "How about it?"

"At this hour?" Jaime exclaimed indignantly. "It is past one A.M., Able! What do you take me for?"

"A smart man," Able said. "So am I. Now, Jaime, what I want to know is—"

"No!" Jaime said, beginning to sound as though he was really enjoying it. "You know I can't say anything about *that!*"

"You don't even know what I'm going to say," Able protested.

Jaime laughed. "I can guess."

"So guess."

"Well, I have already told you I won't talk about it," Jaime said cheerfully. "So good night!"

"Jaime," Able said patiently; and decided on a sudden change of tactic. Jaime could be shrewdly obfuscating when he wanted to be, but no point in letting him get away with it without a good tussle. "Is the President going to give Sidi an ultimatum?"

"For heaven's *sake!*" Jaime exclaimed. "Why?"

"You know why," Able said comfortably.

Jaime laughed. "Sure I do. But you don't."

"So what's Sidi doing, threatening us with atomic bombs?"

"Absolutely not!"

"Threatening Lesser Lolómé with atomic bombs?"

"Oh, come!" Jaime said. "Stop the fishing expedition, please. And go back to bed. You need your beauty sleep."

"You are suspiciously cagey."

"You are suspicious, period." Jaime's tone became earnest. "Able, if there was anything I could tell you, I would. But when there isn't nothing—"

"Oh, sure," Able said. "Oh, sure. How's the boss taking all this?"

"I don't know about 'all this,'" Jaime said. His tone did change a bit, however, becoming more confidential. "I do know, jus' between you and me, that he is a complicated man."

"That's news," Able said dryly. "There's a big headline in that. You find him hard to pin down, do you?"

"Yes," Jaime said. He sighed and became more accented. "He ees won puzzle, sometimes. I don' know what he thinks!" His tone became suddenly, disturbingly, bleak. "I never know whether he will stand firm or give way. It makes it very hard. It is very difficult. It gives me concern for our policies."

"In other words," Able Montague said, "he is like all Presidents nowadays. He hasn't given Sidi an ultimatum. He's waffling, like they all do."

"I wouldn't say that," Jaime objected.

Able laughed triumphantly.

"Then he has given him an ultimatum!"

"Don' say it," Jaime advised. "We would have to deny it, if you do. Anyway, it isn't true. Exactly."

"He's given him one and Sidi has refused to back down."

"Not exactly that, either."

"Well, damn it!" Able exclaimed. "There's got to be some pattern of sense, here."

"He has and he hasn't."

"Who has and who hasn't?" Able demanded, exasperated. "Which one is 'he'? Or are they both 'he'? Or—"

"Now," Jaime said severely, "you do not make sense at all, amigo. Now you are driveling on. That is not like Able Montague, keen master of television and world events . . ." He paused; his tone became more confidential. "Actually, I do not think he really knows himself how he is going to handle Sidi this time."

"No threats of armed response, I hope," Able said with equal severity. "The media wouldn't stand for it. The country wouldn't stand for it."

"Are they different?" Jaime inquired dryly. "If the media tells the country that it is not to support the President, you know the country will not support the President. Is that not so?"

"Not quite," Able conceded, more amicably. "But we can raise a hell of a stink."

"Absolutely," Jaime agreed. "Absolutely. Anyway, he is soundly sleeping at this very moment, I believe. And hope. He will be ready for you tomorrow, whatever happens."

"How is he sleeping these days?" Able inquired. "Sound as a baby?"

"A good conscience means good dreams," Jaime observed.

"Is that an old Cuban saying?"

"It is old Cuban from me," Jaime said with a laugh. "I jus' made it up." He sighed and once again lapsed into complete and disturbed confidence. "He is difficult to deal with. I wish I knew where he really stands on things. Life would be simpler for a national security adviser."

"Simpler for all of us," Able remarked. "Well, if that's all you can tell me—"

"You have enough for hours of television talk," Jaime said. "Do not complain."

"But I won't know what I'm talking about!" Able protested, and joined Jaime in his cheerful laughter.

"Would that be any different from what you and your colleagues do every day?" Jaime inquired. "What else is new?"

"You have me, Jaime," Able Montague said. "Go back to sleep and have good dreams like your boss."

But after he hung up Able stood in thoughtful silence in the silent house. He wondered how good the boss's dreams were. And he wondered how far he should go in reporting and commenting upon the crisis that was obviously beginning to swirl up around the President for Life of Greater Lolómé. Sidi was a tricky character, but so was the President. Jaime had signaled plainly that the White House considered the matter serious. Something atomic, obviously . . . something involving a threat to the peace of the region, and perhaps beyond . . . involving powers in the region . . . or perhaps beyond.

Something the President was obviously going to try to solve with words.

Something that would test just how strong and effective American words were, in the jungle world of the closing millennium.

Something that would disclose how justified was the faith of America's leaders in the power of American words, which in recent decades had sounded so fierce . . . on so many occasions . . . and, when not backed by force and the will to use it if necessary, had been able to achieve so little.

———

*   *   *

He rather fancied Shakespeare, though his was not a mind to quote anyone at any length except when his speechwriters provided the text. He
did not have a student's mind. He had a very quick mind, a very astute
and clever mind, excellent at understanding human aims and foibles
and how to play upon them successfully; but not a student's mind,
unless it be a student of human nature, which for his purposes was quite
sufficient for his time.

So he did not quote Shakespeare often, for he did not really know a
great deal about him, save for scraps of schoolboy memory; and the
things he liked best, those that he felt applied to his own situation, he
did not dare quote to anyone for fear of ridicule.

"Upon the king," for instance . . . upon the king, *"who hath a heavy
reckoning to make . . . all those arms and legs and heads chopped off in a battle."* Upon the king, nowadays, rests caution.

Exactly so, he thought now as he came awake suddenly in the king-
sized bed he occupied alone, listening moodily for a moment to the
stately old house creaking and settling from time to time around him. It
had been gutted and rebuilt internally in Harry Truman's time, but still
it creaked and settled now and then, as if it had a memory of its own of
times long past and Presidents all too often as troubled and uneasy as he.

Not, of course, that he was ever going to indicate to anyone that he
was uneasy and troubled; and essentially, of course, he was not. The
façade of self-confident ease and sardonic parrying that he always displayed in public was more than skin deep. It really represented how he
felt at heart, even though there were times, such as this night after his
hostile exchange with Seedy Sidi, when he did feel, temporarily, a little
uncertain of his course. But he knew from lifelong experience that it
would sort itself out. It always had for him, and he was confident that it
would this time, too.

It had been easy for him, therefore, to turn aside Helen's characteristically shrewd and perceptive probings when they had met in the great
hallway of the second-floor family quarters on their separate ways to
bed. It had been four years since they had shared the same room at
night, except when on the road campaigning, or on state visits at home
or abroad. This was something the public did not know, though of

course the Secret Service did. Sooner or later he expected it would leak to the media. Everything always leaked to the media, and the more venal and titillating, the better. No oaths of secrecy, no pledges of fealty, were ever enough; the possibility of publication and the lure of the talk shows always proved too strong. Not that he gave a damn, really, except that there were always some votes out there that could be affected by such a silly thing—silly to him, anyway, though not, perhaps, quite so silly to Helen. But she was used to it, he thought complacently now. She had accepted, with characteristic practicality, the increasing boredom of physical custom and the occasional, carefully concealed outside contacts he successfully sought to alleviate it. As long as they always appeared in the public gaze hand in hand, and as long as she always draped herself dutifully around his shoulders whenever possible at photo opportunities, it didn't really matter. The show of substance was there. He had learned from a lifetime in politics that the show was all.

For Helen, however, who still knew him better than anybody, and in addition had a really first-class instinct for world affairs, the show as it concerned Sidi was not enough.

"You're worried about something," she said, still tall, svelte, and striking at almost fifty, even in her slightly too frilly Armani bathrobe and the usual protective nighttime swaddlings that encased her normally free-swinging blond hair. "I hope it's not too serious."

"Enough," he said, and told her, as he usually did, the basics of it.

She pursed her lips and looked genuinely concerned.

"He's such a flake," she said. "What will you do if he continues to defy you?"

"He won't," he said. "Not when I get the UN and the allies lined up and he realizes the weight of world opinion opposing him."

"You think 'the weight of world opinion' will be enough to stop him this time? It wasn't last time."

"And he found out about that, didn't he?" he inquired. "He didn't get away with it."

"He wasn't ready, then. He's much better prepared now. And if he really does have the bombs—"

"He wouldn't dare," he said calmly.

"Maybe," she said. "Maybe not. If I were you I would proceed on the assumption that he might. And then what?"

"At the moment," he said frankly, "I don't quite know. But it will work out all right. It always seems to, for me."

"Yes," she said dryly. "Golden boy. Well, I hope you're right. It would be a little unsettling to suddenly find an actual atomic war breaking out. You may have to bluff pretty hard to get him to back down."

"You think so?"

She nodded. "This time I do. I hope I'm wrong, but—"

"You are," he said confidently. "Trust me."

"We all have to, don't we?" she said, reached over, and kissed him lightly on the cheek, and without waiting for response turned away toward her own room.

"You'll see," he called after her, but she made no reply, just tossed a knowing and skeptical look back at him over her shoulder as she disappeared, closing the door behind her.

He stood for a moment almost irresolute, although even when alone as he was now in the empty upper hall he did not like to appear irresolute; and after a moment went to his own bed and fell into a deep sleep from which he presently awakened with a start in the midst of a dream in which Sidi, riding a large flying camel, appeared to be hovering over the White House. This was so ridiculous that it brought him awake laughing. Quickly this stopped. Whatever else it was, it was not a laughing matter, even though he was, as he had told Helen earlier, quite confident that everything would go well for him as it had on so many occasions, about so many things, before.

This was why he sometimes became a little irritated with his team at State. Eulie Montgomery was always consistent, always predictable; no President in recent years had ever been strong enough in his dealings with other nations to satisfy Eulie. They were always, in her mind, ducking their responsibilities, dodging their challenges, attempting to finesse their various challenges without ever really committing themselves or the full weight of their country's power. In her mind they shared the same basic, very simple motivation: they didn't want to risk their own precious political necks. By so much, Eulie felt—and was notorious for expressing it in no uncertain terms within the department—was the United States weakened and diminished in its foreign policy.

And the Secretary, the President thought with some annoyance now, could be equally challenging to his employer's strength with his own conviction, deeply held if more diplomatically expressed, that recent Presidents had used the UN to conceal their own indecisiveness and uncertainty about what to do when challenged. Ray Stanley had rarely expressed this to him in so many words, but indirectly he was inclined to keep up a quiet but nagging barrage. He had recently forwarded to the President's desk a Sunday piece by Tim Bates which had appeared in Anna Hastings's *Washington Inquirer*—"The UN: American Necessity or Presidents' Excuse?" Ray had offered no accompanying comment except to scrawl across it a single handwritten question mark. It had been, the President recalled wryly, a very large, black, and definite question mark.

Well: given all the things he had to worry about in this world, all the endless clamor of nations, causes, and peoples that beat in upon him virtually nonstop around the clock, he was not going to be deflected by this kind of indirect but persistent nibbling at his morale from below. That he thought of Ray as "below," and indeed, in some curious but deep-seated fashion considered everything and everyone "below" him, perhaps said something about the presidential frame of mind. It seemed to go with the office. It certainly indicated that he was possessed of a certainty of power that was not going to be deflected from the pursuit of what he felt to be his responsibility in any given situation.

But what, he wondered now as the mansion gave another slight but definite creak and groan, was his responsibility in the situation now before him? Should he be as tough as Eulie wanted, as cavalier with the UN as would presumably satisfy Ray? Or should he find—as, he had to admit, all recent Presidents liked to do—some middle ground that would put a sufficient gloss on things to ease him past the crisis and at the same time leave him looking as decisive and commanding as he liked to be seen at the end of the day?

So far he had been strong, and he hoped Eulie was satisfied. And he intended to have Ray start tackling the UN first thing in the morning and use it, as he saw it, to strengthen his hand. Meantime, retracing the course of his conversation with Sidi, he was satisfied that he had been more than emphatic in staking out a clear-cut and unequivocal position. It was true that he had concluded with an offer to talk further if Sidi so desired, which Sidi had instantly seized upon as one more example of the weakness of American Presidents; but that, he was confident, was just Sidi being crafty and trying to make debating points. Thus he could rationalize comfortably what at first blush had seemed to be an unnerving contempt in Sidi's tone.

The President did not think for a moment that Sidi would really dare to defy him. Sidi did not have the power or the means to do so for any period of time, even a brief one. Even if he did have atomic bombs and the missiles to deliver them, who was he going to use them on? Lesser Lolómé was certainly not a target worthy of such enormous expenditure of military capital—the heart had seemed to go out of the destroy-Israel group, the idea no longer seemed a worthwhile objective to those who had clutched it to their bosoms over the years—there would be no point in an attack on anyone in Europe—and an attack on America was simply out of the question, so all-obliterating was the annihilation America could unleash in return.

What the President looked for now was the usual chronology of events. First the story would appear in the media—Ray had called him shortly before midnight to report his conversation with Sally, Able, and Jimmy Van—which would get the clamor going so loudly that by nightfall it would be on every show from MacNeil-Lehrer to Larry King and C-Span. Next morning it would be in the *Times,* the *Post,* and everywhere around the globe that print and picture could reach.

Then would come the escalation of statements from himself and Sidi. He was certain he would be backed by Britain, France, and most of the Security Council (Russia and China perhaps being less dependable, but since nothing was going to come of it anyway, what did it matter?). And then would come the swift and inevitable back-down by Sidi, who, confronted by overwhelming world outcry, would see that his latest gamble on American weakness wasn't going to work. He would retreat accordingly, growling and spitting like a cat in a corner, but speedily giving in. After all, he had nothing to support him but bluster.

The President had great faith in his own powers to cajole, convince, and, if necessary, bribe the allies and the UN at large to support the American position. Dutifully, helpful resolutions would come tumbling out of the Security Council (carefully worded to get around Russian and Chinese objections: he would count on his own cleverness, and Ray's, for that). Even at the end of the millennium, the United States was still able to dispense financial and military favors, though it was increasingly unclear how much longer it would be able to do so in an economy that had never really recovered from the recessions and the desperate down-sizing of the early nineties.

(Ironically, much of America's international clout both monetary and military came from a combination of money and the matériel furnished by one of the world's largest armaments industries. There were moments when the President, not a particularly imaginative man, could envisage himself walking a tightrope a thousand feet above the ground, balancing a bucket of dollars in one hand with a fistful of guns, bombs, planes, and tanks in the other. It was not a very pleasant imagery, but what could one do if one wanted to maintain a stable economy and use it to help achieve a stable world?)

"Stable world!" He groaned and turned over. That would be the day. It had never been stable in his entire lifetime and he suspected it never would be. But one had to keep trying. Certainly one had to pay the idea lip service, anyway, if only because elections were not won by leaders who told their peoples the harsh and glaring truth. Not in America, any-way; and America, in general, was the most honest of the lot.

For half a dollar, he thought in exasperation now, he would chuck the whole thing and go fishing. He was too impatient to enjoy fishing, and he knew he couldn't chuck it willingly until he had won the next elec-tion and finished a successful second term; but there were times when he was sorely tempted. If he weren't so convinced that what Helen sometimes referred to dryly as "your fatal charm" could pull off this cur-rent little tussle of wills with Sidi, this might be one of them. It was tire-some and boring to have to go through one more game of bluff with an opponent whose only real aim was to be an international gadfly. He had many more important things to do, including a bill to reform the reform of the health-care system, and a bill to reform the reform of the welfare system. He had observed in his years in politics that presidential highs had to be cleaned up after by somebody, and usually it was the next guy in line who tidied up and tried to put things back in order—if the next guy was lucky. As he had told Helen, he always seemed to be. But he was still mopping up after his frenetic predecessor and, he was sure, would be for quite some time.

In this situation Sidi was a secondary annoyance, if potentially a somewhat more difficult one than the President liked to see. If Sidi indeed had the support of a powerful neighbor, that would be one thing;

if secretly supported and encouraged by Russia or China or Iran or North Korea, or, quite possibly, all four, that would be another. In either event, the President was confident he could handle it, since he could not bring himself to believe that it was actually all that important.

Sidi had acted up before, and the coalition led by the President had slapped him down. Surely any sensible man, confronted by that record and the certainty that it would be repeated if he didn't behave, would give up his stupid little ideas and retreat to his pink monstrosity atop Pointe Sinistre. Of course Sidi was not necessarily a sensible man—far from it. But surely there must be some bounds of rationality within which he felt constrained to act. And surely the necessity of not antagonizing America and her President must be one of the most important of all.

So why didn't the President stop thinking about it and go to sleep? Tomorrow he would talk to the allies, start lining up the UN, chat with Willie Wilson and Johnny Jones on the Hill and start greasing the wheels there. He might also hold a press conference, just to underscore things and get the jump on Sidi.

Right now, he needed his sleep. To quote Helen again (for a man who had become relatively independent of his wife, he reflected wryly, she certainly remained a major presence in his life), he had a mind that he could "turn off like a spigot." And on, too, when needed.

Now it was off.

Thought stopped.

Sleep took over.

Around him the beautiful mansion stirred, and spoke softly from time to time, through the night.

So sleep finally claimed some of the more famous residents of the hub-city of the Western world from which all blessings flowed—to friends, and sometimes even enemies, in times of crisis when they needed help . . . received by friends and enemies with jealousy and snide resentment when crises passed and they felt themselves relatively secure again.

4   The balance, as always, fluctuated sharply. Right now, aside from the President of Greater Lolómé and his sinister friends, it was generally favorable to America. What it would be tomorrow when America's President began telephoning around the world to round up support for another crackdown on Sidi, who could say? It changed in minutes, in today's instantly communicating global society.

For the moment the major players in Washington were all accounted for, resting safely, securely (and perhaps a little smugly, the Secretary of State reflected as he drifted comfortably into sleep).

They were all pretty much agreed, in this latest crisis. They might disagree on details and approach, but as to Sidi himself and the problem he now posed for them, they were at heart unanimous. It would be a comparatively minor episode—it would be handled—Sidi would back down—it would all end comfortably—the world would go on. Everybody from the President on down was quite confident of that.

Eight thousand miles away in Greater Lolómé City, other players in the game were well into their morning occupations.

They were not quite so smug, safe, and secure.

It would not be, for some of them, a good day.

For Creed Moncrief, however, possessor of the funny name the President loved to make fun of but otherwise known as "that fine young man from California" to his principal sponsor, Senator Richard Emmett Wilson, the day began brightly and with supreme good cheer.

He had just received a fax from Pasadena.

In it Anna-Maria Gonzalez, thirty-four, highly successful trusts lawyer, member of the city council, potential candidate for Congress and V.B.G. (Very Bright Girl, as he often addressed her in his letters and faxes), said what he had been waiting six months to hear.

Her message, brief and to the point, said simply "I can stand it if you can. Love, A."

Now as he prepared to leave the embassy, tucked away in the dusty side street where it was barely permitted to exist by the President of All the Peoples of Greater Lolómé, the world seemed a sunny and sparkling place. Actually the sun, as usual, was dimmed by the heavy haze of dust kicked up by the city's constantly moving population of nomad buyers, sellers, and seekers after food and water, with their many camels and donkeys and their few rusting old secondhand American cars. The embassy, surrounded by massive, barbed wire–topped mud walls, electronically controlled gates, and armed guards stationed on the rooftops and at every aperture, could hardly be considered a home-away-from-home conducive to relaxation and peace of mind.

There were constant threats to its personnel, constant "little nibblings," as Big Bill Bullock described them in his reports to the department, harassments all the time that kept them all on edge and made of Greater Lolómé a true hardship post for the thirty or so staff members who lived within the walls of their highly fortified and closely guarded compound.

"Not exactly the fun center of the universe," the ambassador had commented dryly during his most recent appearance, three months ago, before the Senate Foreign Relations Committee. "But we survive."

And so they did, not as comfortably as many of the older Foreign Service and civil service hands on the roster would have liked, but, for younger spirits like Creed Moncrief, a high-tension challenge that satisfied their hunger for excitement. "Living on the edge," as he described it to Anna-Maria, was, simply, fun.

He knew this morning that his enjoyment of it would not last much longer, for she had made it emphatically clear during his last leave home that marriage, when it occurred, would be in Pasadena and that he should arrange reassignment back to Washington because she would not go to Greater Lolómé nor would she permit him to return there.

So now he was faced with the reality that his days here were numbered and his enjoyment of desert distances and silences, and all the teeming life of the mud-brick cities and busy oases, would not last much longer.

"Don't worry," she had remarked. "We can always go to Palm Springs. And I'll be glad to accompany you to the Riverside County Fair."

This had made him laugh, of course, but he still observed wistfully that life in the real desert in the midst of tribes and caravans was also fun.

"And fun, I suppose," she remarked, "to live under the dictatorship of that penny-ante monster in the Pink House."

"We stay out of his way," Creed had replied, "and he stays out of ours, pretty much. It isn't an amicable arrangement, but it works. Most of the time."

It worked for him because, at thirty-six, he was already a thoroughly experienced veteran of the CIA, and whatever he needed to do in Greater Lolómé he had the expertise and knowledge to accomplish— and, he prided himself, the courage, which sometimes, as on this particular bright day, took him into areas where he might not go, to undertake risks he should not invite. The ambassador was always telling him this, always telling him to go easy and not invite danger if he didn't have to. The Agency in Washington was equally cautionary. But Creed was not yet of an age—and had never, really, been of a temperament—to live within the strict letter of safety. He had the extra edge the Agency liked to see in those it sent into the field—but always with the tacit, sometimes plainspoken, understanding that if he went too far, he was on his own and they couldn't help him much. Which was another reason Anna-Maria wanted him safely back at a desk in Langley.

He had to concede that she had a point. Aside from his liking for living dangerously, which in this particular environment really was dangerous, Creed was basically quite a conventional soul. He came of a solid old-line California family which went back on his mother's side to Spanish land-grant days; had gone to Thatcher School for Boys in Ojai; graduated from the University of Southern California, and completed Yale Law School in the top five percentile of his class. From there he had gone directly to Washington, an early obsession, and had immediately joined Willie Wilson's staff as assistant to the Senator's legislative assistant; and from there, after two fascinating years, to the CIA, where he had volunteered for overseas duty and rapidly been given it. Now he was a nine-year veteran of the field, most of it spent in the Middle East, the last two years in Greater Lolómé. But always at the back of his mind was the desire to marry, have a family, settle down. Anna-Maria had come into his life three years ago and now had made all that possible. Suddenly a desk at Langley did not seem so unattractive, after all. It was time; perhaps, at thirty-six, a little past time. Not, he thought happily now, too late to retire most happily to full domesticity and a quieter life.

After this last job that he wanted to do, of course. He had faxed back immediately, "Wonderful. Yes, yes, yes. Will call tomorrow. Love, C." He had not intimated in any way, nor would he, that he just wanted to nail down, as he thought of it, a few more details about Sidi's attempted end run around the U.S., world opinion, and the nonproliferation treaty.

To this end he had put on the native disguise he sometimes wore on special occasions, walked through the secret underground tunnel between the embassy compound and the ubiquitous (and obliging) McDonald's that stood on the opposite corner, and from there had emerged through its kitchen back door into the swirling streets, apparently a garbageman carrying an overflowing can which he emptied into a waiting truck. This attracted, as always, a rush of some of Sidi's happy, gaunt-eyed people to scrounge what they could from the refuse. In the ensuing uproar he slipped into the crowd and disappeared. Or thought he did.

Casually he proceeded along unpaved roads and alleyways toward his objective, rendezvous with a young houseman at the Pink House, an accidental contact he had met on a similar venture a few days ago who had turned out to be one of Greater Lolómé's few hidden but dedicated "freedom fighters" and an invaluable source of information. He was supposed to bring with him today a detailed sketch of the location and launching trajectories of the missiles now in place beneath Sidi's palace.

Singing happily inside with the thought of Anna-Maria's acceptance and the wonderful prospects it opened up, Creed Moncrief spent his last few sentient moments thinking of her with part of his mind while another part, coldly trained, took him slowly, circuitously, unobtrusively but inexorably toward his destination.

Ten blocks from the run-down center of Greater Lolómé City, where the Great Mosque, the two-chambered House of Advisers, and the three main government departments of War, Peace, and Religious Dissemination flanked a nondescript and shabby park, he saw at the far end of an intersection the figure of his contact leaning casually against a wall while a group of children played around his feet. They exchanged no sign of recognition, but as Creed came within a hundred feet the children suddenly rushed toward him, tossing a ball between them, apparently wanting to play.

He stepped aside to avoid their rush, found himself caught, batted the ball back and, laughing, tried to push on through. Suddenly one of the boys, perhaps ten, banged headlong into him, bounced off and landed on his back in the street, where he gave a fearful cry and, apparently doubled with pain, appeared to roll in agony.

The rest of the children circled Creed, yelling and screaming, faces now contorted with fear and hate.

"But I—" he began; became aware that his contact had disappeared from the corner ahead; tried to break free of the children, who surrounded him on every side; and realized too late that one of the government's green-painted weapons carriers, manned by half a dozen soldiers in the government's green uniforms, was roaring down upon him from the intersection.

He made one last desperate lunge to free himself from the dirty little clawing hands that clung to every portion of his loosely flowing robe; failed to do so; found himself suddenly tripped and toppled to the ground; stared up into the barrels of three or four Uzis; and realized that he had been trapped by one of the oldest gambits in the books.

Mentally, he began in that moment to give up the world.

It would, however, be a while.

He was blindfolded, thrown into the weapons carrier, sat upon by several of the soldiers. The children scattered, the vehicle roared away, the street fell still; a lone scruffy dog wandered by and idly sniffed the earth where tumult only seconds ago had taken place. He concentrated on every twist and turn as best he could, trying, as he had been trained, to memorize them, knowing even as he consigned them to memory that he would never have reason or opportunity to use them.

After five minutes of jolting speed, the vehicle swung off what was apparently a main thoroughfare, started up a long ramp of smoothly polished stones, arrived at what was apparently an entryway, stopped and was recognized. He was roughly removed, flung forward, hustled stumbling along a long, smoothly paved corridor. He was almost certain he was in the Pink House. He was shoved into an elevator; it descended. He was shoved out into another corridor, far below the peak of Pointe Sinistre.

He knew now where he was going and began to pray, to God, to Anna-Maria, to his country, knowing as he did so that none of them could help him now.

He was flung headlong into a room and blindfolded. His clothes were stripped from him by hot, hurrying hands. He was flung down upon a cold stone table. Very soon the torture began, mild and almost gentle at first, escalating presently. Time blurred, began to lose form and dimension; swiftly he lost sense of it. Constant pain began to dominate his being. Above him at one point, for several long, lingering moments, the grinning face of Young Sidi stared down upon him. In one last despairing moment he tried to restore some balance of sanity to the world by forcing himself to think, *When I get out of this and Annie and I get married*— But just then rough hands seized his naked legs, forced them far apart. Unmitigated pain, savage, searing, merciless, seemed to swallow his whole body. His last conscious act was to think stupidly, *But I can't get married now. I don't have any*—

At that moment a blinding whiteness consumed the world and the screaming began. He didn't know who was doing it but he couldn't seem to stop it from driving him mad.

Five levels above in his private study, into which such things were regularly piped from below for his personal enjoyment, Sidi bin Sidi bin Sidi listened with a pleased smile as the wailing went on, rising and falling, rising and falling—almost four hours of it, he realized later with satisfaction, during which he had a leisurely lunch with his air force chief of staff, whose loyalty had seemed a bit shaky lately. Sidi, as he put it to himself Western-style, wanted to scare the shit out of him.

The noise from below helped him do this with supreme efficiency and completeness. The general was unable to finish his lunch, but Sidi finished his, quite calmly and happily, before he dismissed his trembling subordinate, deathly pale and reduced almost to gibberish. He need not, he thought complacently, fear trouble from that one ever again.

After the luncheon dishes were cleared away by manservants silent and equally shaken, Sidi was left alone to take his usual nap. But he did not go to sleep for a while. The awful noises emanating from below presently induced in him that physical reaction he most enjoyed, particularly when he could arrange for it to occur to this particular type of accompaniment. It happened to him twice, in fact, before the dreadful sounds ended in one last, choked, animal gurgle.

Sidi smiled, turned on his side, and went peacefully to sleep.

About half an hour after that a large, lumpy burlap bag was flung on the doorstep of the American embassy from a truck whose driver and crew sped grinning away into the city's labyrinth of back alleys, firing rifles exuberantly into the air as they went.

For several minutes the guard on the door did not approach the bag, fearful of bombs. Then he noticed the blood seeping from it, exclaimed loudly, and yelled for help. Two of his subordinates rushed out, retrieved the bag, and carried it inside, dripping now a steady flow.

Ambassador Bullock was informed immediately and ran down the stairs from his second-floor office. He engaged in a brief, sharp exchange with his deputy chief of mission, who wanted the bag tested for bombs before anyone touched it again.

"Hell," Big Bill Bullock snapped, "there aren't any bombs in there. There's a body in there. Let's pray to God it's still alive."

But it wasn't, and when he saw the condition it was in, and with difficulty but with certainty recognized who it had been when alive, Big Bill Bullock, that rough, tough, blunt, pragmatic son of Texas, threw up.

After which, as he told his badly shaken wife in their suite in the compound an hour later, he got on the horn to the White House and began to raise holy hell.

"But—" the President began with some annoyance, although aware that something must be unusually wrong with the world or he wouldn't be aroused from a sound sleep at—he glanced quickly at the illuminated clock face on his bedside table—5:11 A.M. "Can't it wait until—"

The ambassador would have none of it.

"God damn it," he roared, "you listen to me!"—and put it immediately on the basis he thought would do the most to provoke action from this particular chief executive. "That worthless son of a bitch has not only ordered the ghastly murder of one of the finest young men I've ever known, he has flat-out defied you. What are you going to do about it?"

"The first thing I'm going to do," the President said crisply, coming fully awake, "is tell you to calm down and moderate your language. I am aware of the seriousness of this, you don't have to shout at me. *Is that clear?*"

"Well, God damn it—" Big Bill Bullock began again.

The President's tone became cold.

"God damn *you*," he said. "*You* listen to *me*. I repeat, I am fully aware of the gravity of this. How do you know this was done at Sidi's direction?"

"How do I know?" the ambassador demanded. "How do I *know*? I know because any half-ass who knows anything at all about this God-forsaken country knows that you don't breathe in Greater Lolómé unless Sidi tells you to. And you don't die here unless he says the word. That's how I know!"

"If you don't stop that talk and quiet down right now, Bill," the President said, "I'm ending this conversation and directing you to address all communication to the Secretary of State, which is what you ought to be doing anyway. Understand me?"

"Well, God damn it!" Bill Bullock cried. "God damn it, do something!"

"I will do what the circumstances warrant," the President said evenly. "Goodbye, Bill. Ray will get back to you."

And he hung up.

"God damn it," the ambassador said bleakly into the silence. "You won't do any damned thing, I'll bet!"

But in this, as many had before him, he underestimated the President, who was not where he was for nothing, and who did not minimize his duty or evade it when he saw clearly how to handle it. For the moment he did not. Quite properly he resorted to protocol and roused the Secretary of State. The wheels of the government-in-crisis began to spin, while in Greater Lolómé City, Big Bill Bullock took up the phone again and began the task he always hated however effectively he managed it. First came the parents and then came the fiancée. Everybody cried out in horror (although he told them the absolute minimum—"an accident in this crazy traffic we have over here"). Black rage filled his heart again and he began to consider how he personally might do horrible damage to the man who had done such damage to them. He couldn't right now but he promised himself that if it ever became possible, he would. That helped, a very little.

In Washington, in the handsome Washington Harbor apartment, the Secretary of State replaced the receiver after the President's somber message and stared down reflectively upon the broad sweep of the Potomac, rippling and glistening in the first light of morning as it rolled away south and east toward its ultimate destination in Chesapeake Bay.

Black rage filled his heart, too, but in a long life in the Foreign Service he had learned to accept what came when it couldn't be changed, and to submerge his feelings and attend matter-of-factly to the business of the day.

There would be plenty on this day.

The first thing to do, as he and the President agreed, was damage control. And the first step in that was to clamp the lid on Bill Bullock and everyone else in the embassy so that no word would get back to Washington until they were ready to handle it.

"Bill has enough sense to do that on his own, I'm sure," Ray Stanley said, "but I'll get to him in a minute and reinforce his instincts. Meanwhile, I can't conceive that this will pass without some open defiance of you. That wouldn't be Sidi. I think we should prepare some statement and let it, and the news of the death, go out together."

"But not how the death came about," the President said.

"Not unless Sidi reveals it," the Secretary said. "I doubt if he'll want to, at first. Or maybe he will. We've just got to be prepared for whatever." And he echoed the ambassador's furious question, because it was the one they all had to have answered: "What are you going to do about it?"

"Well," the President said slowly. "First of all, you don't bring the dead back to life. And second, you have to figure out, in this killing game we're in everywhere in the world right now, how you make use of the dead as astutely as you can to score for your side." He sighed. "You know, of course, that I am as shocked and saddened as anyone by this horrible crime. I made fun of his name but that was only in jest. Maybe it will fix him in the world's memory as a symbol of a special kind of horror that I'm sure goes on in Sidi's part of the world"—he sighed again—"and many others, of course—all the time, nowadays. For the moment," he said, with a calm acceptance of his own awkward position, "I don't know what to do. We're too big to launch a major effort to stamp out every little bug that bites us, and he's too small, basically, to warrant the kind of effort we would have to make—unless we do use this as an excuse to go after the bombs, in which case the coalition will have to be revived and a major effort launched. Yet he must be brought to book . . ." His voice trailed away, then repeated strongly, "He must be brought to book." He uttered a wry little laugh. "You're my Secretary of State. Give me some ideas."

Ray Stanley, who had given the matter a lot of rapid thought in the few moments since the President had told him of Creed's death, found himself, somewhat to his own surprise, recommending actions much stronger than he had originally considered wise.

"Send a couple of aircraft carriers from the Mediterranean," he suggested. "Don't explain why, let the world speculate. Let me contact Sidi, demand reparations for Creed's death, threaten sanctions if he doesn't comply. Use this as a wedge to demand immediate inspection of his military facilities by the International Atomic Energy Agency. Simultaneously, you talk to the allies, alert the UN, get the Secretary-General into the act, he always likes to throw his weight around and feel important. Sic Penny Sims onto it, he always makes a big deal of his contacts in that part of the world, let him go to work on them. Keep everything off the record as much as possible." (The President snorted, but the Secretary ignored it.) "Make sure he understands that there are going to be the gravest consequences."

"Aside from the aircraft carriers," the President noted, "which would make Arlie McGregor and Bill Rathbun scream like eagles, but that's all right, you've outlined pretty much what we thought about yesterday, haven't you? You aren't being very original, Ray."

"It's a difficult area of diplomacy to be original in," the Secretary admitted, "but it's important that we appear to be decisive. Aside from everything else," he added, deciding like Bill Bullock that it might be necessary to arouse pride to get action, "this killing is a direct defiance of you personally. You warned him specifically against harming Creed, and he went right ahead and did it. It was cold-blooded, deliberate murder, and it's cold-blooded, deliberate, sneering defiance of you. Something's got to be done."

"Oh, I agree," the President said. His tone became thoughtful. "I don't want to make public the nature of his death if I can help it, it would be so hard on his family—"

"And precipitate an immediate major confrontation, which you aren't ready for at this point," the Secretary said.

The President uttered a rueful chuckle.

"That's right. So?"

"For the moment," Ray Stanley said, "I'd suggest using as many back-channels as possible. Then in due course when the timing seems right, issue a public statement setting forth as much as you want to reveal of the facts, stating the penalties we intend to enforce."

"Possibly we underestimated old Sidi yesterday," the President remarked thoughtfully. "But, then again," he added, sounding more upbeat, "maybe he underestimated us."

"What we have to do," the Secretary said, "is get rid of this dangerous assumption that's growing in the world, that you can jerk the United States around and get away with it. We've come dangerously close to letting that impression stand, on a number of occasions in the last two administrations, and we've got to stop it or it will be the death of us yet—and there are plenty out there who want our death, in a pretty specific way. We've got to stop that before it comes back upon us a hundredfold."

"If it isn't too late?" the President inquired in a musing tone; then caught himself up short. "But what the hell am I doing here, sounding like that? I'm the President of the United States, the responsibility is mine, I've never been afraid of it and I'm not afraid of it now. We're letting Sidi spook us. We've nothing to fear from him or anybody as long as we're strong and decisive and know what we're doing. Why, hell, we're not some damned banana republic. We're the United States of America. Which the world is afraid of."

"As long as we keep it that way," the Secretary said.

"Exactly so," the President said.

Silence ensued for what seemed to the Secretary minutes, though possibly only seconds. Finally he said, "Well?" in a tone he hoped would provoke response.

"What?" the President inquired.

"So what shall we do?" Ray Stanley asked. "Shall we proceed along these lines, or—?"

"We'll have to think about that some more," the President said in a thoughtful tone. "Better have another NSC meeting this afternoon, I think. Meanwhile," he added more briskly, "if anyone in the media starts stirring around, we'll stonewall it. Right?"

"Right," the Secretary said, wondering: *Now what's holding him up?* "The last thing we want is to have them break it before we're ready."

But in this, as frequently in Washington, the desire did not delay the deed. In Greater Lolóme City, Big Bill Bullock, riding the wave of horror, repugnance, and furious outrage he had felt when viewing the remains of Creed Moncrief—"like raw hamburger somebody had only half chopped up," he described them to Arthur Reeves Burton in Lesser Lolómé when they talked later that day—was busy, busy, busy on the satellite. And he was not alone.

Results were speedily apparent.

The trouble with a lot of the more famous media types, the ambassador reflected as he waited impatiently for his call to go through, was that they always liked to play hard to get. It was as though *they* were conferring a favor on *you,* not the other way around. This was noticeably true in the case of James Van Rensselaer Burden, with his fancy airs and superior ways. Bill Bullock often told his friends down home in Texas that he had known Jimmy Van for what he was the moment he first met him a couple of years ago. Normally he wouldn't have given him the time of day, but in Washington you took 'em as you found 'em, and the only thing that mattered was what they could do for you and what you could do for them, in the capital's never-ending balancing act of favor/counterfavor.

Jimmy Van was a good man to know and a good man to use for your own purposes of manipulating the media, which is what Bill Bullock was now setting out to do. He was also, the ambassador admitted to friends, really quite a nice guy and not difficult to talk to, even if he was a damned—but at that point Bill Bullock always stopped with a coy chuckle and admonished himself, "Now, now, we don't use that word anymore!" Anyway, Jimmy was useful and never more so than at this moment when the call from far-off Greater Lolómé came through to his pleasant oak-lined study in Georgetown.

"Mr. Ambassador!" he responded, sounding surprised and genuinely pleased. "I was just thinking of you. Something's going on in Greater Lolómé. What is it?"

For a moment the ambassador sounded—or rather, was conspicuous by his lack of sound—quite taken aback. Then he chuckled.

"You're pretty sharp," he said. "Where did you hear that?"

"At Dolly Munson's," Jimmy Van said. "Last night. From Ray Stanley. He wouldn't tell us what, though. Have you called to tell me?"

"Yes," Bill Bullock said grimly, "I have. He was a fine young man and I want you and your colleagues to raise hell."

"Who was that?" Jimmy asked, sounding puzzled. "I thought it might be something really serious." His tone became humorous. "I thought you were going to tell me that Sidi has the bomb and is going to drop it on the poor old Mouse."

"Absolutely," the ambassador said, his light tone matching Jimmy's— after all, he wasn't a fool and had no intention of revealing the real secret until the White House was ready for it. "Except we're going to bomb him first."

"That would be the day," Jimmy Van said with a comfortable laugh. "*That* would be the day. Not that we don't want to."

"I recommend it every day," the ambassador said. "He's an annoying son of a bitch." *He's a monstrous son of a bitch,* he added under his breath.

Jimmy Van, diverted, returned to the chase.

"So what about this mysterious fine young man? Anyone I know?"

"I doubt it," Bill Bullock said, in a tone so dry that Jimmy couldn't help laughing.

"Now, now," he said, "Mr. Ambassador. Don't be mean. I take it this is someone on your staff. What has happened to him?"

"He's dead."

"Oh?" Jimmy Van said, perking up. "When and how?"

"This afternoon, our time."

"Killed by Sidi's men?"

"Yes."

"Tortured?"

"I'm not prepared to go that far at this time," Bill Bullock said. "Let's just say he met with a suspicious accident."

"Leading to suspicions that he might have been."

"Very definite suspicions that it wasn't an accident," Bill Bullock said. "That's about as far as I want to go right now."

"Name?" Jimmy Van said, and Bill Bullock obliged with basic details.

"What was he doing there?" Jimmy inquired. "CIA?"

"He was an expert on demographics and was my assistant," the ambassador said blandly. "He was making a study of the agricultural possibilities if we should ever decide to assist Greater Lolómé in developing some viable crops. Which we aren't going to do," he added firmly, "until the Lolómés get rid of Sidi."

"They show signs of it?" Jimmy inquired dryly.

Bill Bullock said, "No," in a flat, disgusted tone.

"Are you making a formal protest about Moncrief?"

"I hope we will," the ambassador said. "You aren't to use my name, incidentally. Not that I'm afraid of reprisals from the department, I have a hundred thousand acres, five thousand head of cattle, and one hundred and fifty oil wells to go home to; but I don't want to leave here just yet."

"What do you want to do, Mr. Ambassador? Why did you call me? Just to raise hell?"

"I want to get things moving over here," Bill Bullock said. "I don't want this swept under the rug by the pantywaists in the department. I don't want Creed forgotten. He was worth more than that."

"Oh, he won't be forgotten, Bill," Jimmy Van said. "I think I can promise you that. I'll call a few people myself. Any time we can land on Sidi, I'm for it—barring, of course, something just too violent and military that would get us into real trouble."

"He may not listen to anything else," the ambassador said.

"Well," James Van Rensselaer Burden said, "I intend to make very clear in the column I'll write today on this, that along with the indignation all Americans must feel about this awful criminal act against a fellow American, there must as always be a note of caution maintained. We must not make the mistake of reacting too strongly and thereby endangering the peace of the world."

"What peace is that?" Bill Bullock inquired. "We can't see much of it from here."

"Oh, you know what I mean," Jimmy Van said with some impatience. "It's just an expression. But," he added firmly, "one that should be supported by all sensible Americans. What's the President going to do about this?"

"I've recommended the strongest possible action," the ambassador said.

"Recommendation accepted, I'm sure," Jimmy said dryly; and when the ambassador made no response, added tartly, "He's such a—such a wishy-wash."

"I thought you just said in effect that that's what you want him to be. Nothing violent, nothing military. Right?"

"I didn't mean crawl into his hole and hide from it," Jimmy said impatiently. "*You* know what I mean!"

"Not really, no," Bill Bullock said. "Anyway, please keep this as completely confidential and treat it with the greatest discretion when you publish it."

Jimmy Van had the grace to laugh.

"You can count on me, Bill," he said with a chuckle. "You can count on me." He paused for a moment's consideration, then thought, *What the hell, the more the merrier.* "Able Montague and Sally Holliwell were with me last night in that talk with the Secretary. You might want to talk to them too—?"

"By all means," the ambassador said.

"Good," James Van Rensselaer Burden said. "I think you can count on all of us."

And so he could, Bill Bullock thought as Jimmy's plummily confident tones faded from the air. He quickly got through to Able, Sally, and Tim Bates, whom he added to the list because he respected his judgment and his still-potent hold on his older audience. All were much interested; all, he knew, would start digging in D.C. The story would grow almost of its own volition as the news began to spread to more and more colleagues on the omnipresent internet of the media.

All of this, he told himself grimly, to make sure that tricky soul in the White House would "come up in the saddle," as they said on the Triple B Ranch, and *get moving.* Big Bill Bullock, not as disillusioned then as examples of what he considered weakness had tended to make him now, had contributed a couple of hundred thousand dollars to the President's campaign. He hoped what he was contributing now would have some effect.

What he was doing, he thought with a gambler's satisfaction as he looked out upon the compound baking in the sun and noted the extra guards in position on the roofs, was making an end run around the White House in an attempt to stir up public opinion and put pressure on the President. He knew this was all very irregular. But there were ways of doing things, in Washington; there were always ways. He prided himself that he was no slouch when it came to using them.

*   *   *

Nor, though greatly agitated and upset, was the determined young soul who at that moment was waiting in the outer office of the senior Senator from California, chairman of the Senate Foreign Relations Committee, Richard Emmett Wilson.

Willie had heard of her in a general sort of way, as those in politics do hear of potential rising stars who might conceivably someday challenge them. Not that Anna-Maria Gonzalez would ever really do that, particularly since he expected to be out of the Senate long before she might attempt to move in; but it made talking to her an intriguing prospect. He had never met her; now she was on his doorstep. He wondered idly why. The idleness gave way to a sudden concerned alertness as his receptionist showed her in and he realized that she had been crying heavily. When he stood up to shake her hand, looking every inch senatorial, white-haired, stately, fatherly, and calm, she burst into open sobs.

"There," he said, "there, there," at first patting her awkwardly on the shoulder, then, as that only increased her tears, putting his arm around her and leading her to one of the three chairs that faced him across his memento-cluttered desk. (Like most other senators, he had once had a sofa, coffee table, and facing chairs in one corner of his office. That comfortable aspect of the Hill had long been banished in many offices in favor of straight chairs, no sofa, no slightest sign of casual contact. "Can't afford it," one of his colleagues had once remarked dryly. "Sit 'em on a sofa and you're going to have a sexual harassment suit on your hands next morning." It was a male joke, rather grim and not very funny; nonetheless, many no longer encouraged any signs of informality in their inner offices.)

"Now," he said, "tell me all about it."

"I'm so—so—sorry," she blurted out.

He looked surprised.

"About what? Crying? Everybody cries sometime, even senators. I assume you have reason."

"Yes," she said, voice growing a little steadier, though the tears still came as she dabbed at them with a Kleenex.

"Here," he said, handing her a full box from his desk. "Be my guest. How are things in Pasadena?"

"I don't *want* to talk about Pasadena," she said, voice threatening to go out of control again.

"All right," he said gravely, seating himself again behind his desk. "What do you want to talk about?"

"Great—" she began, and even as she faltered, Willie, a very astute man, came fully alert as he knew almost instinctively what she was going to say. "Great—Greater—Lo—Lolómé."

"And what," he said quietly, "about Greater Lolómé?"

"My fiancé," she said, and with obvious great effort of will she brought her voice down again to a steady level and held it there—a very pretty girl, he thought, fine features, dark eyes, dark hair, high cheekbones, generous mouth, obvious intelligence. She took a deep breath and started over. "My fiancé, Creed Moncrief—"

"I know Creed," Willie said. "He used to work for me before I helped him get his job in the Foreign Service."

"He was in the Foreign Service," she said, and again her voice threatened to break; but she held it. "Was. He was m-murdered yesterday."

"No!" he said, completely shocked. "I am so sorry. . . . Tell me about it, if you can."

"Yes," she said. "That's why I'm here. Ambassador Bullock called me yesterday after he spoke to Mr. and Mrs. Moncrief. I took the red-eye last night because I wanted to talk to you about it. I want you to do something."

"Oh, I will," he said. "If I can . . . and I expect I can. Was this just a wanton street attack, as happens in that part of the world—or"—he looked both wry and sad—"on the streets of Washington, D.C., for that matter—or was he—"

"He was CIA," she said, and he nodded. "He was—after something. Ambassador Bullock isn't sure what. He just—went out, yesterday morning, in a disguise of some sort. And then he—he came back—dead."

"Forgive me," the Senator said, "but it will help to have all the facts. Was he tortured?"

"Ambassador Bullock won't tell me," she said, beginning to cry again. "But he won't deny it. I think he wants me to assume so."

"Did he suggest you come see me?"

"He did, but I had decided that already. I knew you would help if—if anybody could."

"Thank you," he said gravely. "I will do my best. So he was on some mission for the embassy or the Agency, or both—"

"Probably not both," she said. "The ambassador doesn't seem to know about it."

"He knows," Willie said. "He's just being cagey. Anyway, Creed was after something, as you say. And they got him. I wonder if— But of course he does. I was going to say, I wonder if the President knows. But I'm sure he does."

"Yes, but will he do anything about it?" she asked, eyes again filling with tears. "Or will he just—just try to ignore it?"

"Oh, no," Willie said flatly. "We won't let him. Do you have a place to stay in Washington?"

"Yes," she said. "One of my classmates from Harvard Law School is in the Justice Department. I always stay with her when I come to Washington."

"Good," he said. "I want you to stay in town until I decide what to do."

"Will you hold a hearing?" she asked.

"Will you testify?"

She hesitated briefly, then nodded; the legal mind, he thought, having one himself: the legal mind! He could see it clicking. Sympathy, sympathy: most potent weapon in the arsenal. She'd testify.

"Yes," she said. "I will."

"Good," he said. "I can't say exactly when at the moment. But it will be soon, I can promise you that. Meanwhile, stay out of sight, don't contact anyone in the media—"

"Does anyone in the media know?"

"They will," he said, "they will. But you lie low, OK? I want your appearance to get the full attention it deserves. Can you trust your girlfriend?"

"Implicitly."

"And her husband?"

"He's in the State Department."

"Does that guarantee discretion?" he inquired, to which she responded with the faint beginnings of humor.

"Not necessarily. But I think Alice and I can sit on him."

"Do," he said. "And"—his tone became both fatherly and emphatic— "try to get some rest and some sleep. Here's my home phone number"— he scribbled it on a notepad, tore it off, got up, and came around to tuck it in the jacket pocket of her smartly cut black suit—"call if you need anything, or just want to talk."

"Will you let me know," she said, and abruptly the tears threatened again—"what—what you find out about it?"

"Surely," he said. "Thank you for trusting me. Go get a cab, go to your friend's apartment, go to sleep. All right?"

"All right," she said with a shaky smile he suspected was the first in a good many hours. "You sound like my father."

"Grandfather," he said as he showed her out. "Old enough to be. Now, scoot."

"Yes, sir," she said obediently, managing another shaky little smile. "I didn't vote for you, but—"

"For heaven's sake!" he said with a glint of real exasperation. "Who gives a damn?"

But it was nice, he thought as he returned somberly to his desk, to have this kind of tribute from the young. He hoped he was kind, had always tried to be, though sometimes failing, as everyone does from time to time; it was nice to have his picture of himself affirmed. Another picture would soon be affirmed also, he promised himself grimly: the scourge from the Senate, one of the people the administration could always depend upon to take an independent and usually discomfiting position on things.

He wouldn't anticipate, though, for the moment; he would let them come to him. Very shortly, they did.

First came calls from his three sparring partners of last night, and with them he sparred again.

Jimmy Van implied he knew a great deal more than he did, which was an old trick the Senator parried with ease. Able Montague went at it head on, as was his direct and generally honest way of getting the news, and the Senator promised he would get back to him as soon as he had "direct and unimpeachable information," which Able chuckled was a good out; he agreed with an answering chuckle that yes, it was. Sally Holliwell, also direct but more challenging, implied as always that if he didn't cooperate she'd blast him out of the water, a threat he had often before turned aside amicably, and did again.

About an hour after he said goodbye to Anna-Maria Gonzalez, the call he was really waiting for came in. He was on the floor in the midst of a debate about giving most-favored-nation status to Iraq, which the administration wanted to do in what he thought was the futile hope of encouraging some unspecified good behavior from the chronically intransigent. One of the page girls called him off the floor to a booth in the cloakroom.

"I thought I'd be hearing from you, Ray," he said. "What's new on Sidi?"

After the Secretary confirmed what Anna-Maria had told him, with specific details, he said bluntly, "Well, Ray, what do you want me to do?"

"Keep the lid on for a few days," the Secretary said.

"Can't."

"Why not?"

"Because the young man's fiancée—former fiancée—was in to see me a little while ago, and I promised her we'd have a hearing."

"Oh, damn it!" Ray Stanley exclaimed. "And I suppose, sentimentalist that you are, you feel you must keep the promise."

"Lots of people in this town don't keep promises," Senator Wilson said. "I'm one of the few who do. It's a record I cherish."

"I wish you'd consulted me before you made it," the Secretary said. "You always have this tendency to become noble, Willie. It complicates things."

"Apparently few things at the moment are more complicated than the problem Sidi is—or soon will be, if he isn't already. How do you interpret this murder?"

"Sheer defiance," the Secretary said. He related briefly the President's conversation with Sidi the previous day during the NSC meeting. "This was just, 'I'll show *you*.'"

"And on that basis, quite frightening, I'd say," Willie observed. "It means that the threat of American power no longer inhibits the brigands of the earth. And we all know why that is."

"Yes, I know," the Secretary said. "You've spelled it out very clearly in a dozen speeches."

"And will again."

"And will again. And I agree with you, we've made too many threats and backed down from them too often. That's why we've got to do something very forceful about this case."

"I couldn't agree more," Willie said. "'We've got to do something very forceful.' But what? Perhaps our hearing will elicit some enlightenment from you and others in the administration."

"I'd rather you left us alone for a few days to try to work it out so we can present something definite to the country when we testify," the Secretary said. "You people on the Hill aren't perfect either, you know. This is another example of how you jump in with both feet and upset methods of diplomacy that really might work if you people weren't there disrupting them and looking for headlines."

"I don't look for headlines at my age," Senator Wilson remarked with some asperity.

"No, but Johnny Jones does and a lot of your other colleagues up there. It makes it very difficult for us down here, sometimes."

"Now I'll play the violin and you whistle," Willie said dryly. "If I hear one more song and dance about the poor old State Department having its brilliant efforts sabotaged by Congress, I'll regurgitate."

"Delicately stated and humorous in the extreme," the Secretary observed with equal dryness. "Nonetheless, I wish you would hold off a bit before you start raising a rumpus. You can rest assured we're making every possible effort to make our displeasure known to the President of Greater Lolómé."

"'Make our displeasure known,'" the Senator echoed. "Kick the you-know-what out of him, would be more like it."

"We may yet try to do that, too," Ray Stanley said. "The President has scheduled another NSC meeting for this evening."

"Are you announcing anything about it?"

"Not yet. We believe it to be the better part of discretion to keep it quiet for the moment. Just as we want you to keep it quiet."

"All right," the Senator said. "I'd rather keep my promise to Creed's fiancée, but if silence up here would really be helpful for a few days . . . will anything come of the NSC meeting?"

"He and I have discussed some preliminary plans," the Secretary said. "Things will be done."

"You'd better move fast," Willie suggested. "Our friends at Dolly's were intrigued enough by what you said so that they're all busy digging today. Particularly since Bill Bullock this morning called them all and told them the basic fact of Moncrief's murder."

"Oh, God damn it!" the Secretary exclaimed, in what was for him a rare burst of open profanity. "I specifically told him he was not to do that. God damn it!"

"Very irregular, I agree," the Senator remarked. "That's what can come of appointing millionaires as ambassadors—sometimes the bureaucracy can't keep them under control. Wealth makes them independent: sometimes they tell the truth. Apparently Bill hasn't told them all the gory details, but enough so that the defiance angle will probably be the lead into all their speculations about what you were actually talking about last night."

"I hope they haven't got that, too," Ray Stanley said.

"They're coming close," Willie said. "When Jimmy Van called me a while ago, he asked point-blank if we had any evidence that Sidi had 'a bomb or bombs,' as he put it. I was able to say that I had no direct personal knowledge of it. For once he wasn't quick enough to ask if I had any 'hearsay' knowledge, which would have been more difficult to handle. Able Montague and Sally Holliwell were equally close to the mark. As was my old pal and fraternity brother Tim Bates. They'll have it all soon, Ray. Better get moving."

"Mmmmmm," the Secretary said thoughtfully. "Perhaps we should issue a formal warning after the NSC meeting, outlining the whole situation—"

"And tie it into Moncrief. You've got to demand punishment for that, as well."

"I think the President and I have already got the outlines of it," Ray Stanley said, thinking, *At least I hope we have.* "It's a matter of timing. We had hoped to keep a lot of it off the record for a few days at least."

"Well, good luck," Willie Wilson said. "It's out of hand already."

But how out of hand neither he nor the Secretary of State could have imagined as their conversation ended. The extent of the unraveling very swiftly became apparent.

Turning on the MacNeil-Lehrer NewsHour, as was his usual custom when other matters did not prevent, the President heard in measured tones the words, "We turn first to the new crisis in Greater Lolómé. There is speculation that President Sidi bin Sidi bin Sidi has come into possession of one or more atomic bombs. In addition to that, Creed Moncrief, a young attaché, possibly CIA, in the American embassy in Greater Lolómé City, has been murdered, perhaps in retaliation for continuing U.S. pressure on Sidi's regime. We go now to our panel of experts—"

Like the Secretary of State before him, the President exclaimed, "Oh, God damn it!" at this new evidence of how difficult it was to keep anything secret inside the Beltway. His annoyance grew rapidly as he heard the speculation, described as commentary, that effectively established in the public mind the very strong possibility that Sidi did indeed have the bombs. And he was not made happier when Larry King followed with that most dramatic of former Secretaries of State, Reginald Pennebaker Sims, the only other man in present or recent diplomatic history who came close to equaling Ray Stanley's physical resemblance to Dean Acheson.

Penny Sims absolutely adored the limelight and could always be counted on to appear at the drop of the hat on any program, any time, anywhere, that would give him a pulpit for his very definite views on foreign policy. These were basically pragmatic, beneath a smooth veneer of what passed for idealism. Actually Penny was, as any of his former colleagues in the department often said, as tough as nails. And always, the President thought with a sigh, ready to try to prod his country into more and more daring feats of brinkmanship.

"I thought you were going to get Penny to work behind the scenes," the President silently accused his absent Secretary of State. "Not make a God damned spectacle of it on 'Larry King'!" But, Penny being Penny, he thought more objectively, what could one expect? They should have known.

"How we can sit idly by and watch this two-bit little twit get away with it?" Penny declared with the free-swinging rhetoric made possible by being out of office, his twin shafts of nose and jaw framing his indignantly quivering white handlebar mustache, "I cannot see and do not understand!"

"You think, then," his obliging host summed it up for him, "that this government should take strong and decisive action at this very moment to stop Sidi once and for all, both for the murder of Creed Moncrief and for the atom bombs Sidi may have."

"I *do*," Penny said, most emphatically.

"Well, Mr. President," his host said, looking directly into the cameras through which he was sure the chief executive was watching, "that leaves it up to you. Thank you, Mr. Secretary, for another great job in keeping our worldwide audience informed on the ins and outs of American foreign policy. Some ins, some outs! We bring you now Tweezela Tonkela, that beautiful African bombshell from South Africa who is sweeping the world of professional modeling off its feet. Don't go 'way!"

Fifteen minutes later, after Tweezela had related the fascinating story of how she had been discovered by an English camera crew in her native Soweto when the new black government of South Africa began the dismantling of all physical barriers between that vast black township and the formerly thriving city of Johannesburg, Bob Alexander came on the regular CNN news broadcast to give the Sidi story another push.

Bob was the veteran correspondent whose broadcasts during the second Gulf war had made him an overnight sensation after thirty years of journeyman slogging around the world's hot spots. Chubby-cheeked, baggy-eyed, soft-spoken, and deadly in his open-faced honesty, he covered Greater Lolómé from his base in Riyadh. His sources were excellent and his moral indignation always high.

It was increased now, he said, "by the cold-blooded murder of a very fine young friend of mine, Creed Moncrief. Those responsible have not yet been identified, but there is good reason to believe that the crime can be traced directly to the door of the Pink House, perhaps to overzealous lieutenants of Sidi, more likely to a cold-blooded order by Sidi himself. And there is another item arousing great concern throughout the whole area: the strong possibility that Sidi may have somehow secured an atomic bomb or bombs from some hidden sinister ally, possibly China or Russia or North Korea, perhaps Libya, perhaps someone even closer to home.

"Both of these events add up to a major crisis for the United States and its not-always-anxious-to-lead President. It seems imperative, looking at it from here, that the United States has no option but strong and vigorous action against the maverick from the desert who holds absolute power in Greater Lolómé."

"Well, the hell with you, Bob," the President said, using his remote to turn off the huge machine in a corner of the Oval Office. "And you, too, Penny! And you, Larry! And you, Robert and Jim! And you too, Jimmy Van and Able and Sally and Tim and all the rest of you!"

But, that said and done, Sidi remained. Within the hour the NSC would be meeting again in the Roosevelt Room, and something public would obviously have to emerge from its deliberations. How little or how much he still did not know; but he expected it would have to be much, given the public attention being generated by the media—and, as Ray Stanley told him when he and Eulie Montgomery arrived from Foggy Bottom, by the Hill.

Passing again under the familiar portico, walking again through the tall glass doors and down the long central hall of the night-hushed mansion, the Deputy Secretary of State felt reasonably encouraged by the way things seemed to be going. From Ray's rather disgruntled remarks in the limousine, giving her the gist of his earlier conversation with the President, and her quick glimpse of the ubiquitous news programs she had found time to see, she gathered that advocates of a strong response to Sidi were already gaining ground. The President was apparently being smoked out. She couldn't help being gratified by this.

That he felt he was being pressured was evident from his rather cool nod as they entered the Roosevelt Room to find the Vice President, Jaime Serrano, and the Defense Department contingent already in place around the table. But his manners, as always, were impeccable.

"How is Herbie, Eulie?" he inquired gently as she took her seat.

"Hanging on," she said.

He shook his head and uttered a sympathetic sound.

"If there's anything Helen and I can do—"

"No, thank you, Mr. President," she said. "You're very kind, but, there isn't much anyone can do, except—think good thoughts."

"You have ours," he assured her, his tone so kindly that it almost destroyed her tightly held control.

It had been a long, trying, desperately wearying night, during which Herbie tossed and turned and called out for her approximately every twenty minutes, or so it seemed. He had the means of releasing the painkillers into his bloodstream himself, whenever the pain became too great; but when she suggested gently that he do so and let her get at least a little sleep with which to prepare for what was certainly going to be a busy day ahead, he had whispered with the stubborn insistence of the dreadfully ill, "I want you to do it."

So she had, and sleep had dwindled to a few hasty catnaps. She had come to her office this morning exhausted and not feeling up to any major battles. She hoped now that the President would yield gracefully and not insist on one. The arrival of Eldridge Barnes, obviously agitated and ready for combat, appeared at first to threaten that.

"Mr. President!" he said tersely, taking his seat and looking around the table with a cursory nod. "I hope we can conclude this meeting with reasonable speed."

"Oh?" the President said, sounding a little edgy in response to the CIA director's peremptory tone. "Why is that?"

"Because I am leaving for Greater Lolómé at midnight," Eldridge Barnes said, "and I don't intend to miss my plane."

"Are you now?" the President said. "I didn't know that."

"I considered it an internal CIA matter," the director said. "I didn't think it was necessary to get your approval on everything."

"Perhaps not," the President said, an ominous little glint in his eyes. "However, as a matter of courtesy . . . What are you going to do in Greater Lolómé, if I am permitted to ask?"

"Escort Creed Moncrief's body home," El Barnes said. "I feel he deserves the honor."

There was silence for a moment, broken when the President, across whose face various thoughts, all quite obvious, had passed, finally said, "Well, well," in a thoughtful voice. "What plane are you going to use?"

"Commercial, over," El Barnes said. "Unless you wish to send me on Air Force One."

"Or Two," the Vice President volunteered earnestly. "I'd be happy to cooperate—er," he added hastily as the President's expression turned to an open scowl, "that is, if—if it's OK—that is—if you agree, Mr. President."

The President sighed heavily and spoke in a tired but amiable tone, his mood, as so often, apparently changed in an instant.

"Everybody is *so busy,*" he said. "And I'm always the last to know. Thank you, Hank, that's magnificent of you. And don't think I haven't thought of something like that, El. I won't send Air Force One—or Two—but I don't object to your going. It would be a very fitting gesture—certainly a dramatic one that would make many of the points I think we wish to make in this situation. I just wish you'd told me earlier, we could have announced it from here in time for the evening news shows. Which were not, as some of you may have had time to notice, particularly kind. However, El, go—go. And God bless. I assume Bill Bullock is making arrangements from that end."

"Oh, yes," Eldridge Barnes said, relaxing now that he had won his point with much less turmoil than he had anticipated. "Army helicopter to Riyadh, air force jet to Frankfort, to Andrews. Along with, I might add, Regina Gates, who has already come down from Lesser Lolómé and is in Bill's embassy. I thought it best to order her home for a while until we see what's going to happen, particularly being a woman in a Muslim country. Not that we expect Lesser Lolómé to be attacked, of course, but"— he paused and gave the President a challenging look—"or do we?"

"Not if I can help it," the President said.

"And how do you propose—?" the CIA director inquired. "Have you and Ray worked it out?"

"Ray has," the President said. "See what you think."

And he nodded to the Secretary of State, who proceeded to outline for them the suggestions he had made to the President that morning. As expected, the Secretary of Defense and the chairman of the Joint Chiefs expressed considerable alarm at the thought of placing two aircraft carriers in what could only be interpreted as a hostile stance.

"Are you sure that's what we ought to do?" Arlie McGregor inquired. "After all, that's a pretty warlike gesture, Mr. President."

"That's what I want you all to discuss," the President said.

"The basic question to my mind is, can you do it?" Eulie Montgomery said. "And if so, how fast?"

"We can do anything we're asked to do," General Rathbun said, sounding a bit starchy. "And in twenty-four hours or less. Is that saber-rattling enough for you, Eulie?"

"I don't want to rattle any sabers," she said, voice tired from her difficult night and tired from having to fight the endless policy battles around which State revolved at an endless pace. "I just want us to make adequate response to both Creed's death and to the presence of A-bombs and missiles beneath the Pink Palace, that's all. If you can do it, and that rapidly, fine, I'm for it. I'm for anything that says: *This time we mean it.*"

"Yes," the President said dryly. "Thank you, Eulie. You do spell it out, don't you?"

"Somebody has to," she said, adding, again in a voice uncharacteristically dispirited, "Mr. President."

"All right," the President said. "So what do we do? Jaime?"

"Unless Arlie and Bill are going to absolutely refuse to send the aircraft carriers—" Jaime Serrano began, and paused to stare at them pointedly.

"Oh, hell," Arlie McGregor responded, looking disgruntled but bowing to what appeared to be inevitable, "of course they'll go if you want them to, Mr. President. Against our better judgment, but—"

"Swatting a gnat with a two-by-four," Bill Rathbun grumbled.

"We'll see," the President said. "I have to stress that this is a planning meeting, not an action meeting."

"Oh?" Eulie Montgomery said, dismay apparent and combativeness reviving. "I thought you called us here because you felt it was time to make some firm decisions?"

"I want to be *ready* to make them," the President emphasized blandly. "A lot of things have to be taken into consideration. I just want everything in place."

"All right," she said, becoming more animated as she rose to the challenge. "How about"—and she began making notes as she spoke, on one of the big yellow legal notepads they all had at their places—"'The government of the United States has received with anger and repugnance the news of the barbaric murder of Creed Moncrief, a member of the staff of the American embassy in Greater Lolómé City.

"'We call upon the Government of Greater Lolómé to bring to justice immediately the perpetrators of this barbaric act, and to make reparations immediately to Mr. Moncrief's family and to this Government for this monstrous and inexcusable act.'"

"Isn't that a little strong, Eulie?" Ray Stanley inquired. "How about 'has received with dismay and deep concern' the news of the murder, leaving out 'barbaric,' of Creed Moncrief, et cetera . . . 'Those responsible for this act,' leave out 'perpetrators' and leave out 'barbaric' . . . 'Reparations for this grievous act,' leave out 'monstrous and inexcusable' . . . Wouldn't that achieve the same result without using unnecessarily inflammatory and provocative language?"

"Why not be inflammatory and provocative?" Eldridge Barnes demanded before Eulie could respond. "It was the barbaric act of a barbaric and monstrous man who deserves every condemnation we can give him, plus adequate, and I do mean adequate, punishment for his crime. I'm with you, Eulie. Let him have it."

"You would be, El," the Secretary of State observed. "Creed was your man. You have a direct interest."

"We all have a direct interest," Eldridge Barnes snapped. "Every decent person on this earth—assuming there are any left—has an interest. Monsters shouldn't be allowed to get away with monstrosities, although of course they always do thanks to people like you, Ray, who don't have the courage of their convictions."

"I think," the Secretary said mildly, "that I have the courage of my convictions. It's your responsibility to contemplate and prepare for the brutal barefaced realities; it's mine to protect all the necessary niceties that hold some sort of civilized discourse together. I think I'm as anxious as you are to discipline this slimy character—this two-bit little twit, as Penny Sims calls him—this monstrous little twit, as you and Eulie see him, and as we all see him, in reality. But I think we can do it more diplomatically and still be just as forceful."

"I don't see how," the director of the CIA said bluntly. "I'm past pussyfooting, myself. I've had it."

"Yes," the President said. "Well. No doubt language can be perfected once we have the basic framework. Go on, Eulie."

"Which means it will be smoothed down to nothing," she observed with a revival of her usual tart honesty.

The President smiled. "You underestimate me. Go on, Eulie."

She gave him one of the "Eulie's looks" that could "make even the stoutest hearts in the department," as Ray put it, "quail before her." But she resumed as directed.

"'Further,'" she said, "'this Government has learned with the deepest concern'—this is the place for that phrase, Ray—'that there is a strong possibility that the Government of Greater Lolómé has come into possession of one or more atomic bombs and the means to deliver them—'"

"Are we ready to go public with that yet?" Jaime Serrano interrupted with real concern.

"I wonder," the Vice President echoed earnestly. "It might not be quite the right thing, do you think? Maybe the two things should be kept separate, I'd think."

"That's what we really have to decide, Hank," the President said. "It's the basic question."

"It seems so to me," the Vice President said, looking pleased.

"I have no doubts," Eulie remarked, "providing—*providing*—we're prepared to back it up with the sternest possible warning. To wit—" she smiled a rather grim smile and interjected, "I don't want to shock anybody, now, particularly you two gentlemen at the head of the government"—the Vice President looked even more pleased at his inclusion—"but, to wit:

"'This Government wishes to warn the Government of Greater Lolómé most emphatically that if the Government of Greater Lolómé does not immediately comply with the inspection procedures of the International Atomic Energy Agency as outlined in the nuclear nonproliferation treaty signed by the Government of Greater Lolómé on November 3, 1996, the Government of the United States will immediately request a meeting of the United Nations Security Council to take such disciplinary action against the Government of Greater Lolómé as the facts may warrant.'

"In a separate statement issued through you at the Pentagon, Arlie," she concluded, "delayed perhaps twenty-four hours, with no reference to this statement at all, I would make the bare announcement that two aircraft carriers, the U.S. what's-its-name and the U.S. whoever-you-are, have taken up new positions in the Gulf.

"Then I would sit tight for maybe another twenty-four hours to give him an opportunity to pull in his horns and comply, and if he doesn't, I'd issue another even stronger statement from this office announcing that we will go to the UN and seek a resolution imposing sanctions."

For a few moments they were silent, studying their own notes which they had made as she went along. Then Ray Stanley cleared his throat almost apologetically and gave her a smile.

"Again, Eulie," he said, "I'm afraid there's a difference of opinion at State. 'Warn the Government of Greater Lolómé most emphatically'—I don't think 'warn' is necessary, it's obvious we're being emphatic—delete 'immediately comply,' simply 'comply' will do . . . 'immediately request a meeting' of the Security Council, 'immediately' not necessary . . . 'Disciplinary' action, too schoolmarmish, 'appropriate' action more suited . . . and I'd hold up the carriers for maybe a week, to allow him full time to comply and not give him the feeling he's being pressured."

She uttered a sarcastic snort. "For God's sake, why not? He should be pressured! In other words, you want to take all the urgency out of it, as much as possible, right down the line. I can't go along with you, Ray. I think we've got to be tougher." She turned to the head of the table and demanded bluntly, "What do you think, Mr. President?"

"Eulie, Eulie!" he said in a fond tone that told her he was preparing to dodge. "You are so positive. We do want to put on the pressure, yes. At the same time, we don't want to get too harsh about it because presumably he is going to back down and we'll still have to be dealing with him on a relatively civilized basis for quite a long time to come." He smiled and glanced at the director of the CIA. "Unless El can foment something and get him overthrown. I'm sure El would like to try."

"You bet I would," El Barnes said. "I'd like to kill the bastard with my own bare hands, if you'd let me."

"You remember what Sidi pointed out last time we were in this room," the President said with an indulgent chuckle as though he were dealing with a recalcitrant child. "Our law won't let you. So there we are. How about that language, Eulie? Let's throw it open and kick it around a bit. How far do we want to go, how tough do we want to be? Bearing in mind always that the chances are one hundred to one that he is going to back down and we may be able to bring him under control without too much extra pressure. In which case, it might be better to be diplomatic. What do the rest of you think?"

There followed what Eulie described to Ray later as "one of his soften 'em up and talk 'em around" sessions, in which they all indulged their finely honed talents for nitpicking and word-changing, each according to personal prejudices and/or fears about the basic dangers of U.S. toughness or lack thereof.

What finally emerged was, as she disgustedly felt and bluntly expressed, almost a slap on the wrist. "A warning," the President insisted. "A tentative admonition," she countered.

They couldn't even agree at that point on whether or not to dispatch the two carriers. "This," as El Barnes remarked with scathing sarcasm, "is presidential decision making at its most profound and best." They took their cue from the President, who laughed comfortably at that one.

They were nearing the end of their discussion, prodded by El's impatience to get off to the airport, tired and snappish after almost three hours of argument, when the phone rang.

The national security adviser took it and heard the lilting tones of the Eunuch calling from Greater Lolómé City.

Jaime's face became blank—then shocked—then angered. He said nothing in response to the Eunuch for several long minutes. Then he simply said tersely, "Thank you, Mr. Secretary," and hung up.

"We might as well have saved our breath," he told them bitterly. "Do you know what that bastard has done?"

Half an hour later it was on television. An hour after that the bulldog edition of the *Post* had it on the streets:

Sidi Claims 4 A-Bombs, Threatens Immediate Lesser Lolómé Strike

---

Defies U.S., UN "Satanists," Calls Muslims to World Jihad

It was not, as El Barnes remarked dryly as they left the Roosevelt Room, America's finest hour.

TWO

TWO

1   But of course it had to be portrayed that way, to the media, to the country, and to the world.

"We have now arrived at another of those things which is known as 'the moment of truth,'" wrote that stubbornly independent thinker Tim Bates, in a thumb-sucker sent out to the 313 client newspapers of the Washington Inquirer syndicate.

"Watch the stirring drama unfold.

"There will now come into play the basic, overriding, implacable principle of the present-day American government:

"The President must always be made to look good.

"This doctrine, begun almost inadvertently in post–World War II years as instant communications made instant impression the most important part of any event, has become refined and institutionalized into an ironclad rule as communication has first linked, then shrunk, then completely taken over, the world.

"In the past three administrations, particularly the last, the necessity to make the President look good has become the defining element of every event, every action, every decision. From the President himself on down, every clever mind in the White House now has one single, all-consuming aim: the creation, care, and tender nurturing of presidential image. Mistakes are never admitted, uncertainties never acknowledged. The reality of human imperfection, while it sometimes cannot be completely concealed, is never allowed to divert or subvert the basic purpose of the executive branch of the American government: to maintain the psychological, if not always the factual, picture of human perfection behind the desk in the Oval Office.

"'Spin' is all.

"Poor, battered Truth lags far behind.

"So, as with all his immediate predecessors, the current President will now be concentrating his efforts on protecting the public perception of himself as the shrewd, all-knowing, all-controlling manager of affairs. He will now be busy salvaging his reputation from Sidi bin Sidi bin Sidi's appalling defiance—for it is indeed appalling.

"For the first time in many a decade, if ever, a foreign leader is treating the United States and its President with utter, jeering contempt.

"Sidi has apparently been warned. And Sidi just doesn't care. The contempt is beyond jeering—it is fearless. Somebody just isn't afraid of the United States any longer. The world has abruptly crossed, in this open defiance from a small desert dictatorship, a profound psychological divide: on yesterday's side, a United States the threat of whose displeasure was enough to make the world's evil ones hesitate and reconsider—on today's side, the threat falling, ridiculed, on empty air.

"To reestablish the credibility of American power is now the most important task facing the President. Many are the past architects of the gradual decline of American credibility. Only one architect, the one now in office, has the present responsibility of restoring it. Hype for the incumbent is not the answer.

"Behind the President's efforts and those of his staff to make him look good, the harsh realities will march on unimpeded. All that, it is devoutly and desperately hoped at 1600 Pennsylvania Avenue, will be concealed by the rosy glow cast by a leader portrayed to be in full command of a chaotic and increasingly insane world.

"It is not enough."

So wrote that tough-minded soul Tim Bates, still able at almost eighty to be savagely indignant about what he perceived to be the shortcomings of his government. Anna Hastings, founder, publisher, and sole owner of the *Washington Inquirer* and its child, the Inquirer syndicate, was as usual blunt and direct in her appreciation. One of her terse little notes came over his fax within the hour after his piece had gone in to the copy desk: "Timmy: Great stuff. Let him have it! A."

As for the syndicate's clients, there was the usual split between genuine conservatives and phony conservatives, genuine liberals and phony liberals. On balance it appeared that there was a deep skepticism concerning the President's ability to pull this one off. Editorial reaction was deeply divided but leaning, on balance, toward Tim's general view.

Meanwhile at the White House, at State, Defense, and wherever Cabinet members or other high appointees of the administration had, or were able to arrange, opportunities to speak, the spin went on.

For the first two days after the issuance of the formal response of the government, the President did not communicate. Unlike that of his immediate predecessor, his face was not omnipresent on every screen and every scrap of newsprint. There were actually moments when his voice did not reverberate from television and radio twenty-four hours a day. He had long ago learned the lesson that some in politics never learn, that silence can actually on occasion be more effective than sound, and that absence sometimes actually does make the public heart grow fonder.

"I'm going to lie low for a while," he told them when the second emergency NSC meeting finally broke up, and true to his word, he vanished behind the protective screen of the White House, which can be either concealing or revealing as its spinmasters decree. Offscreen and out of media view, he rallied his departments and embarked in private upon a busy week. The machinery of the executive branch went into defensive high gear.

Cabinet members fanned out across the country. Audiences that had contracted days, weeks, months previously to hear the Secretary of Labor, say, were startled to learn how closely the successful thwarting of Sidi was tied into the fate of America's declining trade unions. Members of the chamber of commerce of Cleveland were surprised to hear from the U.S. trade representative how closely their support for the administration's handling of Sidi was vital to the ever-rankling question of the trade balance with Japan. The Secretary of Health and Human Services told her audience in San Francisco that welfare reform could not possibly go forward unless Sidi's sinister schemes were defeated. The Surgeon General, in a dazzling verbal sleight of hand, somehow managed to link Sidi with sex education for grammar school children, the distribution of free condoms to teenagers, and the ongoing investigation of the pros and cons of legalizing drugs. The stability of the dollar, the Secretary of the Treasury warned solemnly, hinged on Sidi. The director of the Environmental Protection Agency warned darkly that the fate of titmice in the Arizona desert might well depend upon what happened with Sidi.

Finally, raising it all to the highest levels, James Van Rensselaer Burden accepted a commission from the *Times* Sunday magazine to write a piece for the upcoming issue entitled "Here We Go Again? Pride and Prejudice Clash Anew in the Desert." The Secretary of State agreed to appear with Senator Wilson and Congressman Jones on Sally Holliwell's "Capitol Perspective." And the President, who when the occasion called for it could act as down-home-to-the-max as his immediate predecessor, agreed to appear on Able Montague's "WorldView" and answer the phone-ins of his countrymen.

Some of this solemn thunder made sense, some of it was nonsense; but the drumbeat went on. Behind the public foofaraw, the President and those most closely associated with him in foreign affairs, particularly the Secretary of State, did the best they could to meet the ugly threats to world stability posed by The Wearer of the Two Hats, President for Life of All the Peoples of Lolómé.

Across the country, America reacted as America always reacts—or at least as its noisier and more self-consciously "involved" citizens react.

From Bonnie Terhuitt, president of C.C.A.—Concerned Citizens Against—to Drs. (academic) Random Cruikshank of Harvard and Feemahle Jackson-Washington of Yale, cochairs of W.P.—We Protest—they were on the screen, on the air, in print, or seated at their fax machines spewing forth their statements, manifestos, letters to the editor, petitions to White House, Senate, and House. What Tim referred to as "letterhead liberals" and "copy-machine conservatives"—the minuscule groups, often no more than two or three individuals, who possess a telephone, a typewriter or word processor, a fax, a copying machine, a post office box, and several thousand letterheads solemnifying themselves as the Alliance for This, the Coalition for That—also raised their clamor. National news programs and national publications that would never print a release from a major political group without thoroughly checking its background, members, and financing, dutifully publicized these letterhead fly-by-nights without ever bothering to confirm their authenticity—as long as they supported the programs', or the publications', points of view.

Overwhelmingly, these itches on the body politic were conspicuously not in favor of doing anything about Sidi. Within three days they had generated such a furor in Washington, been quoted solemnly so many times by national programs and publications, that hurriedly taken polls were able to report that 71 percent of the 1,230 Americans questioned out of approximately 280 million were against any attempt to intervene in what one prominent pollster characterized catchingly as "the ever-roiling, ever-boiling, always hopeless Middle East."

In the face of all this, the humor at the White House tended to be somewhat grim.

"How about a swim upstream against public opinion?" the Secretary of State inquired.

"Be my guest," said the President of the United States.

But for the time being they were determined to respond somehow, some way, to the latest démarche from Greater Lolómé City. That way, they were convinced, lay a return to stability, a recapture of public support, a reestablishing of America's reputation for consistency and strength which the President of Greater Lolómé—backed by his secret friends, whoever they might be—was obviously determined to destroy if he could.

Their determination lasted roughly a month. If the pattern of its gradual fading away seemed familiar, it was because American diplomacy in recent years seemed to have become frozen in a sort of foredoomed dance toward failure whose successive steps had become as stylized as kabuki.

Nonetheless, the effort had to be made. It involved most of the world before it was over, and put upon the Department of State burdens it perhaps was not really equipped to handle in the present Age of Disintegration, which the more determinedly optimistic chose to call the Age of Change.

You could not, however, have convinced Ray Stanley and his colleagues in foreign policy of that. They acted with considerable inner trepidation but with the basic conviction that America, though possibly blundering at times, would still emerge triumphant. After all, it always had—or rather, remembering Vietnam, Iraq, Bosnia, Somalia, Haiti, Cuba, North Korea—it *mostly* always had, anyway.

At two-thirty in the afternoon after Sidi's announcement, the President reconvened the National Security Council for its third emergency meeting on the matter.

This time the greatest possible publicity was sought to emphasize the gravity of the occasion. Members arrived openly at the north portico, worried, grim-faced, silent. An air of crisis hung about their arrival. It was made clear to waiting cameras and reporters that the matter of Sidi was portentous, and a thing of state.

When they were regrouped around the table in the Roosevelt Room, the President entered with his quick, determined step. There was a slight tension apparent in his manner, but on the surface—and, they felt, inside as well—he appeared to be his usual sardonic, confident self.

"Thank you all for coming," he said, with the slightly ironic emphasis that conveyed the impression that it was smashing of them but they didn't really have to, which of course they did. "Obviously we've got to respond with a formal statement. With all respects, Eulie, our work of last night is out the window and all your fine efforts are meaningless. What do you suggest now?"

"Make it twice as strong, if possible," she responded tartly, and the debate was on.

Three hours later, after many suggestions, amendments, deletions, corrections—after defining, as Eulie remarked with even sharper tartness toward the end, "the *real* number of angels that can dance on the head of a pin"—they came up with a statement that pleased no one entirely but commanded the public support of all simply because it had to.

"We don't have much choice," noted Eldridge Barnes, disgruntled because he had been forced to cancel his trip to Greater Lolómé and order Creed Moncrief's body sent home accompanied only by a white-faced, deeply unhappy Regina Gates.

The statement was released to the world an hour later by the President himself, flanked by the Secretaries of State and Defense. They appeared in the East Room of the White House before more than 250 members of the media in an evening time slot cleared for them by all the major networks. All three looked grim.

The President read the statement in a slow, deliberate voice:

"The Government of the United States notes with serious concern [*Eulie and El Barnes tried to swing the Council to 'notes with the gravest concern,' but failed*] the statement issued by the President of Greater Lolómé, Sidi bin Sidi bin Sidi.

"Coming as it does fast upon the murder [*originally 'death'—Eulie and El won that one*] of Creed Moncrief, a member of the staff of the United States embassy in Greater Lolómé City, it assumes, in this Government's estimation, even graver import. This Government cannot emphasize too strongly the seriousness of the situation that now confronts the world.

"This Government holds the Government of Greater Lolómé [*Eulie and El proposed adding 'and its President,' but were thwarted by Ray Stanley and the President, who said they should not antagonize him too much personally—'I may have to have him to lunch next week,' the President remarked with wry exaggeration*] responsible for the brutal and totally unprovoked murder of Mr. Moncrief. We demand immediate, full, and unconditional reparations to Mr. Moncrief's family and this Government [*'unconditional reparations, including a formal apology by the Government of Greater Lolómé,' argued Eulie and El, but again were overruled by the argument that this would be 'not diplomatic'*] for this wanton and deliberate violation of international law and the mutual protection of diplomatic personnel that must exist between civilized governments if the comity of nations is to be preserved.

"This Government further views with concern [*'views with the utmost gravity,' Eulie and El suggested, but again were overruled*] the statement of the President of Greater Lolómé claiming that he and his Government are in possession of four atomic bombs and the means to deliver them. We believe that this claim, if true, should arouse [*not 'must arouse,' the Secretary objected; 'some may not feel the same urgency we do'*] the intense concern of the entire world community.

"Possession of atomic bombs by Greater Lolómé would create a threat [*'Not a major threat,' Arlie McGregor objected to Eulie's suggestion; 'we don't want to give the guy too much importance.' 'Which Defense would have to respond to,' she shot back*] not only to the region but to world stability itself.

"Therefore this Government intends to consult at the earliest opportunity with other concerned Governments to seek support for an early meeting of the United Nations Security Council [*Eulie and El: 'to consult with other concerned Governments to demand an immediate meeting, etc.'—overruled*] to explore the possibility of requesting [*'to demand'—overruled*] that the Government of Greater Lolómé agree to the inspection of its military facilities [*'all' its military facilities; Eulie and El, overruled*] by the International Atomic Energy Agency.

"To this end I am directing the Secretary of State to consult with the

Secretary-General and other interested powers on the date and time of such a meeting of the Security Council, which should be held as promptly as possible so that inspection by the IAEA may start as soon as possible ['*at once,*' *final proposal from Eulie, over and out*]."

The President stopped, took a drink of water, stared at them gravely for a moment, then asked for questions. A dozen hands shot up.

"Mr. President," the dean of the White House press corps asked in her direct and bluntly honest way, "is it true that this is basically just a personal feud between you and Sidi?"

The President laughed. Everyone laughed. The tension broke a little.

"Oh, my goodness!" he exclaimed with a humorous air. "What next?"

"Well, is it?" she demanded.

His expression turned grave.

"I hope my approach to foreign policy has a little more substance than that," he said. "In the first place, certain facts are unarguable. One, a fine young man, Creed Moncrief, has been murdered by the government of Greater Lolómé, quite possibly at the direct order of President Sidi. Secondly—"

"Mr. President, does this government have proof that his death was ordered by Sidi?" the *Times* inquired.

"We have reason to believe," the President said, "that this was the fact, as confirmed by Bob Alexander in his CNN broadcast—"

"Bob said circumstantial evidence showed that it must have been ordered by Sidi," the *Times* objected. "He didn't say he had any direct proof."

"That's right," the President said. "I am prepared to take Bob's word for it"—his tone became sarcastic—"since he's some three or four thousand miles closer to the scene than you and I are."

"Mr. President," the *Los Angeles Times* said, as they all laughed a little uneasily at the President's combativeness, "was Moncrief CIA?"

"CIA!" the President exclaimed with comfortable scorn. "Poor old CIA, they get blamed for everything. In the eyes of the world's suspicious minds, does the United States have anybody anywhere who *isn't* CIA?"

"But, Mr. President—" the *L.A. Times* began.

The President laughed, scorn still in his voice.

"Come on, Henry," he said. "We *know* you're not one of the world's suspicious minds!"

"Mr. President," said the *Post* doggedly, "leaving aside Moncrief, what proof do we have other than Sidi's word, which is not notorious for its truthfulness, that he actually has atomic bombs? Isn't your administration overreacting to what may be just bluster or bluff?"

The President became suddenly grave.

"We do not feel that this is an area—or an era—in which we can ignore anything having to do with the possible proliferation of atomic weapons. It is not a subject or a period in which to take chances. If we are overreacting, as you put it, I assume time will disclose that. If we are not, then we are taking what would seem to be the prudent course. I would rather err on the side of overreacting than fall into the error of not reacting at all."

"You do have some private information that there actually are bombs, then," the *Boston Globe* said.

The President looked bland.

"Presidents sometimes do have private information that even you bird dogs don't have," he said, "hard though I know it is for you all to acknowledge and bitterly as it upsets you not to be in on absolutely everything. Obviously," he added, tone hardening, "I and my administration would not be taking this action if we felt we were dealing with a mirage."

"What action *are* you contemplating, Mr. President?" the *Globe* persisted. "This statement doesn't seem to reflect any particular urgency. It all seems pretty casual to me. You'll consult other governments and then you'll get around in due course to calling for a Security Council meeting—and only then will you consider the possibility of asking the IAEA to investigate Sidi's military facilities—and not even all of them. Doesn't that give him a lot of opportunity for ducking and dodging and ultimately getting away with it?"

The President looked annoyed but kept his voice down.

"All I can say is, wait and see. We are prepared to take whatever steps are necessary and appropriate in this situation."

"Even to the extent of blockading Greater Lolómé again and perhaps even engaging in some sort of armed action?" the *Wall Street Journal* asked.

The President shook his head impatiently.

"You people!" he said. "Are you ever in favor of anything your government does?"

The dean of the White House press corps gave her characteristic gurgle of laughter and remarked in her famously characteristic confidentially nonconfidential sotto voce, "Does our government ever do anything?"—and decided to end the conference on her colleagues' burst of laughter even though she hadn't received the standard high sign from the press secretary.

"Thank you, Mr. President," she said dryly. They all echoed it and began to file out, but not before someone at the back of the room shouted out one last parting shot.

"Are you contemplating military action against Sidi, Mr. President?"

The President paused.

"Not at this time," he said calmly. "Not at this time."

"Does that mean, Mr. President—"

"Not at this time," he repeated, and turned away.

"I thought they might ask Ray and me something," Arlie McGregor said in a disappointed tone as the President took his arm and the Secretary of State's and led them from the podium.

"Thank your stars they didn't," the President said lightly, good humor apparently restored. "That's what I'm here for. It was my turn this evening. Yours will come. Before that, though, we all have a lot of work to do."

Following them back down the long central hall, the Deputy Secretary of State and the director of the CIA, who had been standing on the sidelines, gave each other a thoughtful look.

"The cancer's begun," she said.

He nodded grimly.

"It's in the words. It always starts in the words. And from there, it spreads."

They both knew, as veteran observers of their country's often erratic course in foreign affairs, that the word-changes in official statements, the carefully managed casual back-downs from officially stated brave positions, might at first appear small and quite innocuous; but often they were, as Eulie Montgomery and Eldridge Barnes were well aware, the first indications of policy carcinoma.

They knew, with a glum sense of foreboding and inevitability, that it would spread in this instance, as in so many before, unless it could be reversed forthwith; and there had been no indication, from the President or in the questions from the media, that anything would stop the process now.

For some days, however, things seemed to be proceeding with reasonable speed and firm resolve. In the NSC statement they had decided not to make mention of aircraft carriers, but in actuality they had been ordered sent and were already being put in a condition of readiness at the time of the press conference; by midnight that night they were on their way. Simultaneously the behind-the-scenes diplomatic efforts began, and simultaneously, inevitably, the reports in the media grew and flourished.

Tim Bates was not the only one to launch into reportage, speculation, approval, or condemnation. As with everything of major import in the hemorrhaging world of the closing years of the twentieth century, sooner or later the general gist of it saw the light of day. Where facts were not available, shrewd speculation and intelligent guesses furnished the fuel. "The matter of Sidi," as it was soon referred to at State, was dubbed "the crisis" by the media; ergo, it became one. "I think, therefore I am" became, as always, the media's "*We* think, therefore it is."

SIDI CRISIS GROWS, said the *Times*.

SIDI CRISIS GROWS, said the *Post*.

SIDI CRISIS GROWS, said the *Washington Inquirer* and all the rest.

And so it did.

Meanwhile the work of diplomacy, the production of news, and the attempts to influence public opinion on both sides of the issue went on.

2   "Mr. Ambassador," Ray Stanley said, gesturing his visitor cordially to a seat facing his own enormous desk, "you know why I have invited you to come here this morning. I want your invaluable advice on how we should best proceed to defuse the situation created by the President of Greater Lolómé." He passed a hand across his forehead to wipe away mock sweat and smiled at his guest with knowing, between-us familiarity that he hoped would induce some sense of fellow humanity. "It is *most* difficult."

His visitor, who was Vladimir Novotny, ambassador extraordinary and plenipotentiary of the recently proclaimed Second Soviet Republic, gave him one of his small, smug smiles in return and accompanied it with an elaborate, rather bored shrug.

"It does pose a problem," he agreed. "For you. We admire the way you are volunteering to solve it for us all. Without the leadership of America, where would we be!"

And his smile broadened into a comfortable, aren't-you-people-in-a-mess-now grin that did not augur well for any Washington hopes that Moscow might be willing to assist in this latest crisis. Almost a decade of wishful yearnings for friendly cooperation was being swept away by the fast-reviving party machinery. Old empires die hard, and this one, the Secretary of State often reflected with an inward sigh, was unfortunately far from moribund. It was, in fact, reviving by the hour.

First had come the popular election of the New Stalin—or the New Hitler—or the New Whatever-He-Was—certainly the new World's Champion Demagogue, Ray Stanley thought grimly now, vividly aware that almost every morning's news brought some new, wildly hysterical salvo against the West, new ominous demands for the return of former Soviet satellites to the Soviet fold, new massings of an enthusiastically cooperating Soviet Army on their borders, new demands that Russians originally sent abroad to subject states to strengthen the grip of the old empire devote themselves actively to strengthening the new, constant, terrifying evidence of a mind out of control rushing himself and his tragic country toward— what? . . . And of iron dictatorship descending once again, in all aspects of life, upon peoples who could not comprehend, and therefore impatiently opted out of, the slow, awkward, patient, and painful sacrifices necessary to a successful transition to a democratic way of life.

Then had come the final remuzzling of the media—the rewriting of history, at which the new leaders of the state had become so adept during the years of tyranny—the wiping out in the official "histories" of the ill-fated attempts by two blundering leaders to bring political and economic freedom to Mother Russia after so many black decades and centuries of Communist and czarist rule—and so, finally, the shrewd renaming, which, as the Secretary had summed it up in a recent article in *Foreign Policy,* "in three clever words brought transition, obliteration, confirmation, and reaffirmation."

The Stalinist period had now officially become "The First Soviet Republic." The failed time between had become "The Interim Period." The two ill-fated leaders and their deputies of that period had been reduced to one line each in the official records. The new regime had been given a title carefully chosen to echo the past and reestablish it in the minds of their peoples and the world's peoples, who had scarcely had time to absorb the "Interim Period" before the new dispensation returned triumphantly to power.

It was now the "Second Soviet Republic," with nothing except a very hazy, ill-defined, officially forgotten "Interim Period" between it and its predecessor. The name in English slid easily from one into the other: "U.S.S.R."—"S.S.R." Few nowadays referred to the Interim Period at all. It was almost as dead and forgotten as its leaders.

Not for the first time in forty-eight hours, the Secretary wondered if Sidi had received secret encouragement, perhaps even the A-bombs themselves, from the resurgent Soviet state. It would fit the seventy-five-year pattern that so many of America's most fashionable leaders of journalism, academe, Hollywood, and politics had so loudly and fervently—and perhaps a trifle prematurely—proclaimed to be over.

"I am sure America would welcome any assistance the S.S.R. wishes to give us," the Secretary said. "Or, at the least, Moscow's forbearance from any interference that would seek to upset any negotiations leading to a peaceable solution. Russian interventions," he added smoothly, "however well intentioned and peace-loving would, I am afraid, provoke a rather"—he hesitated deliberately—"awkward—reaction from this government."

"What would you do, Ray?" Vladimir Novotny inquired, leaning forward with a genuine, if subtly mocking, show of interest. "Not, you understand, that my government would do such a thing—we have abandoned all that ill-mannered stuff in favor of a more civilized approach. But just as a curiosity, what would you do?"

"We should regard it as a most unfriendly act," the Secretary said, "with all the consequences that would flow from such a miscalculation by your government."

"Yes," Vladimir said, "that is all very well, Ray, and all the world trembles at American disapproval, as you know—or rather," he said with an extension of his grin, "perhaps I should say, all the world except Sidi bin Sidi bin Sidi, which, we do completely sympathize with you, is embarrassing. But even so, what would you do? Impose sanctions upon us, perhaps? Call a meeting of the Security Council to condemn us, which we would veto? I mean, Ray, what?"

"I would not advise finding out," the Secretary said, air of amicability unruffled. "There are methods available to this government—"

"Yes," Vladimir agreed, "you are full of little tricks. So," he sighed elaborately, "we must go ahead blindly, not knowing what the consequences of our actions might be, and trembling in fear thereof."

"Only if they are contrary to the interests of the United States in this most difficult situation," the Secretary said. "For the rest, there is no reason for any disruption of our usual cordial relations."

"Good!" Vladimir Novotny exclaimed, mockery again evident and not so subtle this time. "As long as we are assured that our relations will remain cordial, we can certainly surmount any little awkwardness caused by this stinking camel-lover from the desert. He is a piece of excrement, that one."

"Not a nice man," Ray Stanley agreed with a smile.

"But of course," Vladimir observed, "we can understand his position."

"In what regard?" the Secretary demanded. "In the murder of one of our embassy staff—"

"CIA," Vladimir interrupted. "What can you expect?"

"We expect our people to be respected," Ray Stanley said, permitting his voice to acquire an edge of sharpness. "Do you support Sidi in his treatment of Creed Moncrief?"

"Of course we do not condone that," Vladimir said. "Still . . ."

"And do you support his proposed aggression against Lesser Lolómé?"

Vladimir shrugged. "It might be well to liberate some of the oil the old man is sitting on."

"Or choke it off from the West by working through Sidi if Sidi defeats him," the Secretary suggested. "Oil is always a good weapon, when it is permitted to flow and when it is not permitted to flow. Either way can be effective in the wrong hands."

"'Wrong hands'!" the Russian ambassador echoed. "There you go again, American morality! By whose judgment 'good,' by whose judgment 'bad'? You force these arbitrary categories on the world, Mr. Secretary. It makes life so *uncomfortable* for us innocents who just want to get along and lead our national lives without worrying about living up to America's standards."

"What are your own, Vladimir?" the Secretary inquired dryly. "They don't seem very well defined, to us."

"And there you go again!" the ambassador exclaimed. "Defining, defining! Why do you not just let things happen, without 'defining,' Ray? 'Defining' is not a help. It just confuses the issue. In fact, it confuses everybody. My government would like to assist you in defusing this crisis—if it is a 'crisis'—but how can we, when you persist in putting up arbitrary barriers against us?"

"Now, Mr. Ambassador," Ray said, permitting himself a certain sharpness, "stop trying to divert the argument by attacking America. That is an old, old game we thought had been disposed of along with many other errors of the Soviet system, some years ago."

"Fools!" the ambassador said darkly. "All fools. What did they know of Old Russia and what is best for it? It was inevitable that they fall, in spite of Washington's silly efforts to support them."

"Well," the Secretary said, "I am not going to get into an argument with you about what happened in Russia. That is your problem."

"Your then-President attempted to make it his problem," Vladimir Novotny said, and added with deep satisfaction, "That turned out to be *his* problem." His voice sailed up to grandiose levels. "We are a sovereign state! We decide our own fate! We *have* decided our own fate!"

"So *there!*" the Secretary could not resist, which brought an angry scowl in response. "Anyway," he added smoothly, "this is all very much beside the point. What we want to know now is, are you or are you not going to help us eliminate this new threat to world peace that has developed in Greater Lolómé?"

"Threat to peace of mind," the ambassador remarked. "*Your* peace of mind. Why should we?"

"Because it is in your interest as well as ours to prevent any new outbreak of hostilities in the region," Ray Stanley said. "That is why."

"We will determine whether it is in our interest," Vladimir said. "Not America. Why is it in our interest?"

"The maintenance of world stability is in everyone's interest," the Secretary said calmly. "That seems elemental—or should seem elemental. Even to a state"—he paused, appearing to be giving his next words considerable study, which he had indeed done, but some hours previously—"which may deliberately have contributed to the threat of instability by furnishing the means of instability to a notoriously erratic and unstable individual who may yet turn upon his sponsors."

"We are not among his sponsors!" the ambassador replied angrily. "We did not furnish him with the means of instability! I give you the word of the government of the Second Soviet Republic that this is not true! We did not give him bombs! The government of the S.S.R. deeply resents any such implications!"

"Very well, then," Ray Stanley said calmly, "we expect you to vote with us in the Security Council for whatever means may be necessary to restrain Sidi's adventurism and bring his nuclear arsenal, if he has one, under the control of the International Atomic Energy Agency."

"Why would *that* be in our interest?" the ambassador inquired, giving him a shrewd glance tinged with an almost insolent blandness. "What can America do to make it in our interest?"

"Your government is still seeking enormous loans from this country and from the International Monetary Fund," Ray said in an unimpressed tone that turned suddenly blunt and tough. "Despite glorious new revolutions rolling out of Moscow, you still need money. Your economy is still in shambles. *You need money.* And don't"—he raised a warning hand as Vladimir scowled, turned red, appeared about to explode—"pretend you don't, or give me high-sounding rhetoric, or utter your typical bombastic, empty threats. We've heard all that over and over for endless years, now, minus a brief interlude—"

"A crazy interlude!" Vladimir snapped. "It was not *us!*"

"Well, whoever it was," Ray said, "it was a welcome break in a sad, monotonous tale that we don't want to hear any more of now. It is in the interest of world peace, in your interest and ours, that there be no break in the ranks when the Security Council votes—without argument and without public conflict—to bring Sidi back within the bounds of international law and the family of nations."

"We may abstain," the ambassador said in an ominous tone.

"Abstain." the Secretary shrugged. "That's your privilege. But don't veto."

"That is our privilege too," Vladimir Novotny said. "If we so desire."

"The lingering dream, still, of trying to destroy America," the Secretary said, shaking his head with an elaborate wonderment he knew would infuriate. "How hard these silly illusions die!"

"Illusions!" the ambassador exclaimed. "A dream? Destroy America? Look, Mr. Secretary! There was a time, not long ago, when a President of the United States confronted a crisis in the Gulf and mobilized half the world against it. He threw in great troops and mighty air power and he won a paper victory in a sandpile. Then he turned around and lost it because he was too weak to go forward when he had victory in his hand. Then along came another President and he was equally weak, in Somalia, Bosnia, Haiti, North Korea, China, Cuba, you name it. In six short years, through the inconsistency, the indecisiveness, the shilly-shallying— and, yes, the political and moral cowardice—of your Presidents, America was reduced from world leader to world weakling. And it is *we* who wish to destroy you? Why should anyone else have to destroy you? You destroy yourselves!"

Ray Stanley rose from his desk, came around, and held out his hand. "I believe the IMF will vote on your latest loan request in a couple of weeks," he remarked cheerfully. "Good luck to you, Vladimir! Good luck to the Second Soviet Republic! Good luck to Old Russia!"

"We will not shake hands," Vladimir said, rising also, with an elaborately heavy scowl, "with people who mock us. We do not shake hands with enemies."

"I am sorry," the Secretary said, unimpressed and unperturbed. "I trust you will reconsider, in due time." He paused by a window as he escorted his visitor out. Below, around the Tidal Basin and along the tree-lined streets, the dogwood, the magnolias, and the cherry blossoms were out.

"What a beautiful season," he exclaimed, "in which to have such headaches! But, I suppose, that's life."

"Goodbye!" the ambassador snapped.

"Goodbye," the Secretary said. "Come see me again soon, Vladimir."

But playing verbal Ping-Pong with the Russian ambassador, he reflected with a sigh as he returned to his desk, while perhaps fun in a tiger-tweaking sort of way, probably did not contribute very much to solving the matter of Sidi. If Vladimir's reaction was any indication of what might be expected from the other Communist states, it would be slow slogging in the Security Council. But the effort had to be made. According to the conventional wisdom now virtually unchallengeable in the American government, nothing could be done without the United Nations. It wasn't much of a support, Jaime Serrano had remarked in a moment of wry candor recently, "but it sure is nice to hide behind!"

And, of course, its formal endorsement did carry a certain shaky respectability, even if its impulses were erratic, its means weak, and its ability to launch decisive action as uncertain as its ability to maintain it, once launched.

He was about to have his secretary put through a call to the Chinese embassy when the phone rang beneath his hand. Mary was on the line, sounding perturbed.

"Sorry to bother you at work," she said, "but can you find time to talk to Bets? She and Samir have apparently had a major row and she's devastated."

"She's always devastated," he said with a sudden testiness, alarmed and bothered, as so often, by this high-strung child of his. "All right, I'll talk to her. Is she with you?"

"No, she's at home. Try not to sound too impatient. She sounds really upset, this time."

"What's the problem? Is he staying out late again?"

"Oh, yes. The same problem, but she seems to have tried to precipitate a showdown—which she got, and now she isn't happy."

"I'm not happy," he said. "I have a few things on my mind over here this morning."

"Yes, I realize that," she said. "How are they going?"

"Our friend Vladimir was just in, at my invitation," he said. "Puffed up and important as always—the old gang has come back with a roar, which is a whole other set of problems. If he's an example, they're beginning to throw their weight around just as they used to do. It complicates handling Sidi, unfortunately. We've got to go to the Security Council in the next few days and the S.S.R. isn't going to be any help, I can see that."

"You'll have to be firm."

"I was. I informed him we'd block their loan application in the IMF if they didn't behave. Not quite that language, but he got the sense of it."

"It slowed him down," she said, sounding dry.

"Somewhat," he said. "Maybe it will hold them and maybe it won't. Anyway, it's an example of what we face."

"Who's next, China?"

"Yes. Then Britain and France, ambassadorial level. The President wants to talk to the big boys himself. He leaves the grunge work to me."

"No one better," she said, in the tone in which she paid him compliments. He was never entirely sure that a certain secret amusement, deeply fond but slightly prickly and perhaps even a little jealous, did not underlie them.

"I sometimes think," he said, "that the talk over here is correct: you ought to be Secretary of State, you're so much better than I am."

"I *love* being the power behind the throne," she said with a chuckle. "Don't forget to call Bets. There may be something significant in Samir's increasing absences. She seems to think so."

"I'll get to her," he said. "It may be late afternoon, so tell her to hold her horses. And keep an eye out for anything significant. If another crisis is brewing in the Middle East, I want to know about it."

"It is, for her," Mary said, "and she's your daughter. So don't be snippy."

"No," he said with another sigh. "I'm sorry, I won't. Tell her Daddy loves her, and hang in there."

"You too," Mary said. "Sidi's shenanigans may yet turn out to be a tough one."

"That they may," he said. "Let's don't go out tonight. I want to stay home, watch trashy television, and get drunk."

"Secretary Ray Stanley, that old stuffed shirt?" she inquired with a chuckle. "The department would never believe you just said that."

"I'd never believe it if I did it," he said. "Keep your fingers crossed for me and think good thoughts."

"I always do," she said. "Let me know about China."

"Sure thing," he said. "I can predict it word for word."

And so, as it turned out, he could have: for things did go just about as he expected. He reached the Chinese ambassador, Li Peng Liu, invited him to lunch in the Secretary's private dining room. Li accepted with a suck of breath and the appearance of delight, and arrived promptly at twelve. It was all downhill, as Ray told Mary wryly later, from there.

"Mr. Ambassador," he said as they sipped a small preliminary glass of sherry at a small table set up beside a window, "we are both busy men, so I suggest we get right to the heart of it. I know that isn't always the way in your great country, but we believe time is of the essence here, so forgive me if I appear somewhat precipitous."

Li, a slim and ascetic mandarin of indeterminate mid-sixties and a characteristically ideological approach to life, smiled a rather remote and ironic smile as he bowed his head in agreement.

"It is what we have come to expect," he said gently. "Please proceed."

"It is our intention, as you know from our formal statement, to seek a meeting of the Security Council as soon as possible to consider the crisis precipitated by the President of Greater Lolómé. We would appreciate some indication of where the government of China might stand on the issue of instructing Greater Lolómé to accept inspection of its atomic facilities by the International Atomic Energy Agency or suffer the consequences."

"Your statement did not say," the Chinese ambassador pointed out politely, "that he must agree to inspection of his *atomic* facilities. It simply said 'military facilities.' You did not even say 'all' of his military facilities. Does this not pose a small problem for you—and for the Security Council?"

"I think our statement in the Security Council will make entirely clear what we mean," the Secretary said.

The ambassador smiled again, a rather wry little contribution.

"But, ah, a little late," he said. "You should have said it at the beginning. It would have been much simpler."

"Perhaps," Ray Stanley said, remembering with annoyance the way the President had danced around stronger language all through the statement and finally vetoed it, in order, he said, "to leave my hands free for whatever may develop." Ray remembered that on several points he himself had sided with Eulie and Eldridge Barnes, until the President's annoyance with their opposition became too apparent to ignore, at which point he had dutifully fallen in line and taken the lead in seeking more circuitous language.

"There is a certain lack of urgency in your approach," the Chinese ambassador pointed out as two waitresses entered discreetly, removed their soup dishes, and served the "Chinese chicken salad" the Secretary had ordered. "Why do you not go directly to the Security Council instead of wasting time talking to us, if it is a matter of such concern?"

"We consider it a matter of courtesy," the Secretary said, at his blandest, "to consult with good friends before we move so directly into a crisis position in this matter. Frankly, Mr. Ambassador"—and he gave his politely attentive visitor a confidential smile—"we are hoping to secure pledges of support from our colleagues on the Council so that when the matter comes to a vote there will be a united front and a show of real determination from the United Nations."

"And no veto from anybody," Li said with a sudden cheery smile.

In spite of himself, Ray Stanley had to smile.

"And no veto from anybody," he echoed. "Is that too unreasonable a request, in China's opinion?"

"Perfectly reasonable," the ambassador said with another cheery smile. "Whether perfectly possible is another matter." He dropped the cheery air with startling abruptness. His tone became cold. "Why do you assume, Mr. Secretary, that America can lecture us all the time—yes, harass us—with your boring talk about 'human rights' and then expect us to come running when America waves a finger? Does it not occur to you that this might occasionally make it difficult for China to join a 'united front' with you? And over such a relatively minor episode?"

"It is our contention that the episode potentially could be of the gravest import to the world community," the Secretary said, choosing not to answer the ambassador's principal point, constantly reiterated in every contact between their two countries. No gain in following him down that rocky road on this occasion. He knew it would inevitably come up in the Security Council debate.

"Furthermore," he added in a contemplative, faraway tone as of one considering an interesting but only mildly significant item, "we had thought that there might be some sympathy on the part of China for a move to forestall this crisis before it begins . . . since there might appear to be some parallels in recent weeks with what appears to be imminent in South China."

"Nothing is 'imminent' in South China!" the ambassador snapped, pushing aside the remnants of his salad with considerable vehemence. "Traitors are always attempting to subvert the People's Republic! You know that they have never succeeded!"

"Not yet, Mr. Ambassador," Ray Stanley said in the same judicious tone, "but with the surge of Hong Kong money and influence into Shanghai, Canton, and indeed most of Guangzhou province, it appears there well might be—difficulties—for your government. Hong Kong gives promise of being a troublesome child, now that you have her. Will not your government need some assistance from its friends if South China flares into open revolt? This seems possible to us."

"What could we expect from you if it did?" the ambassador demanded, now genuinely angry. "More talk of 'human rights'? More support for traitors? More attempts to interfere in China's internal affairs and agitate the world community? We will thank you to keep your meddling to yourselves! If," he added hastily, "something happens. I do not say it will."

"We certainly hope not," the Secretary said with what appeared to be grave agreement. "That would be a situation which the world community simply could not ignore, don't you agree? And," he added thoughtfully, "there is always the west. How about Kashi and Xinjiang province and all those Uighurs and Muslims anxious to break away and join their tribal and religious relatives in Turkistan, Kyrgyzstan, Tajikistan, Uzbekistan, and other areas of Central Asia? Isn't it quite possible, Mr. Ambassador, that China is on the verge of imminent dissolution, and that you will need at least some minimal sympathy from the United States and the rest of the world if your government is to maintain itself even in the areas it now controls?"

"Imminent, imminent, imminent!" the ambassador spat out. "Nothing is 'imminent' in China! We have four thousand years of 'imminence' behind us! We will be there long after the United States has vanished from the earth!"

"Possibly so, Mr. Ambassador," the Secretary said, his own tone hardening, "but in the meantime you are going to need us, in one way or another. So don't be so arrogant, if you please. The mountain defied the river, but the river won, I believe your proverb says." (Or does it? he wondered with ironic humor. Damned if I know, I just made it up.) "So do not place too many bets on survival, at least for your government in its present form. You appear to be a monolith on the map, but everyone who has traveled in any depth through China knows that you have many, many problems, any or all of which can explode at any minute. So, as we say in America, cool it, all right? And remember that you may need at least our sympathetic forbearance, any day now."

"I did not come here," Li Peng Liu said, in a voice still quivering with rage but visibly forcing his annoyance under control as he went along, "to receive another lecture from the United States. Your 'forbearance' is something we cannot count on; your lecturing is something we do not value. As far as the Security Council is concerned, it is possible that after we have carefully considered all the facts, we will either abstain or vote with you on the necessary disciplining of Greater Lolómé. That remains to be seen. For the rest, China will thank you, as always, to keep your fantastically foolish imaginings under control."

"Very well, Mr. Ambassador," Ray Stanley said, his own voice becoming again bland and reasonably friendly, "that is all we can ask, that China study the facts and do what seems best to it with regard to Greater Lolómé. If we have your commitment to that approach, we will be content."

"I did not say you have our commitment," the ambassador said, voice again becoming sharp. "I said our final decision 'remains to be seen.' Now I must go. Thank you for the delightful lunch."

"And thank you," the Secretary said, not offering to shake hands as his visitor departed, "for an enlightening glimpse into the thinking of the government of China concerning"—his tone became even blander—"the problems that beset the world—and it. We must consult again soon."

"Perhaps," the Chinese ambassador said with a small, wintry smile. "That, too, remains to be seen."

And after all that was said and done, the Secretary thought as he returned to his desk and began to consider what he should do about his daughter and enigmatic son-in-law, there still was no assurance that the People's Republic, shaky internally with the final departure of its elders and growing unrest everywhere throughout its vast landmass, would be a reliable partner in any Security Council action against Greater Lolómé.

He had not challenged the ambassador on the possibility that Sidi's bombs might have come from Beijing through one of the many devious routes along which China cynically and ruthlessly sold its armaments to inflame the world's trouble spots. To raise the challenge at the moment might only serve to consolidate wavering elements in the P.R.C. into one solid front opposing the U.S. The U.S., he conceded, was not in a position to invite that kind of opposition at the moment because it did not want to do anything to impede the steadily increasing erosions of the central government's authority. Anything developing internally that would weaken China was fine with the U.S., though no one in the U.S. government could say that at this moment.

He was not sorry that he had talked bluntly to the Chinese ambassador. His attitude at the moment was: what's to lose? It was a different age in international politics than it had been when he came into it forty years ago. Spokesmen for governments nowadays frequently indulged in polite, or not-so-polite, billingsgate in their comments about, and to, one another. When used too much, this became juvenile and self-defeating; when applied judiciously it could inject a needed candor into discussions that might otherwise stray a certain distance from the cold realities. Starting with the ill-fated Warren Christopher mission to Beijing in 1994, U.S.-Chinese dialogue had been distinguished by a blunt display of bad temper on the part of the Chinese, desperate rationalizations by the Americans. (Diligently following Principle #1—*The President [and his administration] must always be made to look good*—the then

Secretary of State had remarked soothingly that "We began to narrow the differences." The *Washington Inquirer* used this quote as caption for an editorial cartoon that showed the Secretary on one side of a just-slammed door, the Chinese foreign secretary on the other.)

It was more than time, Ray Stanley thought, for a little astringency on the American side. It wouldn't hurt to be candid: the monolith of central government in China was indeed increasingly threatened with dissolution, particularly in the south and west. He reflected again that this would be fine. It would create many new problems, but at least they would be facing into the future, not backwards in a desperate attempt to prop up a frightened party leadership and a decaying ideology that stood in the way of constructive development.

He was not scheduled to see the British ambassador until late this afternoon, the French directly after that, and to talk to the Secretary-General in New York by telephone after that. Routine departmental matters occupied him for a time—suggested changes in ambassadorial postings in several places, a fiscal scandal in an African post that had to be taken care of before it reached the media and created embarrassments, a sexual scandal in an Asian office whose deputy head of mission had strayed into areas he should have known much better than to get himself involved in.

When he finally got around to calling his daughter, it was almost four o'clock. Before that the whole subject had been forcibly brought to his urgent attention by the Assistant Secretary for Near Eastern Affairs, who descended upon him like a small, furious whirlwind with no other warning than a terse phone call, "Ray, I'm coming up to see you."

"I have a few things—" he started to say, but Joan Cohn-Bourassa would have none of it.

"They aren't important," she snapped. "I've got to talk to you."

"OK," he said amicably. "If you're on the warpath, I guess I'd better see you."

"Not on the warpath," she said, managing a not very amused small laugh. "But I am upset."

"Come ahead," he said. "I'll be here. . . . Now," he said when she had arrived, been shown in, and had taken the chair opposite, from which she leaned forward as though she were about to swarm across his desk at him, "what's this all about? Boo leaving you?"

She reacted so sharply she almost physically started back in her chair.

"No," she said, "he isn't leaving me. But it does concern him. Why have you got Hugo Mallerbie sniffing around? He had the nerve to call me a few minutes ago and ask if I knew 'what Boo is up to.'"

"I haven't got Hugo 'sniffing around,'" he protested mildly, and decided that the best tactic, as always with Joanie, was to be absolutely straightforward. "I did ask him to see whether any of his contacts could turn up anything on why Boo and my son-in-law are apparently involved in meetings with certain members of the Arab community. I thought you were wondering about that too. Bets is."

"I know Bets is. We've talked about it several times. At length. Bets is as upset as I am."

"I know you both are. What's your guess?"

She looked him straight in the eye.

"What's Hugo's?"

"Hugo hasn't reported much to me, really," he said. "I've only had him on it for a couple of days. He says Boo and Samir are apparently meeting at a Georgetown bar favored by many of the Middle East diplomatic corps."

"I know that," she said impatiently. "What about it?"

"That's all, at the moment. There doesn't seem to be any particular pattern. They meet late, talk awhile, the group gradually narrows down to perhaps half a dozen. Then that group, along with Boo and Samir, gradually disbands and appears to go their separate ways. There is some indication, however, that some of them, including Boo and Samir, depart together for some destination unknown—as yet. We'll find out. Meanwhile, that's why Hugo is 'sniffing around.' Aren't you pleased? Maybe we'll have an answer for you soon."

"I don't like the idea of my husband being spied upon," she said flatly.

He shrugged.

"I don't like the idea of my son-in-law being spied upon. But something's a little out of pattern, right? Male Arabs seek male Arabs for company, there's nothing unusual or sinister about that, it's their societal habit and way of life. But maybe not—"

"Not quite as much as they have lately," she finished for him.

He nodded.

"That's why you and Bets are concerned, and Mary and I are concerned. Maybe you'd better suggest gently to Boo that it might arouse suspicions in some quarters if it continues. And we'll suggest the same to Samir."

"Boo knows it," she said. "I've told him. He just laughs and dismisses it."

"He's been around awhile," Ray Stanley observed. "Apparently Samir's a bit touchy."

"Yes, I know," Joanie said. "Bets has told me. Samir's new at whatever's going on."

"Smuggling drugs?" he suggested ironically. "Women? Boys? Belly dancers? Rugs?"

"None of the above," she said dryly. "And hopefully, nothing really sinister, either. Boo's too sensible for that—I *think*. And I don't think he'd lead Samir into anything that wasn't—all right." She sighed uncomfortably, more openly worried than she had ever allowed herself to appear in his presence. "Still . . ."

"Still," he agreed. "We'll let Hugo sniff a bit longer, I think. Meanwhile, I can't expect you to spy on your husband, nor would I want you to. But if anything really egregious comes along—"

"I'll let you know," she said. She smiled suddenly as she stood up. "I've got to go. Thanks, Ray. You're a stabilizing influence."

"Try to be," he said. "But, God, what a world!"

"I know," she said. "How are you doing on Sidi?"

"I've talked to Russia and China; Britain, France, and the Secretary-General are next. Not much help so far. Sparring matches with Novotny and the Chinese ambassador. I think they'll both support us in the Security Council, but at some price we haven't agreed upon yet. Wish me luck."

"Call me if there's anything more I can do," she said. "I'm contacting all the major governments in my area and should have a report for you in twenty-four hours on the general sentiment."

"Thank you, Joanie," he said, knowing other assistant secretaries were doing the same, but very few with her diligence and tenacity.

"Try to be," she said wryly. "T'aint always easy, but I try."

So did his daughter, he reflected when he finally found time to call her shortly after four o'clock. He could tell from her voice that her reserves, at least temporarily, were wearing a little thin.

"Hi," he said comfortably when she came on the line. "Mother tells me you're upset."

"Yes, I am," she said, and promptly began to cry. "Oh, Daddy—!"

"Hey, hey, hey, hey, *hey!*" he said. "Slow down, girl. Slow down. Life isn't all that bad, not even in the State Department."

"Well, it is here!" she said, voice muffled so he could hardly understand her for a moment. "It sure is here. I don't know what's happ-happening. He's so secretive. It isn't l-like him."

"No," he said in a thoughtful tone he hoped would prove calming. "Egyptians are normally a pretty sunny and outgoing people, at least in my experience. Certainly he used to be."

"That's one reason I m-married him," she said. "Always laughing. Always such g-good fun. N-not anymore."

"When did all this start, anyway?" he inquired. "It isn't just lately, is it? He's been a little remote before, hasn't he, and gotten over it? It happens. It doesn't mean the world is coming to an end. Or the marriage, either."

"So it's b-buck up, Bets, right? You're just a typical b-baffled wife, right? I didn't think you'd just g-give me clichés, Daddy."

He could detect a certain returning humor in her voice and breathed a silent sigh of relief. Their daughter had plenty of character; she just let it get away from her, sometimes.

"That's right," he said. "Not battered, just baffled. So be thankful for that."

"If he ever laid a finger on me, I'd punch him out," she said with a sudden asperity that gave him the encouragement to chuckle openly.

"That's more like Battling Bets Stanley," he said. "Now, what's prompted this latest explosion?"

"These mysterious nights out," she said, tears apparently forgotten, he hoped. "He's overdoing it. Why? That's what I want to know. And he won't tell me." For a second her voice started to wobble again, but she controlled it firmly.

"I hear you're not the only one," he said. "Joanie just came to see me about Boo."

"We talk about them," she said. A sudden thought struck her, she actually began to laugh a little. He felt the crisis was over—until the next time. "We're thinking of establishing MEW," she said, pronouncing it like a cat. "The Middle East Wives club." The absurdity of picturing herself and Joanie Bourassa in anything with a name as gentle as MEW made her laugh outright. "Anyway," she said, sobering abruptly, "the thing that really has me upset is that Hugo Mallerbie is sniffing around."

"That's exactly how Joanie described it," he acknowledged calmly. "'Sniffing around.' I asked him to."

"But, Daddy," she protested. "Why?"

"Because of exactly such things as this. You're all upset, you've apparently had a row with Samir, he's staying out too much, and he won't tell you why. I take it that you demanded that he tell you why, right?"

"I've been polite about it for the last month or so," she said. "Suddenly this morning I decided I'd had enough."

"After another late one."

"Another late one. Two A.M., to be exact. That's a little late to be out with the boys. He said they were 'just talking.'"

"Do you believe him?"

"Oh, yes," she said impatiently. "As far as it goes. We love each other, I'm not worried about that. And even if I were, I'd manage somehow for the sake of the kids. The thing that really set me off was how touchy he's become about it. He flared right up."

"And you flared right back."

"That's right," she said, with considerable satisfaction. "Only," she said, threatening to become forlorn again, "it shouldn't have to come to that. I don't like it when he storms out of the house and doesn't c-call me all day."

"Don't you think I should let Hugo go on sniffing, for a little while? If there's anything really—bothersome—going on, shouldn't we know?"

Bets, who had completed adolescence, and married, in the Middle East—who was the knowledgeable daughter of two very knowledgeable diplomats—paused thoughtfully for a moment.

"I hate to even admit the thought," she said slowly, "but—yes. Yes, I suppose we should. I can't believe either of them would be so—so *stupid*—as to get involved in anything really dangerous, but, yes—yes, I suppose we should."

"All right," he said. "Now suppose you just calm down and greet him amicably when he gets home. And if you find out anything, let me know. All right?"

"All right," she said. With a sudden bitterness she added, "I don't like to think of anybody spying on my husband and your son-in-law. *I don't like it!*"

"I don't like the age we live in," he said. "But here we are."

And here we are indeed, he thought as Hugo Mallerbie called a few minutes later to report that what he called "the core group" of what he referred to as "Boo's little sewing circle" seemed to wind up "fairly regularly" at a certain suspect embassy to conclude their evenings.

"That will be a tough one to crack," the Secretary observed.

"Damned difficult and dangerous," the Undersecretary for International Security Affairs agreed. "But I'll stay on it."

"Do," Ray Stanley said. "The world is bad out there."

One would never have suspected it, however, as he greeted the British ambassador promptly at five. They had known each other for a decade, ever since he and Sir Anthony Marsden had been ambassadors together in Athens. Their relations had always been amicable: Tony and Marcia always "dropped by" when they came through Washington. Now his posting there brought them again into frequent contact.

"Well!" Tony said, lounging back comfortably in the armchair by the window in which Ray had seated him, away from the big desk that was meant to, and usually did, intimidate less confident diplomatic visitors. "This is a fine pickle you've got yourselves into, isn't it?"

Ray Stanley gave him an easy smile and a diplomat's answer.

"It might be construed so by some," he said, "but why by you? Surely Her Majesty's Government understands the importance of what we are trying to do."

"It's important, all right," Tony Marsden said. "About as important as a bomb in Piccadilly Circus. We do regret a bit that you chose to set it off so quickly, and without consulting us."

"Why should we consult you?" the Secretary inquired, but amicably.

"Don't *you* think you've been a bit hasty?" the ambassador countered. "A mite precipitous? Prior consultation might have at least prepared the way and made it easier for the rest of us to adjust to being called to arms to do battle with a minor tyrant in the Gulf."

"It seemed best to us to take a stand immediately," Ray Stanley said. "It did not seem wise to wait."

"Well," Tony said, "it would have been. I know why you did it this way, of course. *He* wanted it."

"And *he*," the Secretary said, wryly echoing his emphasis, "is the President. So there *we* are."

"Yes," Tony Marsden agreed. "With egg on your face. It's getting to be endemic. You've taken a stand and you've been openly defied. And now you have to make good on it. You want us to support you in the Security Council and give each other such aid and comfort as we may be able to provide."

"Certainly," the Secretary said with a cheerful smile. "What else would we expect Britain to do? What else *would* Britain do?"

"We might veto or abstain," the ambassador said crisply; then grinned. "But of course we won't. But there are practical questions involved here. What kind of a Security Council resolution do you want? How far are you prepared to go to implement it?"

"To the utmost of our resources," the Secretary said flatly.

The British ambassador gave him a searching stare, intelligent dark eyes peering out skeptically from under bushy silvery eyebrows and a neatly groomed mane of silver hair: Sir Anthony Marsden was a distinguished-looking man, appearing ten years younger than his actual sixty-seven.

"Do you mean that?" he inquired. "Sidi obviously doesn't think so. He's in process of calling your bluff."

"It isn't bluff," Ray Stanley said, with a first hint of annoyance. "We mean it."

"When you have to insist on it," Tony Marsden said, "it's a bluff. There's a dangerous impression around in the world that the United States doesn't have the guts to stay the course when the bugle sounds. I hope, for the sake of some semblance of international order, that this is not true. But how can the world be sure?"

"Because I give you the word of my government," the Secretary said, letting his annoyance become obvious. Old friend or no, Tony was getting into sensitive territory.

"Exactly," Tony said. He stared out the window for a moment with a thoughtful air. Then he swung back with the sudden intent concentration he could project when he deemed it advisable. "You must understand," he said, "that this impression is a very grave thing, which has been growing during the last two presidential terms. It casts a heavy shadow over every ostensible 'firm' stand the U.S. government takes. It is highly dangerous, for you and for all who look to you for consistency and unwavering—and, I might say, courageous—leadership. Are you aware of that?"

And he stared intently at the Secretary, who stared intently back. Ray's eyes did not waver, but he presently gave a nod that was a concession.

"Yes, I know," he said. "I am aware of that."

"Is he aware of it?" the ambassador asked.

Again the Secretary gave him a slow nod.

"He is a very intelligent man," he said. "He knows that." He paused and then spoke with a candor he knew was probably not advisable in diplomatic discussion, even with an old friend; but this old friend represented a sophisticated government that knew what he was going to say as well as he did.

"He is highly sensitive to political realities—domestic political realities—or what he sees as domestic political realities. The foreign political realities beyond our shores are something he is not always as attuned to as—he might be."

"It's the curse of the office," the British ambassador said. "Even the shrewdest of them sooner or later allows the foreign dog to be wagged by the domestic tail"—he smiled—"if you can forgive my mixed-up metaphor. In other words, he always has his eyes on where the votes are. Correct?"

"Correct," Ray Stanley said.

"It is leading the U.S. into perilous waters," the ambassador observed.

"Correct," Ray Stanley said.

"Then why," Tony Marsden demanded, and this time he too stepped beyond polite diplomatic discourse with a concerned directness not so acrimonious but perhaps even more unsettling than the typical blast from China or the resurgent Soviets, "are you not using your influence to try to change this, old friend? Is office that important to you too? Over principle?"

There was a silence while the Secretary for once found himself temporarily devoid of words. This was how the underlying realities of the world sometimes confronted you: they sneaked in in the midst of socially cushioned conversations and socked you in the ribs, as Mary had once put it. It had been a long time since his basic convictions about his own character had been so challenged. His answer when it came was slow and thoughtful.

"Office is not more important to me than principle, Tony," he said. "I hope I would never betray my concept of myself in that way. But I have the same hope that you have when confronted by some policy of your government that challenges your concept of yourself—you add it all up and go along, because you hope that by doing so you can work from inside for changes that might make things come more into conformity with your basic beliefs. I know we're in a dangerous downslide around the world. I know Sidi is trying to take advantage of it, this monstrous little pipsqueak defying the United States, apparently convinced that we won't have the will or the integrity to stand up to him as we're threatening to do. I know there have been too many precedents for that in recent years. I *know* it's almost too late to recover world respect and belief in our word and our intentions. I am devastated by this, as one who has spent all his adult life in the service of our country's foreign policy.

"But I also know that the President knows all this, too—in an intellectual sort of way, not in the gut-instinct way in which he knows things domestically. And I feel I should stay in here and attempt to hold him to it, without wavering and without letting his political sense overcome his moral and historical sense of what is right for this world."

Again the ambassador gave him a long and penetrating look.

"And if you can't influence him that way, you'd go?"

Again the Secretary thought long and hard before his answer.

"I think it is too early," he said finally, "to make a decision on that. We will have to see what develops when—"

"Then you wouldn't," the British ambassador said, and was on his feet holding out his hand, which the Secretary took automatically in a farewell grasp. "Good luck, old friend. You can count on us in the Security Council, of course. May your tenure here continue to be all that you wish it to be."

"Now, wait—" Ray Stanley said. "Wait a minute. I didn't say—"

"What you didn't say was quite enough," Tony Marsden said, not unfriendly but in some subtle way not as respectful as he had been. "Give my love to Mary. We must all get together soon."

"But—" the Secretary said.

Tony waved aside his protesting tone.

"Good luck to you, Ray," he said. "Don't bother to see me out. I'll just run along."

And did so, with a wave and a brief departing smile as he went out the door. It closed and the Secretary was alone.

But not, of course, for long.

Not long enough to think, just use the bathroom, return to his desk, and compose himself in sufficiently statesmanly stance to receive the French ambassador, who was ushered in within ten minutes after the British ambassador left.

The Secretary was glad at this moment that he didn't have time to think. Tony had penetrated his armor most directly; he needed a little time to adjust. He didn't want to face up immediately to the moral and ethical complications of what his ultimate course might be. He wasn't ready yet to throw the world away for principle—nor by the same token was he ready to abandon principle, which in the last analysis had always guided his life.

Perhaps a big defiance by the small tyrant of a small country was not the point on which the decision should turn. Surely there were more important issues.

He wanted to talk to Mary, and perhaps to Eulie, though he knew what both would counsel.

He stood up with a warmly welcoming air. Suave and smiling, Georges Marranne, former foreign minister, former prime minister, presently, "in the twilight of my years," ambassador to the United States, came slowly peering in with his air of a scaly but immaculately turned out old turtle. He was, as always, beautifully dressed, "a real d.o.d.," as Bets referred to him, meaning "dapper old dandy." Ray Stanley found him boring, pretentious, smug, and often quite insufferable, which, he often thought wryly, made Georges the perfect ambassador: one of his major jobs, after all, was to reflect his country.

"Georges!" he exclaimed, with his most fulsome, practiced cordiality.

"Raymond!" exclaimed Georges, equally hearty. "How nice of you to invite me to visit!"

"I would have come to see you, Georges," Ray Stanley said, "except that this has been a very busy day."

"Ah, yes," Georges Marranne said. "Washington is in a bit of turmoil, is it not? Little Sidi has this big country"—he paused and with a twinkle used one of the startling bits of American slang he liked to throw in to shock people—"by the balls. Yes?"

"That's right, Georges," the Secretary said. "They're really clanging. Have a seat."

"Thank you," Georges said, moving with sure instinct away from the big desk to the more intimate armchair by the window just vacated by the British ambassador. "Now," he said, having carefully arranged his elderly bulk in its comfortable confines, peering at the Secretary across the top of the cane over which his beautifully manicured hands were draped, "what can our modest efforts contribute to the solution of this difficult problem for you?"

"Not only for us, Georges," Ray Stanley told him, taking the chair opposite, "but for all of us who value decency and stability in the world—or perhaps I should say *of* the world. I know France has always been in the vanguard of such efforts."

"Of course!" Georges said, accepting the compliment serenely as France's due. "You can bet the farm on that."

"Consider it bet," Ray told him. "Now we approach a discussion in the Security Council."

"Ah, yes," Georges said. "And you wish us to support you in the condemnation of this piece of *merde* in Greater Lolómé."

"Not only the condemnation but the actual control of this piece of *merde*," the Secretary said. "Including, if necessary, the punishment of this piece of *merde*. Can we rely on France to join us in that?"

The ambassador looked profound, wiggled his eyebrows, pursed his lips. *Oh, knock it off,* Ray Stanley thought, but forbore. Presently, having mugged enough, Georges responded.

"I think," he said, slowly, "I—think, that we had best take it a step at a time, should we not? Let us see how the condemnation goes, and if that proceeds in order, then we shall see about punishment. If he continues to be defiant, that is. He may surprise us all by agreeing to inspection."

"I'm afraid that is not his mood," Ray Stanley said.

Georges Marranne shot him a suddenly shrewd glance.

"You have had some direct contact, then?"

"Yes," the Secretary said, and added blandly, "Hasn't France?"

The ambassador stared at him for a moment. A slow smile began and spread. He looked more than ever the knowing old turtle.

"I am informed there has been a brief exchange of views." His expression became more serious. "It was not encouraging."

"No, he's quite intransigent," the Secretary said. "So the question remains: will France support us on the resolution and, if need be, after?"

"I can only reiterate," Georges said, "one step at a time. When will you desire the Security Council to meet?"

"The President hasn't indicated."

"Ah, yes," Georges remarked. "The President. Well, we shall see. It has been indicated to me that we will support you on the resolution. After that"—he raised his shoulders and looked skeptical—"*qui sais?*"

"It will be of no value unless it is fully implemented," Ray Stanley said, "and unless it is made emphatically clear to him that it will be implemented by the full weight of a united world community."

Again the ambassador gave his skeptical shrug.

"America, America!" he said with a smile. "Always absolutes! Always end-of-the-world decisions! Why not wait and see, Raymond? Have faith in France! More importantly"—his smile became fatherly if not downright patronizing, his tone gently chiding—"have faith in yourselves! Don't be so nervous."

"We aren't nervous," the Secretary said, unable to keep a certain irritation out of his voice: they were always so smug. "We just like to know where we stand."

"Guarding the ramparts of freedom!" the ambassador said, beginning a slow struggle up out of his chair. "Is it not always so?"

"We hope so," Ray Stanley said, rising to place a hand under Georges's arm and give him a boost—perhaps not quite as gentle as it should have been, for the old turtle gave him a sudden penetrating glance. "We hope you'll be with us, Georges."

"Oh, yes," the ambassador said impatiently. "Thank you. Oh, yes, we will be there—as far as you go."

"All the way," the Secretary said firmly, a conviction in his voice that he did not entirely feel, at the moment.

"We await it," Georges Marranne said, "with interest. Keep us *au courant*."

"*D'accord*," Ray Stanley responded dryly. "Don't take any wooden nickels."

"Or the Brooklyn Bridge," the ambassador said with a chuckle.

"You're dating yourself, Georges," the Secretary told him as they reached the door. "That hasn't been for sale for years."

And so, lastly, came his conversation with that high and mighty, imperious and contentious, excruciatingly sensitive soul who was always hearing slurs in the most innocent remarks, the Secretary-General of the United Nations, the Hon. Kwazze Kumbatta of the Republic of South Africa.

Kwazze Kumbatta was also one of those whom Ray had met in his travels around the world—the first time, when the Secretary had been a member of the official U.S. delegation to the inauguration of the new multiracial government in Pretoria.

"Call me Kwazz," he had urged everyone on that wildly exuberant (for the victors) occasion, but it was obvious that the nickname, and indeed most remarks, had to be spoken carefully and in just the right, respectful tone, or Kwazz would take umbrage and bridle—which, Ray had observed, might be said to apply to the entire new government. They were still very skittish with power. Many ominous cracks were beginning to appear in the cobbled-together contraption they had created with the whites, Indians, and coloreds. The Secretary's prognostications for the future of southern Africa were not optimistic, though the United States was doing all it could to encourage stability.

Soon after the new government took office, the post of Secretary-General had unexpectedly fallen vacant. Kwazz, who had been a very active figure on the darker side of the African National Congress, had been nominated by the government as South Africa's candidate. The UN, in a characteristic spasm of symbolism, had promptly accepted the recommendation on a unanimous vote. The Hon. Kwazze Kumbatta ("KWA-zee Koom-BAH-tah," as he had it printed directly beneath his name on all his official letterheads) took over administration of the United Nations and had been riding high ever since. Talk about us lecturing the world! Ray Stanley often thought, mindful of the Secretary-General's frequent disparaging remarks about racial conditions in America: we aren't in it with that one.

However, diplomacy was still diplomacy on many occasions, and for many reasons having to do with the need for stability in that part of the world, the market for American goods down there, and the vast mineral wealth of the country, now largely under control of its new masters—to say nothing of Kwazz's own sensitivity—the Secretary's tone was friendly but guarded now. In mind's eye he could see Kwazz's handsome high-cheek-boned face, intelligent gray-blue eyes, and lighter than normal skin, all inherited from some wandering Afrikaner, now lost to history, who had contributed to the family bloodstream a century ago. The expression, he knew, would be as cautious and guarded as his own. So was the voice.

"Yes?" the Secretary-General inquired carefully. "Who is this, please?"—although Ray of course had identified himself to the S.-G.'s secretary.

"This is Ray Stanley," he said. "Is this the Secretary-General?"

"It is he," the S.-G. said gravely. "It is my pleasure to hear from you, Mr. Secretary."

"Mutual, Mr. Secretary-General."

"You wish to discuss a date for the Security Council meeting on the problem posed by President Sidi," Kwazze Kumbatta said. "Right?"

"Right."

"Next Friday would be the earliest," Kwazz said. "Is that agreeable to your government?"

"We would prefer it sooner," the Secretary said, "but if prior commitments make it impossible—"

"You know how it is," Kwazz said, deep voice sounding politely regretful, though the Secretary knew, from past experience, that Kwazz, like all Secretaries-General, was secretly quite pleased with anything, however minor, that would annoy the United States. "There are still flare-ups in Palestine—the wars in Sudan and Kenya may require action—Northern Ireland—Korea—Haiti"—his voice trailed away, there was a heavy sigh. "One never knows. It never ends, does it? It keeps us jumping."

"Like a cat on a hot tin roof," the Secretary said.

There was an instant loss of cordiality at the other end.

"Funnily enough," the S.-G. said, not sounding as though it were funny at all, "my tribal name as a child was 'Little Jumping Cat.' You did not know that?"

"How could I?" the Secretary inquired calmly.

"You should," Kwazze Kumbatta said in an accusatory tone. "It is in my official biography distributed through this office."

"I am sure our ambassador to the United Nations has read it with great care," Ray Stanley said. "It just has not happened to come across my desk."

"Ah, well," the Secretary-General said, "I suppose your remark was not meant critically."

"It is just an expression we have," Ray Stanley said.

"Oh," Kwazze Kumbatta said. "Very well, then. What position will the United States take on this matter of Sidi?"

"I assume you have read our official statement as presented by the President," Ray said.

"You will file copies of your resolution prior to the meeting so that we may consider it?"

"Of course," the Secretary said, permitting a slight impatience to enter his voice. "Don't we always comply with UN procedures?"

"On the many occasions when you seek Security Council support?" Kwazze Kumbatta said. "Yes, that is correct. Very good."

"What seems to be the sentiment up there regarding Sidi?" Ray inquired. "Have you had a chance to find out?"

"It is my duty to find out," Kwazz said stiffly, sounding attacked again.

"And you have," Ray Stanley said.

"I have."

"Well?"

"I really do not feel," the Secretary-General said, "that I have the right as Secretary-General to reveal the contents of confidential conversations I have had with members of delegations."

"For heaven's sake—" Ray Stanley began in a tired voice, then dropped it. "Of course you are right, Kwazz. I suspect they have not revealed much to you, anyway. I think you are still regarded as the new boy—sorry, I mean the new man—on the block. They would probably not confide in you, anyway."

"I am privy to many of their secrets!" the Secretary-General said angrily. "And not as a 'boy,' either!"

"I amended that," the Secretary said. "Calm down, Kwazz. Nobody's criticizing you, but it does seem to me that you would know more about their sentiments than you are telling me. If, as I say, they really confide in you."

"Yes, they confide in me!" Kwazze Kumbatta said angrily. "Many of them do not approve of the United States position this time. They feel Sidi has been punished enough."

"Even if he is threatening the peace of the world—" the Secretary began, but was interrupted by the S.-G.'s heartily sarcastic laugh.

"What is that?" he demanded. "And where do you see it? Does such a thing exist? Where, Ray? Where?"

"And even," the Secretary continued in a level voice, "if he really does have A-bombs that pose a threat to the entire region, if not to the entire world—"

"Oh, well!" Kwazze Kumbatta exclaimed, scornful laughter deepening. "Everybody has them, nowadays. What difference does that make?"

"If that truly represents your sentiments, Kwazz," Ray Stanley said, finally provoked, "you strike me as completely unfit for your job. 'The World's Conscience' did the *Times* call you a few weeks ago in that Sunday magazine puff piece? What a conscience! What a world! And how snugly—and smugly—do you fit together!"

"Now," Kwazze Kumbatta said, "I am really angry, Ray. I do not accept that kind of remark from you, or—"

"Or any other white man," Ray Stanley interrupted.

Kwazze Kumbatta's voice actually shook with anger.

"Or *any* man," he grated out. "This is not amusing, Mr. Secretary. You are offending me. I hope your resolution fails! I hope your efforts fail! I hope you are humiliated!"

"You said Friday?" the Secretary inquired, unimpressed.

"I said Friday," Kwazze Kumbatta snapped.

"We will begin circulating the resolution tomorrow," the Secretary said in the same unemotional, unimpressed voice. "Please notify the members of the Security Council that I will appear in person this time. Say that we urge other foreign ministers and heads of government to attend, if they so desire."

"You will lose," the Secretary-General predicted, still angry. "China and Russia will veto."

"Then we may have to act independently of the United Nations," the

Secretary said, in a voice so cold and matter-of-fact that the Secretary-General was genuinely at a loss for words.

"You would not dare," he said at last.

"Tell them to try us," the Secretary said in the same cold voice.

"You would not dare," the S.-G. repeated.

"You don't know what we would do, do you, Kwazz?" Ray Stanley inquired blandly. "Hadn't the UN better think twice before it really tries to find out?"

"You wouldn't dare," Kwazze Kumbatta repeated, sounding still half-stunned. "You just wouldn't dare."

"I hope you all don't have to find out," Ray Stanley said cheerfully. "See you next Friday, Mr. Secretary-General." And hung up before Kwazz could rally himself for another riposte.

He only wished, the Secretary thought with a frustrated annoyance after he had hung up, that he was as certain of America's course as he professed to be—as he had to be, given his position. He was dealing with an uncertain and unknown quantity on which he was not entirely sure he could rely. Act alone if the Security Council did not agree?

Promise or bluff?

He picked up the phone that linked him directly to the Oval Office and asked the White House operator to put him through. Perhaps he could prod the uncertain and unknown quantity in the direction he felt to be the right one. All he could do was try. The decision rested elsewhere.

"Ray!" the President's cheerful voice came over, apparently without a care in the world. "What are you up to?"

"I'm up to exactly what you told me to be up to," the Secretary said, unable to keep a certain starchiness out of his voice. "What else would you be expecting me to do?"

"Tut, tut," the President said comfortably. "I can tell it's been a long day. The Big Four and the S.-G., right? All being obdurate and uncooperative and frustrating and generally acting like bastards, right?"

"Not Britain," the Secretary said, "and, basically, probably, after they've satisfied their egos by trying to make us sweat a little, not the French. China and the S.S.R. will be problems, yes. And Kwazz Kumbatta—you know how he is."

"He's a flouncer," the President said. "Afrikaner obduracy used to be hard enough to deal with. Mix it with black hypersensitivity and you've got a real combination on your hands. What date for the Security Council?"

"He says next Friday, but of course we can insist on an earlier date if we want to. Do we?"

The President thought for a moment. Ray imagined he could hear the wheels turn with an audible click.

"No," the President said finally. "I think Friday will be fine. That will give us time over the weekend for the programs, and time for a little reaction to build up in our favor. This first wave of opposition was to be expected from people like Concerned Citizens Against and We Protest, but there's bound to be a groundswell. And also, it will give me time to dicker with Sidi a bit."

"I thought you were going to talk to the Prime Minister, and the President of France, and the Chairman in Beijing, and the President in Moscow," the Secretary said, reeling them off with deliberate emphasis. "Have you given up that idea?"

"Nooo," the President said. "Not exactly. I'd like to try some personal diplomacy with Sidi first, though."

"What makes you think it will be any more successful than it has been so far?" the Secretary inquired.

"He'll begin to think better of it as the international pressure grows," the President predicted.

"Oh?" the Secretary said, and took a chance on bluntness. "So far, he's responded by announcing he has four A-bombs, threatening to jump on Lower Lolómé, and ordering the murder of Creed Moncrief. How successful can personal diplomacy get?"

"Nonetheless," the President said, beginning to sound a little irritated, "I still think the personal approach can do a lot, particularly when it's backed by united world opinion."

"Which is the furthest thing from what we've got," the Secretary remarked, a little surprised by his own independence; but Tony Marsden had perhaps hit home harder than he knew. The President chose to remain optimistic—or sound like it to his Secretary of State, anyway.

"Nonetheless," he said again, "I think I'll keep on working on it. We can ratchet up the pressure along with it. There are the aircraft carriers, after all. There's a good bit of pressure right there."

"Have they reached Greater Lolómé yet?" Ray inquired. He could sense a sudden reserve in the President's tone. He knew from experience that an evasion was coming.

"Nooo," the President said, in the same thoughtful tone he had used before. "Not—exactly. I'm holding them at Suez, for the moment."

"What?" Ray Stanley demanded, too startled and annoyed to be polite. "I thought we agreed in the NSC that they would go straight through and take up stations off Pointe Sinistre just as they did a couple of years ago in the second Gulf war—"

"They're only five minutes away by jet," the President said calmly. "What's the difference?"

"The difference is—" Ray began in an exasperated tone, then caught himself up more mildly, "the difference is that in this kind of game, physical presence is all. Out of sight is out of mind. If Sidi can use a pair of good binoculars and see them sitting off Pointe Sinistre, that's one thing. If they're invisible, except by radar, off there on the other side of the landmass, their presence isn't going to weigh too heavily."

"I understand all that, Ray," the President said mildly. "I'm not a fool, you know. On the other hand, as I've arranged it now, I can ratchet up the pressure with a one-two punch. I've sent orders through Bill Rathbun at the Pentagon that they're to maintain open communications for the moment and do a lot of talking about their plans to depart soon for Sinistre. If Sidi doesn't come around, he knows that all I have to do is say the word and they'll be on his doorstep in twenty-four hours. Let's try it my way for the moment and see what happens. Carrot and stick, you know. Carrot and stick."

"What's the carrot?" Ray inquired.

The President's tone became positively airy.

"Oh," he said cheerfully, "probably money. Money always works, doesn't it? A big loan from the World Bank, a big line of credit from us—'financial assistance,' in all its myriad, wonderful forms. You know the sort of thing. We've done it before."

"So many times," the Secretary said dryly, "that it must make the world's collective head swim. To say nothing of the potential recipient's. And if that doesn't work, then—"

"Then there are the carriers," the President said.

"Yes," the Secretary said. "The stick. And when they're on his doorstep, then what will they do? Anything? Or will it just be another threat from the U.S. that never comes off—as, again, so many times?"

"You're being very critical," the President observed, "for a Secretary of State. Do you want to resign, Ray? Am I getting too far out of sync with the State Department?"

"If you want to fire me, Mr. President," Ray said with a calmness he did not entirely feel, but he seemed to be on some sort of roll, so unexpected he couldn't quite define exactly where it came from, "go ahead. Meanwhile, part of my job as I conceive it is to be the devil's advocate. And to try to maintain some strength of policy out of Washington."

"I'm not strong?" the President inquired, amicability gone, an ominous note in his voice.

"No one doubts it," the Secretary said, amazed at his own serenity in the face of his formidable employer's annoyance; he seemed to be buoyed up by a confidence in his own position that he hadn't felt in quite some time. Mary and Eulie would be proud of him now.

"Words are beginning to be not enough. Lately, American words are beginning to be not enough. It's a problem—for us and, I think, for the world, which ought to be able to depend on some degree of American strength and consistency."

"I intend to be strong and consistent," the President said, more mildly. "Hang in there, Ray. You're doing a fine job of keeping me on track. Just let me do it my way though. You tuck in the edges."

"Mr. President," Ray Stanley said, starting to laugh, "you're something else."

"I'm President of the United States," the President said with an answering chuckle. "That accounts for a good deal."

"Even when it doesn't explain a great deal, sometimes," Ray said.

"I love being an enigma," the President said with another chuckle.

"Fine for you," Ray said. "Not always so easy for us."

"Poor things!" the President exclaimed with mock commiseration. "I feel for you. Good luck with Sally Holliwell's show if we don't talk before then."

"And good luck with Able Montague and the call-ins," the Secretary said.

"I'll snow 'em," the President said with a cheerful certainty that carried, still, the elusive note of mockery that held them all captive to the fascinations of his erratic but powerful charm. "I'll just absolutely snow 'em."

But when he prepared to leave the Oval Office and go upstairs to join Helen for one of their rare private dinners alone, he was not at all sure. And despite the teasing fun and games he liked to play with subordinates such as Ray who were inclined to be, the President felt, too serious when he himself wanted to be light and facetious, he was not at all sure that the gamble he was taking with Sidi would pay off.

"Light and facetious" was a false description, anyway. Underneath it all he was dead serious and approached his job that way. It was just that lightness and facetiousness, after all these years, were such a habit that he was not entirely sure himself where they ended and the seriousness began. He had realized often in his successful political life that this could be a handicap. Helen often told him so.

Tonight she did so again. She performed her usual duty of mixing "the best martini in Christendom," as he often told their guests, set it down on the end table beside his armchair, took her own armchair opposite with her usual mild vodka and tonic. In the kitchen the staff was busy preparing the light meal that would presently be served them on television trays.

"Well," she said, "have you had a busy day running the world, today?"

"Call me Atlas," he said, lifting his glass in toast and taking the first, stomach-thumping sip. "What did you do?"

"Nothing so dramatic," she said, returning the gesture with her usual relaxed, self-contained smile. "Visited a school in Maryland for retarded children—'disadvantaged,' as they call it, one of those words we hide behind these days to escape the world's realities. These kids, however, were really retarded, but most of them nice and lovable, as they often are. Then I had lunch with the Supreme Court wives and the two lady Justices here at the house, very relaxed and pleasant, they're a nice group. Took a nap, called up a limousine and had the Secret Service take me shopping at a couple of bookstores in Georgetown, causing a minor traffic jam and dazzling a few tourists. Came back, went over some White House accounts, read awhile, watched the news, wondered what my husband was doing to save humanity from its errors. Checked the social schedule, saw we were free tonight, ordered dinner in here, relaxed, and waited for the arrival of my lord and master."

"Ha!" he exclaimed with an amicable grin. "That would be the day. Sounds as though you managed to keep busy."

"Oh, I do," she said. "I'm not shy, like some, or brash, like others. I try to keep a balance between fading into the woodwork and climbing a new mountain every day."

"You're an effective First Lady," he acknowledged with a smile. "Any time you feel you aren't busy enough, let me know. In fact, there are a couple of things coming up soon on the Hill where I'd like your help in the way of testimony and perhaps some quiet lobbying among your friends."

"Yes," she said. "The new environmental legislation and the National Endowment for the Arts. I'm available."

Aware of her extensive influence in both areas, he smiled again with real affection and approval.

"You're good," he said. "And a great help. You really are. I don't know what I'd do without you."

"You'd manage," she said with a certain characteristic dryness. "However," she added with a smile that softened it, "a girl does like to hear words like that . . . So what about Sidi?"

"Oh, Christ," he said with a sigh. "Seedy Sidi! Yes, what about him? I just heard from Ray a few minutes ago and he's had an annoying day talking to the Big Four on the Security Council, and our flaming spear carrier in the front office, Kwazze Kumbatta. Rather frustrating, I gathered, particularly the Russians and Chinese and Kwazze Kumbatta."

"Not cooperating?"

"Not exactly rushing to support the boy who has his finger in the dike, you might say."

She smiled and offered an imaginary quote.

"'Nice finger, nice dike. We'll watch.' That it?"

"At the moment," he acknowledged. "There isn't exactly a great rush to support us."

"Support you," she corrected.

He shrugged. "In this office, it's the same."

"That's right," she agreed. "Do you ever stop to realize the truly enormous power you have to change the world?"

He nodded thoughtfully.

"I do; indeed I do. That's why I can never understand Presidents who make a big show of insisting that they just want to be 'domestic.' They can't escape the world, it's the height of naïveté to try. All their busy plans to stay out of it come to nothing: they can't. Whether they like it or not, they sneeze in the Oval Office and somebody blows his nose in Borneo. Or the equivalent. It's amazing." He frowned, half-amused, half-regretful. "Except when it's 'Nice finger, nice dike. We'll watch.' Then it isn't so easy."

She considered this for a moment; she had always been one of the shrewdest political minds he had ever known. Her expression now was thoughtful, concentrated on the problem of Sidi.

"You can pretty well lay down the ground rules at this stage, though, can't you? When you go on Able Montague's show on Sunday, you'll have the world's attention. At that moment you'll be in sole control of world opinion. It will be up to you then."

"Oh, sure," he said. "I intend to frame the debate. But when the major pieces on the board come into play, it's going to take a lot of hard-slogging diplomacy, plus a lot of bribery in some form or another, to bring everybody into line. They can all be bought sooner or later, some with money, some with flattery, some with appeals to self-interest—but it's generically all bribery, whatever it's called in polite society."

"And you think it will work this time?"

He looked complacent for a moment, in a way he never permitted himself to do in public, where he had found earnest concern to be a more popular stance.

"It always has."

"Well, don't get too confident," she said.

"I'm not," he said, "but I've found that when what you do is based on a bedrock of principle and integrity, it works, more often than not."

"It does," she observed, "if you stick with it."

"Well!" he exclaimed with a half-laugh. "Are you implying I won't stick with it—or just being the devil's advocate like Ray, to prop me up so I won't start to waver?"

"Is Ray doing that?" she asked. "I'm glad to be in such good company. . . . I don't see how you can waver. You've taken a position, in the statement, that you've pretty well got to maintain, haven't you? Or make yourself and the country look pretty weak and wishy-washy."

"Some people think the statement was wishy-washy," he said. "Eulie Montgomery and El Barnes, for instance. We had quite a go-'round in the NSC. They wanted it to be much stronger, at certain key points, than I did."

"Yes, you told me about that," she said. "I didn't say anything then because it was a matter of record by that time, the statement was out, but I was a little curious as to why it wasn't stronger, myself."

He gave her a long, shrewd look and the disingenuous smile she knew very well.

"I have to have room to maneuver," he said.

She gave him a skeptical glance. "Maneuver for what? What are you going to do, let Sidi get away with it?"

He looked annoyed.

"No, I'm not going to let Sidi get away with it! But there are a lot of points of view that have to be accommodated in something like this. Eulie thinks it's a fundamental turning point. I don't take that view, myself. It's important but not *all*-important. As I say, I believe in leaving myself room to maneuver."

"How?" she inquired, sounding genuinely puzzled. When he told her about his step-at-a-time policy with the carriers, and remarked with satisfaction that "by having Ray deal with the allies at his level, I've left my options open as to when I can appeal to heads of state—if I should need to," the puzzlement deepened. With it came a skepticism he knew well. It had greeted many of his political assumptions over the years and was still there even though many of them had come true.

"But," she objected, "you obviously think Sidi's going to give in. How do you know that? What makes you so sure?"

"Oh, my political instinct," he said comfortably. "He'll come around."

"You're always so confident," she remarked. "Supposing he doesn't, will *you* back down? It seems to me you've put yourself in a position where one of you is going to have to."

He smiled.

"It won't be me."

"That implies that if he doesn't, you're going to have to force him to, right?"

He leaned forward, half-humorous, half-earnest.

"Listen, lady! I'm not going to back down, he's going to back down. You're like too many Americans, you know—you're too absolute. It's either/or from the git-go, with no room to maneuver. That's what I'm leaving myself, I'll say again, room to maneuver! *Don't worry.* I'll work it out." He smiled. "Have faith in the President of the United States. He won't let you down."

"He doesn't think he will," she said, "but he just might be mistaken. Anyway," she added, rising and holding out her hand for his glass, "have another martini. It helps the world stay rosy."

"I'm not being rosy," he protested, but humorously. "There's a realistic situation here, I'm trying to handle it realistically. . . . About half, thank you. If Sidi and his friends bomb Washington tonight, I want to be alert."

"No doubt you'd joke your way out of it," she remarked, handing back his glass half full as requested. "But they just might. It's a strange world we live in."

"That's right," he agreed as two members of the kitchen staff came in with a food trolley and began to prepare their trays. "But not that strange."

It was this eternal confidence of his that made him sometimes so difficult to work with, the Secretary of State told his wife as they, too, settled in for a rare meal at home—"off the circuit," as Mary put it.

This seldom-possible luxury always began, weather permitting, with drinks on the terrace of their Washington Harbor apartment overlooking the Potomac, now dark and deserted in the soft spring night. On the other side the highways sparkled with the steady stream of lights from the incessant flow of traffic, homeward-bound into Virginia.

"Self-confidence in a President," he said, "is fine, but there are times when he overdoes it. He's convinced that Sidi's going to give in, so all he has to do is charm the daylights out of the world and all will be well. It isn't going to be that easy." He smiled, rather ruefully. "At least, that's the way I hear it. From my contacts. Which haven't been too helpful, today."

"Bets appreciated your call," Mary said. "She was glad you had time to be a father, along with all your other headaches."

"A welcome note of human reality," he remarked wryly, "'midst th' encircling gloom.' I hope that doesn't turn out to be something really serious. I can't believe Boo and Samir would do anything foolish."

"Men," she said with equal wryness. "They love to play games. We'll just have to hope . . . Did you have a nice talk with Tony Marsden?"

"Oh, yes," he said. "When all's said and done, Britain's still the most reliable friend we have in the world." He gave her a candid look. "He upset me a little, though."

"Oh? How so?"

"He asked me if I would resign if the President took a course in this matter that I couldn't conscientiously support."

"What did you tell him?"

"I said I'd have to consider it very carefully and weigh a loss of influence through resignation against what I could do if I stayed in there and pitched for what I believed, in the hope that I could turn things around. He seemed to think this was equivocating. It seemed only realistic to me. What do you think?"

"It may be something you'll have to face one of these days," she said. She gave him a long and thoughtful look. "I'm surprised you haven't faced it with this one before now."

"Well, you know I haven't," he said. "So far, we've managed to see pretty much eye to eye on things."

She smiled.

"And in the State Department they don't train us to be radicals. It would take a very substantial difference of opinion for you to do anything like that, I would think."

"It's not inconceivable, though," he said, sounding suddenly rather anxious, as though she, too, were questioning his integrity.

She smiled again.

"No, no," she said. "I know that. What's your particular worry with this President? How might it come about, would you think?"

"The same thing we've discussed. Take a stand and then run from it . . . issue a threat and then weasel away from it . . . demand adherence to principles and then betray them . . . state a moral position and then abandon it . . . destroy a little further the credibility and the moral and psychological strength of the United States . . . continue the pattern of recent years, made even more obvious and more devastating by the fact that this time we're being blatantly challenged as never before, and by a pipsqueak country at that."

"And that's what he's proposing to do?" she inquired. "I haven't seen any signs of it—yet, anyway. Are you sure you're not worrying unnecessarily?"

"Maybe I am," he said. He smiled. "Maybe it's Eulie's influence. She's so convinced he's going to waffle that she may have worried me into seeing things that way too."

"But of course if you did think there was an irreconcilable difference—"

"Then I would have to restudy my position with great care," he said gravely.

She gave him a sudden amused look.

"Which is Statespeak for maybe I will, maybe I won't. I'm afraid if it comes to that point I'll be siding with Eulie. I think then you had better restudy your position—hard—and then do it."

"It would depend on the circumstances," he said.

Her amusement deepened.

"It's just as well I'm *not* Secretary," she said. "I still don't quite fit the mold in spite of all my years in the Foreign Service. You're much more the organization type than I am, at heart."

"I'm surprised the bureaucracy never caught up with you," he remarked, also with amusement. "You're such a radical."

"That's me," she said. "And if I didn't have so much faith in your integrity, I'd really raise hell. But I suspect that if it really came to a basic moral point, you'd be true to yourself. You always have been, after all."

"I've tried," he said. He stood up and started toward the built-in bar at the other end of the terrace. "How did we get into this sanctimonious talk, anyway? Have another drink."

"Just build up the ice and the tonic," she said. "Forget the gin. That will do fine. . . . When do you go to the UN?"

"Next Friday, Kumbatta tells me. Want to go along?"

"Sure," she said. "It's always interesting to watch the circus in action."

"You can help me lobby for our resolution."

"Is it going to be a strong one?"

"I hope so," he said. He frowned as he returned her glass, refreshed his own. "We haven't got the final language worked out yet. I'm not sure the President knows exactly the wording he wants."

"More importantly," she remarked, "what wording do *they* want? That may be the determining factor."

"Not if we can help it," he said flatly.

"That sounds very secretarial," she told him with a smile that removed most of the sting—not quite all, but most. "Is it really going to be that easy?"

"No," he confessed glumly, settling back in his chair. "It may be a hell of a fight."

"If the President sticks with it," she said.

"Which is where we came in," he agreed wryly.

Later, when they were eating the cheese soufflé she had prepared, still on the terrace, so mild was the night, the phone rang. He answered and found it to be Reginald Pennebaker Sims, calling from his place on the river up in Potomac, Maryland, just over the District line.

"Ray!" he exclaimed with his usual flamboyance. "Have you and his majesty really thought through what you want to do with this Sidi bastard?"

"Pretty much," Ray said. "But I'm sure you have some invaluable insights for us, Penny."

"Don't be sarcastic," the ex–Secretary of State advised. "Are you folks alone? Are you eating?"

"Yes and yes," the Secretary said, "so make it brief, please."

"Oh, I'll call you back later, then."

"No," Ray said firmly, knowing that the prospect of free time later would only encourage Penny to fill it to the limit with his characteristic orotundities. "Let me have it right now."

"I'll be brief," Penny promised.

"Do," the Secretary said.

"Stand firm!" Penny said. "Stand firm! Smite the bastard hip and thigh! De-nut him, Ray, de-nut him!"

"I would like to," the Secretary said grimly, thinking of poor Creed Moncrief, poor savaged body now mercifully reduced to ashes and scattered on the Potomac near Key Bridge by his grieving family. "But it isn't that simple."

"Make him an international pariah!" Reginald Pennebaker Sims urged, and Ray could see the bristling handlebars of his glorious mustache jumping up and down and vibrating in the winds of righteous indignation. "Isolate him, devastate him, destroy him!"

"We're going to do our best, Penny," Ray Stanley said, "allowing for all our friends at the UN who appear to want to be more gentle with him than we do."

"Oh, those," Penny said, scornfully dismissive. "They never had any doubts where *I* stood, Ray. They jumped when *I* said jump!"

"Yes, well," the Secretary said, "the situation is very fluid at the moment. Even more so than in your day, Penny. They don't jump quite as easily as they used to, I'm afraid. We've got our work cut out for us."

"Do you need any help?" Penny asked, trying to sound offhand and casual, which was not easy for him. "I would always be glad to come to New York and help you lobby, either as a member of your official party, or just as a private, interested individual, or—"

"No, thank you, Penny," Ray Stanley said hastily. "You just stand by and hold yourself available for whatever appearances you're asked to make down here, and help us that way. That will be an invaluable contribution."

"I have been invited to go on MacNeil-Lehrer with a panel next week, and there's a possibility of Able Montague," Penny said. "If any of the shows come to you for suggestions, you might bring up my name. My new book, *The Consequences of Indecision,* will be out in August, remember. It's getting some very good advance blurbs, from you among others."

"And so it should," Ray said sincerely, reflecting that Penny was like Oliver Goldsmith, whose friends said, "He writes like an angel but talks like Poor Pol." "They all know you," he said. "I'm sure your name is being kicked around in a dozen offices. I'll certainly push it along if they come to me."

"And you're going on with Sally Holliwell on Sunday," Penny said. "She's a bright young thing." (All of forty-three, the Secretary thought.) "I hope you're going to give 'em hell, Ray."

"I shall certainly try to make our position entirely clear," the Secretary said. He placed a hand half over the mouthpiece and called out, "Yes, Mary, just a minute. I just have to say goodbye to Penny."

"Well," Penny said, unperturbed but conceding, "I must run along and let you get back to your meal. Give her my love, Ray. She's the one who ought to be Secretary, you know, not you!"

"Very diplomatic, Penny," Ray said dryly. "That's what everybody says. Thanks so much, I'll tell her. And thanks for calling. Your advice is always welcome."

"Anytime," Reginald Pennebaker Sims said comfortably. "Anytime."

"One who wants you to stand firm, anyway," Mary said with a smile.

The phone rang again, she picked it up this time, said, "Yes, dear, just a minute," and handed it to him. "And another."

"Eulie," he said warmly. "How goes it?" His expression changed, became grave; Mary put down her fork and listened. "I am so sorry," he said finally. "Yes . . . yes, I understand . . . yes, of course . . . no, you mustn't try to do that. You just stay right there and . . . no, you mustn't, Eulie. You just stay there. Don't try to come in, he needs you there . . . Well, OK—whatever you think best. But I still wish you'd—all right, whatever you like. Would you like Mary to come by and sit with him when you—oh, all right. If you need anything, call us day or night. And let us know if—if anything changes. Love to you both from both of us. . . ."

He put down the phone, frowned, and shook his head.

"That was probably clear enough, right?"

She nodded. "He's gone into a coma?"

"Yes. And of course she wants to come in to the department tomorrow as though nothing has happened."

"She mustn't do that," Mary objected.

He smiled ruefully.

"You know Lulie. When did she ever take anybody's advice or welcome anybody's concern. Young Herbie's already come down from New York prepared to stay for the duration, which she says will probably be anything from a day to two weeks, so the doctors tell her. She's inclined to think it will be more like a day, which would be best for poor Herbie and for everyone concerned, and would permit her to get this over with and concentrate on worrying about damned Sidi, which she feels her duty requires." He sighed. "How long have we known them, Mary? Forty years? Time is drawing on."

"Yes," she said, eyes suddenly filling with sympathetic tears. "For thee and me, as well . . . Well!" she said briskly. "Let's finish up and get you to bed and let you get some rest. You're going to need it. Nothing's going to get any easier, for a while."

"No," he agreed. "That's for sure."

*   *   *

Later that evening, around ten-thirty, when the President and his wife, the Secretary and his, and most of the others most directly concerned with the matter of Sidi were either in bed or getting ready for it, Boo Bourassa and Samir Hashimi were preparing to leave their respective homes for another of those late evenings that so bothered and upset their Western wives, who would never completely understand their male-oriented Arab ways.

And in far-off Greater Lolómé, The Wearer of the Two Hats, President of All the Peoples of Lolómé, etc., was meeting with his powerful friends to discuss the final timetable for the surprises—of which they had in mind several, all unpleasant—that they intended to inflict upon their Western adversaries.

And at a certain friendly (to them) port, a nondescript tramp steamer of uncertain registry began its long, circuitous journey to other friendly ports and thence across the Atlantic to landfall in New York harbor and a rendezvous with an always complacent and unsuspecting America.

Presently, inevitably, and as planned, the Georgetown meetings, the Greater Lolómé conferrings, and the tramp steamer would come together.

But not for a while yet.

First, the stately, accustomed ballet of world diplomacy, the hallowed dance of stern advance and soft retreat, must proceed upon its stately, inevitable, all too predictable way.

And first in that, as always in the communications-ruled world of the almost-twenty-first century, came the by now inevitable obeisance to the great god television.

High and mighty were its suppliants, and into the homes of many millions around the globe came their august personages, bearing offerings to lay before the multitudes.

To a considerable extent, an aging, acerbic, but still powerfully influential columnist in Georgetown, though he was not of television and was almost an anachronism left over from an earlier day, framed the debate; perhaps even more than the President, for he was able to do it hours before the President was scheduled to appear, in the one publication that could still compete—if only just barely, now—on equal terms with television.

As on several notable occasions before, and as shrewdly as Tim Bates from a different point of view, James Van Rensselaer Burden set the tone.

The article in the Sunday *Times* magazine was Jimmy Van at his most moralistic, most indignant, and most powerful.

THREE

1

This was The Other Side of the Argument, as Jimmy thought of it. He had no doubt it was the best side. He intended to give it the strong support he felt it deserved. He had read Tim Bates's column in the *Washington Inquirer*—as everyone had, Tim in his difficult way was part of the Washington establishment, too—and he didn't think much of it. He and Tim had been "friends" for many years in the press corps, as much as two smart men with strongly opposed opinions could be friends in Washington's ideologically sensitive climate; but while Tim's standing with the P.C.B.Y.T.s (Politically Correct Bright Young Things, as Jimmy characterized them sarcastically in the privacy of his own mind) had never been solid and now was fading into history, Jimmy's was still relatively secure.

Since he was usually to be found on The Right Side of Things, he was generally regarded as a "grand old man." Since Tim had always swum upstream against the compliant and complacent tide of the politically correct, he was an "old has-been."

Nonetheless, Jimmy knew, Tim still carried a lot of weight with a sizable segment of the country. If his views in this instance could not be censored and suppressed by Right Thinkers, as they had been on many occasions in a long and controversial career, he could at least be given strong opposition. To this Jimmy had devoted his considerable talents in the three days the paper had given him in which to produce "Here We Go Again? Pride and Prejudice Clash Anew in the Desert."

The gist of it summed up the arguments of all those—very many, he was sure—who did not favor what Jimmy thought of as "going after Sidi again"—those in whom the President would find his most vigorous and vocal support if he decided to proceed with what Jimmy regarded as statesmanship instead of hysteria. Hysteria, he felt, had far too often clouded America's conduct in foreign affairs. The U.S. and the world, he reflected sternly as his fingers flew over the old, familiar keys, could do without *that* this time.

"The President of the United States," he concluded, after a lengthy review of the first Gulf War and a carefully minimized "second Gulf war," "is now confronted with the question: Is a 'third' Gulf war—and the satisfaction of temporary national (and perhaps personal) pique—worth the satisfaction of that national, and personal, pique?

"Rational consideration would seem to suggest that it is not.

"Not only would such an adventure probably be extremely difficult, if not downright impossible, to organize on the scale of the First, or even the 'second' Gulf war, but its outcome in all probability could only end in another ignominious 'victory' for the United States as empty, open-ended, and inconclusive as the first and second such 'triumphs' proved to be.

"Americans can remember all too vividly the long, drawn-out, ultimately failed aftermaths of the first Gulf War—the endless wrigglings of the enemy after his 'defeat,' when he successfully evaded, one by one, the strictures placed upon him by the United Nations at United States behest, thereby making the United Nations and the United States look like fools (as indeed they were) in the eyes of a world whose respect is vital to the success of U.S. and UN policies.

"Americans can also remember the similarly trailed-away, blown-away, thrown-away 'victory' in the 'second Gulf war,' when a comparable lack of will and tenacity on the part of the 'victors' permitted President Sidi to similarly, successfully, evade the punitive after-measures sought by the U.S. and the UN.

"To mount still another such venture in the face of the ultimate failures of the first two would only be to confirm the skepticism and contempt with which many of the world's aggressor states and their bandit-leaders regard the United States.

"Given what the world has now come to see as the almost certain outcome of such American adventures, it would in all probability be impossible for this President to muster the international military force that was such a wildly hyped aspect of the first adventure and such a feeble if not downright pathetic aspect of the second. The will to support another such futile gamble (or gambol) in the desert is nowhere to be found. Not a clarion trumpet but a universal raspberry, one might expect, would await another such American call to arms.

"Therefore America would be attempting, virtually alone, to impose its will upon the rest of the world in the pursuit of one who is, after all, essentially a tin-pot tyrant in a minor patch of sand. Why, then, should the world heed an American call to bestir itself to thwart his puny ambitions? Why should America care?

"It is argued, and presumably we will hear the argument much in days immediately ahead, that the possession of atomic bombs by the President of Greater Lolómé seriously threatens the peace of the world. Perhaps, by some determined stretch of the imagination, it does; although the possession of those weapons in the hands of a rapidly growing number of states both large and small, both democratic and tyrannical, has not as yet resulted in any final Armageddon. The likelihood is that it never will.

"But the President, presumably, believes sincerely in the threat, and will sincerely attempt to use it to persuade the United Nations and the world in general—to say nothing of his own country—to condemn President Sidi. Such condemnation, one supposes—if, indeed, it can be secured, which seems highly doubtful—will be the limit of permissible action in present circumstances.

"Certainly it seems best that it should be so. Because there is no other action, in all reality, that this country or the United Nations can take.

"A massive military onslaught upon Greater Lolómé would seem to be both futile and ridiculous. Already there are many indications that such a misadventure would not be supported by a majority of the American people. Its failure would once again emphasize to the world the shaky foundations of American power. Ultimatums without teeth and bombast without bullets add up to futility and ridicule. It seems safe to say that, in the opinion of most Americans, we cannot afford it.

"Therefore it seems likely that both militarily and psychologically the answer to the question: 'Here We Go Again?' is: No, we should not.

"Americans, it is hoped, will join in persuading the President that he must stand firm—not, as some more irresponsible elements in politics and the media would have it, stand firm in a belligerent, warlike, intractable position toward President Sidi and, by extrapolation, any individual leader who happens to challenge a position of the United

States, no matter how minor the challenge may be, or how ill-advised the position.

"Rather, the President should stand firm in a posture of reasonable discussion, peaceable solution of controversies, the mature and thoughtful consideration and calming of differences between states.

"That way, one suspects, lies the true genius, and the true validation, of American democracy and its necessary and worthy place in a changing world."

Which, Jimmy Van felt as he concluded his piece and faxed it off to the paper's Sunday magazine, was as good a statement of the sensible view of things as he could muster on short notice; and damned good it was, too, he told himself. As he had indicated to Ray Stanley and Willie Wilson at Dolly Munson's party, he did not have any great respect for what he regarded as the equivocal individual who sat in the Oval Office. If he could pin him down to the course of action Jimmy considered wisest for the country, by the simple expedient of giving it such fulsome praise that the President would feel that for the sake of his own popularity he could not escape doing it—then Jimmy felt he would have achieved a lot for the United States of America.

Since "helping the country," as he thought of it, had been his basic and quite genuinely sincere purpose ever since he had begun to achieve a major voice in the formulation of American opinion, he was pleased with his present effort. In his own rather pompous and self-important way, James Van Rensselaer Burden considered himself a genuine patriot; and in his own rather pompous and self-interested way, he was.

The fact that others such as Willie Wilson, Ray Stanley, and Tim Bates believed themselves to be equally patriotic did not deter or particularly concern him. They had their vision and their duty as they saw it. He had his. Making the incumbent toe the mark was, as Jimmy Van saw it, the most constructive thing he could do for America at this particular moment.

Sally Holliwell and Able Montague had similar agendas, and on the weekend proceeded to put them in place.

For Sally, her original plan for a general free-for-all on "Capitol Perspective" that would include her major colleagues "and a cast of thousands," as she put it humorously to herself, had quickly narrowed down to a more manageable (and more self-emphasizing) formula. In one brisk twenty-minute period of telephoning which signaled clearly how important—and how powerful—she was inside and outside the Beltway, she had lined up the Secretary of State, the Secretary of Defense, Senator Wilson, and Congressman Jones. That was enough. And one interlocutor, herself, was enough. This was an occasion, she told herself, where Little Sally had earned, and intended to exercise, the right to take center stage by herself. She was convinced that she was in a position, one of the most powerful in Washington, to head off another futile war in the Middle East. As determinedly as Jimmy and Able, she intended to do it.

"So, Mr. Secretary," she began after introducing her guests, who faced one another at an inverted-U table, herself in the open end, Ray Stanley and Jimmy Jones (barely shaking hands on arrival) on her right, Arlie McGregor and Willie Wilson facing them from her left, "is the United States entering another major crisis over Sidi bin Sidi?"

"bin Sidi," Ray Stanley added with an easy smile. "Don't forget the third 'bin Sidi.' No, I don't think we are, *if* the United Nations and our major allies will stand firmly together in our approach to it."

She turned to Arlie McGregor.

"I agree," the Secretary of Defense said with the rather winsome, deprecating, chipmunky smile he could produce when he wanted to generate support, "providing, as Secretary Stanley says, that our allies and the United Nations—and NATO, which must figure in any decisions that include the possibility of military action—are in agreement."

"So far, so good," Sally said with a brisk smile. "Senator Wilson?"

"I think the chances of such agreement are slight," Willie said crisply. "I think it may come down to a matter of American will and American staying power, which essentially means the will and staying power of the administration and particularly of the President. Of them, I am not at the moment so sure."

"There speaks our leading Capitol Hill skeptic," she said, with the smoothly practiced smile that enabled her to make a lot of points she wanted to make without antagonizing her guests too much. "And I assume you're another, Congressman?"

"I think," Johnny Jones said with a scowl, "that the President and the administration will be just as strong as the State Department here allows them to be. And that, in my opinion, like as not will not be very strong. Isn't that right, Mr. Secretary?"

And he half-turned in his seat to direct an ostentatiously unimpressed glance at Ray Stanley, who drew back and returned it with a nicely calculated balance of disagreement and distaste.

"As usual," he said, with a mildness that didn't remove the sting, "the Congressman has a rather unique view of the almighty influence of the Department of State and a rather unusual understanding of the structure and functioning of the American government. We in the department would like to think we're as all-powerful as the Congressman apparently does, but I assure him we're not. Not only would that go against the grain of what State Department people are trained and permitted to express, but it would violate the constitutional provisions that make the President head of government, superior to State as he is to all other departments and agencies of the executive branch. He is subject to no one's manipulation. Least of all," he added with an amiable smile that made his words even more startling, "a bunch of lily-livered, cookie-pushing, panty-hosed perverts, which I believe were among the most recent complimentary things the Congressman said about us."

"Whew!" Sally exclaimed with the exaggerated laugh she used when guests became too heated. "There's a mouthful! I'm sure the Congressman didn't mean all that as harshly as it sounds, Mr. Secretary."

Johnny Jones hunched his shoulders, jutted his jaw, and shook his shaggy graying locks.

"I did," he said grimly. "I surely did."

"I rather thought so," the Secretary said, amused and unperturbed, which he knew would annoy. "I was surprised you managed such restraint, Johnny. That wasn't like you."

"Now, now," Sally said with an amicable firmness. "I will have to remind the Secretary and the Congressman that we're here to discuss the dangers of fighting Sidi, not each other. And I think all Americans are agreed that we want to avoid those dangers. Don't you think so, Senator?"

"Clever girl," Willie said with amusement, wagging an admonitory finger. "Clever, clever girl. Ah, what a verbal web we weave when first we practice to deceive! Suddenly we're not discussing the *possibility* of fighting Sidi, we're already into it and discussing the *dangers* of it as though you were calling us to battle against it. You are, aren't you?"

"Well, Senator," Sally said, pointed little face looking a bit strained and not so amiable—she wasn't used to having her techniques exposed, particularly not in front of the estimated 20 million people who customarily watched her show—"I'm not here to call anyone to battle. I am concerned that America not do battle, certainly. I think that's a perfectly legitimate stand. And," she added with some asperity, "I believe that as a citizen of America, I'm allowed. Right?"

"Oh, yes," Willie said. "I'm not challenging your right on that at all, Sally. I had thought, though, that we were here to analyze the justification, or lack of it, for responding to Sidi's challenge—which, we mustn't forget, he has given us, we didn't initiate it. How we can respond short of battle, that is."

"Very well, Senator," she said, still looking ruffled. "So tell us. What *can* we do?"

"I'm interested in that," Willie agreed. "But I think that, even more than what we do, I'm interested in the spirit and the will with which we do it. We mustn't do it halfheartedly, it seems to me, and we mustn't lose our determination somewhere along the line. No more Bosnias. If we go in, we should go in the first time around with maximum force and with the determination to stay there until it's over."

"You say 'go in,'" Sally noted, a certain triumphant gleam in her eyes. "That sounds pretty aggressive to me, Senator."

Willie smiled.

"Yes, I thought you'd pick up on that." He chuckled. "That's why I said it, just to get you going."

"And not only me, Senator," she said, beginning to sound a little annoyed by his seeming flippancy: he had never been as respectful of her influence as she would have liked. "There must be millions of Americans out there who are already alarmed by the administration's apparent desire to plunge us into a third Gulf war."

"Oh, I wouldn't call it that!" Arlie McGregor exclaimed, sounding alarmed.

"Nor I," Ray Stanley said, allowing a certain steel to enter his voice. "I assure you that it is not the administration's 'desire' to 'plunge us into' a 'third Gulf war,' nor is it the administration's intention, nor can the administration imagine a situation in which such a course would be even remotely possible."

"You certainly contemplated something the other day in that official statement," Senator Wilson remarked. "What was it you contemplated?"

"They don't know," Johnny Jones said darkly. "They don't know what they want, over there in the department where all the crazy stuff comes from. They don't know their—well, anyway, from a hole in the ground. That's how competent *they* are."

"What would you like them to do in the Sidi situation, Congressman?" Sally inquired quickly—so quickly that the Secretary of State gave her a wry glance.

"Don't worry, Sally," he said. "Comity will be maintained between the Congressman and downtown. The Congressman has his own ideas, as always. Like you, I'd like to hear them."

"I'd bomb the hell out of the miserable bastard," Johnny Jones said flatly, again with his characteristic out-jut of jaw. "I wouldn't pussyfoot around."

"Would we be able to do that on short notice, Mr. Secretary?" Sally inquired of Arlie McGregor, who had raised a quick hand in protest. The Secretary of Defense smiled at the Congressman, with whom his relations in general were a lot better than Ray's.

"It would be difficult to mount the kind of attack Representative Jones seems to visualize," he said. "At least on any short-term basis. Physically and in an armaments sense, yes, we could do it. But to take care of all the possible political contingencies—"

"And then, too," Willie Wilson could not resist, "you might invite an atomic bomb on your aircraft carrier."

"What aircraft carrier?" Sally demanded sharply. "Have you sent an aircraft carrier to Greater Lolómé?"

"There is no aircraft carrier in the vicinity of Greater Lolómé," Secretary McGregor said hastily, giving the Senator, at his side, an annoyed look.

"Is one on the way?" Sally demanded.

Arlie hesitated for a moment. The Secretary of State stepped in. Sally filed the hesitation for future reference.

"Aircraft carriers are frequently on routine duty in the Mediterranean," he said in a calm, comfortable voice. "That does not mean that one is en route to Greater Lolómé." (Thinking: A necessary lie, but not *really* a lie because the ship isn't "en route," it's anchored off Suez.)

"Will it be?" Sally persisted, in the hammering, demon-newshen tone she had often found useful. "And if so, when?"

"There are many options open," Ray Stanley said in the same unhurried, comfortable fashion. "That might be one of them—or it might not. In any event, if and when it were to happen you can be sure it would be announced at the proper time and in the proper place."

"Well," she said, a rather strained smile on her face, "this may or may not be the 'proper time' as you see it, Mr. Secretary, but I can tell you that I, and I am sure the American people, would consider this a 'proper place.' Any place that brings out vital news involving their own destiny is a 'proper place,' it seems to me."

"What about Sidi's destiny?" Senator Wilson inquired with an amiable smile upon them all. "I thought we were supposed to be concerned about that this morning?"

"We are," Sally said, "but I find it hard to separate the two, particularly if the President is contemplating a major military strike against Greater Lolómé."

"I would be interested to know that, too," Willie said in the same amiable way, "particularly since it may be necessary for the Senate Foreign Relations Committee to get involved sooner or later." His smile increased. "We always do."

"My House Appropriations subcommittee is going to want to know a few things, too," Johnny Jones remarked with an ominous scowl. "Somebody's going to have to answer for it."

"For what?" the Secretary of State demanded with his first show of real annoyance. "Nobody's done anything so far, except issue a statement of U.S. intentions to try to persuade Sidi to adhere to international standards of behavior, if possible. Surely you don't object to that."

"I don't object to it," Johnny retorted, "but I sure don't see anybody doing anything."

"It's just beginning," Ray Stanley said shortly. "Give us a little time, please, Congressman."

"Speaking of time," Sally said, "I think we'd better try to summarize some points of view here. Suppose you two gentlemen from the Cabinet tell us how you see this. Then you can give us your view, Congressman, and you can wrap it up if you like, Senator."

"I may say nothing at all," Willie Wilson said. "But," he added with a smile, "don't count on it."

"No," Sally said, not sounding very amused. "Mr. Secretary of State?"

"As I see it," Ray Stanley said, "leaving aside the murder of an American citizen at the almost certain direction of President Sidi—"

"But you have no real proof of that," she interrupted.

He frowned.

"Enough. Leaving that aside, there is the threat posed by the aggressive ambitions of Greater Lolómé toward its weaker neighbor Lesser Lolómé—"

"Which involves oil," she said.

"—and the stability of the region and, in a broader sense, of the world community. Leaving aside those two factors, there is finally the greatest problem of all, and that is President Sidi's announcement that he has four A-bombs and the missiles to deliver them, and, by implication, that he plans to use them—"

"He hasn't said that," she noted.

This time he simply ignored the interruption and went on.

"—which poses an enormous threat to world stability, whose consequences would be vast and far-reaching and perhaps could not be contained.

"Therefore we have begun consultations with fellow members of the United Nations to find a solution, which may extend to sanctions—" he paused and then concluded quietly, "but may not necessarily end there."

"The Secretary of Defense?" Sally inquired.

Arlie McGregor looked both earnest and good-natured, a combination he had mastered at an early age and always found helpful.

"From where we sit in the Pentagon," he said, "this of course presents a strategic as well as political situation. I leave the latter to my good friend and colleague the Secretary of State, who always handles such matters with great skill in coordination with the President, whose expertise in foreign policy continues to grow and amaze those of us who work most closely with him."

"Thank *you*, Mr. Secretary!" Sally said with a laugh. "How many more billions do you want in your next year's budget? Just ask!"

"Well, he *is* amazing," Arlie said, looking a little nonplussed. "Isn't he, Ray?"

"Sui generis," the Secretary of State agreed blandly. "Unique."

"Right!" Arlie said with satisfaction. "So, we have the strategic worry, which I hope we will always discharge as efficiently as we have in the past—"

"Watch it, Arlie," Senator Wilson warned with a chuckle. "Might get an argument there. Might start a whole other debate."

"I know we have to watch out for you, Willie," the Secretary of Defense rejoined with a slightly nervous laugh. "Always . . . Anyway, looked at strictly from a military standpoint, all I can say, or should say at this moment, is that the Pentagon is prepared for whatever may happen in Greater Lolómé."

"You ought to be," Johnny Jones interjected in a tone that was not as friendly as the Secretary had obviously hoped. "You sold him the weapons."

"But not the bombs!" Arlie said quickly. "Not the bombs or the missiles, which pose the biggest problems. But those, too, we are confident we can handle. Greater Lolómé is under constant surveillance by satellites so sophisticated that they can literally distinguish from orbit the hairs in his ears, so to speak, so we know what he's doing—"

"Yes," Willie murmured, "but will you do anything about it? That, as they say, is the question."

"In coordination with our allies in the United Nations and NATO," the Secretary of Defense said rather stiffly, "we will do whatever the situation requires."

"Will you send American troops?" Sally inquired.

"There is no intention to do that," Arlie said. "We do not contemplate that it would be necessary at any point in the future, under any circumstances."

"But if the circumstances were there?" she persisted.

The Secretary began to look a little annoyed, the chipmunky cheeriness a bit frazzled.

"I do not believe the President, or I, could conceive of a situation in which circumstances should prompt such an action," he said flatly.

"It would be air strikes only, then," Sally suggested.

Arlie's footing slipped a bit, as Ray Stanley, concerned, had known it would.

"Air strikes might be a possibility," he said; then added hastily, "except, as I say, we cannot conceive of such a circumstance." And added further Washington Mantra No. 1: "Air strikes alone can't win a war."

"*Anything* can win a war if there's enough of it," Willie said. "Send in a couple of bombers for a ridiculous pinprick predesigned to fail, it's nonsense. Send in two hundred determined to kill, it's over. It's a matter of mass. Anything can win a war *if you send in enough of it and have the will to prevail.* Neither element can stand alone, however, I grant you that. The massive strike without the will or the will without the massive strike are fruitless."

"That's a fascinating subject right there, Senator," Sally said, and meant it. "Will you come back and help us with a discussion of that?"

"With pleasure," Willie said. "But excuse me, Arlie. I didn't mean to get us off the track. You were saying about Sidi?"

"Oh, that's all right," the Secretary of Defense said with a rueful smile. "Whoever said Senator Wilson's purpose in life was to make people comfortable? You always were a hard man to keep on the subject. . . . As I said, Sally, if I had to sum it up I'd say Sidi has presented us with an awkward diplomatic problem, maybe, but not with a strategic one. We can handle him."

"I can see the headlines," she said, knowing they would be exactly as she predicted. "MCGREGOR THREATENS AIR STRIKES ON SIDI. 'WE CAN HANDLE HIM.' Is that fair enough?"

"Not quite," Arlie McGregor said with an uncomfortable smile. "But you're probably right, that's how they'll be."

"Most likely," she agreed, with an impersonal, that's-your-problem smile. "Congressman?"

"I've said what I think," Johnny Jones said. "Bomb the bastard to hell."

"With how many bombers?"

He shrugged.

"As many as it takes. If the Senator's right, let's use two hundred. Or three hundred or five hundred or whatever it takes. But let's get it done."

"Succinct and to the point," she said. "When will you hold your hearings?"

"Haven't said I'd hold any," he said. "Let's see what happens next."

"You will," she said. "How about yours, Senator?"

"I had thought we might have some right away," Willie said, "but on reflection I think we, too, will wait a bit to see how things develop. They may not be necessary."

"When was a Foreign Relations Committee hearing not necessary?" she chided. "You folks are into everything."

"And so we should be," he said comfortably. "It's a big world out there. Do you want to know what I think about Sidi?"

She smiled.

"Please."

"I think the President's course so far is the correct one—as far as it goes. He has issued his statement, he has put Sidi on notice, he has decided to take the matter to the United Nations, with which I assume you and he have already been in contact, Ray—"

"I have," the Secretary said. "He'll be talking to heads of state very shortly, I believe."

"Good," Willie said. "The administration is going through the chairs. So far, so good. So we come back to the possibilities, which seem to me to be three: either Sidi backs down—or he doesn't—or we do. I do not like to contemplate the third possibility, but I think it has to be taken into account. Not, I hope, by Sidi. Assuming all goes well and we are able to muster sufficient support from our allies—and enough spirit and determination from within the presidential heart and others most directly involved—then possibility No. 1, a Sidi back-down, should be in the works and will lead to a peaceable disposal of the issue. Which do you think is most likely, Mr. Secretary?" And he turned to Ray Stanley with an earnest air whose basic sincerity the Secretary couldn't gauge but knew he must answer effectively.

"I think I can assure you, Senator," he said firmly, "that all our efforts are directed toward achieving possibility No. 1. I am sure neither the President, nor I, nor Secretary McGregor, nor anyone else in this administration 'most directly involved,' as you put it, is prepared to accept any less."

"I am glad to accept that assurance," Senator Wilson said. "I am pleased with it. And I assume it wipes out all chance of possibility No. 3, a back-down by us."

"Absolutely," Ray Stanley said, sending up a small silent prayer inside that it would be so. "I think you and I are in complete agreement on that."

"Another headline for you, Sally," Willie said, "to follow Arlie's two you predicted: STANLEY SURE OF U.S. SUCCESS IN NEW MIDEAST CRISIS."

"It may not have the right letter-count to fit the space, Senator," she said with a smile, "but I certainly hope it fits the facts. Now if I could just get somebody to say '*peaceful* success,' I'd be happy."

"That goes without saying," Arlie McGregor said.

———

"It had better," Senator Wilson said with a rather grim smile.

The Secretary of State nodded and smiled also, but in the quick glance they exchanged as the cameras focused on Sally preparing to end the show, it was apparent that neither he nor Willie was overly sanguine.

"That wraps it up," she said. "I want to thank you all very much. It's been a real contribution."

"I hope so," Ray Stanley said, smiling, as they faded from the screen. "A lot is at stake."

And so it was, he reflected as he drove back through Sunday's deserted streets to Washington Harbor to join Mary, Bets and Samir, and Joanie and Boo Bourassa, to watch the President on Able Montague's show and have a small pickup supper on the terrace. Sally had succeeded quite well, he thought, in emphasizing it.

"I simply won't stand for another ridiculous and foredoomed use of American military force!" she had told him at Dolly Munson's party. "I just won't have it!"

She hadn't been that openly arrogant on her show, of course, but he was sure her sentiments were quite clear to her viewers. He expected she had carried millions of them with her; probably almost all, for it was a sane objective and all sane Americans were in favor of it. Everybody wanted peace, that was a given. It was a very simple proposition except for two questions: (1) how do you get it? and (2) how do you keep it after you've got it? Nobody yet, in ten millennia of increasingly "civilized" society, had found the answers, though every generation had to keep trying. And now it was his turn, and the President's and the administration's, and the path was no clearer than it had ever been.

At the apartment he found Mary alone. Bets and Samir had been delayed by the last-minute defection of a baby-sitter; a substitute had been found and they were on their way. Joanie and Boo were expected momentarily.

"You did very well," she said, "as did everybody but that obnoxious Jones. What a travesty and a tragedy he is, to hold the power he does in the House!"

"The voters send him," he remarked in the old, exasperated Washington cliché, "and we have to take him, right down to the last lovely shoelace, barring some truly egregious malfeasance. Are Bets and Samir speaking? And Joanie and Boo?"

She laughed.

"Barely, I gather. Why don't you see if you can sound out the boys privately? I'll have the girls help me in the kitchen and you three can talk."

"The Middle East," he observed, "doesn't talk unless it wants to, as you know very well. Samir has never been the most forthcoming of young men, and Boo sometimes obfuscates by being too forthcoming, and it means nothing."

"Samir's the weak link in Boo's chain," she said, "whatever it may be. Go after them! After all, that's why you asked me to invite them here together, isn't it?"

"It never occurred to me," he said solemnly. "Never occurred to me."

Fifteen minutes later, everybody having arrived, and Boo and Samir circling him a bit warily, Mary said brightly, "Come on, girls, help me with supper. These men want to talk."

"We do?" Boo inquired with a humorous air. "I didn't know that, did you, Samir?"

Samir, his normally frank dark eyes looking withdrawn and clouded, his thin, wiry frame held even more tensely than usual, managed an uneasy smile.

"I wasn't aware of it," he said.

"Well," the Secretary said comfortably, "let's go out on the terrace and think about it. Anything to drink, anybody? The usual orange juice and soda, Boo? Tea, Samir?"

"Nothing, thank you, Ray," Samir said politely.

Boo grinned.

"You're really going to make me lose all my inhibitions, aren't you, Ray? Orange juice and soda will be fine."

"I," the Secretary said firmly after he had served Boo, "am going to be a dissolute infidel and have a gin and tonic. Light, though. I don't want you outsmarting me, Boo."

"That will be the day," Boo said, chuckling. "Now," he said seriously when they were seated, the river at their feet, Virginia and the Pentagon beyond, "what's all this about, Ray?"

"You know," the Secretary said, stretching out comfortably in one of the chaise longues, Boo facing him in another, Samir perched stiffly on one of the white plastic straight-backed chairs. "Bets is very worried about you, Samir. And Joanie's concerned about you, Boo. It seems you're going out on the town too much." He smiled at them with an easy humor that relieved his next words of insult. "More than good little Arabs should."

"I didn't know there were any 'good little Arabs,'" Boo said with a smile. "Maybe Samir's one. I never claimed it."

"Oh, come," Ray Stanley said. "Don't be disingenuous, Boo. Lots of people at State think Arabs are great and side with them all the time. I've been known to, myself. Anyway, the girls are concerned."

"Did they appoint you their spokesman?" Boo inquired, a slight edge in his voice but still amicable, easygoing Boo. "I think Joanie can speak for herself." He gave a sudden wry grin. "She certainly has on this one."

"So's Bets," Samir echoed with a shy smile that seemed to break his tension a bit. It returned instantly at his father-in-law's next remark.

"Tell me about your little discussion group, Boo," the Secretary suggested. Samir shot a suddenly worried glance at his older friend and tried to cover it, unsuccessfully, by glancing quickly across the river. "What are you plotting?"

"How to blow up Washington," Boo said with amiable scorn. "You know *that*, Ray."

Samir managed a loud, startled laugh and shook his head as if to say, What a joker this Boo is.

"I'm sure," the Secretary said, amused but not quite entirely, looking thoughtfully at his son-in-law. "Nothing would surprise me in this day and age. Aside from that, what?"

"Isn't that enough?" Boo inquired with an easy grin. "No," he said, suddenly serious, "we're just talking, as I've repeatedly told Joanie, and as I'm sure Samir has told Bets." Samir nodded emphatically. "It's quite innocent. After all, there's so much going on in the Middle East—I mean, there always is, but now, what with Sidi and all, it's an even bigger mess than usual." His grin returned. "Us Ay-rabs, we *are* a mess. Aren't we, Samir?"

"That's right," Samir said, nodding vigorously. "A real mess."

"And the visits to the embassy afterwards?" the Secretary inquired casually, watching his son-in-law, who had begun to look increasingly tense again. Samir almost visibly jumped at his words. Boo, as always, remained calm, unruffled, and in command.

"We have our concerns about Sidi, too," he said smoothly, ignoring the fact that their meetings had apparently begun before Sidi's latest eruption on the scene. "He's a bad one, that man. We have to keep an eye on him. We talk about that too."

"And this embassy is planning some anti-Sidi move?" the Secretary inquired, sounding genuinely intrigued and not skeptical at all, though he was, entirely. "That's interesting."

"I'm sure they'll let you know," Boo said seriously. "Isn't that right, Samir?"

"Oh, yes," Samir said earnestly. "Oh, yes, that's right."

"Well, I thank you for clearing that up," the Secretary said, apparently convinced. "It's good to know there's some support being developed for our position on Sidi." He gave them both a confidential smile. "We're going to need it."

"Yes," Boo agreed with an answering, rueful smile. "It shouldn't be that way, it should be easy, he's a *bad* man, but, yes, I think you will need a lot of support. I'm glad we can help," he concluded earnestly. "Right, Samir?"

"Oh, yes," Samir said. "Oh, yes."

"Mary!" the Secretary called. "What's holding you girls up? We're hungry!"

"Coming," she said, as they appeared carrying table settings and the beginnings of food, and the conversation turned general and innocuous. "We want to listen to the man on a full stomach."

At nine P.M. Eastern time, six Pacific, they returned to the living room, turned on the set, settled down with a vast segment of their countrymen and the world's population into the all-embracing arms of CNN. Into focus came an earnest Able Montague, a seemingly relaxed and easy President.

"He looks good," the Secretary noted. "Give 'em hell, partner!"

And by and large, he did.

"Mr. President," Able said, "thank you for being with us. Would you like to make a general statement first, or shall I just plow ahead?"

"'Plow' is not the word for you, Able," the President said with an expansive smile. "First of all, thank you very much for having me on your most distinguished and valuable show. One of our great national treasures, in my estimation."

"As if I would object," Able said with an answering grin. "It's always the thrill of a lifetime to have you on my show."

"The kindness is all yours," the President assured him, passing smoothly over Able's implicit indication that he had asked to be on the program. "It's a great honor for me, a great opportunity to talk to all your vast audience in this country and your vast audience of concerned citizens throughout the world, and to have a chance to put this new crisis in perspective on your justly famous forum."

"A little more of this," Mary murmured, "and Constant Viewer is going to fwow up."

"Hush, Mother," Bets said with a chuckle. "You know how much they both mean it. When two old con artists get together, you know—"

"Disrespectful," her father admonished with mock severity. "Listen to Able, now. He'll jump in with both feet."

"Mr. President," Able said, polite but determined, "why are you so concerned about President Sidi? Why do you think America should be so excited about one who is, after all, a third-rate dictator in a third-rate country a long way away?"

"That," the President said with a comfortable laugh, "is the no-frills way to look at it. It is not, perhaps, the most realistic or the most pertinent to the best interests of this country or to those of a stable, peaceful world. Atomic bombs are not a joke. Long-range missiles are not a joke. Irresponsible dictators in charge of weapons of mass destruction are not a joke. Bloody irresponsible tyrants professing themselves to be completely free of all restraints and completely contemptuous of world opinion and world peace, threatening to destabilize their regions and launch attacks on their neighbors, are the farthest thing from a joke. It seems to me the answer to your question is very clear."

"But why us?" Able inquired, still polite and also still determined—he always was, which was one of his chief strengths as a reporter, he didn't snipe, snarl, confront, or impute in the modern manner. He just asked, politely and persistently.

The President gave him a bland look.

"Why not us?" he responded. "Somebody has to. Who has greater responsibilities in the world?"

"Very true, sir," Able said, "but I'm sure a lot of our countrymen must wonder why the administration—why you—must almost seem to volunteer to be the cop on the beat when Sidi runs amok. Particularly when it is not, you might say, our beat."

"Unhappily for us," the President said, looking genuinely saddened by it, "the whole world seems to have become our beat in recent years. This government is constantly asked to involve itself in many world events far beyond our shores. Many states and nations seem to feel better if we're involved with them in trying to solve major problems that threaten world stability and peace."

Able looked respectfully puzzled.

"Don't some states, sir, sometimes rather resent our involvement? Isn't there occasionally some wish that we would refrain from getting involved in quite so many things? It sometimes seems to me that not a sparrow can fall, not a noticeable event of any prominence can occur anywhere on earth, but what a moral pronouncement doesn't come zinging out of Washington approving, deploring, denouncing, or warning. Other countries don't do this. Why are we always in there sounding off?" He smiled his deprecating, ingenuous smile. "You understand I'm playing the devil's advocate here, but I know it must seem that way to other peoples and probably to a lot of Americans as well. Frankly, it does to me, too."

The President smiled, not at all hard-pressed.

"I appreciate your candor," he said, "and I know that, as always, you speak for an intelligent, informed, and highly responsible segment of opinion here and overseas. In recent years our worldwide responsibilities have seemed to put upon us the burden of furnishing an example, of trying to adhere to certain standards, of trying to further such causes as international stability and the advancement of human rights. Recent administrations have seemed to feel, and I feel, that one way to do this is to make our position very clear on events that seem to be threatening these desirable goals."

Able looked apologetic but soldiered on.

"You don't think this could be regarded as arrogant and overbearing, American ego carried to insufferable extremes? You don't think it arouses more resentment than approval?"

"If no one set a standard," the President said, "if no one enunciated a principle, where would the world be? If there were no one at all to express concern, no one would care about anything. Our efforts are feeble sometimes; perhaps sometimes they may seem a bit egotistical and even overbearing, as you say, but without some attempt to define decent behavior as opposed to bad, what then? Would the world be better off or would it be drifting even further toward the anarchy that threatens in so many places? I submit we have a duty to speak out. I certainly don't intend to shirk it."

"No, sir," Able said with a smile. "That is certainly obvious. . . . What, then, should we do about Sidi? Sanctions? An embargo? Armed conflict? A 'third Gulf war,' as some are already warning us against? How do you answer these critics?"

"Whoa!" the President exclaimed with an easy laugh. "You're throwing too many things at me all at once. Shall I tell you what we should do about Sidi, or do you want me to tell you what I think about those uninformed souls who criticize what seems to me to be the only valid course for a decent man and responsible world leader to follow?"

"Mr. President," Able said with a chuckle, "you do have a way with words. I think you've disposed of your critics in that one well-thought-out sentence with the stinger in its tail. Now, what do you propose to do about Sidi?"

"That's the trouble with you, Able," the President said with a smile he made warm and affectionate. "You're so *persistent*. Which of course is what makes you the great reporter you are. What do I propose to do about Sidi? I propose first to go to the United Nations—"

"Why?" Able interrupted innocently. For just a second the question hung in the air; for just a second the President for the first time looked, fleetingly, a little nonplussed. Recovery was instantaneous though. He laughed again, friendly and intimate.

"There you go again," he remarked. "Because the United Nations is the body through which the United States and all reasonable nations must work in the endless quest for a stable and lasting peace."

"Why?" Able inquired.

The President looked a trifle less chummy but still comfortable and cozy.

"Because that's the way it is," he said. "Isn't it? What other body is there? What other international peace-keeping organization do we have?"

"Some critics might argue," Able said, "that as peace-keeping bodies go, the UN is not the greatest—"

"Human nature," the President interjected blandly. "What is?"

"—and that it has been given undue and perhaps crippling importance in recent administrations by Presidents who either lacked the courage or the foreign policy skills or the simple brains and guts—or maybe all of the above—to chart an independent course for America and then invite the UN to go along—rather than go first to the UN and concede to that fractious and fumbling body the right to tell America what it can or cannot do."

The President chuckled.

"Talk about *me* uttering sentences with stingers in the tail," he said, not at all disturbed or bothered. "I've met my match! I thought you were a great defender of the UN."

"I am," Able said, for the first time pushed a bit on the defensive himself. "As an abstract concept and as an 'all we've got' proposition. Many people here and abroad nowadays seem to feel that recent Presidents have used the UN as a shield to hide behind to conceal their own mental and emotional shortcomings and their inability to think through, and follow, a consistent, broad-gauge, long-range, *American* foreign policy. I take it," he concluded amiably, "that this is not your intention, Mr. President."

"Certainly not," the President said calmly. "Certainly not! I have my own policy, I think, ably aided by a team of top-flight foreign policy advisers including the Secretaries of State and Defense and their staffs, and my national security adviser, Jaime Serrano—"

"All dear friends," Able interjected, "and"—with a twinkle—"all excellent off-the-record news sources, which endears them further to me."

"They aren't supposed to be," the President said with mock sternness. "But I suppose that's Washington. . . . No," he went on more seriously, "I would not readily accept the charge that I am a President who doesn't have a long-range, consistent policy designed to be in America's best interests, because I believe that is what we have. You may not agree, Able, other less objective and disinterested critics may not agree, but that is what I think we have. But I am getting pretty far away from your recent questions. What would I propose to do about Sidi? Go to the United Nations with a request for a strongly worded resolution putting him on notice that unless he abstains from any new attack upon his neighbors, specifically Lesser Lolómé, and agrees to accept inspection of his alleged newfound atomic arsenal by the International Atomic

Energy Agency, he will face sanctions and a most stringent trade embargo."

"And?" Able inquired.

The President looked a little surprised.

"Then we shall see. But I would think the resolution, if strongly enough worded, and strongly enough applied, will be quite sufficient to make him draw in his horns and decide to be a decent, responsible, well-behaved member of the international community."

"No military action, then," Able persisted.

The President smiled.

"I wouldn't want to telegraph *all* our punches, Able, even though you literal-minded members of the media won't rest until you've got us to enunciate and disclose every last possible move we might make on the international chessboard. I'm not threatening military action nor am I ruling it out. Let Sidi guess. Let the media guess." He looked amiable, but for the first time spoke with a certain sting in his voice. "It will do you good."

"It may do us good, Mr. President," Able said, not at all inhibited, "but the question is, will it do Sidi any good? Suppose he continues to defy you despite a UN resolution—what then? Or suppose you can't get the UN to go along with as strong a resolution as you would wish—what then? That may be the likeliest thing. So far there doesn't seem to be any wild scramble of world opinion to come to America's support in this matter. Suppose the UN just balks. Will you apply pressure to get it to support American policy, or will American policy once again be voluntarily subordinated to UN policy because an American President doesn't have the tenacity or the temerity to use the means of persuasion he has?"

"Doesn't have the guts, you mean," the President said with a smile. "Spell it right out, Able. Well, I do."

"So you will insist that the UN pass a strong resolution supporting your policy toward Sidi, no matter what," Able said thoughtfully.

"I don't think insistence on my part will be necessary," the President said comfortably. "Anyway, members have a right to their own opinions and it will have to be a decision of the Security Council based on the unanimous agreement of the five permanent members. I shall use every means at my disposal to persuade them to our point of view, yes. That, it seems to me, is the limit of what I can do. I would hope that would be enough."

"But you're not certain."

"What is certain, in this crazy, mixed-up world?" the President inquired with great good humor. "I'll do my damnedest, you can be sure of that."

"You haven't quite answered me, Mr. President," Able said, "but, then"—he smiled, just on the verge of overly cordial insolence—"I suppose we of the media *do* always look for too many absolutes. It's a tough world. . . . Will China and the S.S.R. veto?"

"The positions of China and the Second Soviet Republic will have to be stated by them," the President said. "I would hope they would agree with the American position. Secretary Stanley has already had substantive talks with all of the other permanent members of the Security Council, and with the Secretary-General, and I think they understand our position." He uttered an amiable laugh. "Isn't it about time to go to questions from the viewers? Haven't you grilled me enough?"

Able laughed too.

"I think we may have stirred up some interest. Fargo, North Dakota, *hello!*"

"Mr. Able," Fargo said, sounding young, a bit intimidated but earnest, "I want to congratulate you on your show. It's always wonderful, and today, with the President on, well, like, wow, it's really great, you know?"

"What's your question, Fargo?" Able inquired, firm but fatherly.

"I'm in the army, Mr. President," Fargo said. "My folks and I want to know, are you going to send me and my buddies to the Gulf to fight old Sidi?"

"Like, wow, man!" the President said with a chuckle. "You speak right out, don't you? You really tell it like it is."

"I hope so, sir," Fargo said earnestly.

"You will go far in this man's army," the President predicted. "But not"—his face and voice became solemn—"*not* as far as Greater Lolómé. You may tell your folks and your buddies from me, Fargo, that I have no intention of sending you or any other American boy or girl to fight old Sidi. That is the farthest thing from my mind. Here and now, I rule out the most obvious military option. There will be no 'third Gulf war.'"

"Thank you, sir," Fargo said fervently. "You've, like, cleared the air for me and my folks and my buddies. We, like, thank you, Mr. President."

"Thank you, Fargo," Able said. His tone became slightly ironic. "I'm sure, Mr. President, that for Fargo and most Americans you have, like, eased a lot of fears. You don't think you have also very substantially eased old Sidi's?"

"Not if Sidi knows what is good for him," the President said crisply. "I wouldn't want anyone to be under any misapprehensions about that."

"But, Mr. President," Able said gently, "how does that jibe with what you just told me a few moments ago?" And he touched a button and produced an instant rerun of the President saying firmly, "I'm not threatening military action nor am I ruling it out."

The President, not at all nonplussed, favored him with a broad smile as the rerun ended and they were back, as Able put it sardonically to himself, from virtual *past* reality to virtual *present* reality.

"Ah," the President said in a fondly chiding tone. "There he goes again, that demon newshawk! You will note that I specifically did not say 'ground troops,' nor did I specify in any way what action might be possible for us. I have, I admit, just ruled out for young Fargo and his parents, and for all other loyal, patriotic American mothers and fathers and their sons or daughters who may be in service, the possibility of *ground* troops in action in Greater Lolómé. But look at all the options! There is air power. There is naval power. There are smart bombs and Patriot missiles. And there are other options too sophisticated and at present too secret for me to divulge. Rest assured, the options are open. Rest assured, also, that it is not intended or even contemplated that any ground troops such as young Fargo and his buddies, both male and female, will be sent to fight in another desert war."

"But there may be young airmen, both male and female [Able could not resist echoing his tone] who may conceivably be at risk if Sidi remains obdurate. To say nothing of young sailors and marines, male and female, who may be equally in harm's way. You would advise them to stand by and be ready for action, Mr. President?"

"Able!" the President said, producing what the media had termed in his predecessor's time the Earnest-Honest Look, straight into the camera. "Able, Able! How you put words in my mouth! I must repeat, I am not threatening military action nor am I ruling it out. It is simply an option. The final decision on what may happen rests with President Sidi. And don't you—or President Sidi—or anyone—but particularly President Sidi—forget that. OK?"

"San Francisco," Able said impassively. A female voice, intense, dedicated, full of Good Thoughts, Love of Humanity, and Endless Devotion to Great Causes, zeroed in from Dreamworld on the Pacific.

"Mr. President!" she said, grim concern for all of poor, suffering humanity in every syllable. "How can you justify an attack on such a small, weak power as Greater Lolómé, which under the enlightened leadership of President Sidi, even though one of the most poverty-stricken nations on earth, with an annual estimated income of only $180 for every man, woman, and child, still has an estimated seventy-five hospitals and clinics in good condition and has achieved one of the highest levels of literacy in the entire area and which, just this past year, was reported to have sixteen libraries containing an estimated 1,230,000 books, serving an eager reading public on one of the most generous schedules of any libraries anywhere, staying open from eight A.M. to ten P.M. with an estimated readership of 500,000 adults and 750,000 children of all ages from grammar school to college or college equivalent?"

"Wow!" the President said with a chuckle. "Lady, your statistics are simply staggering—and, of course, I am sure," he added, expression instantly sober and respectful, "completely accurate. Your assumption that an attack on small, weak Greater Lolómé is either contemplated or imminent, however, is completely mistaken."

"But, Mr. President—" she began.

"Sarajevo, Bosnia," Able said. "Hello!"

"Mr. President," Sarajevo said, "why should we believe you, any more than we had cause to believe your predecessor, when you say America will take firm action against President Sidi? Isn't this one more American bluff destined to become nothing?"

"All I can say," the President replied calmly, "is that I am not my predecessor. All I can say is, wait and see. Look at it again a month from now and tell me if it is a bluff."

"Don't you think, Mr. President," Sarajevo persisted, "that America's reputation for consistency, and America's good faith and integrity, are involved here as much as they were in my own poor country?"

"American consistency, good faith, and integrity are involved in everything I do," the President said, still calmly but with a slight trace of controlled and calculated asperity that came across as completely spontaneous and sincere. "I will not abandon them. I am not concerned with what others have done. My responsibility is now and what I do. I assure my friends in Europe, you need not worry."

"We do," Sarajevo said bleakly. "On the basis of the past, we do."

"Johannesburg, South Africa," Able said. "Hello!"

"Mr. President," said Johannesburg, "would you be as determined to attack President Sidi if his skin were white?"

"Now, see here," the President said, tone suddenly cold and genuinely angry, "stop dragging in tiresome, phony old clichés to confuse the issue. If I have to dignify your question by spelling it out as though you were in grammar school, President Sidi's skin may be darker than mine but unless I much misread your voice, it is still considerably lighter than yours. Right?"

"That is right, man," Johannesburg said.

"Very well," the President said. "Try to be objective, if possible. The answer to your question is yes, I would be as determined to stop President Sidi's dangerous ambitions and his extremely dangerous possession of atomic bombs and delivery system if his skin were white. Is that clear?"

"Clear as mud, *baas*," said Johannesburg, and laughed.

"Baghdad, Iraq," Able said. "Hello! Keep it short, please, we're running out of time."

"Mr. President," said Baghdad, "will America stand firm in this situation? And why do you think it should?"

"America will," the President said flatly. "As to why, because it is in the best interests of the region, and of the world community as well, that President Sidi be restrained from military adventures and that he submit to international inspection of the atomic arsenal he professes to have."

"But it is only a small one," Baghdad observed.

"One bomb in the wrong hands is one too many," the President said.

"And you think too many wrong hands now have too many bombs," Able interjected, "and that is why it is necessary to restrain Sidi, as an example?"

"And as a threat in himself," the President said.

"We do not worry about such things too much over here," Baghdad commented in an indifferent tone.

"No," the President said dryly, "I imagine not. Someone has to act responsibly, however, and that is what I intend for America to do."

"Thank you, Mr. President," Able said smoothly, reaching to shake his hand across the respectful distance that separated their armchairs. "It is always a great pleasure to have you on the program and a great responsibility to be able to transmit your views to our worldwide audience. I trust its members now have a clear picture of where you stand and what you intend to do."

"I hope so," the President said, comfortable smile restored. "It's always my pleasure to bring them to the country and the world through your splendid show." He produced again the Earnest-Honest Look, straight into the camera. "I hope our viewers do understand now where we stand in this latest crisis to threaten the peace and stability of the world. Firmness without belligerence, is our policy. Strength through diplomacy. Peace by peaceful means."

"Yes, sir," Able said pleasantly. "I am sure that is all very clear now. . . ." His face suddenly crinkled with the pixieish little smile with which he couldn't help telegraphing his punches when he thought he had his targets sufficiently relaxed. "By the way, Mr. President, one last question before we close—"

"Fire away," the President said comfortably, though with a slight wariness in voice and expression. "Knowing you, Able, it will probably be a last-minute zinger."

"No, sir," Able said, smile broadening into a grin. "Hardly that. However—"

"I knew it," the President said.

Able laughed, then turned serious.

"You probably didn't notice, sir, but just a moment ago they put on the little screen that I have inset in my desk here the results of four major polls that are being released for use in tomorrow morning's papers. There are slight variations, but overall they show an overwhelming public sentiment that Sidi is not worth a major American effort. The highest figure supporting your position is only 17 percent nationwide, and only 4 percent in all four polls approve of any kind of military action. When the question is put negatively, a very emphatic 63 percent—as high as 71 in one poll—are strongly opposed to the use of any kind of American force, ground or otherwise, in any confrontation with President Sidi. How does that jibe with your own position, sir?"

"Well, in the first place," the President said calmly, "the sound instinct of the American people is always against the use of force and, insofar as possible, for the use of peaceful diplomacy. These positions coincide with my own. I thought I had made that quite clear."

"Well, sir," Able said politely, "not quite. You are prepared to abide by these popular sentiments, then?"

"Sentiments change," the President observed. "The opinions may be different after the public fully understands the issues involved."

"As a general rule," Able said, "you do not think a President should be bound by the sentiments of his countrymen when they conflict with his own informed view of what is best for America?"

"I didn't say that," the President said, patience beginning to sound a little thin.

"There are some who would say that was leadership, sir," Able pointed out, still politely. "To do what one believes as President is best for the country, and to educate and lead rather than consult the polls and follow. Or, as some might see it, consult the polls and retreat."

"I'm not retreating," the President said sharply.

"So we can expect, then," Able said gently, "that you will continue to pursue your policy toward Sidi on all fronts irrespective of what public opinion may be in this country, is that correct?"

"Consistent with the best interests of America and the best interests of world stability," the President said finally. "Always consistent with those. The country will have to be the final judge of the wisdom of my course. I think I have made my position abundantly and completely clear."

"Yes, sir," Able said pleasantly. "I think you have. Let us hope so."

And again they shook hands and faded, a little more obviously wary of each other now, from the screen.

"Well," the Secretary said as he switched off the set, "what do you think?"

"Clear as mud, *baas*," Boo Bourassa said with a grin. "Clear as mud. Is this the policy you helped formulate, Ray?"

"He wants to keep his options open," the Secretary replied, rather lamely.

"He lost me somewhere along the line," Mary said. "But, then, he always does. So what else is new?"

"First he rules out the military option," Joan Bourassa summarized, "then he reinstates it sans ground troops, then he waffles on other military means, then he winds up reaffirming a strong stand—almost. Or did he? He's got me confused, that's for sure."

"He wants everybody to be confused," Bets remarked. "Maybe it's all part of his strategy to keep Sidi off base. Is that it, Daddy?"

"As I understand him," Ray said carefully, "it is supposed to confuse Sidi."

Boo snorted. Samir nodded solemnly in agreement.

"It sure confuses me," Boo said. "How does he get away with things like that?"

"Presidents who have mastered the art of saying contradictory things with a straight face can get away with almost anything," Mary observed. "The public is so impressed with a President who is Just Like One of Us"—her capitals were verbal but emphasized and sarcastic—"that when he apparently stumbles a bit in a human fashion, it is shrugged off and forgiven and forgotten. They don't realize that sometimes behind the stumbling and bumbling a careful strategy is being put in place. Boo has a good question, Ray. Is this the policy you've advocated in your private talks with him?"

"They *are* private," the Secretary remarked.

Bets laughed.

"Which means he'll tell you later, Mother. Not in front of the children. Aren't you going to call and congratulate him, Daddy? Isn't that what faithful Secretaries of State are supposed to do?"

"I'll get to it," her father said. "Don't rush me." He was starting to add, "Would anybody like a nightcap?" when the phone rang.

"Don't call me," Boo said wryly. "I'll call you."

But it wasn't the President. It was Hugo Mallerbie at State. His voice was grave.

"An urgent call for you, Ray," he said.

An almost incoherent Big Bill Bullock was on the line from Greater Lolómé City.

Next morning the President had his headlines. But he had to share them.

Lead item, all news programs, right-hand column, page 1, all major newspapers:

———

239

PRESIDENT RULES OUT TROOPS AGAINST SIDI, CALLS FOR UN SANCTIONS IF HE REFUSES TO PERMIT ATOMIC INSPECTIONS

Second-lead item, all news programs, adjoining right-hand column, page 1, all major newspapers:

SIDI BOOTS U.S. EMBASSY, MASSES TROOPS ON BORDER, DEFIES BOMB INSPECTIONS, RAPS "PUNY U.S. THREATS"

Almost a decade of American retreats from firm positions, of loud American threats followed by hesitant American actions, were coming home to roost.

Deeply aware of his responsibilities, the Secretary wondered how he and the President would handle things now.

Somehow the world must be reconvinced that American words were backed by strong and unwavering American purpose; somehow the world must be induced to care again about what America said.

He hoped devoutly that it could be done.

He hoped, devoutly, that it was not already too late.

FOUR

1   The winds of spring blew along the East River, softening the memories of another harsh winter, bringing to the denizens of the great, tumultuous, contentious, impatient, impolite, cruel, and exciting city the revival of spirits, the encouragement of hope.

Against their better judgment, for the brightening season had much to do with the steadily growing chaos of the world—it was, as the Italian ambassador put it with urbane realism, "perfect killing weather everywhere"—the delegates to the United Nations entered in almost cheerful mood their vaguely phallic buildings, the Secretariat rising straight and rigid against the sky, the rounded contour of the Security Council and General Assembly bulging below.

It never took long for their illusory cheerfulness to dissipate, as all the problems of a global society racing headlong to chaos crowded in on them. They knew their efforts were at best feeble, their capabilities minuscule when measured against the enormity of the peace-keeping tasks they faced.

"Yet we must *try*, we must *try*," the elderly ambassador of Norway, this month's Security Council president, could always be counted on to admonish earnestly in moments of disillusion and despair.

"It is our responsibility, yes!" the plump little female ambassador of Pakistan could always be counted on to support him, with equal earnestness.

Arriving for the opening of the Security Council debate on "The Matter of Greater Lolómé," the U.S. Secretary of State and the Deputy Secretary paused for a moment in the lobby to contemplate the two-hundred-pound, gold-plated Foucault Pendulum given by the Dutch, which hangs from the ceiling on its seventy-five-foot stainless-steel wires and slowly, endlessly swings back and forth across a metal ring below, in response to the rotation of the earth.

Engraved on the pedestal supporting the ring are the words of Queen Juliana on the occasion when the pendulum was presented to the United Nations:

It is a privilege to live this day and tomorrow.

"How like the Dutch," Eulie Montgomery murmured, "to remind us always of how petty we are in the face of the forces of nature."

"That's nothing compared to how petty we are in the face of the forces of *human* nature," the Secretary responded glumly. He gave her a shrewd look. "How are you doing? Seriously, now. You didn't have to come with me, you know. I'll send you home in a minute if it gets too much for you."

"I'm fine," Eulie said stoutly, though her eyes for the time being filled with tears at the slightest show of kindness, the slightest tone of sympathy. "I'll get over this. It comes and goes."

"But mostly comes," Ray Stanley said. "It was only last Saturday after all, and this is Friday. You shouldn't have forced yourself."

"It was a beautiful funeral," she said firmly, "and everybody came. He would have been very pleased. I was very pleased. And now back to work. It's the only way."

"You're quite a gal, Eulie Montgomery," he said.

"They say I'm tough," she said with a wan little wryness that touched his heart. "But I'm not. I just rise above, rise above . . ." She dabbed vigorously at her eyes, blew her nose, shook her head in annoyance with herself. "Enough of that. Don't try to make me weak, now. We have a lot to do here."

"I wouldn't dream of it," he said with a smile. "We need all the strength we can muster."

"Particularly since we don't know what our marching orders are," she remarked, as the ambassadors of Malawi and Romania walked by together and bowed. "Or do we?"

"Pretty much as he outlined on Able's program," the Secretary said, taking her arm as they joined the growing crowd of delegates, staff, and public moving along to the Council chamber. "An admonition to Sidi to back off—an insistence that he permit the International Atomic Energy Agency to inspect his atomic weapons, if any—and sanctions if he balks."

"He's already balked, hasn't he?" she inquired dryly. "I don't know how much balkier he could get."

"The President obviously hopes a strong resolution here will give him pause."

"Is that all," she demanded, "'give him pause'? That doesn't seem a very strong approach, to me. Nor does it seem a very strong resolution if it's only going to 'admonish,' as you say. You're backsliding, Ray. What's been going on in the department while I've been away?"

"I can only move as fast as he will let us," he said, lowering his voice as they entered the chamber and immediately became the focus of intense delegate and media attention. "And we can't push too strongly here, as you know."

"Why the hell not?" she responded, maintaining a fixed smile but speaking in an intense whisper. "This pack of second-rate scum-bums just out of the jungle, plundering and slaughtering their own peoples all over the continent of Africa! What are we afraid of?"

"I'm glad you said that," he whispered back with a chuckle, "and not me, because I couldn't. Nor could you, publicly. And of course there are many who don't warrant your kind description."

"Oh, of course not," she said impatiently. "But I do get fed up with them."

"Control yourself if I ask you to speak, please," he urged, not entirely in jest. "We need the votes."

She nodded and moved along to the seats of the U.S. delegation at the big round table, with its space in the center for secretaries and stenographers, which houses the Security Council in public session. Most of their work nowadays was done off-camera in a private conference room off the Council lounge, but the public didn't know that. The public wanted a show, and most of the delegates wanted to give them one, so the preliminary skirmishing on The Matter of Greater Lolómé would occur here. What Big Bill Bullock described as "the real nut-cutting" would come in the conference room later.

He was already in a chair behind the Secretary's, looking rumpled and tired from his two-day journey from Greater Lolómé but as combative as ever. He jumped up and greeted Eulie with a big hug when she came along to take a seat beside him.

"How ya doin', babe?" he inquired, trying to be simultaneously jovial and sympathetic.

"Nobody's called me 'babe,'" she said, with what began as a smile but instantly became tears, "since—since—"

"Oh, hell, I'm sorry," he said, looking stricken himself. "I didn't mean to—"

"No, no," she said firmly, sitting down beside him and patting his arm. "No, it's my fault. I'm still a little—a little rocky, I guess."

"And understandably so," he said. He lowered his voice and became determinedly brisk. "So what's going to happen here today, anyway? Are we going to get clobbered?"

"I don't think so," she said, accepting the diversion gratefully. "I think we'll get pretty much what we want. If we fight for it."

"Exactly," he said. "And what is it we want? And how hard is he going to let us fight for it?"

"Ray is talking about 'admonishing' Sidi," she said, trying to be dutiful but unable to keep concern out of her voice. "That doesn't sound like much of a fight to me."

"Hell, no," the ambassador said, forgetting for a moment to keep his voice down, lowering it hastily when he became aware that the ambassador of Zimbabwe, nearby, was glancing curiously their way. "That bloody murdering son of a bitch is going to take more than 'admonishing,' I think. We've got to tromp all over him."

"I agree," she said, "but can we get them to do that here?"

The ambassador frowned.

"We can if the President will really let Ray put on the pressure. But will he? That is the question."

"I think Ray would like to," she said, and they both looked thoughtfully for a moment at the Secretary, who had paused near the door to greet with great cordiality the ambassadors of Ecuador and Argentina, entering together. "But, you're right: will he be allowed to? He isn't sounding very positive."

"Sh—ucks!" Bill Bullock said, amending himself in mid-expletive. "Do you know what I think about that guy in the White House, Eulie? He's a coward."

"Shhh," she admonished, glancing about with a determinedly comfortable smile at the curious faces studying them. "Keep it down, Bill. But you're right, I think. It's perhaps the worst legacy of Vietnam. The Soviet Union won a greater triumph than they perhaps ever imagined, when they supported the Vietcong. They left us with a new generation of military leaders, and a new generation of Presidents, who are scared to death of using American power."

"They'll be the death of us yet," Bill Bullock predicted gloomily.

"Oh, I hope not," she said with a laugh that was designed for public consumption; underneath, as he knew, she was as worried as he was. "We'll see. He may have more guts than we think."

"Hmph!" the ambassador snorted. "All I can say is, hmph!"

"What are you two cooking up?" the Secretary inquired as he took his seat at the table and swung around to clap Bill Bullock on the knee and give Eulie's hand a squeeze. "Something subversive, I'll bet."

"Bill was just outlining our program here for me," she said with a smile. "He says we've got to tromp all over Sidi."

"Wouldn't I like to," Ray Stanley said. "Wouldn't I like to!"

"Well—?" Bill Bullock inquired.

Ray shook his head and waved an admonitory finger.

"Diplomacy, diplomacy! We can't be quite as tough as Texas here."

"A damned shame," the ambassador observed. "Having just had to scramble like hell to get everybody out of Greater Lolómé safe and sound and in one piece, I'm not in much mood for diplomacy."

For the time being, however, things proceeded with reasonable decorum as the Secretary-General bustled about getting everybody settled, finally persuading Norway to call the meeting to order, in typical UN fashion, almost an hour after the scheduled time of three P.M. Kwazz ("KWA-zee Koom-BAH-tah") had chosen to dress today, as he sometimes did on occasions when he expected to be in the public eye, in the full regalia of a minor Zulu chief, which he was. This made him a dazzling figure in the midst of the soberly dressed delegates who, with the exceptions of Kuwait in flowing white and gold, and Zimbabwe, also tribal, were in Western business suits. Ray thought of the President's comment on Kwazz—"He's a flouncer"—and reflected that so he was, but today he was doing it in style.

"The Council," Norway said in his politely tentative voice, "will be in order. The Council is now seized of The Matter of Greater Lolómé. The chair recognizes the delegate of the United States."

"Mr. President," the Secretary began quietly, "first I wish to express my appreciation for the consistently excellent work of the permanent

United States ambassador to the United Nations, the Hon. Rufus B. Birdwell." He turned and bowed to the elderly little figure, looking as always anxious, earnest, gray-faced, and more dead than alive, who had unobtrusively taken his seat beside Eulie as the gavel came down; a former Secretary of State himself, of the Milquetoast persuasion; a leftover, a political debt of the President's, moderately helpful within the limits of his modest abilities.

"Normally he would have presented the American case to you. However, because of the great gravity which the President of the United States attaches to this matter, he has asked me to come before you to present the facts which we believe make imperative strong and decisive action against an international renegade who now threatens the peace of his own region and, indirectly but most inescapably, that of the world community as well."

And he proceeded, in ten minutes and several thousand well-chosen words, to lay out the reasoning behind "the proposed resolution offered by the United States, which has been circulated to you all and which you now have before you." He concluded his presentation, and prepared to read the text.

A hush fell on the Council, on the media, and on the visiting members of the public, who sat in the tiers of seats rising upward from the round table with earphones adjusted and expressions intent. Proceedings today were being rendered by the UN's corps of skilled translators into English, French, Chinese, Russian, and, as a concession to subject matter, Arabic.

"Whereas," he read in a firm and steady voice, "the President of Greater Lolómé has announced his intention to war upon a fellow member of the United Nations, his neighbor Lesser Lolómé; and,

"Whereas, he has announced that he has received, from a source or sources presently unknown, an indeterminate number of atomic bombs and the long-range missiles with which to deliver them, and has threatened to use them upon a target or targets presently unknown if he decides to engage in hostilities; and,

"Whereas, this would pose the gravest possible threat to the peace and stability of his own region and of the world community as a whole; and,

"Whereas, he has violated all norms of civilized conduct between sovereign nations by ordering the murder of a member of the United States embassy staff in Greater Lolómé, and has summarily expelled all other members of the United States embassy staff; now, therefore,

"Be it resolved:

"That the Security Council deplores and denounces the use of force by neighbor upon neighbor; is alarmed and greatly concerned by the alleged proliferation of atomic weapons and missiles in the hands of Greater Lolómé; and deplores and denounces the cruel and shameless violation of civilized relations between sovereign states demonstrated by the murder of Creed Moncrief, a member of the United States embassy in Greater Lolómé, and by the subsequent expulsion of the entire United States embassy staff from that country;

"That the Security Council demands that Greater Lolómé desist forthwith from any further aggressive gestures or actions toward its neighbor or neighbors; that Greater Lolómé, a signatory of the international nuclear nonproliferation treaty, abide by that treaty and permit immediate inspection of its alleged nuclear weapons and facilities by the International Atomic Energy Agency; and that Greater Lolómé enter immediately into negotiations with the United States looking toward adequate compensation for the family of Creed Moncrief.

"On penalty of Security Council response, including the imposition of sanctions and such other measures as the Security Council may deem sufficient, unless this resolution is promptly honored by Greater Lolómé."

He concluded and looked gravely around the table, expression bland but inner thought specific: *Which one of you ornery bastards is going to challenge us first?* As he had anticipated, Vladimir Novotny, always anxious to needle the United States, raised his hand. The Secretary was pleased to note that many members had acted upon the President's suggestion that they send their top people to this debate. It showed some respect for the U.S. evaluation of the matter's gravity even if it did not necessarily mean success for the U.S. position.

"Mr. President," Vladimir said, broad, pugnacious face challenging and combative, "if I may inquire: what does the distinguished Secretary of State of the United States think can be gained by the tone of his proposed resolution at this date, when the President of Greater Lolómé has already, in effect, defied any action the Security Council may take?

What is the point of all this? What purpose does the Secretary and his government think can be served by—"

"Mr. President," Ray Stanley interrupted calmly, "if the distinguished delegate of the Second Soviet Republic is going to indulge in an ad hominem attack upon me personally, then I think he will be wasting the time of the Council. I am sorry he has such obvious personal worries and tensions in the matter."

"I am not engaging in ad hominem argument!" Vladimir Novotny said indignantly. "I am addressing the issues! I am perfectly at ease, I will say to the Secretary! I am not tense at all!"

"Well," Ray said in a fatherly tone he knew would annoy, "I think we had better try to stick to the substance of the resolution, nonetheless. I can understand the delegate's intemperate attitude, Mr. President—"

Vladimir looked as though he might explode, round face flushed and exasperated—"but if we can stick to the point it will permit us to move along with our very serious task here, and not go on all day picking nits."

"Picking nits?" the *Times* murmured to the *Globe* in the media gallery. "Who's picking?"

"Picking noses, is more like it," the *Globe* said in a tired tone. "Stanley can only do what he's told to do, that's the problem. Apparently that's why he's so aggressive all of a sudden, which isn't his normal operating procedure. The President wants action now."

"Or does he?" the *Times* wondered wryly. "I'm not so sure in this case."

Nor was the Secretary; but he pushed on firmly despite his private doubts, being not the first Secretary of State nor the last to proceed with outward confidence and inward uncertainty about the real intentions of his employer in the White House.

He ignored a further splutter from Vladimir, caught the eye of the Secretary-General, and unobtrusively raised the index finger of his right hand, the signal they had agreed upon for a requested adjournment. Kwazz billowed over, robes flashing, to Norway, bent down to whisper in that earnest oldster's ear, and billowed back to his seat.

"Mr. President," Ray Stanley said, "I move that this public session of the Council be adjourned to eight P.M. tonight."

There were exclamations of surprise around the table and in the media, some movements of protest among the delegates. Li Peng Liu, obviously annoyed, raised his hand.

"Mr. President!" he said sharply. "This seems most irregular to China. I must protest this attempt by the United States to shut off democratic debate. We object, Mr. President!"

"We most strenuously object, Mr. President!" Vladimir Novotny echoed angrily. "It is typical of high-handed U.S. practices. It is dictatorial! It is undemocratic! I demand a vote on the motion of the United States delegate!"

"Is it the wish of delegates—?" Norway inquired hesitantly, uttering a nervous little cough and clearing his throat. "The chair must point out that this will be a vote on a procedural matter which, unlike matters of substance, can be decided by simple majority with the concurrence of the five permanent members. In other words, the veto will not apply." He peered over his glasses at China and the S.S.R. "Is that agreeable to delegates?"

"A voice vote will suffice," Li said quickly before Vladimir, looking disgruntled, could respond.

"Mr. President," Ray Stanley said calmly, "the United States asks for a roll-call vote."

"Yes," Norway said. "Well." He peered about, found no support for further delay, cleared his throat again. "Will the Secretary-General be so good as to call the roll."

"Argentina!" Kwazze Kumbatta said in his deep, resounding voice. "Belgium! . . . Ecuador!" By the time he had concluded with "Zimbabwe!" the result was overwhelming: ten members of the Council in favor, China, the S.S.R., France, Pakistan, and Romania in opposition.

"Not so good if it had been substantive," Bill Bullock murmured to Eulie, who looked worried but shrugged.

"We'll see," she said. "There are leverages . . . if we use them."

"Exactly so," Bill Bullock said. "Exactly so."

"The Council," Norway said obediently, "will stand in recess until eight P.M." Kwazze, who had come to sit beside him during the vote, murmured again in his ear. "It is suggested," he added, "in the interests of adhering to a reasonable schedule for this evening, that delegates might be willing to forgo any social engagements they might have and repair to the conference room, where a light supper will be served to those who desire it."

This was another understood signal: time for a private session. Time for nut-cutting, as Bill Bullock described it.

251

The few faithful members of the public still present looked puzzled and disappointed but went dutifully away. The media, whose members also understood the signals, looked annoyed but had no choice but to go away with the rest, grumbling. The only consolation was that they would have time for a really good dinner somewhere in Manhattan before being recalled to duty.

"And it really doesn't matter, anyway," the *Times* remarked. "We all have our sources. We'll get to them later."

Knowing delegates' love for the limelight and their eagerness to stay on the good side of the media, he and his colleagues laughed and looked less annoyed.

Fifteen minutes later, refreshed by trips to the rest rooms, the Council reconvened in the drably utilitarian private conference room off the lounge. There was indeed a light buffet available; delegates carried sandwiches and coffee to their seats around the horseshoe-shaped table that substituted here for the round table of the public chamber. Brown leather armchairs soothed diplomatic bottoms. Fifty-five straight-backed blue chairs ringed the walls, accommodating aides, two per country, UN staffers, and special guests, among them Eulie Montgomery and Bill Bullock. The atmosphere was comfortable, informal, and intimate. The nut-cutting began.

Again Vladimir Novotny was first off the mark.

"Mr. President," he said, still looking annoyed, "when I was so rudely interrupted, I was interrogating the Secretary of State." His tone became emphatic, he looked defiantly at Ray Stanley. "I shall do so again."

"Please do," Ray said, barely looking up from the sandwich he was demolishing. "I'm ready."

"If I may repeat," Vladimir said sternly, "what does the distinguished Secretary of State of the United States think can be gained by the tone of his proposed resolution, at this date, when the President of Greater Lolómé has already, in effect, defied any action the UN might take? Why should we not make the threat valid and impose sanctions immediately or, in contrast, not bother to threaten at all? The first course would leave no mistaking the Security Council's intentions. The latter would at least relieve us of the embarrassment of another overt defiance by President Sidi. What is the United States attempting to achieve here? My government is puzzled. We are also puzzled by the United States' language, to wit, Sidi's 'alleged' bombs. Is the U.S. conceding that we do not actually know that he has them?"

"The delegate perhaps knows more about that than we do," Ray Stanley said, ignoring Vladimir's immediate indignant reaction. "The ignorance of the Council—or most of the Council—as to the truth of President Sidi's boast is the reason why the resolution demands that the IAEA be empowered to investigate. I am surprised at the delegate's reasoning—or lack of it, rather."

"Well, Mr. President," Vladimir said, face flushing, while Norway as usual looked flustered by any show of asperity among his fractious colleagues. "I shall not dignify the Secretary's completely spurious and offensive slur upon my country, but will simply say that it is the logic of the United States which must be justified here, not mine. The U.S. obviously wishes us to force Sidi to accept IAEA inspection and thereby, he hopes, support for the United States' obvious desire to take punitive action against the President of Greater Lolómé. He has no proof and no justification so he would send the IAEA to find proof and justification. It is a rather backward way to proceed, it seems to this delegation."

"Mr. President," Georges Marranne said, peering about at his most turtle-like, "my government to a considerable extent agrees with the contention of the delegate of the Second Soviet Republic concerning the rather reverse procedure proposed by the United States. However, we can also appreciate the need to secure some definite knowledge of what atomic weapons, if any, are now in the possession of President Sidi. And how else to do it, than through the International Atomic Energy Agency?"

"I wonder, Mr. President," Tony Marsden said, "what inspires the delegate of the United States to think that the IAEA will be permitted by President Sidi to conduct an inspection with a freedom that will guarantee accuracy? We have had experience in the past, North Korea for instance, in which the IAEA inspections were constantly blocked and obstructed and were not allowed to achieve any trustworthy results. What makes anyone think that inspection of Greater Lolómé will proceed any more smoothly or accurately than similar inspections of recalcitrant states in the past? Her Majesty's Government is thoroughly sympathetic to the proposed objective of the government of the United States, but how is it to be achieved in a fashion we can believe in?"

"That is why we propose sanctions for noncompliance," Ray Stanley said.

"And what makes the Secretary think that the threat of sanctions, or sanctions themselves, will be any more effective with President Sidi than they have been with anyone else?" Pakistan's plump little lady inquired. "It is more of the sameness. Sanctions hurt people, not leaders. President Sidi's people would be hurt, not President Sidi."

Kuwait's princeling spoke up with a wry expression.

"He does not seem the slightest bit uneasy," he said. "We are another of his neighbors, and we have never observed the slightest degree of either conscience or unease. Kuwait is inclined to agree with the S.S.R., Mr. President, why not impose sanctions immediately and argue about it later? It is the only language he understands."

"We cannot act on mere assumption of guilt," Li Peng Liu said sternly. "There must be an action before we can respond. Otherwise it becomes entirely illegal and unwarranted on our part and exceedingly beyond any mandate conferred upon or illegally appropriated to itself by this body."

"So we pass my resolution," the Secretary of State suggested calmly, "and see what happens."

"On the assumption of guilt," Li said.

The Secretary shrugged.

"Assumption or presumption. They aren't valid, in your view?"

"They have not occurred," Li said, still sternly unamused. "We do not have proof—"

"We can wrangle on that point all night," the Secretary snapped, suddenly fed up and with a rare public impatience. "Mr. President, I suggest we get on with it!"

"Mr. President," Li said angrily, "one does not lecture the People's Republic, which has more than one billion people and at least five thousand years of history, as though we were schoolboys. Some of your Presidents have been immature enough to try that. It does not work. I shall proceed in my own way and in my own time. The delegate of the United States may withdraw from the debate if its pace does not please him."

"Get on with it," the Secretary repeated, in a tired tone, with a tired wave of the hand. "Get on with it for all our sakes, please. Incidentally," he added, leaning forward with a sudden intent interest that brought an immediate hush, "perhaps the delegate of the People's Republic after all *is* the one who can tell us whether President Sidi's boast of atomic weapons is true. Perhaps the delegate knows more than the rest of us do whether Greater Lolómé has actually received atomic bombs from some kindly supplier. They must have come from somewhere, Mr. President. Could the delegate of the People's Republic tell us where he thinks that was?"

"Mr. President," Vladimir Novotny cried before a suddenly white-faced Li could muster his indignation and reply, "China is the second state whom the delegate of the United States has accused here of furnishing atomic bombs to Greater Lolómé." He looked about the table, expression as tight and bitter as his Chinese colleague's. "Does anyone else wish to qualify? Welcome to anyone!"

"Mr. President," Tony Marsden said with a fatherly air into the angry silence that ensued, "this is not advancing our consideration of the resolution. My delegation regards Greater Lolómé's possession of atomic capability as indeed the gravest possible threat, and not only to his own region but to the world community as well, just as the United States contends. If any delegation wishes to suggest other language, let its representative bring the language forward and present it to us."

"Very well!" Vladimir said triumphantly. He shuffled among his notes, held up a heavily scribbled piece of paper, and began to read:

"Whereas, the Council notes the claim of the President of Greater Lolómé that his country may have a small, undetermined number of atomic bombs and the missiles with which to deliver them; and,

"Whereas, if true, this might conceivably pose a threat to world peace if the President of Greater Lolómé were to employ these weapons irresponsibly; now, therefore,

"Be it resolved, that the Council urges the President of Greater Lolómé, in the interests of peaceable relations with other states, to disclose whether or not he does indeed possess atomic weapons and missiles and, if so, to assure the Council that he does not intend to use them in a hostile fashion against any state.

"The delegation of the S.S.R.," Vladimir concluded with satisfaction, "thinks that this is perfectly reasonable language which adequately covers the situation faced by the Council."

"Mr. President," Ray Stanley said, "the United States objects to the gently absolving language proposed by the Second Soviet Republic. In effect it removes all responsibility from the shoulders of President Sidi. In effect it relegates his possession of atomic weaponry to the realm of kindly maybe's and could-be's. In effect it tells the world that this Council is not really much concerned about it. In effect it weakens this Council still further as a world peace-keeping body. Aren't we weak enough already?" He leaned back, one elbow resting on an arm of his chair, the other hand resting on the other arm, and looked with deliberate exasperation around the table. "Think about it!"

"We have thought about it," Li Peng Liu said coldly. "Mr. President, China seconds the language offered by the Second Soviet Republic and requests an immediate vote."

"Roll call, Mr. President," Georges Marranne suggested.

"Second that," Tony Marsden said.

For a second the Secretary of State obviously contemplated raising hell; as obviously rejected it; shrugged and nodded.

"Second also, Mr. President," he said. And added, interrupting Kwazze Kumbatta just as he prepared to launch himself into another sonorous roll call, "Parliamentary point, Mr. President. I would remind the Council that this is a substantive matter. The veto applies."

Norway looked perturbed. Others looked upset. There was a silence.

"Mr. President," Pakistan said finally, "it seems to my delegation that unless the Council wishes to commit itself immediately to an all-out confrontation with Greater Lolómé, with all that entails in the way of agitating the world and the media, then we should think most carefully about our language. My delegation is inclined to agree with the delegate of the Second Soviet Republic. We think his language is sufficient to cover the situation as it exists now. We can always meet later to take further steps if that should be necessary."

"We are always having second-thought meetings, Mr. President," Belgium said wearily. "It grows tiresome."

"Tiresome or no," Pakistan's lady said with some spirit, "it is better than rushing headlong to inflame situations that might be better left untroubled, is it not?"

"Atom bombs in the hands of a lawless international renegade is a situation that can be described as 'untroubled'?" Ray Stanley inquired of no one in particular. "Well, well."

"I have requested a roll call," Georges Marranne reminded. "The Secretary of State is right. The matter is substantive. The veto applies."

"The Secretary-General will call the roll," Norway said.

By the time the vote got to the United States, all ten of the nonpermanent members had voted for it, many of them simply because it seemed the easiest way out at a late hour; of the five permanent members, China and the S.S.R. had voted for it. France and the U.K., after several moments of thought and some show of reluctance, finally said, "Abstain."

The Secretary of State also made a show of thought and reluctance, turning to Eulie and Bill Bullock and pulling them into a confidential huddle with his arms around their shoulders while he whispered, "That's a good-looking dress you've got on, Eulie," and "Hang in there, Bill, we'll be out of here soon and you can get to bed." Both winked and muttered something innocuous in return. He whispered, "I think I'll save the veto for the whole shebang when we get back into public session."

His whisper turned suddenly serious.

"Do you realize," he murmured, "that Novotny forgot to offer his language as an amendment? As it stands, it's separate and unrelated."

Eulie looked pleased and Bill Bullock grinned.

"Don't anybody breathe," he urged with a gleeful relish. "*Don't anybody breathe.*"

And nobody did; and for some reason, nobody caught on; and the American delegation felt for the moment that it was in better shape than it had thought it was.

The Secretary turned back with a cheerful smile to the room, which had begun to murmur with interest at the little American confab.

"Mr. President," he said, "the United States will not veto. The United States abstains."

"The language of the delegate of the Second Soviet Republic is agreed to," Norway said in a tone of obvious relief that prompted amusement.

One other pitched battle occurred when China and the S.S.R., joined with some reluctance by France and Britain, moved successfully to delete the language of the American resolution referring to the murder of Creed Moncrief, the ouster of the U.S. embassy from Greater Lolómé, and the demand for compensation to Creed's family.

"With all respects," Tony Marsden summed up, "it does seem to this delegation, and obviously to others, that the United States is attempting to use the United Nations as a medium for the redress of its own grievances. It seems to us that such matters should better be left to direct negotiations between the United States and Greater Lolómé. We would hope the United States would not insist on this language. It seems that the United States is attempting to establish a whole new area of UN concern, as if"—he smiled placatingly at the Americans, who did not look impressed—"the UN did not have problems enough."

"It is all part and parcel of the same package, Mr. President," Ray Stanley said, unamused. "It seems to the United States that it would be good for the UN to strike a blow for civilized intercourse between nations—there is so little of it left anymore. However," he added matter-of-factly, "it is obvious there is not sufficient sentiment in the Council at this time for such a declaration of purpose or accretion of responsibility, so my delegation will withdraw that part of the proposed United States resolution. You all," he predicted dryly, "will regret it sometime in the future when it gets to be your turn somewhere around the world, but if nobody wants to bite the bullet with us, we will not insist."

"These delightful Americanisms!" Georges Marranne exclaimed with a chuckle.

They returned to the public chamber, somewhat bleary-eyed, shortly before ten P.M. Aided by assorted miracles of the electronic age, the UN secretarial staff had copies of the American and Soviet proposals printed and ready at their seats.

"What a crock!" Bill Bullock murmured to Eulie as they resumed their seats behind the Secretary.

She smiled grimly.

"You can be thankful this isn't taking place while actual bloodshed is going on. There have been times when literally hundreds of thousands of people have died while the UN wrangled over points like these."

"God help us," Bill Bullock growled in disgust.

She smiled a wry smile.

"Sorry," she said. "He isn't on any of the delegations. He doesn't have a vote."

"The Secretary-General," Norway directed, "will read the proposals before the Council."

"Mr. President," Kwazze said, obviously relishing the way his resonant voice boomed around the room and surged through the earphones (most volume controls were hastily turned down), "the texts of the two proposals are as follows—"

"The cancer is in the language," Eulie had remarked to Eldridge Barnes at the President's press conference ten days ago; and after it had metastasized its way through UN hesitations, doubts, and timidities, both proposals were subtly different, subtly weaker, subtly "acceptable" in a way they had not been before.

Kwazze concluded, Vladimir immediately raised his hand.

"Mr. President," he said loudly, "I request a vote on my proposal."

"That is quite agreeable to the United States," Ray Stanley said. "I would point out that this is now a substantive matter, therefore the veto applies. I ask for a roll call, Mr. President."

But it was not to be, quite yet. The tiny red light, concealed under the edge of the desk and visible only to the occupant of the chief delegate's chair, blinked on. The Secretary picked up his special phone; a familiar voice was on the line. Ray's face was impassive, but Eulie, who knew him better than anyone outside his family, saw the familiar tracery of tension in his jaw.

"Mr. President," he said calmly to Norway, "I ask for a recess for fifteen minutes."

"Mr. President," Vladimir cried indignantly, "it is approaching eleven o'clock. We have been here a long time. Is the delegate of the United States going to insist—"

"Fifteen minutes, Mr. President," Ray Stanley said, picked up his copies of the resolutions, nodded to Eulie and Bill Bullock to follow, and stalked out of the chamber.

"Well," Norway said uncertainly; then capitulated in a small, flustered voice. "Well, under the circumstances . . . the Council stands adjourned until eleven-thirty."

"My God," the Times said to the Post. "What now?"

"Big Brother in Washington has been watching C-Span," the *Post* said dryly. "Last-minute instructions for the Secretary."

"Veto the bastards—or, saved by the bell?" the *Times* wondered with a chuckle.

"Whichever," the *Post* said solemnly, "you can be sure it is dictated by the highest principle and integrity, with no relation to domestic politics, world politics, or the personal political fortunes of a certain individual in the White House, what—so—ever."

"Now you play the marimbas for a while and *I'll* whistle," the *Times* said with a dry humor. "What crap this all is, anyway."

"Oh, it could mean something," the *Post* said. "That's what's so sad so often, up here. It *could* mean something."

For the Council, and particularly for the members of the American delegation, it did mean something. Words mattered, actions mattered. Principles, the Secretary thought grimly as he picked up the phone in the Secretary's private room behind the podium, mattered. And the reputation of the United States, for firmness, for reliability, for strength—and for courage—*that* mattered.

He shooed a hovering Kwazze out, to that flamboyant figure's obvious annoyance; gestured to Bill Bullock to lock the deadbolt on the door; looked thoughtfully at Eulie, Bill, and frail-looking Rufus Birdwell, more gray-faced and ghostlike than ever; and lifted the receiver.

"Mr. President," he said flatly.

A comfortable chuckle responded.

"Now, Ray," the President said. "I can tell you're annoyed. Not with me, I hope?"

"Should I be?" the Secretary inquired, not giving an inch.

"I hope not," the President said.

"Why are you calling?"

"You *do* sound bothered," the President said, still perfectly amicable. "You aren't protesting before you're hurt, are you?"

"I hope not," the Secretary said in his turn. "Either you want me to veto, as I've indicated I'm ready to, in which case there would probably be no reason for you to call; or you want me to back down, which would require a call."

"You've always had a way of clarifying things," the President said admiringly. "I like that."

"Good," Ray Stanley said. "I hope so. As you know, we've got a fifteen-minute recess."

"But surely they won't object if you're a little late," the President said. His tone became a little less cheery. "Surely you won't object if your President runs over a little."

"No, sir," the Secretary said, "but I'd like to keep the momentum rolling."

"Or tension rising," the President said. "Let 'em sweat, Ray! That's the ticket."

"You want me to veto, then," the Secretary said, and winked at the Deputy Secretary, who shook her head and looked dismayed.

"I didn't say that."

"Well, don't shadowbox, Mr. President," Ray Stanley said. "Please. This is serious business here."

"Oh, indeed," the President said, "and nobody more aware of it than I. No, I don't think I do want you to veto."

"You don't?" the Secretary demanded incredulously.

His three colleagues looked at him in dismay.

"I don't think so," the President said in a reasonable tone. "Look, Ray, I've been following this, it's on C-Span, you know, and it's quite apparent even out here in the boondocks that sentiment is against us as far as your original resolution is concerned."

"Yours, too, I was led to believe," the Secretary said evenly.

The President dismissed the thought.

"Oh, well," he said comfortably, "that was probably true at one point, but, as I say, the sentiment's against us, so why take a public licking on it?"

"There could be a matter of principle involved," Ray Stanley said coldly. "And there could be some advantage to the United States in standing firm for what we believe—as a matter of principle."

"Oh, I'm not backing down," the President said. "What I want you to do is abstain on the Soviet language—then resubmit our original—and then when that's been vetoed by China and the S.S.R., announce that we wish to reconsider our vote on the Soviet—and ask for another roll call—and surprise the hell out of everybody by voting for it."

"Very clever," the Secretary said. "That puts us on both sides of it, doesn't it?"

"Sure," the President agreed, not at all abashed. "We make our strong disapproval of the Soviet language known—try again for ours—and then gracefully give in to majority sentiment and go with the crowd. At least we'll have something anti-Sidi on the books and we can go from there."

"Not very much on the books," Ray Stanley said bleakly, "and we can't go very far from there. How will I explain this to the world?"

"You're the diplomat, Ray," the President said cheerfully. "You're the Secretary of State. I'm sure you'll think of something."

"I hope you will too," the Secretary said grimly, "because you're certainly going to be asked about it next time there's a photo op in the Rose Garden."

"Tomorrow morning at ten," the President said with a chuckle. "I'll use your remarks as a text."

"As long as you don't use my true sentiments as a text," the Secretary said.

His employer gave a whoop of laughter.

And went off the line, still chuckling.

"Why, the miserable son of a bitch," Bill Bullock said into the silent room. "He's cutting us off at the knees."

"I hope he knows what he's doing," Eulie Montgomery said grimly. "I hope he has a lot of tricks up his sleeves, because he's going to need them. Or Sidi's going to win this one, hands down and going away."

"Well, Ray," Rufus Birdwell said in his tentative little voice, tentative little smile flitting across his tentative little face, "I'm glad it's you and not me."

"Let's go," the Secretary said tersely. "Let's get it over with. No gloom when we go out. In fact," he added with a grim humor, "it might help if we were all roaring with laughter."

"They look pretty comfortable," the *Globe* remarked as they filed in and resumed their places. "Maybe he's told Ray to go ahead and veto."

"Don't bet on it," CNN remarked dryly. "This guy is as tricky as the last one. And about as reliable when it comes to keeping his word and standing firm."

"You're a cynic," the *Globe* told him.

CNN snorted. "A realist, I prefer to call it," he replied.

"Mr. President," Li Peng Liu inquired with heavy sarcasm, "if agreeable, may we be permitted, finally, to vote?"

"The United States welcomes the opportunity to make its sentiments clear," the Secretary said crisply. "Roll call, Mr. President, please."

"The Secretary-General will oblige," Norway said.

In quick succession, Kwazze, looking, like all of them, a little tired now from the long afternoon and evening, read off the names.

Voting in the affirmative were Argentina, Belgium, Chile, Ecuador, France, Kuwait, Malawi, Norway, Pakistan, Romania, the Second Soviet Republic, Thailand, the United Kingdom—

"The United States," Kwazze said.

"Mr. President," the Secretary said, thinking: at least I can make them sweat a little, isn't that what he told me to do? "The United States wishes to withhold its vote for the moment."

"The United States withholds its vote," Kwazze echoed; and added dryly, "For the moment. Zimbabwe?"

"Zimbabwe joins its thirteen colleagues in voting Aye," Zimbabwe said, "and awaits with great interest the vote of the United States."

"Don't wait," the *Times* murmured.

"Want to bet?" the *Post* inquired.

"We'll veto," the *Wall Street Journal* guessed.

"You wish," the *Post* told him. "We abstain, is more like it. . . . You see?" he said triumphantly a moment later. "What did I tell you? He didn't have the guts."

"Stanley would have vetoed if he'd had his druthers," the *Journal* said. "Look at him. He looks as though he's been eating sour pickles."

Which was a description of the Secretary more journalistic than accurate; but though he was determined to remain bland he did not, in fact, look overjoyed.

"Mr. President," he said matter-of-factly, "on this vote the United States abstains."

"Fourteen ayes, one abstention," Norway said with a tired sigh. "The Soviet resolution is approved. If there is no further business—"

"Mr. President," the Secretary said, "I wish to call up the original resolution proposed by the United States, and I ask for a roll-call vote."

"What the hell—" somebody said loudly in the media gallery.

"Mr. President," Vladimir Novotny cried indignantly, "that is most improper procedure."

"Not at all," Ray said sharply. "If the Soviet resolution had been offered as an amendment to our original resolution, and had been approved, the substitute would automatically have replaced the original, and that would be that. You chose not to proceed that way. Our original resolution is still on the table. I call it up and ask for a roll-call vote." His tone became emphatic. "If—you—please."

"This seems somewhat irregular," Norway began hesitantly.

Vladimir snorted. "This is the UN," he said. "Call it up. Put it to a vote. It does not matter. We will veto."

"And we," Li Peng Liu said with rigid disapproval.

"Call the roll, Mr. Secretary-General," Tony Marsden said with an exaggeratedly hearty yawn. "It is past my bedtime."

Which brought a murmur of amusement: it was almost midnight.

Kwazze ran through the roll again in his most important voice.

"The vote," Norway announced, "is thirteen for, two of the permanent members, China and the Second Soviet Republic, against, and the United States resolution is not agreed to."

"Mr. President," Ray Stanley said, "the United States is now prepared to vote on the Soviet resolution. The United States has reconsidered its abstention and now wishes to vote Aye on the substitute resolution."

"I told you!" the *Post* said triumphantly.

"Roll call, Mr. President," Li Peng Liu said, expressionless, and Kwazze once more went patiently through the list.

"The United States," Ray announced in a firm voice, "votes Aye."

"Zimbabwe," Zimbabwe said cheerfully, "votes Aye—again!" And joined in the relieved laughter as the Secretary of State waved amicably at them all, picked up his papers, and prepared to lead his delegation out. Eulie looked pensive, Rufus Birdwell, eyebrows lifted until they almost joined his hair, glum. Big Bill Bullock openly scowled.

In the penthouse apartment in Washington, Mary turned to Bets and Joan Bourassa, who had spent the evening with her, watching the session. Boo and Samir were quietly absent.

"How humiliating for Ray," she said, close to tears. "How humiliating!"

But not as humiliating as it swiftly became in the morning's papers and news broadcasts.

UN Rejects Tough U.S. Stand on Sidi, Expresses Hope He Will OK Atomic Inspection

Chinese Scoff U.S. "Climbed Up Hill and Slid Down Again"

And, almost predictably now, the latest from Greater Lolómé City:

Sidi Withdraws from World Atomic Treaty, Blasts UN "Meddling"

Will Meet U.S. Media on International TV

"There are many things we can do under the resolution," the President said cheerfully at ten A.M. in the Rose Garden in response to a challenging question from UPI. "There is, for instance, a new dialogue which we hope to open with President Sidi which could lead to substantial economic assistance by the United States and its allies and much closer trade and diplomatic ties with Greater Lolómé which would be of advantage to everyone."

"Will President Sidi consider that sufficient to meet his demands?" UPI inquired. "Has he shown any interest in closer ties with us?"

"We can only hope," the President said with a comfortable smile. "We can only hope—and try!"

"Good luck," she said with her characteristic little gurgle of laughter.

He laughed too and responded at his most charming. "We'll need it!"

"You sure will, honey," she murmured to Able Montague, who had caught up with her on the walk back to the press room.

Able laughed.

"I think we'd better find out what's really going on, don't you?" he suggested. "This guy is as slippery as six eels in olive oil. And *that,*" he added with a grin, "is *really* slippery!"

But after Sidi's appearance on world television Sunday night, in which, to his great surprise, Able found himself included, they were forced to agree that the President had met his match.

2   Six weeks later, on his way to a private meeting with the chairman of the Senate Foreign Relations Committee (at the chairman's request—"a command performance, you might call it," Willie Wilson had said with a chuckle that brooked no argument), the Secretary of State had to admit ruefully that Sidi had done his work well. His swarthy, smugly smiling face was displayed on a group of T-shirts where the Secretary's limousine stopped for the light at Constitution and Fourth; as he approached the Senate side of the Capitol he saw a small scraggle of demonstrators, parading listlessly in the brutal heat and humidity of summer, with banners that read, in part:

U.S. STOP BULLYING! PICK ON SOMEONE YOUR OWN SIZE! LAY OFF SMALL NATIONS! GOOD LUCK, SIDI AND GREATER LOLÓMÉ!

Similar indications of public disapproval were appearing elsewhere, in too many places. By so much, Ray Stanley thought, was measured the current depth of knowledge about the foreign affairs of the United States of a sizable segment of the American public.

And by so much, the effectiveness of a modern tyrant when he was shrewd enough to call to his assistance the media's inexhaustible appetite for sensation, and use their global network of communications for his own purposes.

The event had begun in the afternoon in Greater Lolómé City, after midnight in New York, when Sidi had finally turned off CNN's coverage of the Security Council, which he had been watching for hours, and announced to his foreign minister:

"I shall talk to the world."

The foreign minister, momentarily taken aback but fond enough of his own hide to conceal his misgivings, immediately responded, "But of course, Mr. President. Tell me how I can help with this auspicious event."

"It may be auspicious," the President for Life of All the Peoples of Lolómé said with a grim little chuckle, "but it will also confound them in Washington, which is the important thing. What I will do is—"

An hour later, first Able Montague, then James Van Rensselaer Burden, and lastly, as befitted a woman in Sidi's scheme of things, Sally Holliwell, were awakened by insistent telephones.

In the Eunuch's piping voice they all heard the same words:

"His Excellency the President of Greater Lolómé!"

"Are you kidding?" Able demanded. "Who is this?"

"Who is trying to be funny?" Jimmy Van inquired testily.

"And I'm Eleanor Roosevelt," Sally snapped. "Get off my line, jerk!"

"I repeat," the Eunuch said sternly, "His Excellency the President of Greater Lolómé! Be silent!"

All three started to protest once more but were overridden by a terse, emphatic voice they recognized. Astounded but alert, they listened.

It was his intention, he told them, to submit himself to their questions in an hour-long global telecast which he had already arranged with CNN. They would be flown to Greater Lolómé City at his expense, accompanied by a representative of the State Department, selected by the Secretary, as earnest of Sidi's good faith and guarantor of their safety. They would go on a scheduled airline due to leave Dulles International Airport for London in an hour and a half, and then on to Cairo. From Cairo they would be flown on LolóméAir to Greater Lolómé City, which would get them there in time for a reasonable rest before the program. All expenses would be paid, and if they wished he would stake them to a couple of days at the Dorchester in London on their way home. He had already spoken, at the Secretary's suggestion, to Hugo Mallerbie, who had agreed to make the trip. What about Able, Jimmy, and Sally?

"Are you kidding?" Able demanded again. "I wouldn't miss it for the world."

"What a great opportunity, Mr. President," Jimmy Van said gravely. "I shall be glad to accept."

"Count me in," Sally said, "but I warn you: I may have some questions you won't like."

"And I may have some answers you and your President won't like, madame," Sidi said with a chuckle, and went off the line.

Their immediate instinct was to call one another, but there wasn't time. They had barely finished flinging clothes into suitcases when a limousine from the embassy of Greater Lolómé (whose staff, following the expulsion of Bill Bullock and colleagues, expected to be booted at any moment, in the customary tit-for-tat characteristic of current diplomacy) stopped first at Jimmy's door, then Able's, and so across the river to Sally's, and on to Dulles. There in the softly suffocating darkness of the sleeping Virginia countryside, the great terminal as always blazing with light, they were transferred to a State Department car and whisked to their plane, where they joined Hugo Mallerbie, were escorted to first class, and made comfortable. For the first few minutes after they were airborne, they exchanged rather nervous jokes about their personal safety.

"We're counting on you, Hugo," Able said with a laugh that was just a little uneasier than he had intended, "to get us in and out in one piece. I'm damned if I want to wind up like poor Creed Moncrief."

"I don't think we need to worry," Hugo Mallerbie said. "He may be a madman, but he wouldn't dare do anything to you. Me, he might dispose of if I went alone, but the shoe is on the other foot now. He wouldn't dare harm anyone under the media's wing. That would destroy his whole strategy."

"Which is to fight it out on television," Sally suggested with satisfaction.

"And the columns and editorials," Jimmy Van hastened to assert.

She laughed and patted his knee.

"Don't worry, Jimmy," she said. "I intend to have you and Able on my show next week for a postmortem."

"I thought I'd do that," Able said quickly.

Hugo Mallerbie snorted, lowered his seat back, and arranged a pillow behind his head. "I'll hold the straws and you can draw for it," he suggested; and added, "After we're all safely home."

"Now, stop scaring us, Hugo," Sally said, jesting but not entirely. "You just assured us—"

"Who knows?" Hugo inquired of the air. "I'm going to catch a quick nap, thank you. We have a grueling flight ahead."

"Good idea," Able said, and started to arrange himself for napping. But they were all too keyed up to sleep.

"Hey, Sally," he said, leaning forward to tap her on the shoulder. "What do you want to ask him?"

They speculated, gossiped, and planned most of the way across the Atlantic and only fell groggily into fitful dozing when they left London for Cairo. It was already Sunday noon when they reached Greater Lolómé City. There they found some 173 correspondents already gathered from around the world to watch the event in the small auditorium of the Pink Palace. It was approximately eight hours to broadcast. They were taken to adjoining bedrooms and went thankfully to bed. At eight P.M. local time they were roused and given a few minutes to freshen up. Sally missed her usual studio hairdresser but emerged spic and span nonetheless. Able and Jimmy made do with quick shaves and a quick comb.

"We look damned authentic," Able murmured as they were taken backstage at the auditorium. "The quintessential media, grimy but game."

"Speak for yourself," Sally said. "I feel great—may collapse any moment, but I feel great."

"I, too," Jimmy said. "I'm not afraid of the big, bad wolf."

"We'll blow his house down," Able agreed cheerfully.

They emerged smiling from behind the curtains, were greeted by a burst of genuine applause and fellow feeling from their colleagues, and were ushered to a small table at the left turned slightly toward the audience, Jimmy at the near end, Able at the far, Sally between. Opposite approximately fifteen feet, on a small dais raised two feet from the floor, stood a comfortable overstuffed armchair and two much smaller, straight-backed chairs which caused puzzlement and speculation. In front of them on a small table stood an elaborately scrolled silver decanter and three obviously fine crystal glasses, one large, two small.

Silence fell and tension grew.

Finally, after ten minutes or so when the assorted coughings and rustlings and settlings had completely subsided, a youthful general in the full uniform and decorations of the Peoples Army of Greater Lolómé (financed, equipped, and trained, through one commercial or diplomatic stratagem or another, by China, France, Great Britain, the United States, Iran, the Second Soviet Republic, North Korea, Libya, Japan, and God-or-Allah knew who else) appeared from behind the curtains.

He walked quickly to the small table, poured a red liquid of some kind ("Chk juice," scribbled 173 pens and pencils onto 173 notepads), and came down center stage to peer out with an arrogant blankness at the fascinated throng below.

("Isn't that Young Sidi?" whispered someone in the media. "By God, it is!" whispered someone else. Tension immediately rose. "Hit it!" ordered someone else. Lights flared and cameras rolled.)

"To the peoples of the world!" Young Sidi said with great portentous- ness. "It has pleased my father the President of Greater Lolómé to speak to you today concerning the crisis confronting the nation of Greater Lolómé as a result of the insufferable actions of the President of the United States of America taken to threaten this small, poor, innocent nation.

"My father has been pleased to invite three distinguished American journalists to participate in the question-and-answer formula"—his expression and voice became sarcastic—"so popular with American journalists. Their names and affiliations are"—and he gave them, Jimmy first, Able second, Sally third.

"If you will please be silent, ladies and gentlemen, for the President of Greater Lolómé!"

And with a terse little bow he turned smartly and strode offstage.

Silence again settled, tension again rose.

Without further warning, a dark, chunky, medium-sized, bearded figure in a sober dark blue Western business suit, completely devoid of decoration, set off only by a subdued red tie, stepped forward from behind the curtains and made his way purposefully to the armchair on the dais. Holding him by the hands, staring wide-eyed at the audience, were a beautiful little girl, perhaps eight, and a handsome little boy, perhaps six.

Automatically the assembled media rose. Jimmy, Able, and Sally rose too, exchanging a quick glance as they did so. They could not help but feel a rush of excitement and adrenaline, but also a great annoyance as they realized they were about to be cleverly upstaged by two child stars.

"Thank you, ladies and gentlemen," Sidi said with a friendly smile. "You will forgive me if I do not come unaccompanied. You have just seen, and honored by your respectful attention, Sidi bin Sidi bin Sidi bin Sidi, the son of my first wife. These are the children of my third wife. This is my daughter Shareen—bow to the ladies and gentlemen,

Sharry—and my son Iskander—a salute, Isky, if you please . . . Good. Now we will all sit down and have a nice talk with the nice gentlemen and nice lady at the other table."

Abruptly the lights were cut, the brightness of the two single spotlights trained on the tables turned up. The banks of cameras at the sides and back of the auditorium stirred and whirred, the air was filled with the frantic clickings of the photographers sitting or squatting just below the platform's edge.

The children shifted a little, uneasily, but Sidi shushed them gently and waited patiently for the flurry to die down. When reasonable silence had been secured, he suggested, "Say hello to Mr. Burden, Mr. Montague, and Miss Holliwell, children."

Obediently they did so, Shareen rising to give a little curtsy, Iskander a little salute.

"Miss Holliwell?" Sidi inquired blandly.

She was momentarily thrown off balance by his abrupt reversal of order, but recovered instantly as she thought: *I will be God damned if I am going to play his cheap, obvious little game with the kids.*

"Thank you, children," she said dismissively and turned quickly to him. "Mr. President, what is your reaction to the action of the United Nations Security Council on Friday, threatening sanctions if you do not comply with inspection of your atomic facilities by the International Atomic Energy Agency?"

"Was that a threat?" he asked dryly. "If so, it was not stated in language that impressed me as a threat." He reached in his vest pocket, pulled out a sheet of paper, put on a pair of glasses, cocked his head back—all this very slowly and deliberately, while his children and his audience watched fascinated—and read in the same dry, sarcastic voice:

"The Security Council 'will, if terms of this resolution are not respected by those to whom it applies'—I wonder who that means, they do not say—'consider most seriously what actions, possibly including sanctions, may be taken by the Council.' They do not even say who it is supposed to apply to, Miss Holliwell. They do not actually promise sanctions. They only say the Council will 'consider most seriously what actions, *possibly including sanctions*'—my emphasis—'*may*'—my emphasis—'be taken by the Council.'

"Anyway," he said, tone scornful and dismissive, handing the paper to

Iskander, who promptly began to crease it into an impromptu airplane, "I have withdrawn from the nuclear nonproliferation treaty, so what does this have to do with me? *Iskander!*" he added with mild disapproval as the boy sailed his plane into the audience, where a mad scramble ensued. Several people actually shoved and punched as the media vied for this souvenir of an historic occasion. The *Frankfurter Zeitung* finally emerged triumphant after a vicious elbowing of *El Aram* of Cairo and the lady correspondent of America's National Public Radio.

"I am sorry, Miss Holliwell," Sidi said with a charming smile as Sally began to look uptight and openly annoyed. "Did I answer your question?"

"You did, Mr. President," she said tersely. "So you are going to deliberately defy both the UN and possible unilateral action by the United States. With an air force," she could not resist adding, "about as effective as *that*."

This drew blood. The suave pose snapped. Sidi decided to come back with real anger.

"I have other means," he snapped. "Other means. And, unlike your timorous President, I have the will to use them."

"And invite the destruction of your country?" she demanded, as Hugo Mallerbie cautioned from the front row, too late, "No, no!"

"So!" Sidi exclaimed, while the children looked alarmed at his tone. "You speak for your President on that, I take it. I was not aware he was prepared to go so far."

"I do not speak for him," she said rather lamely, "but I think great risks for your country are apparent in the actions he has already taken."

"Which are what?" he demanded scornfully. "Words, words, and more words. It does not do to make threats and then be too timorous to back them up. We have come to expect that from Washington. He sounds like your other Presidents."

"Nonetheless," she said, beginning to appear flustered but dogged, "it seems to me that you are risking great dangers if you defy the United Nations. You do not worry about those dangers?"

"Again," he said, still scornful, "words, words, and more words! Why should I worry? My conscience is clear."

"Is it clear about Creed Moncrief?" Able asked suddenly, in an obvious attempt to rescue Sally, who rarely floundered but obviously was this time.

"A CIA agent," Sidi said indifferently, air of calm command restored, "who unfortunately became involved with some unknown criminal element in Greater Lolómé. We do our best to control them, and compared with the record of the United States, we do quite well. A stoning in a public square carries a powerful message. But some few do evade us, unfortunately."

"You did not order his murder, then?" Able asked.

Sidi's composure remained unshaken.

"Do you have proof of that?" he inquired blandly.

"I do not, personally, no," Able said. "Our government seems to think it does."

"'Seems to think' is correct," Sidi replied. "Your government 'seems to think' a lot of things, all the time. What a thinking government! It baffles the rest of us."

"Mr. President—" Able began, and Sidi raised a hand with an exaggeratedly gratified smile. "I am glad you finally call me that. It is my title, after all."

"Are you planning to attack Lesser Lolómé, Mr. President? Perhaps we could get a straight answer on that."

Again Hugo looked a little alarmed, although not noted for diplomacy himself; but Sidi again seemed serenely unflustered.

"I will not tell you what I plan to do or not do," he said calmly. "What kind of strategy is that?"

"I am sure that would involve the United States even more directly," Able observed, and added pointedly, "as it did a year and a half ago."

"Oh, yes," Sidi said airily. "Oil . . . What is it?" He turned abruptly to his daughter, who was tugging at his sleeve; bent down, smiled, nodded. "Surely, dear, of course you may." Shareen got up and trotted offstage. He turned back to Able with a comfortable smile.

"You know children," he said. "She will be back."

"Yes, sir," Able said. His tone became bland. "If you would like to, too, sir, feel free. We will wait."

A startled laugh came from the audience. For a moment Sidi stared at him as if he did not know how to reply; but a hearty chuckle indicated that he did.

"No chance, Mr. Montague," he said cheerfully. "All I have had since six A.M. is two sips of this cranberry juice." ("Cran juice" noted 173 pens and pencils.) "I am quite content, thank you. And you?"

"Super," Able said. "Simply super. So how soon do you plan to attack Lesser Lolómé?"

"What?" Sidi exclaimed. "No more intimate discussions? You are losing your famed aggressiveness, Mr. Montague. I repeat, I am not discussing strategy with you."

"But you do intend to invade," Able said, and added with a touch of sarcasm, "Mr. President."

"Maybe," Sidi said calmly. "Maybe not. Mr. Burden, you are noticeably silent. Are your colleagues to do all the work for you?"

"They are not," Jimmy Van said, flushing with annoyance. "I want to make sure they are satisfied." His tone became sharp as an approving little murmur came from the audience. "Let *me* control the interview for a moment, Mr. President." Without waiting he turned to Sally and Able as Shareen tripped daintily and captivatingly back into the room to complete the small distraction her father had planned. "Sally, have you finished your questions for His Excellency?"

"For the moment," she said coldly, which brought a smile and ironic little bow from Sidi.

"And Able?"

"I'll work on a few for later," Able said, giving Sidi a smile as cordial, and ironic, as his own.

"Very well," James Van Rensselaer Burden said, drawing himself up with a dignity to match his name, which he could do when the occasion warranted. "I would like to turn, if I may, Mr. President, to the more long-range, and perhaps more world-troubling, aspects of your policies."

"You are noted for your world view, Mr. Burden," Sidi said with an admiration just this side of mockery. "Please proceed."

"Yes," Jimmy Van said. "Do you think the United States is overreacting—"

"The President of the United States is overreacting," Sidi interrupted. "You and your countrymen have an odd habit of shouldering the blame by saying 'the United States' does this or that in foreign policy, whereas under your Constitution it is the *President* of the United States who does this or that. Thereby you remove the responsibility from his shoulders and, nobly but surprisingly to many of us, put it squarely on your own." He looked thoughtful. "I wonder why this is, Mr. Burden. I wonder why this is."

"Well, Mr. President," Jimmy said, "you are very clever, but you are not going to divert me. Perhaps it is because in the last analysis we all have to stick together. Anyway, whoever it is in Washington, D.C., somebody is alarmed. That's apparent—"

"But not, perhaps," Sidi interrupted again, with satisfaction, "in the entire United States. There seems to be quite a difference of opinion developing in the United States, in the whole country."

"I repeat, Mr. President," Jimmy said firmly, "do you think person or persons unknown, within the geographical confines of what is known, politically, socially, and diplomatically, as 'the United States of America' is, or are, overreacting to the accretion of atomic weapons in the hands of someone who is widely regarded, by one or all or some of them, as an irrational, irresponsible, murderous, worthless, international thug?"

There was a startled intake of breath followed by a storm of applause from the media. It was lent an extra thrill and satisfaction by the fact that they were doing it in Sidi's capital, in Sidi's palace, and literally in Sidi's face.

For a moment he looked genuinely angry, livid, and apoplectic, so disturbed that his children also became greatly disturbed and began to cry. Shareen seized his hand, Iskander plowed his face into the side of his coat. He lifted Iskander into his arms, hugged Shareen close, looked defiantly—and nobly—into the cameras.

"In the presence of my children," he began—hesitated—caught his breath as if overcome—allowed his lips to tremble, his eyes to moisten. "In the presence of my children," he repeated, voice quivering just enough, "and on their innocent bodies, I swear that I do not deserve these monstrous charges of yours, Mr. Burden. I am a simple man, yes; I lack the sophistication of clever people of the media from Washington, D.C., yes. I must work only on my instincts as a decent and honorable son of the desert, raised to my present eminence, such as it may be, and maintained there, by the free will and great love of my peoples, who recognize that my sole aim in this world is to improve their lot and guide our beloved country successfully through these troubled times—these troubled times when we are beset on every side by enemies and adversaries, and when the President of the greatest power of all seems to be determined to destroy us with all his overwhelming force and ruthless greed for oil and world domination. Yes! These are the things I plead guilty to, not to your foul charges, Mr. Burden!"

And defiantly yet tenderly, he held Shareen and Iskander even closer to his side, kissing their tousled heads, first Shareen's and then her brother's, as they looked up soulfully into his loving eyes.

"My God!" Able said, making no attempt to keep his voice down. "*East Lynne* and then some!"

"I am overcome," Sally said with a harsh little laugh. "Whooo-*eee,* I am overcome!"

"I am not," James Van Rensselaer Burden said with the cold, precise contempt of the Hudson River Valley confronted by a slug in the garden. "Mr. President, I must press you further. Obviously you do feel that the President of the United States is overreacting to your possession of atomic bombs. How do you think he should react?"

"I am glad you have decided to place the responsibility for overreaction, finally, where it belongs, on one man," Sidi said, calm and bland again, disengaging himself gently from his children and urging them to resume their seats. "One hysterical man who does not, I am convinced, represent the great majority of his countrymen, who surely cannot regard with any pleasure their President swaggering around the world trying to bully the leader of a small, helpless power who is only trying to lead his people faithfully and honestly—"

"Yes, Mr. President," Jimmy interrupted in the same cold, unimpressed tone. "You do not concede, then, that there is any merit in anyone being disturbed by your possession of atomic bombs—if indeed you have them—"

"Oh, I have them," Sidi said with equal coldness. "Do you wish a demonstration? What would you like me to destroy today, Tel Aviv or Cairo?" He chuckled suddenly. "Or maybe even Paris or London? I can manage them all very nicely." He turned and surveyed the audience, expression and voice heavy with sarcasm and taunting. "Perhaps I should arrange for you all to stay on for a few hours. I am told by my atomic experts—who come from many nations, I will tell you, Mr. Burden—that it will take them perhaps twelve hours to prepare an effective strike. Shall I give the word? Will you stay and be my witnesses?"

"Mr. President," Jimmy Van said, still speaking in a quietly calm tone, refusing to be deflected, "can you grasp the reason why my President, and a great many in our country and throughout the world, are worried about your possession of atomic bombs? Do you have any appreciation at all for the concept that everyone is threatened by the increase in atomic weapons? That atomic bombs are so fearful that their appearance anywhere is a danger everywhere? That just as a principle of common sense and common safety, the world community should unite, if it can, to stop nuclear proliferation, wherever it can?"

For a moment Sidi looked at him impassively. Then he shrugged.

"In the hands of those who are truly irresponsible," he said, "such as your great President who can deploy the enormous power of the United States with nothing but conscience to restrain him, then I agree with your thoughts. Especially when your President apparently does not possess any restraints of conscience when it comes to threatening small, helpless powers—"

"Are you still small and helpless if you have the bombs, Mr. President?" Jimmy inquired. "Doesn't the possession of the bombs give you equality?"

"Equality of protection," Sidi said quickly. "That is all I seek, equality of protection against bullying by the President of the United States and the destruction of my poor, threatened people."

Able raised his hand. Jimmy nodded.

"Mr. President," Able said, "would you be satisfied if the United States were to work out with you a program of substantial economic aid and development for your country and at the same time enter into a specific one-on-one security arrangement so that you would not feel threatened, as you claim, by U.S. military power?"

"Would that reunite the Lolómés?" Sidi inquired. "Would the word of the President of the United States actually be enough to make us rest easy? Why should we trust it?"

"Then you do intend to attack Lesser Lolómé," Sally said.

He gave her a bland stare and shrugged.

"Maybe so, maybe not. I have already said that."

"It is obviously a dream of yours."

"And a dream of Sheikh Mustafa's," he said with a cruel little smile. "Perhaps he will cooperate with me and there will be no need for— unpleasantness. Are you all finished?"

"I am," Jimmy said in a disgusted tone.

"And I," Sally said. "I think the situation is clear enough."

"Thank you for bringing us here and permitting us to question you on this global broadcast, Mr. President," Able said. "I am sure the world understands you better now."

"I hope so," Sidi said solemnly. "You have helped me make clear to the world that I am simply a dedicated leader of my own peoples, who wishes only the greater good and safety of Greater Lolómé—that I have no aggressive intentions and desire only its security from outside attack—that whatever modest stock of atomic weapons I have is in good and responsible hands—that I am not a threat to the United States or to anyone else who does not deserve to be threatened—and that any honorable power which wishes to live in honorable peace with Greater Lolómé is free to do so, and I welcome it gladly. I am only a humble man whom great good fortune has placed at the head of my country. *But*"— his jaw became set, his tone stern—"I do not intend to be swayed from my mission or the protection of my country by the designs of envious outside powers who apparently wish to challenge everyone who dares try to keep an independent, unaligned, peace-loving course in the world. Greater Lolómé is no man's lackey! Sidi bin Sidi bin Sidi is no man's lackey! Take that home to America, ladies and gentlemen!" And with abrupt transition, "Now children, go and say goodbye to Mr. Burden, Mr. Montgomery, and Miss Holliwell, these nice people from America. Off you go!"

And dutifully little Shareen and little Iskander trotted across the stage, bowed and curtsied and pumped their annoyed elders' hands while Sidi looked on with fond fatherliness and the assembled media, for all their collegial sympathy, could not help but chuckle at the expressions on the faces of three of the Washington press corps' finest.

"God damn it," Able muttered as he gave Iskander a push back toward his father which was not quite as gentle as the child expected— in fact, he let out a startled bleat of protest, which made his father glare at Able and hold out his arms protectively as Iskander ran into them. "God damn it, what a show! We've been had, friends."

"The only saving grace is that the whole world has now seen what a fraud and danger he is," Sally said as she gave Shareen one of her most vinegary smiles and a pat on the head so heavy that it brought a vocal reaction similar to Iskander's as the little girl turned in alarm and ran back to her father.

"If the whole world will believe it," Jimmy Van said grimly, having looked so forbidding that neither child had dared approach him, only waved and curtsied from a careful distance. "That's what we've got to hope."

And now, six weeks after Sidi's performance—"the telecast," as it was still shown or referred to a dozen times a day, without other identification, in major news programs and publications—it was obvious that the hope had been ill founded.

There was something that went deeper than T-shirts and scraggly demonstrators; it was an infection, similar to many others in recent years, that had swept the country while the President conducted his particular version of what Ray Stanley thought of as "The Great Smoke-and-Mirrors Dance of Modern Presidents Unsure and Uneasy with Their Power," and Sidi went his way in smug defiance and security.

It was to these two sharply contrasting modes of conduct that the Secretary knew he must address himself when he arrived at the Senate Foreign Relations Committee for his date with the chairman.

His was the job of justifying the President's increasingly erratic course in the face of Sidi's increasingly defiant one.

It was not an appetizing prospect. But he was, after all, Secretary of State.

It went with the territory.

3   "Sidi's playing the President like a fish," Senator Wilson remarked with a mixture of disgust and admiration as he and Ray Stanley settled down at the big old-fashioned committee table. "He's the cleverest international operator since Kim Il Sung. And he doesn't have a wide-eyed angel from Atlanta winging in to help him, either. He's doing it on his own."

"With a little help from his friend—or friends—unknown," the Secretary demurred. "And," he added dryly, "the White House, just between us." He sighed. "Where does it end, Willie? How do we get out of this without stronger leadership at the top? That's what I want to know."

"It hasn't been a good record in recent weeks," Willie agreed. "I asked the staff to put together the major events and headlines, in chronological order, for me. One tends to miss the cumulative effect, living with them day to day. It's a rather sorry picture that emerges."

There was a projector at his elbow, a small screen at the far end of the table. He started the machine. The first frame appeared and froze: the front pages of the *Times*, the *Post*, and Anna Hastings's *Washington Inquirer*. Their headlines matched almost word for word:

Sidi Charges U.S. Designs on Greater Lolómé, Defines UN in Global TV Interview

President Says Sidi Makes "Nonsensical" Accusation,

Will Reply on CNN Tonight

The President, giving his summation with his most sincere and candid expression—the "Earnest-Honest":

"My countrymen, it is, as you know, almost impossible to prove a negative. However, you have my personal assurance that the United States has no designs on Greater Lolómé and no hidden agenda except to preserve the peace of the world. President Sidi's charges are ridiculous. We do intend to see to it that Greater Lolómé does not misuse its stock of atomic bombs to threaten its neighbors, its region, or the peace and stability of the world. We will continue to insist that Greater Lolómé cooperate immediately with an inspection of its military facilities by the International Atomic Energy Agency. Otherwise, the sanctions approved by the Security Council will be imposed."

Secretary-General Rejects U.S. Plea for Tough New Sanctions Against Sidi

Sidi Ups Ante, Claims Right to Lesser Lolómé

President Claims "Vital U.S. Interest in Lolómé Issue," Denies Oil Charge

Kwazze Kumbatta, at a press conference in his UN office, looking regal and sternly disapproving, tone disdainful:

"It seems to me that the United States President is attempting to do by speech what he failed to persuade the Security Council to do in fact.

The Council resolution, you will note, does not specifically impose sanctions. And it only holds out the possibility of sanctions if the terms of its resolution of warning are not honored. And then it only provides that it will consider, and I quote, 'what actions, possibly including sanctions, may be taken by the Council.' I am authorized to say that there is no disposition here to review or strengthen the resolution of warning adopted by the Council. The language we adopted, by a vote including the affirmative vote of the United States, seems quite clear to us here at headquarters."

The secretive face and glib tongue of Greater Lolómé's ambassador to the United Nations, one of Sidi's innumerable desert cousins, invited by the Secretary-General to share the press conference with him; the words of Sidi, savage and bitter, denouncing the United States and setting forth for the first time in specific language his rationale for threatening Lesser Lolómé:

"The natural right of myself, my heirs, and my countrymen, to work diligently and relentlessly for the reunification of our land, artificially divided by past colonial rulers without consulting the interests and wishes of the peoples of all Lolómé."

The President, at a photo opportunity in the Rose Garden with the visiting Japanese prime minister, responding to a question from the Chicago Daily News:

"Any attack on Lesser Lolómé is essentially an attack on the vital interests of the United States."

Question from the UPI:

"Does that mean because it would be an attack on one of our principal sources of oil, Mr. President?"

Follow-up from the *Philadelphia Inquirer:*

"Would you be as strong in your statements if oil were not involved?"

The President, flatly:

"Certainly. Certainly. A matter of principle is involved here. The United States cannot sit idly by while a member of the United Nations threatens a fellow member with open aggression. That is counter to the charter of the UN and counter to all the necessities of a stable world."

From the *Los Angeles Times:*

"But aren't *you* threatening a fellow member when you threaten Greater Lolómé?"

The President, calmly:

"We are not threatening Greater Lolómé. We are simply asking Greater Lolómé to abide by the rules of civilized conduct between peace-loving nations. Which I assume, unless President Sidi tells me differently"—a fatherly, patronizing smile, comfortable and confident—"Greater Lolómé is. I want him to have the benefit of the doubt."

Sidi Blasts "Another U.S. Threat to My Poor Country," Reaffirms "Obligation" to Reunite the Two Lolómés

Caption inserted by committee staff:

PRO-SIDI, ANTI-PRESIDENT REACTIONS GROW AT HOME AND ABROAD. TYPICAL STATEMENTS BY OPPONENTS:

Bonnie Terhuitt, president of C.C.A. (Concerned Citizens Against), before Rep. John Jones' House Appropriations Subcommittee: plump, earnest, humorless, glasses pushed back atop unruly gray hair, thrown-together clothes, looking like a disheveled housewife—but oh, how sincere:

"We of C.C.A. cannot support the kind of crude, imperialistic, colonialist brutalizing of a small state advocated by the President of the United States. He is using the pretext of President Sidi's alleged 'aggression' against Lesser Lolómé—which in reality is simply reassertion of the age-old right of the two Lolómés to be incorporated in a single country—as a means to conceal the real reason. The real reason, the real motive, the real objective, Mr. Chairman, is oil—pure and simple oil! What danger can Greater Lolómé pose to us if it is not to threaten one of our major sources of oil, pure and simple? What excuse can better hide a grab for oil than pious appeals to international order and morality? Who is challenging international order and morality, Mr. Chairman? It is not President Sidi, head of a small, poor, helpless country many thousands of miles from our shores. It is our own President, who, under the guise of high international morals, seems set upon protecting, and no doubt soon controlling if he can, the oil of Lesser

Lolómé. Are we to send American boys and girls to die for the oil of Lesser Lolómé, Mr. Chairman? Shame on our President, if that is his deceitful game!"

Dr. Random Cruikshank of Harvard, cochair of W.P. (We Protest), speaking at a Council on Foreign Relations symposium on: "Is U.S. Imperialism Rising Again?"; mid-seventies, white-haired, slight, wiry, bone-thin, strained, intense, obviously eaten up by a lifetime devoted to Worthy Causes and Vital Concerns:

"Mr. Chairman, we of We Protest cannot protest too strongly against the reckless, peace-threatening activities of our President. We have examined his motives, we have heard his excuses, we have attempted to give him the benefit of every doubt—and still we cannot find it in our hearts or consciences to forgive his present irresponsible course in threatening to attack the poor, helpless nation of Greater Lolómé, whose only crime seems to be its President's desire to reunite his country with its historic sibling Lesser Lolómé and thus erase ancient colonial wrongs and injustices. The two Lolómés are one, Mr. Chairman, they are not the artificial two devised by ancient colonial masters. President Sidi's aspirations are entirely understandable and justifiable, as we of We Protest see it. Rarely have we registered a protest which, in our estimation, is more solidly grounded and more worthy of the support of all decent Americans. We protest, Mr. Chairman! Let us all unite against this conscienceless attempt by our President to revive shameless imperialism in the pursuit of oil! Let us stop him *now!* We protest his actions and we shall continue to protest!"

Dr. Feemahle Jackson-Washington of Yale, cochair of We Protest; mid-forties, beautiful, highly intelligent, famous author of books, articles, appearances, speeches, scholarly papers; delicately feminine in appearance and about as flexible, said both enemies and friends, as a sledgehammer; famous for her brains and famous for her name, which came about when her unlettered but lovely mother, whom she adored, was asked to sign the county clerk's certificate of the baby's birth: "Female Jackson," it said. "I was plannin' on Jane," her mother said, "but I like 'Feemahle'"; and so it became. Delivering the commencement address at Stanford:

"Ladies and gentlemen of the graduating class, we of We Protest have never had a cause more devoutly supported by us than the cause of calling a halt to our President's ruthless and inexcusable attack on the defenseless nation of Greater Lolómé. He has chosen to twist and turn and misrepresent the perfectly legitimate and reasonable desire of the President of Greater Lolómé to reunite his country, tragically torn apart early in this century by ruthless former imperial exploiters such as our own President, now long out of date, apparently wants to be. Oil may be one of his reasons when he takes up the cause of Lesser Lolómé, but sheer imperial greed and desire for dominance would seem to be an even more imperative motive for him. He is not doing so well in domestic legislation; what easier out than a foreign adventure! What bigger sop—he thinks—to toss to disenchanted voters than a new imperial conquest long after the days of imperial conquest are done!"

There followed a mélange of editorials and columns, most of them opposing what one writer (too young to know where the phrase came from, but recognizing it as a good one for his purposes) called "a misbegotten imperialist adventure" in a "little country far away of which we know nothing." There was a reasonable attempt at balance—a column by Tim Bates favoring a stern approach to Sidi flashed past, followed, interestingly enough, by a column by James Van Rensselaer Burden and two excerpts from comments by Able Montague and Sally Holliwell on their respective television programs. All three favored stronger action against Sidi and urged the President to "stand firm and not yield an inch to his bluster," as Able put it. There was a definite tone in the comments of all three of "We've been there, and we know." They had, and they did, and had come home, surprising many of their readers and viewers, as converts to the anti-Sidi camp.

"Once you've seen that son of a bitch face-to-face," Sally told her colleagues in the Washington media, "you don't want to give him an inch. He's a madman. A very clever madman, but a madman."

It was a major shift in position for all of them, which carried a lot of weight in Washington, however scoffed at and rejected by such as Bonnie Terhuitt, Random Cruikshank, and Feemahle Jackson-Washington.

Several more columns and editorials followed, most of those pro-Sidi coming from major publications on the east and west coasts of the nation, many of the anti-Sidi from lesser lights mid-country.

Then came a quick sampling of foreign reactions, generally favorable to the President in Britain and France, opposed elsewhere in Europe, Africa, the Middle East, and Asia.

And then, to conclude, the headlines of the past ten days as the crisis suddenly seemed to revive and escalate toward some new and ominous turning:

President to Ask Stronger UN Support for Punitive Sanctions Against Sidi

China, Soviets Reported Blocking Stronger Action Against Sidi in Council

President Says Stand on Sidi "Not Subject to Pressure from Any Outside Source," Renews Demand for Atomic Inspection

President Threatens U.S. Unilateral Action if UN Doesn't Restrain Sidi. Rules Out Use of Force.

**Sidi Says "Sanctions
Mean War," Defies U.S.
"Colonial Imperialism"**

**UN Bows to U.S. Request,
Orders Sidi A-Inspection**

**Atomic Inspectors Arrested,
Sent Home as They Attempt
To Carry Out UN Mandate to
Check Sidi Weapons Supply**

**President Says Sidi A-Ouster
"Validates Threat of Force"**

**Sidi Says "Go Ahead, Use Force."
President Says It's "Worth Study"**

**Sidi Renews Threat of A-Bomb Use
"If America Forces Me to Defend
The Sacred Soil of Lolómé."
Appeals to UN for Its
Protection against U.S.**

**Sidi Orders Troop Build-Up,
"Defensive Maneuvers" on
Border of Lesser Lolómé**

**Sheikh Mustafa Appeals to UN
For Protection Against Sidi**

**Sidi Reaffirms "Holy Right"
To Reunify the Two Lolómés**

**Lesser Lolómé Reports
Major Border Clash as
Sidi Troops Raid Deep
Into Oil-Rich Region**

**President Threatens "Destruction"
Of G.L. but Rules Out Force,
Hints at "Other Options"**

**Sidi Scoffs at U.S. as
"International Weakling,
A Failure as a Friend,
And a Joke as an Enemy"**

President Orders Two
Carriers into Waters
Off Greater Lolómé
But Again Bans Use
Of Force or First Strike

Sidi Says "I Am Prepared to Meet My Destiny.
The Final Order Will Be Given.
All My Peoples Are Ready."

U.S. Polls Find 67% Oppose
Attack on Greater Lolómé

Report Secret White House Talks
With Chinese, Soviets to Seek
Face-Saving Way out of Crisis

"And in the Pink House," Senator Wilson remarked as the machine whirred to a stop, "Sidi says, *'Gotcha!'* Right?"

"Oh," the Secretary said uncomfortably, "I wouldn't say that."

"What would you say, Ray?" Willie Wilson inquired. "Do these final headlines reflect what we're going to do, after all the big talk? Put our tail between our legs and slink home? If so, he'd better get those carriers out of there damned fast or Sidi's going to sink them, just to show he's won."

"With what?" Ray Stanley demanded with some asperity. "He doesn't have the naval power or the air power—"

"We don't know what he has in those areas," Willie interrupted. "We do know he has atomic power and the will to use it. That would be quite enough, I should think."

"He wouldn't dare," the Secretary protested.

The Senator gave him a grim little smile.

"I wouldn't bet on that." He frowned. "What are we going to do with this man in the White House, Ray? He's following the pattern all too closely: all bluff and no follow-through. We're supposed to be so all-powerful, but our Presidents duck and dodge and wriggle and waltz around their responsibilities—and the United States goes down—and down—and down in the eyes of the world. The perception of our weakness dogs everything we do. I don't like it!"

"*You* don't like it!" the Secretary echoed with a sudden, rare bitterness. "How do you think I feel?"

"How long can he go on in this fashion?" Willie Wilson countered moodily, "without doing America irreparable damage? Threatening—blustering—chasing some juvenile will-o'-the-wisp of trying to throw his weight around as a substitute for genuine leadership—until Sidi calls his bluff. Do these end-of-century Presidents ever stop to think things through, or is it all just smoke and mirrors, ad-lib, and catch-as-catch-can? It's destroying us, Ray. It's devastating."

"What would you suggest?" the Secretary demanded angrily. "A public hearing? One of the Senate Foreign Relations Committee's famous 'reviews of foreign policy,' a public relations quickie that culminates months later in a five-hundred-page report that nobody pays any attention to? Save us from that, if you please. Give us an alternative, if you don't like the way we're handling it."

"You're too generous in taking the blame," Willie remarked. "It isn't 'we' who are handling it, it's 'he.'" He shot the Secretary a sudden shrewd look. "I'll bet he's consulted you damned little in the past few days. . . . Yes, I could hold a hearing—you remember I was going to six weeks ago when this all began, but you asked me not to, as a favor 'while the administration works it out.' So I didn't. He's been free to perform his presidential dance of the seven veils. But I could do it now, all right. I could give the public five days of spun-sugar candy while you and all the other administration top brass came up here and paraded across the witness stand with all the customary phony excuses to protect his precious skin. But what good would that do? It would just give him another screen to hide behind."

"For whom to hide behind?" Ray Stanley demanded sharply. "Who's the enemy here, Sidi about to run amok or the President of the United States, trying to hold the line against a crazy aggressor armed with A-bombs?"

"Exactly," Willie Wilson said. "That's exactly the line." His expression was bleak. "These end-of-the-century Presidents are the enemy. The President is always the key to everything. How he acts and reacts— or doesn't act and react. His character, or lack of it, is what controls matters in the end—he's the decisive element. And character, I'm afraid, is not what's been outstandingly notable in the White House in these recent years. . . . Look!" he said, as the Secretary appeared frustrated yet unable to argue honestly with this old friend with whom he basically agreed, "I would tell him all this to his face if he'd let me, but he's afraid to do it—he doesn't like face-to-face confrontations with people who tell him they disagree. I have tried for the past two weeks to get an appointment, but he's dodged me every time. He finally sent Jaime Serrano up here yesterday to apologize for him and tell me he's just been 'too busy' to see the chairman of Foreign Relations, which is his mistake. Jaime understands the world effects of all this wavering and wandering and two-bit posturing in the headlines, but he's trapped like you are. You're all trapped. So you all go along, and try to rationalize and pretend to the country that all's well, while America keeps on going down." He made a bitter gesture of contempt. "And *he* congratulates himself that words are more important than deeds. He's a fool. He ought to put up or shut up. He ought to grow up sometime and realize that you don't say it unless you really have the will to do it if you have to. He kids himself that he's getting away with it. And America goes down. And Sidi wins."

"All right, Willie!" the Secretary said, shaken by Willie's argument but true to his obligation. "Give me that phone."

He dialed, listened for a moment. His tone became cold and unchallengeable. "This is Raymond Cass Stanley. Put me through to the President, please . . . Mr. President, I am on the Hill with Senator Wilson. He wants to talk to you. I suggest we come down right now, all right? . . . Yes, I know. But I suggest that it would be well to talk to the Senator." His tone turned dry. "His influence in this place is substantial. . . . Yes, sir. Thank you, sir. In ten minutes, sir. We're on our way."

Next day there was a new headline to add to the rest:

Congressional Leaders
Urge President to Seek
"Reasonable Compromise"
In Greater Lolómé Crisis

On the Hill, Senator Wilson made wry note of the way carefully managed White House leaks can control the press. What appeared in print as "Congressional Leaders Urge President to Seek 'Reasonable Compromise'" had begun as his own individual admonition to the President that concluded their bristling confrontation.

"God damn it," Willie had said, after twenty minutes of indecisive sparring, "fish or cut bait. Put up or shut up. If you feel you have to have some reasonable face-saving compromise to get yourself out of the mess you've got yourself into, *get to it*. But for Christ's sake, stop misleading the country and making a fool of yourself by continuing this game of bluff and bluster. You're dragging your own credibility in the mud and taking America's down with you."

The President had stared at him with a bland and unrevealing thoughtfulness for several seconds. The explosion Willie fully expected did not come: the President was too clever for that. Finally he spoke with what appeared to be an obliging acquiescence.

"Thank you, Willie," he said gravely. "I do appreciate your great concern and I do appreciate your coming down here to tell me so in person. I've been wondering why I haven't heard from you—"

"*What?*" Willie demanded, tenuous politeness and protocol finally terminated by his genuine shock at such monumental gall from one young enough to be his son, young enough so that he had been an adolescent when Willie first came to Congress. "You've been wondering why you haven't heard from me? What the hell do you mean by that, may I ask? I've tried for two solid weeks to get through to you—"

"Oh, of course," the President said with a dismissive wave of his hand. "I was just joking. Jaime has told me every time you've called, but you just have no concept of how busy I've been with this Lolómé business. Our friend Sidi has really kept my nose to the grindstone, I can tell you—"

Willie used a term he did not often use. "Bullshit," he said. "Knock it off."

And he stared at the President with an annoyed contempt he made no effort to conceal. But still the President did not reply in kind, only uttered a startled little laugh and turned to an obviously startled Ray Stanley with a chuckle.

"Our Willie doesn't pull his punches when he gets mad, does he? I thought you could take a little joshing better than that, Senator. Of course I understand your concerns, and believe me I think about the problem Sidi has created all the time. I try to think how I can, as you suggest, find a reasonable compromise that will permit everybody to come out of this in good shape."

"Who do you mean, 'everybody'?" Willie demanded. "Are you including Sidi in that? How can he be satisfied with a compromise if it doesn't permit him to claim some sort of victory over you? How can you be satisfied with a compromise that doesn't give you a real victory over him? Honor and integrity would seem to demand nothing less for you—assuming," he added tartly, "you're interested in honor and integrity at this point."

"Now, Willie," the Secretary said, feeling desperately that he must at least get a word in edgewise in this cauldron of dislike that had suddenly boiled over in the Oval Office. "I don't think you mean to impugn the honor and integrity of the President. That type of argument," he added hastily as Willie seemed about to snap, "Hell, yes!," "doesn't help at all in the situation we're in. I'm sure you don't mean it."

"We wouldn't be in the situation we're in," Willie retorted, not yielding an inch, "if he had given an ounce of attention in his busy day to the consequences of his actions. Actions do have consequences, you know, nowhere more so than in the Oval Office. For no one more inescapably than for the man who sits in it."

"Thank you for lecturing me," the President said, still keeping his tone calm though obviously angered. "For *this* man who sits in this office, honor and integrity are not simply rhetorical abstractions but the very foundation of his conduct as chief executive of this great country."

"That's a fine statement," Willie said. "I hope it means something in the next few days. I hope it's remembered when that famous 'compromise' comes out of the hat. What will it consist of, if I may ask, Mr. President?"

"I am not yet prepared to give you specific information on that," the President said, "*but*"—as Willie looked openly skeptical—"I think I can promise you solemnly—in fact, I give you my word—that it will be a compromise that preserves the honor and integrity—and the best interests—of the United States. As well as my own," he added dryly, "which does not seem to be of much concern to you at this point."

"Oh, but it is, Mr. President," the Senator said. "Believe me, it is. The honor and integrity of the man supports the honor and integrity of the office, which in turn supports the honor and integrity of the country. Which is a very elemental lecture," he added with a dryness to equal the President's own, "but something forgotten in our history. The language goes to the heart of America. Don't *you* forget it."

"I won't," the President said coldly. "I have given you my word. Now, I *am* busy, and I must respectfully ask you to give me the privilege of returning to my duties. It has been, as always, delightful to talk with you, Willie, but I suggest you hold your fire up there until you find out what I have in mind. All right?"

"I'll wait," Willie said. "And I'll try to keep the troops in line—for a reasonable time. A reasonable time for a reasonable compromise. All right?"

"Fair enough," the President said, making his tone more amicable with an obvious effort, but pointedly not rising to show his visitors out, or shake hands. A real rift, Ray Stanley thought unhappily, but what could one do? The personalities were strong, the issue vitally important—and the dilemma for the President, and for the administration whose chief spokesman in foreign affairs Ray had been appointed to be, a grave and dangerous thing.

"Now we'll see," Willie said grimly as they left through the east entrance to avoid members of the media who lurked as usual on the west lawn, notebooks, microphones, and cameras at the ready.

"I think he would genuinely like to find a compromise now," the Secretary said earnestly.

"To get himself out of the situation he himself created," the Senator said.

"Not entirely," Ray retorted, more firmly. "He had plenty of help from Sidi and his friends, whoever they may be."

"Sidi hasn't flip-flopped," Willie noted as they got into the State Department limousine that would drop Ray off at his office and then take Willie on to the Hill. "Sidi's been completely consistent. There's never been any doubt where he stood. His unwavering position from the first has been: 'Screw you.'"

"There hasn't been any doubt where the President stands either," the Secretary said stoutly, ignoring Willie's derisive smile.

"That's right," Willie said. "'I'll threaten you but I won't use force on you, I have other options.' What crap!"

"Well," Ray said, "you've had your chance to give him advice and he's told you he'll work something out. Give him a chance. He's ready to move, now."

"Very late in the day," Willie noted. "But I suppose better late than never. I suppose you want me to hold everybody in line on the Hill and not do anything that might upset what I have no doubt will be a brilliant piece of diplomatic legerdemain."

"It would be a help," the Secretary said. "How about it?"

"There are a few who want to jump ship," Willie said thoughtfully as he turned to contemplation of his own beloved bailiwick, "but I can probably keep the lid on for a little while longer. Johnny Jones called me yesterday to announce that he's going to raise hell in the House about the President's 'damned wishy-washy policies,' but I daresay you folks down here can buy him off if you have anything to do it with."

"We may have," the Secretary said. "The list of overseas indiscretions is very long and very well documented. But I doubt if we'll bother. He's lost most of his nuisance value, he's hit us so often. It's the Senate we worry about. So if you can persuade people to keep quiet a little longer—"

"I'll try," Willie said, "but I warn you he'd better come up with something brilliant."

"He'll think of something," the Secretary predicted with more confidence than he felt.

"You hope," the Senator said. "What will you do if he doesn't? Resign?"

"That's something I haven't thought about," Ray said firmly.

"Think about it," Willie suggested. "You may be confronted by the possibility, one of these days."

"I hope not," Ray said.

"I hope not, too," Willie said, "but it's possible he may come up with something you couldn't in good conscience support."

"I can't conceive of him doing anything I wouldn't be able to support," Ray Stanley said. "I can't believe he would be that Machiavellian. How could he, if he's as incompetent as you seem to think he is?"

The Senator snorted.

"Dream on, Ray," he said. "He's not incompetent, he's a very bright man. He's just stupid in the sense of having no judgment. Machiavellianism can come very easily when you think your political future is being threatened. . . . Promise me something."

"What's that?" the Secretary inquired cautiously.

"If it really becomes too much for you, get out. *Go.* Then we'll hold that hearing and you can tell the whole world about it. OK?"

"I don't think it could ever come to that," Ray said doggedly.

Again Willie snorted.

"We shall see," he said. "We shall see."

Resignation, the Secretary thought as he got out at the department and waved Willie off to the Hill in the limousine, was something he had contemplated far more often than Willie could ever dream, although he suspected that this old friend could sense some of it. Only Mary and Eulie Montgomery knew, in these recent days, how often it had come to mind.

He, too, had been deeply disturbed by the "presidential dance of the seven veils," as Willie put it, and had consistently urged the President to moderate his threats to Sidi unless he was prepared to back them up fully. He had not gone quite so far as Willie had in urging him to "fish or cut bait, put up or shut up," but he had made it clear, in more diplomatic language, that he did not approve of the free-swinging, almost happy-go-lucky promises of "destruction" of Greater Lolómé, harsh UN sanctions, and all the rest of it—unless the President had a genuine willingness to use force. He had never thought for one moment that the President intended to do so (unfortunately, Sidi had received the same impression), but he could not seem to convince him that constantly saying without doing was not a wise process either for his own reputation or that of the United States.

Ray's advice had been almost blithely ignored, although he was expected to defend the consequences when called upon. Willie's suggestion that he might "get out. *Go*" was not a new thought, but it was something he was not yet prepared to do. The next few days, he knew, would not only decide the crisis but in all probability his own future as well. It was not a prospect he contemplated with much equanimity as he walked the corridors of Main State and took the elevator to his beautiful office on the seventh floor to a constant respectful chorus of "Good morning, Mr. Secretary. How are you, Mr. Secretary?"

He scanned his messages quickly. One from Mary, one from Bets, one from Joanie Bourassa—all on the same subject, he was afraid. One "urgent" from Hugo Mallerbie and Eldridge Barnes—he thought that was odd, why would Hugo and the head of the CIA want to contact him jointly? Several "Please call—routine" from members of the administrative staff. One call each from James Van Rensselaer Burden, Able Montague, and Sally Holliwell.

He would answer them soon enough. For the moment he simply breathed a sigh of relief to be out of the acerbic atmosphere in the Oval Office. He told his secretary to bring him a cup of tea and walked over to stare moodily out the window at the familiar outlines of summer-sweltering D.C. laid out before him.

In some future time—if, he thought gloomily, there *was* a future time—histories might well look back and regard The Matter of Greater Lolómé as one of the most notable and most typical foul-ups of American diplomacy in the concluding years of the unhappy twentieth century.

Three Presidents of the twilight had contributed, each in his own way, to the downward slide that now had inevitably produced the blatant insolence of a pipsqueak tyrant grown big with bombs. One was the mile-wide, inch-deep, eternally juvenile, lifelong preppie. Next was the burbling, bumbling, without-a-clue, eternally juvenile amateur. And now came the eternally twisting, turning, now-you-see-him-now-you-don't manipulator who currently sat in the White House. The actions of each had flowed inexorably out of the immediate past. None had possessed the innate wisdom, breadth of mind, imagination, or simple elemental courage to reverse the trend or do it differently. The Matter of Greater Lolómé was the inevitable child of them all. It was, he thought bleakly, the final result of all their weaknesses. It was a classic.

First had come the eternal preppie, playing Sir Galahad on a white horse as he bought the support of nations in a great crusade against a crafty despoiler (who among the general public knew, even to this day, what bribes had been given, what pledges of future military preference had been made, what future policies put in pawn to reluctant "allies" to get them to participate?). The conflict ended, the white knight led his puzzled and frustrated troops home, climbed down off his horse and immediately succumbed to the political judgment rendered upon Presidents who appear to have no real gut involvement in their country's problems. The evil villain remained in power, essentially untouched. The pattern of war without resolution was established, and the aura of weakling began to gather, subtly but unshakably, about the United States.

The white knight left, the amateur took over; the law of political contrast seemed to dictate that domestic interest was the surest guarantor of power. Image became all. Never had an administration clung so grimly to the belief that words, words, words were the answer to everything. For a little time this seemed valid; then international interests, inevitably and as always, once again took over. The United States sank deeper and deeper into one international morass after another because its President had no long-range understanding and no long-range plan for the conduct of foreign policy, and was too afraid to use his own power to cut the many Gordian knots that entangled him. And the aura of weakness grew and became a miasma that clung as tightly as a skin to the great Republic, whose leaders told its people the United States was "the world's sole remaining superpower" even as those leaders acted as though it were the world's sole remaining superpower with terminal self-paralysis.

And finally came the present incumbent, inheritor of weakness and the steady deterioration of strength, handed on to him by his immediate predecessors and now being increasingly followed by himself: the feeble stab at a "second Gulf war" which left Sidi as entrenched as the earlier villain; and now the return engagement, full of bombast, empty, so far, of result—and none in sight.

Sooner or later it had been inevitable that some small unimpressed power, armed by parties unknown, all of them eager to further the decline of the United States, would challenge directly the uncertain giant of the West and its wavering, uncertain leaders. The challenge had come. It had not been answered. The Secretary of State wondered bleakly whether it ever could be, now; whether the United States could ever regain a position of moral authority and actual strength with which to lead the world. But Secretaries of State and other dignitaries charged with the burdens of leading the Republic do not admit this in public and only very rarely to themselves or their intimates. Power is too tenuous, the balancing act too precarious, the chances for the final deadly slip and irreversible fall too great.

It was as though America had long ago set out to cross a chasm on a tightrope; increasingly the tightrope was being eroded away, in many places, now, it was no longer there. But with a deep breath, a refusal to admit reality, and the desperate hope that by pretending the journey could still be made on thin air across the chasm, the nation's leaders kept staggering forward in the hope that no one would notice and that somehow they would arrive safely on the other side and, from there, repair the rope for future use.

Except that, in the challenge of Greater Lolómé, there appeared to be a chilling chance that this could no longer be done; that the tightrope could never be repaired; that the balancing act was almost over; and the final deadly slip and irreversible fall were finally under way and could not, even with the greatest of miracles, be reversed.

National strength depended on many things, the Secretary believed, but on nothing more than the will to use it; and it seemed to him that the will no longer existed, in the country but more particularly and most fatally in the White House. It was too easy, too popular, too politically advantageous, too comfortable and undemanding, to abandon principle and shirk international responsibility if principle and responsibility meant a real possibility of force. The rigors of being strong were too much for a people who didn't want to be bothered or hurt, and their politically flexible Presidents who thought they understood which side their electoral votes were buttered on.

It was no wonder, perhaps, that Sidi was so dangerous and so defiant. He and his friends and secret backers had analyzed their target all too well. The long chain of weakness from Bosnia to Somalia to North Korea to Rwanda to Haiti to the "second Gulf war" and so on into the darkness, built up to an overwhelming certainty in their minds: the United States was no longer a great power but a great weakling, and its Presidents and its people would no longer make the tough choices and do the tough things that would assert and maintain America's power, since those things would inevitably at times threaten their fighting men and women, their material comfort, and their self-centered way of life.

"You seek safety in your cocoon," Sidi had declared to Larry King three days ago (having savored the uses of worldwide television and finding that its leaders were begging him to make use of them to advance his cause against their country), "but we will pierce it. There is nothing but a dead butterfly inside."

"That's chilling stuff," Mary had remarked when she and Ray watched this latest example of what their daughter called "Sidi-ism."

"Verbal brinkmanship," he said dismissively, managing to sound more unconcerned than he felt.

"He seems very confident," she observed. "The tone is becoming more positive the more the President wavers. And don't tell me he isn't wavering. The whole world knows it."

He had not been able to offer any strong rejoinder at that moment. Now he thought perhaps he might be able to. He was more hopeful than Willie had been, after their Oval Office contention.

"Hi," he said now, returning her call. "What's up?"

"The usual," she said, sounding exasperated. "Samir's disappeared."

"Damn it," he said, "what's the matter with that boy? How long?"

"Almost two days," she said, "and Bets is frantic. Boo seems to be alive and well and in his usual cheery good shape—Bets called Joanie and all's well there. He has no idea where Samir is, saw him 'last night or the night before,' quote unquote. Predicts comfortably that he'll turn up safe and sound. Scoffs at the idea that he isn't safe and sound. Joanie's unperturbed. Bets, as I say, is frantic. I'm a little uneasy myself. Have you talked to Hugo Mallerbie?"

"He's left a call for me," the Secretary said. "I'm planning to get to him as soon as I've finished talking to you. Meanwhile tell Bets to keep calm. We'll get on it. I suppose she's talked to the police."

"Not yet. She wouldn't want to embarrass you."

"For *heaven's* sake," he said, exasperated; would nothing ever go forward without a fuss in that household? "Of course she won't embarrass me. Anyway, it will take them a while to make the connection."

"Unless somebody in the media gets hold of it."

"That goes with the territory. I'm sure this is just an elaborate extension of domestic dramas. Tell her we'll look into it and everything will be

OK. Meanwhile, back at the ranch, I've just come from 1600 Pennsylvania, where Willie Wilson and our boy had a shoot-out in the Oval Office."

"Who won?"

"I think Willie may have, though the opposition concealed his bleeding skillfully. He did indicate, however, that he is going to offer a compromise to end the current agitation. Which was a concession, of a sort."

"Of what sort?" she inquired. "Did he tell you and Willie what it's going to be?"

"No," he confessed, "but he did give Willie his word that he would have something to offer very soon."

"How much is his word worth at this juncture?" she inquired.

The Secretary was amused but serious.

"That remains to be seen, but I really think this time he means to stop all the fun and games and get down to serious business. I'm beginning to think we've reached a turning point—maybe Willie did it, or maybe he was just ready to be more practical and Willie furnished the right impetus at the right time. I am, however, more hopeful than I've been for some weeks that we're going to come out of this mess in good shape."

"I'd like to agree with you," she said, "but I'm afraid I remain skeptical. He's too tricky. Did he give you any indication that he would like your help on this?"

"No," he admitted with some discomfort, "but I assume that will come along in due time."

"It had better," she said stoutly. "You're the Secretary of State. Jaime Serrano is a nice Cuban boy but he's not exactly the most experienced of diplomatic advisers."

"Jaime's all right," he said, adding humorously, "for a boy of forty-seven. We work together well. We can work it out between us."

"If you're given the chance," she said. "If the President doesn't pull it out of his hat and surprise you along with the rest of the world."

"He may do that," he admitted, "although I think he's shrewd enough not to."

"We'll hope so," she said, unimpressed. "You do sound hopeful. The United States comes out of this with honor and respect and real achievement, thanks to the statesmanly solution devised by its brilliant President. Is that what you think?"

"We all have to think that, don't we?" he asked simply.

"Yes," she agreed, but less confidently. "I suppose we do."

He called Bets, told her he was sure Samir was just being dramatic and would be home soon, and seemed to calm her down considerably by telling her that he would get Hugo onto it if Samir wasn't home by nightfall; told his secretary to call Hugo and Eldridge Barnes and tell them he would see them at one-thirty; told her to inform the kitchen that he would like a light meal, alone, at noon; and filled in the interim by turning to the reports on a troubled world's crises that came across his desk all day and all night twenty-four hours a day in a tide that never stopped.

Promptly at one-thirty Hugo and Eldridge came in. He could sense at once that something was troubling them; two things, as it turned out.

"Hugo," he said, "El"—gesturing them to the chairs by the window—"it must be something pretty serious for you two to gang up on me in tandem like this. What's the problem?"

"Your son-in-law and Boo Bourassa," Hugo said as they sat down.

"And a little boat, outbound from a port in the mysterious Middle East to the great big city of New York," Eldridge said.

The Secretary looked at them for a moment.

"Are they connected?"

"We're not sure just yet," Hugo said.

"Something's fishy," El Barnes said. "Unusual registry and an unusual pattern of ports visited en route. Something doesn't quite scan right."

"Tell me," Ray Stanley said, prepared, as one had to be in such a world, for anything.

"I'm not sure," Hugo Mallerbie said, "that there is any connection at all. Probably there isn't. But Boo Bourassa's little gatherings are a little more serious than we thought, apparently."

"And the ship is not a pleasure cruise," Eldridge Barnes said. "We have good reason to believe some of the cargo may be atomic."

"It wouldn't be the first time," the Secretary observed. "But why New York?"

"That," El Barnes said, "is the question."

———

"And the answer might not be so pleasant," Hugo Mallerbie said.

"Are you sure that kind of cargo's aboard?" the Secretary inquired. "We can raise hell about it, of course, but it would be nice if we could be sure of our facts. We've been trapped by that ploy before, apparently designed just to make us look foolish—which it has. I'm sure the President would want to be very certain before he authorized us to do anything."

"Would he authorize us to do anything?" El Barnes inquired dryly. "He seems to be good at making a noise, not so good at following through."

The Secretary looked wry.

"You noticed. In instances like this in the past, making a lot of noise has been enough. If you think your information is sufficient—"

"I think it is," El said. "We have some first-rate informants in that part of the world. I don't think it would hurt to put up a holler. And even stop it, if necessary."

"I'll pass it on," the Secretary said. "What about Boo? Samir's missing, incidentally."

Hugo looked alarmed.

"How long?"

"Going on a day and a half," Ray Stanley said. "He and my daughter had one of their rows and he left and hasn't come home. I told her that if he hasn't come home by nightfall tonight, you'd get on it."

"We're already on it," Hugo said. "He contacted me day before yesterday, very hush-hush—didn't want you to know about it—said he had some information he felt the government ought to have—was supposed to come see me yesterday afternoon—didn't show or call—I haven't heard from him since. I'm worried, too. I've asked the FBI to check."

The Secretary, surprised and upset, felt for a moment as though the world had been swept out from under him.

"Why didn't you tell me?" he demanded. "You must consider it very serious, to bring the FBI into it."

"Most of Boo's playmates are atomic scientists," Hugo said, "although they came into this country in several guises, principally diplomatic. Four more have just arrived from various countries in the region, all carrying diplomatic luggage that customs couldn't challenge. We have three possible embassy connections definitely identified."

"And two more possible," El Barnes said.

"So you can see why I'm concerned about your son-in-law and his 'information,'" Hugo said.

"Yes," Ray Stanley said. "So am I. Damned concerned." He struck one fist into the other. "God *damn* it, isn't there enough to worry about in this worthless world?"

"It never stops," Eldridge Barnes said. "It just never stops. You'll tell the President about the ship?"

"Immediately," the Secretary said. "And you"—he looked at them with a mix of confidence and appeal—"will tell me about Samir?"

"At once," Hugo Mallerbie said; and Eldridge Barnes echoed, "At once."

Five minutes later they were gone, and he was on the phone to the White House. The President was not immediately available, but he reached Jaime without delay and told him about the ship—withholding the rest "for the time being," he told himself; struggling not to think, as an old Washington hand, of how the puzzle of Samir might ultimately be solved; dreading what might be, telling himself he was foolish and melodramatic to entertain such thoughts, but in his bones almost certain . . . almost sure.

He did not call Mary then, did not call Bets. It was, after all, in the realm of wild speculation—really wild, he told himself sternly. But Mary had said she, too, was "uneasy," which meant that all the instincts sharpened by her own long diplomatic career in the Middle East were at work, probably reaching the same conclusion as his.

I've got him dead already, he told himself with a deeply worried self-mockery. This is insane. *He isn't dead.* I won't believe it.

And indeed, until yesterday, he had not been. He had been simply an earnest, rather confused, rather explosive, temperamental, and somewhat flaky young man who had thought, under the jovial persuasions of Boo Bourassa, that he was involved with a harmless social group of fellows from the same area who shared the same religion and the same way of looking at things. It was not the way his wife or his in-laws saw them, and that only gave his nocturnal adventures an extra defiance and excitement that were quite delicious. It had all been quite innocent, from his point of view. Nobody, after all, was advocating blowing up any-thing. It wasn't as though they were plotting an attack on the govern-ment of the United States, he had remarked at their last meeting.

Everybody laughed.

A week ago, however, all this had changed. Four new members had suddenly joined the group. They had just arrived in the country, it was explained, as newly assigned staffers of their respective embassies. They had been unanimous in their amazement at how easy it had been to bring through U.S. customs the heavy briefcases that each of them car-ried. Diplomatic immunity, they agreed amid general amusement, was a wonderful thing. The contents of their briefcases, when put together with various items brought in piecemeal, by other members of the group over the past three years, would have, they all agreed with more happy laughter, "quite an impact" on Washington.

It was then, a bit late, that Samir began to become alarmed. But still he was not entirely frightened. Boo always drove him home after their social gatherings, and four nights ago Boo had exerted all his glib per-suasiveness and famous charm to soothe any worries Samir might have. Boo pointed out that the group had always liked to joke a lot; what the newcomers had actually sneaked in was some expensive home electron-ics equipment for various friends, girlfriends, and superiors in the embassies. Boo recalled that he and Samir had been getting a lot of flak at home about their little gatherings; what they should do now, he sug-gested, was tell Joanie and Bets and the Secretary and Mary about these innocent smugglings and let them know how silly it made the two of them, Boo and Samir, feel to be criticized for something that was per-haps a little shady in the eyes of U.S. law but was essentially really quite innocent and really just an amusing prank.

From now on, Boo added, so casually that it seemed a reasonable transition, it might be a good idea for Samir to report anything and everything he heard in family conversations about the plans and atti-tudes of the Secretary. He himself was already doing that, as Samir might have noticed (he hadn't, because Boo hadn't been doing it in open meeting), about the activities of the Assistant Secretary for Near Eastern Affairs, Joan Cohn-Bourassa.

Boo was a persuasive man, and when he dropped Samir off at home around two A.M., he felt with complete self-confidence that he had

Samir convinced. He was accordingly much disturbed a couple of days later, though concealing it behind the joking presence that endeared him to his students, to receive an anonymous telephone call in his Georgetown University office informing him that Samir was known to have called the Undersecretary for International Security Affairs and to have been given an appointment to see him the following afternoon. Why, Boo's informant did not know, but, he suggested, better safe than sorry. And when in doubt, act.

That night Boo had called Samir and urged him to join the group again. Samir had seemed a bit reluctant—he was, deeply so, but didn't dare appear too doubtful—and certainly he did not dare refuse the invitation outright for fear that would definitely arouse suspicion. Having made the leap himself from trust to suspicion, for some reason he could not quite define unless it was something a little too effusive in Boo's manner that had not rung true, he was suddenly, absolutely convinced that what he suspected was true. It was with an uneasiness she sensed that he left a protesting Bets and departed for the meeting.

He was, frankly, terrified; but he went through the motions bravely and, for all his friends of the evening could ascertain from his manner, there was nothing for them to fear.

But they knew now that there was; and, as one of them managed to whisper again to Boo during the evening, better safe than sorry.

When Samir complained of a headache and said reluctantly that he must leave early, there were protestations but no one really tried to detain him. Boo offered to leave early, too, and drive him home, but Samir said he'd rather walk. This caused some amusement and jokes about the perils of walking alone in nighttime Washington, but it was agreed, amid more laughter, that someone of his ethnic background was certainly far less conspicuous in Washington these days than a lot of other people of other ethnic backgrounds; and so he set out, along tree-lined streets and charming old alleyways, to make his way home through the deserted quiet of late-night Georgetown.

He was proceeding at a good clip, feeling apprehensive but determined to walk off his fears and his headache—which, brought on by tension, had been quite genuine though it served his purpose neatly— when he became conscious that a car was approaching behind him. Instinctively he began to hurry, until he heard Boo call his name and being by that time tired and beginning to think about finding a taxi if possible at that late hour, he turned around thankfully. He could not see the driver but could see Boo waving vigorously from the passenger's side. He started to step forward, assuming the car would stop. It did not. The last thing he saw before it hit him was Boo's smiling face, arm raised fraternally, friendly voice calling his name. Then the world stopped.

His body was taken across the river to Virginia and hastily buried in a shallow grave in a clump of trees off a country road near Dulles. Boo got home around two A.M. and tiptoed to bed on a sofa in the living room, as was his custom when late, not wishing to disturb Joanie who was, as usual at that hour, sound asleep.

Two days later a country boy and his dog found Samir's body. Headlines flared, the Secretary and his family wept, a private funeral was held, investigations by FBI, State, and CIA began. Twenty-four hours later the sensation was swept away to less prominent pages and much reduced coverage by the news that began to come from the White House.

Matters portentous and a thing of state, hitherto stalled by apparent presidential bluffing and indecision, began to move in Washington, Greater Lolómé, and New York. What the media promptly dubbed "the Lolómé Compromise" took over the front pages and major newscasts.

In Georgetown, Boo and his friends continued to meet quietly, regarded with suspicion by State, CIA, and FBI, but protected by diplomatic immunity and the absence of proof.

In distant seas what Eldridge Barnes referred to wryly as "our own *Marie Celeste*" made its last call at a friendly port and began its slow progress across the Atlantic. It too was protected by absence of proof. Its cargo remained suspicious but not absolutely identified; no overt challenge could be justified. Kept under surveillance by satellite but immune from interference, it chugged slowly along on its mysterious way, due to make landfall in New York in about two weeks.

In the White House the clever occupant of the Oval Office regarded the future with confidence and satisfaction. Everything, he felt, was back on track. The world was looking to him, and to America, for leadership, and he was about to provide it.

The first step, carefully leaked to the media, was suddenly on all the world's front pages:

President Moves to Break Lolómé Impasse

Report Secret White House Talks With Chinese, Soviets to Find "Acceptable" Way Out of Crisis

World Breathes Sigh of Relief As Head-On Clash Seems Averted

There were, however, a few little details that remained to be worked out. Some of them were quite surprising. The President was quite sure, however, that they would leave the honor and integrity of the United States, as he saw them, intact.

FIVE

1 Such, indeed, had been his intention from the first; and looking back upon it now, while he and Helen had their usual "nightcap chat," as she called it, before retiring, he could not find much fault with his actions in the past two months. There had been some exaggerations here and there, some blusters that in retrospect might not have been too becoming, but on the whole he was pleased with his record as it stood to date.

His satisfaction must have been apparent in his face, for she challenged him on it as she often had during their long, companionable climb to power. It was her way, she said, of keeping him humble.

"Does it?" he had once asked her, amused.

She had laughed.

"Not so anyone could notice," she said. "But I'm going to keep trying. There must be room for humility in there somewhere."

"There is," he responded, suddenly serious. "I'm not really the arrogant son of a bitch some of my critics seem to think."

"Mmmmm," she murmured thoughtfully, refusing to give him the absolution he still, after all these years, liked to have from her.

Tonight he did not feel arrogant; just relieved at the way things seemed to be turning out.

"You're pleased with the way it's going," she suggested.

"Finally," he agreed. "Aren't you?"

"Oh, yes," she said. "I'm not exactly sure where you're heading at the moment, but at least you seem to be heading somewhere. There's been the impression in the last couple of months that you were stalled on dead center. There hasn't seemed to be much movement, or any new ideas."

"I made the mistake of thinking Sidi was a sensible man who could be persuaded by reason and logic," he said.

She gave him a wry look.

"You made the mistake of thinking Sidi was a man who could be intimidated by raw threats of American power," she said. "He wasn't. And isn't. If you'd analyzed him correctly in the first place you wouldn't have adopted that tactic and made yourself look like a fool."

He gave her a sharp look but had learned long ago that anger in response to comments like that simply didn't work. She would just laugh and probably repeat it later, having found it drew blood.

"Only a wife," he remarked, "would dare say something like that to the President of the United States."

"Who thankfully has only one," she said with a chuckle, "so he's used to it. Just imagine if you were Sidi! Four, and a harem. The poor man must really be henpecked."

"It doesn't seem to have made *him* humble," he remarked with a ruefulness that came out sounding less humorous and more envious than he had intended.

"So what are you going to do now?" she inquired, refreshing their cups from the pot of decaf the staff had left for them. "Go to war?"

"The country wouldn't take it," he said. "Or the media, or the UN, or the allies, and every other damned kibitzer on American foreign policy, around the world."

"So?"

"So I'm going to use diplomacy. And there, I think, I'll have him."

"What can you offer him diplomatically?" she asked. "He doesn't seem to be overwhelmed by the idea of a financial bribe"—he winced slightly at the word—"and he obviously intends to eliminate poor old Sheikh Mustafa and grab his country and his oil, if he can get away with it—and I'm sure he sees nothing in your actions in recent weeks that would indicate to him that he can't. So what now? A humiliating surrender on your part? A tacit agreement that he can do whatever he wants? And what about those bombs? How do you propose to neutralize those?"

He made a wry face.

"You ask so many questions."

She smiled.

"They're certainly not original with me. And they certainly have to be answered, in some way or another. Did your Chinese and Soviet friends have anything to suggest this morning? I notice the papers and the newscasts are making a big deal of your 'secret talks' with them. Was that just more window dressing, or is something specific going to come out of it—something 'acceptable,'as the buzzword has it?"

"I think we're starting down the right road," he said, so smoothly and confidently that if she had not known him so well she would have been persuaded, as so many were, of his complete sincerity and good faith.

As it was, she simply gave him one of her disconcertingly candid glances and inquired, "At whose expense?"

"Not at ours," he said firmly, "and that's for sure."

"You made that clear to your friends this morning? You didn't leave anybody in doubt?"

"I think I can say to you without hesitation," he said solemnly, "that we reached a clear understanding about what comes next in this most difficult situation."

"That sounds like the photo-op remark you'll soon be giving us to explain what's happened," she said wryly. "And about as close to an answer as I can see I'm going to get." She rose gracefully from her chair in the single, flowing movement that was still characteristic of her at almost fifty, came over, and kissed him lightly on the forehead.

"Sleep well," she said, and added, again wryly, "I assume we all can, now that everything has been taken care of in a way so satisfactory to the United States, its honor, integrity, and general standing in the world. And, of course, those of its President."

"I think I'll emerge in good shape," he said comfortably. "And so will the country."

She paused at the door.

"And Sidi? And Mustafa? And oil and bombs and world stability and all the rest of it?"

"Go to bed," he ordered with a chuckle. "It will all become clear in the morning."

"I can hardly wait," she said. "Will I see you at breakfast?"

"Up to you," he said. "I'm having an early meeting of the National Security Council. Juice, coffee, and sweet rolls on the house, in the Roosevelt Room at eight. You're welcome to attend if you'd like."

"No, thanks," she said. "I'd like to, but I think perhaps not in a crisis situation. It's always so easy for the media to charge me with interfering. I'm always good for a think-piece on a dull day."

"They'd never know," he said, "and anyway, it won't be a dull day, I assure you. I really do think we're on the right road."

"If you can present it that way to the country," she said, in one of those rather oblique remarks he never knew quite how to interpret, "then I'm sure that's how it will be."

And blew him a kiss and moved, with her usual self-contained, cool elegance, out the door and across the hall to her room.

He sat for a long time reviewing the events of the morning and the clear path he thought he now saw ahead to end the crisis created by obstreperous Seedy Sidi. He was thankful he had not let himself be provoked into open retaliation. That would have entailed monstrous strategic difficulties, warned against every hour on the hour, it seemed to him, by the Secretary of Defense and the chairman of the Joint Chiefs. To have taken such action would also have been to severely damage his reputation as statesman and lay him open to the charges of "warmonger," "egomaniac," "irresponsible gambler" so readily applied by many of the media to those of whom they disapproved. His ticket was to keep the peace, preserve the vital interests of the United States, and help maintain the stability of the world—simultaneously.

A big order, he thought with a sigh as police sirens along Pennsylvania Avenue wailed across the lawn below his window, momentarily reminding him of the problems of the everyday world. Upon the king . . . upon the king. Upon the king rested many burdens and, if his diplomacy did not succeed, the fearful reckoning of repudiation at the polls.

Aided by the suggestions—virtual demands, though he would never acknowledge that publicly—of the People's Republic of China and the Second Soviet Republic, he was confident now that success was inevitable. It was all beginning to fall into place, thanks to their "helpful suggestions" to which he knew he would be paying tribute when he made his summarizing speech to the country and the world sometime in the next week or so.

That speech would set the crisis at rest and permit humanity, as he planned to say, "to proceed upon its peaceful and constructive chores." He would have been hard put to say where he saw anything peaceful and constructive in the way humanity was progressing at the moment, but half the business of national leadership was the mouthing of suitable clichés. The President of the United States above all others was required to mouth them, for of no one else was so much expected and no one else, so it was constantly reiterated by the nation's commentators, had such power to calm the frictions and factions of the world.

Thinking back over this morning's conference with the Chinese and the Russians, he found that he was still experiencing the bite and humiliation of being talked to like a schoolboy. He was thankful Helen had not probed too deeply or he might have let go and unburdened himself of the frustration he felt at the disrespect and near-contempt his visitors had shown him. The outside world would never know, but he knew, and it annoyed him still, even though in effect the conversation gave him clearance to get gracefully out of the corner into which he had painted himself. Getting out of that corner might entail damage to others who would presently emerge as the scapegoats, but the reputation of the United States would be reestablished in good shape. More importantly, as he saw it, so would his.

It had begun at six o'clock this morning when he had been awakened by a call from the Secretary of State. He had not bothered the Secretary in the last few days—the murder and burial of a son-in-law, the President felt, was quite enough for Ray to handle. But Ray, bless his heart, was already back on the job. He reported that Li Peng Liu and Vladimir Novotny had just called him; both had just heard from their governments in Beijing and Moscow; both wanted urgently to see the President to convey official messages. He would recommend most strongly, the Secretary said, that the President receive them at the earliest possible moment.

"This may be the break you're looking for," Ray said.

The President accepted this remark, and the assumption behind it, without comment; urged Ray to continue to take it easy, and sent his love to Mary; and said he would see the ambassadors promptly at eight A.M. Promptly at eight A.M. they were there. He offered them coffee, settled them informally on a sofa facing the Rose Garden window, and took his seat in an armchair opposite.

"Now, gentlemen," he said briskly, "what do you have for me?"

"A message from my government," they said simultaneously; smiled slightly at their unexpected chorus; and handed him official envelopes heavy with the seals of government.

He opened the envelopes, read their brief contents without comment, though a flush of anger mounted steadily as he proceeded; finally tossed them on the coffee table in front of him; looked at the ambassadors with a bland and unyielding expression and said, "So?"

"My government would appreciate your comments, Mr. President," Li Peng Liu said.

Vladimir Novotny agreed with a resounding, "Da!"

"You mean I am expected to dignify this kind of bullying nonsense?" the President inquired. "Now, why would I want to do that?"

"You are being given the best advice of the People's Republic of China," Li snapped. "It is not nonsense!"

"Neither is the advice of my government!" Vladimir cried with equal indignation. "It is not 'bullying'!"

"It is not the type of language which I, as President, feel it is necessary to accept," the President said. "What is the purpose of these two extraordinary documents, apparently framed conjointly by your two governments? Are you presuming—*do you dare*—to threaten the President of the United States? Are you presuming—*do you dare*—to tell me what to do? And if so, gentlemen, can you think of any good reason why I should pay the slightest attention?"

"Because you are in an impossible situation," Li Peng Liu said quietly, "and you want to get out."

"Yes," Vladimir Novotny said spitefully. "Having created it for yourself with your futile blustering, you want to get out."

For a moment the President considered ordering them out of the White House, except that some early bird in the press corps would be on duty and would get wind of it. It would make a grand story—"President Kicks Chinese, Soviets Out of Oval Office"—and he didn't want any of that. Instead, with a considerable, but successful, effort of will, he suppressed his anger and continued to address them with reasonable dignity. More, he thought scornfully, than they deserved.

"I am impressed," he said dryly, "by your astute analysis of the current situation. I gather from these two communications"—he paused and rephrased with relish—"these two *impudent* communications—that I am being threatened with some sort of reprisal from your governments if I should proceed with any form of military action against Greater Lolómé. Is that the gist of it?"

"The People's Republic," Li Peng Liu said, "would be forced to act under its treaty of mutual defense with Greater Lolómé."

"When was that signed?" the President inquired sharply. "I don't recall any such document."

"We do not tell the world everything," Li said with a show of asperity. "Only when it becomes necessary."

"We, too," Vladimir said smugly, "signed a similar document exactly"—he paused and went through an elaborate charade of counting on his fingers—"six days ago. We would also feel constrained to come to the aid of our gallant ally if he should be attacked by the United States."

"No one is going to be attacked by the United States," the President said impatiently.

"We were convinced by your statements that it was imminent," Vladimir said.

"It was our distinct impression," Li agreed.

"I have said specifically from the beginning," the President noted with some annoyance, "that I ruled out the use of force."

"Yet you threatened 'other options,'" Li remarked, "which made no sense unless force, as a last resort, was to be used. That was always the assumption with which we all heard your loudly repeated threats. We could not believe that a President of the United States would be so naive as to make such profound assertions unless he intended, if necessary, to back them up with force."

"Why would I possibly want to attack Greater Lolómé?" the President inquired with apparent bewilderment. "It could be done, we have the means, but it would be a most difficult and unpopular thing to do. It would be foolish. By the same token," he added bluntly, "it would be absolutely foolish for the People's Republic and the S.S.R. to attack the United States. If an attack by us on Greater Lolómé is foolishness, an attack by your two governments on the United States would be complete insanity. And you know that as well as I do."

"Nonetheless," Vladimir said with a certain relish, "our united hostility could make it very difficult for you in the world."

"There would be no need for declarations of war or military actions," Li said. "We would simply block you at every turn, everywhere, in every way."

"So what else is new?" the President inquired dryly; and for just a second his visitors had the grace to permit the smallest of smiles to break through their disapproving solemnity. The smiles disappeared in a second and all was solemnity again.

"Suppose we agree," he said, "that the chance of military action, in whatever context, on whichever side of this issue, is minuscule. And also ridiculous. But let us agree that the situation does demand some sort of solution within a reasonable period of time. What do you suggest, gentlemen? I am obviously not going to permit Sidi to achieve a perceived victory over the United States. What, therefore?"

He sat back and studied them, expression earnest, intent, completely bland, and unperturbed.

For several moments they returned his gaze, equally unimpressed, equally bland. Then Li spoke softly.

"Why do you not accept the divergence of his energies elsewhere?"

"I will not permit raw aggression to occur," the President said flatly. "It would be contrary to everything I believe and stand for."

"It need not be made to appear that way," Li suggested, still softly.

"It can be made to appear a diplomatic triumph," Vladimir agreed. "You would emerge with great honor."

"It would not really be honor, however," the President said slowly.

"Who cares," Li inquired gently, "if honor accrues?"

Again there was silence.

Finally the President rose and his guests perforce did likewise.

"Thank you for coming by and sharing your wisdom," he said, and shook their hands. His tone was light and ironic. He had to make it so to preserve the appearance that he was in control of things.

But he knew after they left, and had known all day, and knew now as he sat alone in his room in the silent White House, that a compact with the devil of political ambition had been suggested, and he knew that he was very probably going to take it and use his enormous powers of office and personal persuasion to make it pass into history as the triumph he needed at this time.

What it might do to the reputation and standing of the United States, and to its influence in the world, he glimpsed briefly but did not dwell upon. In the manner of his immediate predecessors, his own political advantage was, at this point, paramount. He was confident he could sell his solution to the country, and that was what mattered now.

He thought for a moment, picked up the telephone. The White House switchboard, its operators prided themselves, never slept; nor did they ever fail to track down anyone the President wanted, however exalted the person, late the hour, or remote the geography. In this case there were no problems. They had all just returned to their homes from a lively mariachi-band party at Dolly's in honor of the new Mexican ambassador. As with their call from Greater Lolómé, they accepted this one with alacrity.

"I know it's terribly late," the President admitted with becoming contrition (it was about eleven-fifteen), "but I *would* like your advice."

"Nonsense!" James Van Rensselaer Burden said stoutly, putting his studs back in. "I'll be there in fifteen minutes. Delighted!"

"I'm a night owl," Able Montague said cheerfully, abruptly wide awake although he had really been about to collapse from the sheer social fatigue of six black-tie dinners in seven days. "Count me in."

"I'll be up for hours yet," Sally Holliwell informed him, hastily resurrecting the evening gown she had just tossed in the hamper to go to the cleaners. "I'll walk across the river and be there in no time."

The President uttered a delighted little laugh.

"I'll bet you could, at that," he said. "I'll bet you could! . . ."

"Now," he said after they had all arrived inconspicuously by cab at the east entrance and been whisked swiftly up to the Lincoln Study through the silent mansion, "what will anybody have?" He swung open the doors of a handsome antique rosewood liquor cabinet and gestured at its sparkling array. "I've also ordered coffee from the kitchen, which will be along in a minute."

"Nada," Sally said.

"Coffee, please," requested Able and Jimmy Van.

"Oh, come on," he chided humorously. "Surely you're game for at least one mild little nightcap."

"We've been to Dolly's and are plumb liquored-out," Sally explained. "However, a very light crème de menthe and soda."

"That sounds good," Able said.

"Likewise," said Jimmy Van.

"Now," the President said after he had served them and himself with a concoction he secretly considered rather insipid and hardly worthy of a hard-drinking town, "I saw your famous TV show with old Seedy, of course, and I've read your various comments since, but I want to get a real, absolute, inside fix on him before I proceed with what I want to do."

He could sense three pairs of reportorial ears pricking up, and reflected with some amusement that it was very easy to manipulate members of the Washington media if you just expended a little thought and care on it. They lived at the seat of power, were often on a first-name basis with its principal players, and yet when you came right down to it, the allure of Really Being in the Know was the greatest carrot anybody could dangle in front of them. All their ostentatious little skepticisms and self-protective barriers toppled at that ultimate flattery. He could never understand why some Presidents had difficulty with the press. All you had to do was take a leaf from the Kennedy book: be sure at regular intervals to scratch their heads and pat their tummies, and they'd lie down and roll over for you anytime.

"What *are* you planning to do, Mr. President?" Jimmy Van inquired cautiously.

"I asked you first," he said with a grin that was intimate and flattering. "However, if you insist. How do you think Sidi would react if I"—and he proceeded to outline in the most sketchy terms, just enough to send them out tomorrow morning trumpeting it to the world, what he had in mind.

When he finished there was a long and increasingly uncomfortable silence. Perhaps his inspiration of inviting them at this unusual hour in the hope his dramatic confidence would win their support was not going to be so successful after all. He decided to plunge right into it, having discovered long ago that this was the best tactic in moments of public uncertainty.

"What's the matter?" he demanded with a carefully calculated hint of asperity. "Don't you like it?"

"Unto the just shall be their just rewards," Jimmy Van murmured.

"But, golly," Sally remarked tartly, "reward *this* one? Are you sure that's what you want to do, Mr. President?"

"I'm not rewarding him," the President protested, beginning to be genuinely annoyed now; perhaps this really had been a mistake, although surely he could make them see it his way. They had all been generally supportive in their treatment of him, if a bit restive in their private comments, which had been carried back to him from Washington's endless gossip mill. "I'm trying to give him a reasonable out that will permit him to retreat gracefully from the confrontation he has forced upon me in these recent weeks."

At this they all looked a little blank. Able could not resist a gentle murmur: "*He* has forced upon *you?*"

"Certainly," the President said sharply. "Have I been the one threatening Lesser Lolómé? Have I waved atom bombs in *his* face and heaped scorn upon *him?* Let's get your priorities straight, please, and your memories as well. Where have you been in the past couple of months?"

"Watching," Able said.

"With a mixture of awe and apprehension," Sally said.

"And a decreasing measure of hope," Jimmy Van suggested.

"Definitely decreasing," Sally agreed.

"Well, I'll be damned," he said. "I—will—be—damned." He decided to play the humor card, which often worked when things became solemn. His tone became much lighter. "I'm starting to get us out of this. That ought to have you all jumping up and down with glee. You ought to be doing cartwheels on the south lawn, Sally. Accompanied by you, Able, and you, too, Jimmy. If you two spavined old warhorses aren't too tired to prance."

At the mental picture this evoked they all laughed. Tension diminished.

"Seriously," he said, "I did want your advice on this. And I was hoping you'd help ease the way with your colleagues and the country. There'll be an NSC meeting early tomorrow morning; you can play this as a leak from that, if you like. Or maybe it could be something you heard at Dolly's, one hears everything at Dolly's. But spread the word. It will help get things rolling, help create the public mood I want. Build some programs around it, you two; write us a sermon in your column, Jimmy."

"Fly a trial balloon for you," Sally said dryly, "so you can yank it back if it doesn't fly."

"It will fly," he said with a sudden grimness. "I'm committed to it. It will fly."

"What if the NSC doesn't—" Able began.

"It will fly," he repeated. "Do you really have any doubt?"

"It's desperation time," Able said thoughtfully. "You do need something. Maybe this will be it. After all, as Lyndon used to say, you're the only President we've got."

"Good," he said with a chuckle, confidence resurging. "Remember that. And thanks for coming by at this ungodly hour."

"It was worth the price of admission," Sally said.

"Every bit," said Jimmy Van.

And off they went, not, of course, committing themselves to him one way or the other on what they would do with the information. Downstairs at the east entrance, waiting for their cabs, they were more candid with one another.

"What do you make of that?" Able inquired.

"Complete surrender, I call it," Sally said.

"That's what *you* call it," Jimmy Van said wryly, "but wait until he gets through selling it to the country."

"He won't have to sell it much," Able said. "He knows his constituency. When did Americans ever want to really disturb themselves over something that far away and that inconsequential?"

"*Inconsequential?*" Sally demanded as the first cab pulled up under the portico and they moved to help her into it. "A-bombs? An international wild card like Sidi?"

"That's the way *they* regard it," Able said.

"Wait and see," Jimmy agreed bleakly. "Able's absolutely right. Americans won't care until the bombs come here someday and then it will be too late."

"Write us a sermon as he suggested, Jimmy," Sally said as she got in and prepared to close the door. "Maybe it will save the day."

"I'll write it out," Jimmy said grimly, "but it will take more than that to wipe out the long-range consequences of this little episode."

"I'll call you tomorrow," Sally said. "I think the three of us ought to do a program together about it."

"I come first," Able pointed out with amicable insistence. "I'm on Saturday, you're on Sunday. Why don't you two join me?"

Sally rolled down the window as her cab started to pull away.

"For once," she called out, "I'll yield. I think it's that important."

"So do I," Jimmy Van called back.

"And I," Able sang out as two more cabs rolled up. "I'll talk to you guys tomorrow."

Upstairs, the President returned to his room along the deserted corridor, its utter silence almost physically haunted by the ghosts of so many strong characters, so many great events.

He had some inner doubts about the course he proposed to follow, and he knew Helen would have some, too, but he honestly did not feel that he was betraying the past or failing to live up to the heritage of his office.

Sometimes things had to be done. It was all in how you sold them to the country. On many occasions, he felt, history was what the President said it was. He intended that the history of this eventful moment should blend seamlessly into the pattern of what had gone before.

He intended it should show him as he pictured himself, a leader wise and courageous and ever conscious of his high responsibilities to his troubled, uncertain land.

2 When the Secretary of State met with his inner group of advisers, "the usual suspects," later that day, he told them the National Security Council meeting had been one of the most extraordinary—and disheartening—he had ever attended. This judgment was endorsed by the Deputy Secretary, who said she had never participated in an event since entering the Foreign Service forty years ago that had so dismayed and disillusioned her.

"Lordy," Basil Rifkin said, starting to be humorous but realizing instantly that this was not what was called for on this occasion, "it really *must* have been something, the way you two are reacting."

"Very strongly," Hugo Mallerbie observed.

"Better tell us," Joan Cohn-Bourassa said, "if State's going to be involved. And I suppose it is."

"That's why we're here, isn't it?" asked Gage McGregor with his ineffable giggle.

"That's right," Ray Stanley said soberly. "State will be involved."

"As long as—" Eulie Montgomery began, then stopped. They all looked at her blankly.

"You're being a mystery woman, Eulie," Joan Bourassa remarked. "Tell us, tell us! We can't stand the suspense."

"It isn't funny," Eulie said, as soberly as Ray. "It's really *very* discouraging."

"Contrary to everything we've always believed and done our best to exemplify in this department," the Secretary agreed.

"Good heavens," Joanie said, "out with it!"

It had begun, the Secretary related, with their arrival at eight A.M., as requested, in the Roosevelt Room. Juice, sweet rolls, and coffee on the house were already in place. So also, much to their surprise, was the

First Lady, whom they all greeted, with respect, as "Helen," which had been her expressed desire to the top officials of the government from her first day in the White House.

"His Nibs will be here shortly," she said with a smile. "He almost overslept. It must have been the sleep of the just."

"It couldn't have been anything else," the Vice President agreed with a certain nervous eagerness which she accepted with a comfortable laugh that put him at ease.

"Of course, Hank," she said in a kindly tone. "What else?"

"There you are," the President said, coming in the door with his characteristic confident stride. "And there *you* are," he said to his wife, bending to kiss her cheek as he passed her on his way to the head of the table. "You changed your mind."

"I got curious," she said with the sort of relaxed good humor he knew from experience indicated an extra attention he should be wary of. "I thought maybe you might need to be kept in line."

And she looked around the table with an amusement in which they were invited to join. Very cheery, the Secretary of State thought, alert, as they all were, to these little presidential undercurrents.

"Hah!" the President said. "I guess that tells me. Well, gang"—he looked around the table at Ray and Eulie from State; Secretary Arlie McGregor and chairman of the Joint Chiefs Gen. Bill Rathbun from Defense; Eldridge Barnes, director of the CIA; the Vice President—"I think we're about to approach a turning point in our dealings with little Mr. Sidi."

"Is he going to let us get off the hook, Mr. President?" Eldridge Barnes inquired, startling them all with his audacity, but then, El was an officially recognized character and allowed his accepted range of outrageousness. No one else would have dared such a remark, except possibly the First Lady.

For just a second it appeared that the President, this time, would not be amused by El's sanctioned audacities. But he laughed, quite comfortably, and gave as good as he got.

"I see the joker's on the job," he remarked with a chuckle, "early in the morning though it may be. No, he's not going to let us off the hook, El. Nor are we going to let him off the hook. It's going to be a mutual business."

"Mr. President," Arlie McGregor inquired in a frankly puzzled tone, "what does that mean?"

"It means," the President said firmly, "that we are working very hard on a compromise for which I would appreciate the endorsement of the National Security Council."

"As long as it doesn't involve the commitment of American troops," Arlie McGregor said solemnly, as though he had a choice.

"We could do it," Gen. Rathbun agreed, "but only as a last resort."

"Don't you people keep up with the news?" the President demanded with some exasperation. "How many times in the past two months have I said that I would not, repeat *not*, use force in this matter?"

"We have always assumed that it was there as a last-resort option," Bill Rathbun said.

"At Defense we always have to assume that it is a last-resort option, no matter what the White House may say," Arlie McGregor agreed.

"You always assume the President is lying," the President said tartly. "Well, thank you very much!"

"We have to make that assumption," Arlie said, "because we have the responsibility to make good on it if the assumption becomes fact."

"Well, well," the President said, tone becoming sarcastic. "Little did I know I had such sophisticated thinking backing me up. Very comforting."

"It would be," General Rathbun said, unabashed, "if you ever needed us."

There was silence for a moment. The President obviously had not anticipated this particular turn in the conversation.

"But you have been diverted, Mr. President," Ray Stanley said smoothly. "You were about to tell us of your compromise."

"Thank you, Ray," the President said. "And thank you, Eulie, thank you both for being here, so soon after your recent family tragedies. It shows an admirable devotion to duty and we all appreciate it. I appreciate it."

"We are here to serve you, Mr. President," the Secretary said simply.

"That's our job," Eulie Montgomery agreed. "All of us here would do the same."

There were murmurs of agreement around the table.

"And your compromise, Mr. President?" Eldridge Barnes reminded in a tone unimpressed by pleasantries.

"Ah, yes," the President said. "Back to business, back to business. Always keeping our noses to the grindstone, eh, El? I am awaiting at this moment a call from the national security adviser. You've probably wondered why he isn't here."

"Where is he?" El inquired. "Mars?"

"He should be in the U.S. embassy in Lesser Lolómé," the President said, and could not conceal a certain lighthearted pleasure at their obvious surprise. "After having had a conference with that stout defender of social justice, democratic principle, and unalienable human rights, Sheikh Mustafa, known to those who love him as The Mouse."

Instinctively Ray looked at Eulie and El. Arlie McGregor looked at Bill Rathbun. The Vice President looked carefully at no one. And no one looked at Helen. Her expression, had they done so, would have been seen to be curious, attentive, and completely noncommittal. This, though they would not have realized it but he did, was for the benefit of the only one whose eyes went instinctively to her face, her husband.

The Secretary of State finally broke the silence cautiously.

"I assume there was some reason for not notifying the department of this mission?" he said.

The President gave him a smile that could almost have been described as carefree.

"We're all part of the team," he said lightly. "We all contribute our efforts to the same end. It all goes into the same pot, right? If it works, we all share the same glory."

"Some of us more than others," El Barnes murmured.

"If it is glory," Eulie Montgomery remarked. "What exactly is Jaime expected to accomplish, Mr. President?"

"Wait," the President said. He glanced at his watch. "Any moment now"—and the phone rang.

"Probably," Ray whispered to Eulie, "he's had Jaime's call on hold for the past ten minutes."

"Probably," she agreed. "But it makes an impressive bit of business."

"Jaime!" the President exclaimed heartily. "Are you exhausted?"

"Yes, Mr. President," Jaime's voice boomed over the amplifier. "I *am* tired. Eet ees a long trip. But I 'ave seen him. Ambassador Burton will tell you."

"Mr. President," came the gravely dignified tones of Arthur Reeves

Burton, "your special envoy is exhausted but he has done his duty. He has seen the Sheikh. In my company, as you requested."

"And—?" the President inquired.

There was a noticeable hesitation at the other end.

"It was not an entirely satisfactory interview," Arthur Reeves Burton said carefully.

"He ees peessed off," Jaime said, which broke up the solemnity in the Roosevelt Room for a few moments.

"What's the problem, Arthur?" the President demanded when they had settled down again. "Did you boys tell him we would support him financially in any way he requires?"

"His Majesty does not seem to think that is sufficient under the circumstances," Ambassador Burton said.

"He ees an old bandit," Jaime remarked. "He wants millions—billions, probably. He also says he weel not budge out of 'my 'istoric 'omeland and my ancien' royal heritage.'"

"He is indeed quite adamant, Mr. President," Arthur Burton observed. "Very hostile to your proposals."

Ray looked again at Eulie; something profoundly uneasy was growing in their minds. This time they both looked at Helen. She returned their glance with an almost imperceptible but definitely quizzical shrug. They all went back to listening intently.

"Did you outline them in full to him, Jaime?" the President inquired.

"Oh, yes," Jaime said in a tired but exasperated tone. "He is a steenking old camel-lover. I don't think we can deal with him."

"It is not we who have to deal with him," the President said, voice suddenly cold. "It is he who has to deal with us. Tell him that."

"We have told him virtually everything we could think of," Arthur Burton said, "except possibly that—or, at least, not quite that bluntly. He is not impressed."

"I want to talk to him," the President said flatly.

"We thought you might," Arthur Reeves Burton said. "He is here."

"In the next room," Jaime said. "Probably cooking cheeken on the floor."

"Get him in," the President ordered. "Tell him I demand to speak to him."

"Oh, he's ready," Ambassador Burton said. "He wants that. Be prepared, Mr. President."

Jaime uttered a cheerful laugh.

"He called me so many bad names in Arabic I gave up counting," he said. "I couldn't understand him anyway, the old fart, but he understood my expression. . . . Wait a minute. Here he is."

"Your Majesty," Ambassador Burton said politely. "If you will take a seat here by the telephone. Mr. President, His Majesty will speak through an interpreter, as he knows very little English."

"How convenient," the President remarked. "Put the old fart on. Your Majesty!" he exclaimed, voice firm but respectful. "What an honor it is to speak to you directly today!"

A slither of liquid Arabic erupted from the amplifier. For approximately one solid minute, by Ray Stanley's watch.

"His Majesty say," the interpreter reported, "that he considers it a *dis*honor to speak to you, traitorous infidel."

"My, my," the President said, winking at his wife. "Does he really? To what do I owe the honor of these kind words?"

Again the liquid verbal lightning rushed forth, perhaps half a minute this time.

"His Majesty say," the interpreter reported, "you are faithless, worthless liar. He say you always promise to defend him and now you want him to surrender to that piece of camel dung from the desert, Sidi."

"*What?*" the Secretary of State demanded, too startled and dismayed to be diplomatic about it. His deputy looked equally dismayed. El Barnes looked cynically unsurprised. An expression of growing relief appeared upon the faces of the Secretary of Defense and the chairman of the Joint Chiefs. The Vice President struggled to look earnest, attentive, and devoid of thought, which, the First Lady reflected, was probably an accurate depiction of what was going on inside. Her own expression remained impassive though her private reaction was every bit as dismayed as Ray's and Eulie's.

The President placed his hand over the mouthpiece.

"You must admit," he said blandly, "I have to do *something*. This seems best for all concerned."

"But to surrender Lesser Lolómé to Sidi?" Ray demanded with increasing dismay. "To give Sidi everything he wants without a fight? To condone aggression? To leave his atomic arsenal untouched and uncontrolled? To lie down and let a two-bit nothing walk all over the United States of America?"

"And its President," Helen murmured, just loud enough to be heard.

Her husband shot her a sudden sharp glance.

"We will fight this out in a minute," he said, beginning to look annoyed as he realized the depth of the opposition he was arousing. It had literally not occurred to him. "Please let me finish with this character first, if you will." He returned to the phone.

"Tell His Majesty," he ordered in a voice abruptly hard and unyielding, "that His Majesty knows that I defended him successfully against Sidi before. Tell him that it is impossible for me to defend him in the same way this time. Therefore we must all make compromises. Tell His Majesty that he may fight Sidi if he wishes, but the United States will be unable to come to his assistance. Tell His Majesty I wish him well. May Allah give him victory, because the United States cannot."

And he gave his listeners a look both annoyed and defiant.

This time the Arabic lasted almost two minutes. Its liquid flow was interrupted at regular intervals by a series of explosive gutturals whose meaning was not in doubt.

"I don't think he likes you," Eldridge Barnes observed.

"Tiresome old son of a bitch," the President said.

Presently the flow stopped. The interpreter cleared his throat. It was obvious from his voice that he agreed with his ruler.

"His Majesty say," he said, "that he despises you, Mr. President. His Majesty say you are a worthless coward who becomes less than a man in the face of battle. He say you are a coward who becomes a woman when Sidi threatens you. His Majesty say—"

"Listen to me!" the President snapped. "Tell His Majesty to listen carefully! My representative, the Honorable Jaime Serrano, national security adviser to the President of the United States, has offered His Majesty all that His Majesty will get from me and my government. We are offering him money to aid him and his family if they feel they must leave Lesser Lolómé, though we are well aware that His Majesty and his family have plundered his innocent people until they are beggars in the streets, and have taken from them so much gold it would make Aladdin blush with shame. If His Majesty wishes to remain in Lesser Lolómé in the hope he can work out some arrangement with President Sidi, we are willing to offer our good offices in working out such an arrangement, and we will guarantee it when it is put in place. Mr. Serrano has explained the details of these suggestions to His Majesty. His Majesty knows them. I will not repeat them here. It is enough to say that His Majesty now has my pledge to see that his interests and those of his family will be protected in the event of a full-scale invasion of Lesser Lolómé. His Majesty may accept them or reject them as it suits him. It is entirely up to His Majesty. But remind His Majesty of one thing: if he rejects these proposals and Lesser Lolómé is invaded, and if by some awful chance, which Allah forbid, his stubbornness should force President Sidi to use the atomic weapons at his disposal, then His Majesty and he alone will be responsible for calling down upon Lesser Lolómé, and perhaps a far greater area of the earth, all the horrors of hell. Tell that to His Majesty!"

For several moments there was silence, in Lesser Lolómé and in the Roosevelt Room. Finally there was a very short rejoinder in Arabic, and more silence.

"His Majesty say," the interpreter said finally, "that your word is as worthless as a snake in the desert. He despises you and has no more to say to such a perfidious one."

More silence, and then Arthur Reeves Burton said in his usual dignified tones, filled now with an obvious regret, "His Majesty is now leaving the embassy. I am sorry your talk proved so fruitless, Mr. President. I shall continue to try to persuade His Majesty to take a more reasonable line, although," he hesitated and then went on, "although I must confess, Mr. President, that your proposals are far from what a reasonably self-respecting head of state, even a small one such as this, would normally be expected to accept. And, I must add, far from what your previous statements in this crisis have led the world to expect."

"Good for *you,* Arthur," Eulie murmured to Ray.

"You can always resign if you want to, Arthur," the President suggested with a calculated indifference. "Put Jaime on the line, will you. Thank you for your assistance. . . . Well, Jaime, I guess we now go to Phase Two, right?"

"Whatever," Jaime said.

"You don't sound very happy about it," the President said with a defensiveness they could all sense, a sensitivity to implied criticism that they had not anticipated.

"I am here, Mr. President," Jaime said simply. "Whatever you direct, I do."

"Very well," the President said with a sudden sharp impatience. "Do it!"

"Yes, sir," Jaime said. "You will notify him I am coming, please. I would not want Air Force Two to be shot down by mistake."

"He will be notified," the President said. "Let me know what he says."

"I would expect," Jaime said dryly, "that his reaction will be quite obvious to the whole world. But I will call."

"Thank you, Jaime," the President said. "Keep in touch."

"Yes, sir," Jaime said, reluctance now quite clear. "As you direct."

He went off the line; silence ensued. The President hung up.

"Well," he said, looking around the room with an almost defiant satisfaction, "that's that."

"Where is he going, Mr. President?" Ray Stanley inquired.

"Greater Lolómé City," the President said. "Is that all right?"

"No, Mr. President," the Secretary of State said crisply. "It is not."

"You can always resign too, you know, Ray," the President said as the tension in the room suddenly shot up.

The Secretary gave him a long, thoughtful look.

"I will take your permission under advisement, Mr. President," he said levelly.

"Good for you," Helen said quietly, and ignored the look her husband gave her.

The Vice President gasped audibly.

"What are the other details of the proposal you have made to Mustafa, Mr. President?" Eulie Montgomery inquired after a moment. "Are we permitted to know?"

"Not at the present time," the President said. "They will all become clear when His Majesty"—he gave the title a sarcastic twist—"finds that he must bow to the pressure of world opinion."

"Do you think world opinion will be on your side in this, Mr. President?" Eldridge Barnes inquired.

The President smiled comfortably, back on top of things.

"Of course," he said. "Where else can it be? Surely not on the side of a—to quote Jaime—steenking camel-lover from the desert. Right?"

"I'm not so sure, Mr. President," El said. "But it will be interesting to watch. I assume Jaime is going to Greater Lolómé City to unleash Sidi and tell him to go to it, right?"

"He will be informed of what has transpired with Mustafa," the President said. "That is only simple diplomatic courtesy."

"And when Sidi strikes, that will force Mustafa to accede to your demands," Arlie McGregor said in a bemused tone, as though he was just now beginning to grasp all the implications of what was happening here and in the far-off Lolómés.

"I have made no demands," the President said blandly. "Only proposals. How he reacts to them will be up to him. Meanwhile, Ray and Eulie, I want you to contact the UN tomorrow and arrange for them to appoint the United States as their agent to negotiate a lasting peace between Greater and Lesser Lolómé."

"Is that an order, Mr. President?" Eulie inquired.

"As long as you remain on board," the President said with an indifference so well acted they could almost believe he meant it, and was not secretly fully aware of the domestic political implications if he suddenly lost several of his top diplomatic people over an issue of conscience. "You can line that up, can't you, Ray? It isn't as though it would be a major crisis they're convening for."

The Secretary studied him a moment.

"Isn't it?" he inquired thoughtfully. "It was, up to yesterday."

"But now it's all being solved," the President remarked; and added with an almost cruel challenge in his voice, "Don't you agree?"

But Raymond Cass Stanley refused to rise to the bait; just stared back at the President expressionless, until the President, flushing, finally glanced away.

"Well," he said with a sudden busy briskness, "thank you all for coming. You now know where we stand. We'll all close ranks and see it through." He gave his wife a mischievous, charming look. "Isn't that right, Helen? You'll help us see it through, won't you?"

She shrugged and gave him an enigmatic little smile; but, like the Secretary of State, did not speak.

"I'll hear from that later!" the President predicted with a jovial laugh as he rose from his chair and started out. "As all you husbands know full well!"

"And," Eulie Montgomery said with a certain angry relish as she and Ray reported to their department colleagues, "I hope to hell he does hear from her. How she stands it, I don't know."

"She's one tough lady," Basil Rifkin said. "That's how. . . . So the fix is in, right, and he's going to solve the great crisis with the great compromise of turning tail in the face of Sidi's bluster and throwing Mustafa down the well as the sacrifice. What a triumph!"

"So it appears," Ray Stanley said bleakly. "The details, as he told us, will develop as the triumph unfolds."

"How can he do such a barefaced thing?" Joanie Bourassa inquired in a disbelieving tone.

"He can do it with the arrogance of Presidents," Ray said. "Not all of them have enough arrogance to get away with it, but when they do, watch out. When they have it, they *have* it. They can convince the country the moon comes up in the morning and the sun rises at night. It's all in the confidence and the manner."

"And the words," Eulie said glumly. "The cancer is in the words."

"So are you two going to quit?" Basil Rifkin inquired bluntly.

The Secretary sighed and looked at Eulie. She sighed and looked at him. Then they both began to laugh, ruefully, and with the almost despairing wryness of two old friends who find themselves caught, after many years of success together, in the same dilemma.

"Give us a little time," the Secretary said.

"We've got to consult," Eulie said. "Meanwhile," she added sternly, "I don't want to see any speculation popping up from this quarter, please. This is a difficult time for us, and we have a right to work it out without distraction."

"Right," Hugo Mallerbie said. "You have our word."

And apparently the secrecy held, for no speculation emerged in the next few hours from either the department or the NSC; no speculation, either, about what might be happening in the Lolómés. By some miracle in the age of universal prying, Jaime's mission and the consequences flowing from it slipped by, for the time being, unreported.

In New York the next afternoon the Security Council took time from routine matters to approve a sense-of-the-body resolution that "The President of the United States, or his accredited representative or representatives, is hereby designated to represent the United Nations in negotiations leading to a permanent solution of the crisis existing between Greater and Lesser Lolómé."

Delegates were pleased to hear, from Li Peng Liu of the People's

Republic of China and Vladimir Novotny of the Second Soviet Republic, of their complete confidence in the President of the United States in these negotiations, and their absolute certainty that the outcome would be satisfactory to the United Nations and beneficial to the whole world community.

A broadly smiling Kwazze Kumbatta ("KWA-zee Koom-BAH-tah") announced the unanimous vote. Thus, he thought happily, were the mighty brought to heel and the arrogant humbled.

Above the Atlantic, Jaime Serrano flew home, staring out the window between spells of fitful sleep, wondering if he had done the right thing in being such an obedient servant to his devious master in the White House.

Across the border of Lesser Lolómé the troops of Sidi bin Sidi bin Sidi were already beginning to move north in a slow but steady advance into the Middle Range of the Mountains of Lolómé. The range was a jumble of harsh, barren peaks, some rising as high as seventeen thousand feet, and harsh, narrow valleys that could easily be used to block invasion if the will was there. It did not seem to be. In any event, Sidi was not particularly concerned. The land advance was basically a show for the television anchormen who would soon swarm onto the scene from their bunkers in New York; he wondered if it would last long enough to make their trips worthwhile. His air force, strengthened by the fifteen new fighter jets he had just been given, was already pounding the capital of Lesser Lolómé in an unrelenting assault that promised to reduce it largely to rubble in another twenty-four hours if the attack continued in its present fury.

In The Matter of Lolómé, the final nut-cutting, to use Big Bill Bullock's term, was about to begin. The public, as always, would not be allowed to see it. They would not have believed it anyway. Reality is much too cynical for the innocent to comprehend. The great majority cannot grasp, even could they know, the brutalities that all too often lie behind the stately march of historic events.

Behind the scenes, which is where the basic bloody work of politics and government takes place—when it has to be bloody, which is far more often than the public realizes—there were small cries of futile protest and helpless terror, rather like the small rodent whose namesake was most directly involved. No one outside the abattoir heard them;

only the most sophisticated observers drew the logical conclusions from the way events unfolded. The Mouse, caught in the middle of a game he understood all too well but was powerless to escape, was about to utter his last futile squeaks before he and his colonial-accident country passed from the international scene forever.

Sidi Issues Twenty-Four-Hour Ultimatum to Lesser Lolómé: Surrender or A-Bomb Falls

Mustafa Makes Urgent New Appeal To United Nations. He Is Told It Is in Recess Until Next Week

3

"Ray," the President said next morning, "get over here and bring Eulie. I think we're approaching the end of our little episode in the Lolómés."

And so obviously they were as the NSC gathered for the last time to consider The Matter of Lolómé, which had now become, if only very briefly, The War Between the Two Lolómés.

State was there, the Secretary and Deputy Secretary looking deeply concerned and not happy; Defense was there, Arlie McGregor and Bill Rathbun looking relieved that the turn of events had removed them still further from responsibility; the CIA, Eldridge Barnes looking cynically unsurprised and unperturbed; the Vice President, looking troubled as his personal instincts told him he did not like such ruthlessly cynical proceedings, while his political instincts told him he had no choice but to pretend approval and support; Jaime Serrano, still tired and jet-lagged, obviously uneasy and unhappy about the part he had played in the past two days' events; and the First Lady, who had canceled a luncheon with two female friends of hers in the Senate because, as she told her husband, "I want to watch how you perform the surgery on poor old Mustafa."

The President did not like this, and had come to the meeting in an unpleasant humor as a result; but it was obvious by the time they were all in place around the table that his equanimity was restored.

"Thank you all for coming," he said with the unnecessary but flattering deference with which he always started their meetings. "As you gather from the news, things have moved very fast in the Lolómés since we met a couple of days ago. Mustafa is obviously on the run, Sidi is clearly winning; it will be only a matter of hours. The specific reason I called you together is because Arthur Burton called a while ago and said

Mustafa wanted to speak to me. I imagine this is to seek my active inter-
vention, which I am ready to give. The UN resolution gives me authority to propose a settlement, and I am ready to do so. I wanted you all here
as my witnesses and also, of course, to put forward any suggestions that
may occur to you to help clear up this most unfortunate business."

He looked around the table as if he expected challenges; and got one.

"Mr. President," Ray Stanley said, "did you ask the UN to put off
Mustafa's appeal so the Council couldn't debate it until it was too late?"

"I have had no contact with the Council this morning," the President
said flatly.

"That isn't what I asked you, Mr. Pre—" the Secretary began.

The President cut him off.

"I know what you asked." His voice turned cold. "Does it matter?"

"Yes, it matters!" the Secretary said, not giving an inch.

"I don't see how," the President said. "The outcome is inevitable.
Why prolong it? Anyway," he added as the Deputy Secretary, the First
Lady, and Jaime Serrano all appeared visibly disturbed, "the Sheikh has
been in the embassy waiting for me for the past two hours—"

"Have you deliberately kept him waiting, Mr. President?" Eulie
inquired.

"I had to have time to round up you people," the President said. "It
hasn't hurt him to wait."

"He's only desperate," the First Lady remarked.

"I'm putting it through now," the President said blandly. "Excuse
me." And he picked up the phone, contacted the Signal Corps, sat back,
and waited.

They all felt a rising tension, compounded partly of suspense about
what Mustafa might say and do, partly, on the part of the more sensitive,
a feeling of disgust at what they were apparently about to witness, the
murder of a small, helpless country to save the reputation of a major
world leader. History was full of examples: it was not the first time international decency and morality had been sacrificed for such an objective.
But it was shocking to have to be present and witness it firsthand; and
even more shocking to have to accept that it was one's own President
who was doing it.

"Mr. President," Arthur Reeves Burton said, dignified tones undis-
turbed by the fact that the thump of conventional bombs dropping on

the capital could be clearly heard in the background. "His Majesty wishes to speak to you."

"Yes, Your Majesty," the President said; and could not resist adding dryly, "I hope I shall not be too perfidious for you today."

"Oh, stop it!" Helen exclaimed angrily. "Just stop it! Of all the unworthy, unbecoming—"

"All *right!*" her husband snapped, momentarily pressing the mute button. "All *right!*" He waited for a moment, breathing heavily; took his hand off the phone and resumed in a calmer and more businesslike tone.

"Yes, Your Majesty. What can I do for you in this unfortunate situation?"

Again the slither of Arabic, urgent this time, openly anxious, frightened, beseeching; no more insults now.

"His Majesty say," the interpreter said, voice equally distraught, "he cannot continue to submit his country and his people to such punishment by the forces of the evil one of Greater Lolómé as you can hear happening right now. He say he must surrender unless he have help right away from you and your great country. He urge you to intervene and save our poor, helpless country. He beseech you, Mr. President. He beg you."

"Tell His Majesty he need not do that," the President said. "We will do what we can. Would it help if we were to send Lesser Lolómé planes and troops from the two carriers we have in position off Greater Lolómé—"

"Mr. President!" Arlie McGregor exclaimed in alarm.

The President winked and held up a restraining hand; mouthed the word "Wait"; and did so, an expression of bored patience on his face.

A silence in Lesser Lolómé followed, then a murmur of consultation. Ambassador Burton came on the line, voice for the first time showing a trace of urgency.

"His Majesty says he did not mean sending help to Lesser Lolómé, Mr. President. He says he means an attack on Greater Lolómé. He says this is the only way to stop Sidi. He says if you will launch an attack from the carriers immediately upon Greater Lolómé City and the military airfields around it, and simultaneously bomb troops now advancing in the Middle Range, it will effectively stop him. That is what he meant."

"Oh," the President said, sounding disappointed but friendly and concerned. "I had not contemplated aggression myself, which would violate everything I stand for and believe. I had thought that if I were to provide arms to Lesser Lolómé, then Lesser Lolómé would be able to defend itself and could defeat Sidi on its own as any self-respecting sovereign state should be able to do. His Majesty does not believe himself capable of that, even with arms from me?"

Again the Arabic rose and fell, rose and fell, melancholy and beginning to sound hopeless.

"His Majesty say," the interpreter said finally, "that his people are not prepared for war, Mr. President. He and his family are not prepared for war. They look to you to save Lesser Lolómé. There is nowhere else to turn."

"I see," the President said thoughtfully. He paused, and allowed the pause to grow until his wife, the Secretary of State, Eulie Montgomery, and Jaime Serrano all began to shift restlessly in their chairs. Then he spoke with a sudden decisiveness.

"I tell Your Majesty what I can do," he said. "I will renew my offer of two days ago which you saw fit to reject so summarily out of hand: I will see to it that you and your family are rescued from your capital by my planes and paratroops from the carriers, and I will see to it that you have safe transport to some other country of your choosing—"

He was interrupted by a burst of excited Arabic.

"His Majesty say they can go to England," the interpreter said. "He say they go often to London."

"Yes," the President said dryly, "don't we all. A lovely city. But"— there was a sudden dismayed silence in Lesser Lolómé—"but before His Majesty starts packing, a few things will be required of His Majesty."

There was another silence, followed by a short burst of Arabic, obviously protesting at first, sinking almost immediately into an acquiescence despairing and devoid of fight.

"His Majesty say," the interpreter relayed, sounding equally bereft of heart, "what are they?"

"I have been in contact during the night with President Sidi," the President said, ignoring the reaction this caused in the Roosevelt Room. "I wanted to explore with him under what conditions he would be prepared to enter into an agreement with Your Majesty to terminate his present attempt, singly, by himself, to right the wrong which he sees as having been done by former colonial oppressors to your mutual ancient homeland, Great Lolómé. He assured me that he believes that you and he have the same objective, the same desire to right this wrong, and reunite your tragically shattered nation into the single Great Lolómé which once was the pride of your ancestors and the dream of all your peoples. He says he is confident you agree with this."

He paused. This time the response was excited, emphatic, obdurate.

"His Majesty say," the interpreter reported, "that he is the sole bearer of the flame of Great Lolómé, and he and he alone has Allah's charge to reunite it. His Majesty say he denies utterly any right of Sidi, who comes from a desert tribe that never held power in Great Lolómé, to be part of this. He say Sidi is a liar and a criminal. His Majesty say he will die in the glory of Allah before he will accept partnership with Sidi, whom no man trusts and who kills as he smiles and would kill His Majesty as quickly as any man."

The President looked thoughtful and for a moment did not reply.

"And yet," he said presently, "and yet—I hear the bombs falling at this very moment on Lesser Lolómé. And just a few moments ago, I was told by Your Majesty that you could not hold out against President Sidi without my help, which I am unable to give you, to attack President Sidi. And I heard Your Majesty say that you would accept my safe conduct for you and your family to go to London rather than stay and fight President Sidi with the weak and inadequate forces Your Majesty has—to say nothing of the terrible vengeance that may be wreaked on you and your family by the people of Lesser Lolómé when your weakness becomes apparent. What am I to make of Your Majesty's contradictions?"

Again there was silence in Lesser Lolómé, followed by another spurt of Arabic, but, again, flat, dull, dispirited.

"His Majesty," the President said softly, again touching the mute button, "is apparently a realist." And winked at his wife, who, staring down thoughtfully at the table's polished surface, did not respond.

"His Majesty say," the interpreter said finally, "what are the conditions Your Highness suggests? And why should His Majesty trust Sidi, who is less than a dog's turd in the path of the righteous?"

At this the President could not resist a quick smile, nor could the others refrain from amusement. The moment passed immediately and he responded with suitable solemnity.

———

"Very well, I shall tell Your Majesty. These are Sidi's conditions. I urge you to consider them most carefully.

"First, I am afraid that President Sidi, on penalty of using one of his atomic bombs on your capital, as he has promised if you do not comply, will require that Your Majesty leave the throne of Lesser Lolómé. He does not require that you leave the country, you may remain if you so desire—"

There was a sudden harsh snarl, scathing, scornful, mocking.

"His Majesty say," the interpreter said, "that he would not live one hour after Sidi entered the capital if he were to stay in the country."

"That would be for Your Majesty to decide," the President said. "I have told you we would assist in your departure if you deem it necessary. At any rate, your abdication is the first condition of President Sidi.

"Second, President Sidi is agreeable that Your Majesty, if you so desire, may appoint a council of regents to preserve the throne of Lesser Lolómé until such time as the reunification of Great Lolómé is complete and all its peoples have a chance to choose their own form of government.

"This council would consist of twenty members, of whom twelve would be appointed by President Sidi"—again the bitter response, no translation, none necessary—"and eight might be appointed by Your Majesty. Of Your Majesty's eight, four might be drawn from Your Majesty's family; the remaining four would be leading citizens of Lesser Lolómé whose names would be approved by the twelve members of the council appointed by President Sidi."

The President paused. Again the scathing sibilance but no translation. He continued.

"In addition to the regency council, President Sidi agrees with me that it would be advisable to appoint an economic council to administer the oil revenues from the bountiful fields of Lesser Lolómé."

There was a sudden angry burst of protest. Before the interpreter had time to report, which was not in any event necessary, the President responded firmly.

"I must point out to Your Majesty that by your own account you are in desperate straits. You are in no position to impose conditions of your own or to reject President Sidi's. I am here to give you the guarantee of the United States that whatever is agreed to between yourself and President Sidi will be honored and maintained. I have his assurances of this."

"Are you—" the Secretary of State started to demand, but did not quite add the word "crazy?" although he obviously thought it.

The President gave him a bland look and continued.

"The economic council will dispose of the oil revenues of the present country of Lesser Lolómé, and its successor country, reunited Great Lolómé, on the following basis:

"Thirty-one percent to the present national bank of Lesser Lolómé and its successor national bank of Great Lolómé, to be used solely and entirely for the betterment of the people of Lesser Lolómé; one percent to Your Majesty's Swiss bank account for the personal use of Your Majesty and Your Majesty's family, wherever you may be; and sixty-eight percent to the government of a reunited Great Lolómé, which shall have the right to enter into such international contracts for the development and distribution of the oil of the present Lesser Lolómé as economic necessity and political advantage shall dictate."

The rush of syllables burst out and this time were translated.

"His Majesty inquire," the interpreter asked, his own tone sympathetically acid, "what percentage President Sidi has agreed to give to the government and oil companies of the United States?"

"That is subject to negotiation," the President said.

"But there will be such concessions?" the interpreter pressed.

"There may well be," the President said crisply. "I would not want to betray my responsibilities to my country and my people by not securing whatever just compensation I can get for my assistance in solving the problem which faces Your Majesty. Finally," he went on, ignoring the abrupt silence at the other end and in the Roosevelt Room, which held such a mixed-up whirl of emotions that no one there could have defined them exactly at that moment, "President Sidi has assured me that within two years of the end of present hostilities there will be a free, open, democratic referendum of the people of Lesser Lolómé to determine, one, whether they wish to remain a separate nation under the rule of Your Majesty's family or, two, whether they wish to join the peoples of Greater Lolómé in a single reunited Great Lolómé under some form of government to be chosen by all the peoples at a later suitable date in a similarly free, open, and democratic election.

"These undertakings to be set forth in the form of a Declaration of Understanding to be signed at the White House by Your Majesty and President Sidi one week from today."

At this there was a real explosion, loud and sustained.

"His Majesty say," the interpreter related presently, voice frigid with his own outraged disapproval, "that he will not sign anything, ever, with President Sidi. His Majesty demands to know what assurance Your Highness has that Sidi will do any of these things even if he does sign such a declaration of understanding."

"It's 'Excellency,' not 'Highness,'" the President corrected almost absentmindedly. "He has given me his personal word," he said calmly; and added before there could be further explosion, "and I have already given you my personal guarantee that the United States—and I think I can speak for the United Nations as their representative on this occasion—together will monitor his compliance. We will even, if you like, append such a statement of guarantee to the body of the declaration."

Another lengthy stream of syllables, scathing and sarcastic.

"His Majesty say," the interpreter reported, "that Sidi's word is worthless. Why should His Majesty trust the guarantee of the United States, which has guaranteed so many things in recent years and has failed so many of them? Why should His Majesty believe that the United Nations, which has been so weak so many times, would be strong this time? His Majesty does not understand, either, what advantage there is for him in going through a play-act on the White House lawn to satisfy the ego of Sidi and Your Excellency."

"The advantage for Your Majesty," the President said with a blunt finality that indicated he was about to wrap it up, "is your life and that of your family, together with a reasonable portion of the enormous fortune you have stolen from the people of Lesser Lolómé. Your Majesty and your family do not deserve to be rescued, but I am prepared to rescue you. Do you wish to remain in Lesser Lolómé and take your chances against the advancing forces of Sidi, which are even now raining bombs upon your capital, to say nothing of the vengeance of the people of Lesser Lolómé when they realize that you are beaten? Or do you wish to get out alive—now—and go to London, if that is your desire?

"I shall await Your Majesty's answer, but I must point out that if you have more than two or three hours to make up your mind, I shall be very surprised.

"Let me hear from you, Your Majesty. I am here. But not forever. . . . Arthur," he added, voice matter-of-fact, "get yourself and your people ready to leave. I shall order the helicopters to land at the embassy and remove you from Lesser Lolómé in exactly three hours."

"Yes, Mr. President," Arthur Reeves Burton said, tone calm and devoid of comment. "We are ready to go."

"Good," the President said, and broke the connection with a decisive emphasis that must have brought further dismay to the royal Loloméan heart.

"What can he possibly do, after that?" Eulie Montgomery asked into the ensuing silence in the Roosevelt Room.

"He can do exactly what he is going to do," the President said. "If you all wish to return to your offices now, I will inform you of his answer the minute I get it. Or you are welcome to remain here until he calls." He uttered a dry little chuckle. "I predict it will not be long. . . ."

"Exactly ten minutes and twenty-three seconds," Eldridge Barnes reported presently, having followed it second by second on his watch. "During which there must have been a lot of royal soul-searching."

"Not much," the President said.

They heard for the last time the long, looping, liquid Arabic, dispirited, disheartened, dismayed.

"His Majesty say," the interpreter said, voice trembling with emotion, "he and his family will be ready to leave with the embassy staff in three hours."

"Good," the President said, expressing no emotion one way or the other. "You leave with them, too, interpreter."

"Thank you, Your Highness," the interpreter said, openly sobbing, apparently with gratitude. "I am small, minor cousin. I did not do any of those bad things."

"I know," the President said soothingly. "Good luck to you. Arthur, stand by."

"Yes, sir," Arthur said. "We are."

"I will be advised of your safe arrival on board," the President said. "Goodbye for now." He hung up and turned to the Secretary of Defense and the chairman of the Joint Chiefs.

"Arlie and Bill," he said, "give the order to the carriers, please."

Arlie McGregor and Bill Rathbun hesitated.

"Will the helicopters be safe, Mr. President?" Arlie inquired.

"Do you want them to respond if attacked?" General Rathbun asked.

"They won't be attacked," the President said.

"Of course not," El Barnes said with a wry little laugh. "Everything's all arranged. Right, Jaime?"

The national security adviser looked uncomfortable but answered honestly.

"I told Sidi what we want," he said.

"And Sidi," El said, "overcome with sheerest amazement and profoundest gratitude at how surprisingly well everything has turned out, snapped to attention and responded smartly, 'Yes, sir! Your wish is my command!'"

"Not exactly," Jaime said with a wan little smile. "But he agreed."

"Of course," Eldridge Barnes said. "What else?"

"Arlie and Bill," the President said, face impassive but tone clearly relieved at the way things were going—saved by the bell again, his wife thought in familiar frustration—"hop to it. Get downstairs to the situation room and talk to the carriers direct from there. They're alerted and waiting for you."

After they had left, another silence fell on the Roosevelt Room. Those remaining seemed almost reluctant to leave; almost as though if they stayed in place it would somehow be as if it had never happened; as though they had not been party to something none of them had contemplated when they originally entered the service of this clever, twisting man who had just pulled himself back from the brink of what would have been an embarrassment at best, a genuine disaster at worst—as though they had not been witness to something which some past occupants of his office would have rejected in moral revulsion, but which some others, particularly in these recent years when the world had become increasingly dog-eat-dog, would have recognized and approved as an example of the grim realities that were more and more necessary for the sake of the occupant's political survival and the wider survival of the United States of America.

The Secretary of State finally broke the silence in a voice in which genuine wonder and moral repugnance were mixed.

"What have you achieved, Mr. President?" he asked. "From the point of view of what I thought the United States stood for—and"—his voice became bleak—"what I thought *you* stood for—nothing has been ended, nothing has been resolved. With the single exception of a change in the map of the Lolómés and a different and more hostile hand on the spigot of Lolómé's oil, what has been achieved?

"Nothing has hurt Sidi, certainly.

"He has achieved *his* goal of capturing Lesser Lolómé and its oil— with your help and virtually without firing a shot.

"He still has his atomic bombs and his missiles, and we still do not know who gave them to him. We still do not know who his backers are.

"He is still free to follow their orders, whatever they may be in future, to threaten the stability of the region and the peace of the world.

"He still is an international renegade, encouraged by the enemies of this country and of world peace, restrained by no one, a loose cannon free to do as he will."

His listeners were very still, the President most of all, face impassive as he followed the Secretary's words intently but without visible reaction.

"And he has achieved," Ray went on, "what obviously was one of his major objectives, and of the people who are behind him: he has defied, humbled, and humiliated the United States of America and its President. Aided by your own ill-conceived bravado and your own ill-conceived attempts to substitute bluff for power"—the Vice President gasped— "aided most of all by your ego-driven willingness to tempt fate by putting yourself in an untenable position you could not support and could never have made good on—which was a bluff, as he knew and the world knew, and so he called it—Sidi has won.

"And what of the future, Mr. President? Any realist knows what it will be. The busy world's attention will swiftly turn elsewhere. Other crises and challenges will grab the television and the headlines. And quietly and shrewdly, without fanfare, convinced, and rightly so, that there will be no reprisal, Sidi will proceed to tear up your precious 'Declaration of Understanding.' And who will stop him? The world will have other concerns, and you won't want to be bothered, and you will see to it that you *aren't* bothered. Who will say him nay?

"First will come the so-called regency council. It may meet once, but that will be all. A minor news item out of Great Lolómé City, or whatever Sidi decides to rechristen it, 'Sidiville' maybe, or maybe just 'Sidi,' will report that the council has been disbanded 'at the request of the people' or some such touching democratic phrase. Who wants to fight the people for a regency council?

"Next will come the cancellation of Mustafa's retainer, which nobody will cry for, the old thug doesn't deserve it—except that its termination will be another independent abrogation by Sidi of the terms of your declaration.

"The national bank will never see any of the oil money. It will all go into Sidi's own tightly controlled economic council and from there into his pockets and Swiss bank accounts and those of Young Sidi and of all the next generation of royal or semi-royal robbers. Any pledges to you of fair access for American firms will be forgotten. One or two minor American companies may be given a small bite of the pie just to appease you, but that will be it—again, by 'the democratic will of the people.'

"And finally, it will be the will of the people that any pledges of free and fair elections—or any elections of any kind—will be put on the shelf and forgotten. This will be described as the overwhelming wish of the people, which is democracy, and so democracy will die stillborn in the name of democracy. And who will object, or really even notice? The world will be too tired, and preoccupied with other things. You will be running for reelection, and preoccupied with other things. . . .

"You will portray this as your triumph, Mr. President, but the decent, the honest, the truthful, and the thoughtful, when this begins to sink in, will know it for what it has been: a failure of honor, a failure of will, a failure of moral purpose, which is almost gone in this world of ours, and to whose further death you have contributed.

"And so it will all come to nothing. And overriding everything else, fundamental to our own future, and to the times we live in, the record will stand in history: the word of the United States, the threats of the United States, the bluffs of the United States, the so-called principles and ethical standards of the United States, do not exist. They are frauds. Your recent predecessors have shown them to be so, and you have continued their great tradition. And America will slip a little more on the long downward slide which may take a few more decades to complete but which only a miracle, now, it seems to me, can reverse.

"And so, Mr. President," he concluded quietly, "I *am* resigning. I could not stay longer to be made party to such a shabby betrayal of my country and of all the principles I have always believed in and tried to adhere to in my many years of service to the United States."

Into the silence that followed, no one moving, no one speaking, no one even looking at anyone else, Eulie Montgomery spoke, beginning with a slight touch of humor, ending as seriously as her old friend.

"And I too, Mr. President," she said. She smiled briefly. "Ray was always the most eloquent of us, even 'way back in Riyadh so long ago, when two young folks, along with Mary Stanley, his wife, started out on the long diplomatic road we have walked along pretty much together all these years. So I'll let eloquent Ray speak for me, too.

"I can't swallow this, Mr. President. It's too much. And I'm too old and too tired to fight any longer in an age that doesn't honor my kind of honor. I think that you have done great damage to yourself, to your office, and to the United States of America, though I suspect you will be able to present it to the country as a great victory. But in this room, and in many other places where thoughtful and decent men and women discuss it, it will be known for what it is. It will be known. . . .

"I thank you for your trust in me in giving me this appointment. I only wish I still had the trust in you with which I accepted it."

And she sat back quietly, a big, statuesque, aging black woman, face as plain and honest as the day is long, eyes brimming with tears and lips quivering with the pain with which she had spoken.

"Anyone else?" the President inquired, as Jaime Serrano made a slight movement, apparently thought better of it and sat back, eyes and face deeply troubled. "Then listen to me. I will give you a little primer in politics and the necessary requirements of leadership, late twentieth century."

He passed a hand across his eyes, suddenly looking some years older than his actual fifty-one. They all aged, the Secretary thought; it got them all, no matter how secure, how ebullient, how convinced of their righteousness, how sure of their infallibility. Mother Nature kept the score and nothing altered it, not even the defiant egos of Presidents.

The President settled back in his chair, arms in an inverted V, chin resting on his folded hands. He looked slowly at their attentive faces, one by one. He let the moment run for a bit. He terminated it according to his own sense of timing, which, as always, was excellent. He spoke in a casual, friendly tone, though he was clearly on the defensive. At the same time it was obvious that he was convinced that the ultimate truth of it was on his side, and that he would be able to make them see it; or if not they, then the worldwide public for whom this was basically a brief preliminary rehearsal.

"I've taken quite a pounding here in the last few minutes," he remarked, not sounding angry, just stating the fact. He looked again around the table.

"What would you have done?" he inquired rhetorically, not really asking.

Nobody responded. He didn't expect them to; would obviously have been annoyed if they had. It was his time at bat. They let him have it, listening with fascinated interest.

"I was confronted by a threat from Sidi, announcing his atomic bombs and missiles, which most probably came from China, Russia, North Korea or Iran or Iraq or Libya—or who knows, possibly from all of them, just to spread the game and give each some say in what he did with them. He was the selected cat's-paw. The object was to do as much damage as possible to world stability, and as much as possible to the United States.

"You obviously think that, with my help, he *has* done damage to the United States. But look at it from where I sit."

He paused as Arlie McGregor and Bill Rathbun tried to tiptoe in unobtrusively and resume their seats. He smiled.

"We see you," he remarked, and for a moment the tension eased.

"I was just saying," he repeated, and it returned, "that Sidi and his friends have obviously been out to damage this country, and most of you think that, with my help, he has succeeded. But see it my way for a minute.

"I thought at first that the threat of American power would be enough to stop him. I expended quite a lot of time and effort on that. I know most of you thought I was badly mistaken—you, Ray, and Eulie and El—and certainly Helen, who either thought I would soon see the error of my ways, or come a cropper, which would be good for me." He smiled at his wife, who returned his gaze steadily and without expression. "But I felt I should try that for a reasonable time and see what happened. It didn't work, obviously. He hung me out to dry, as you all tried to point out from time to time. So I had to find some other means of bringing him to heel.

"He kept talking about how he had a claim on Lesser Lolómé, all that stuff about historic Great Lolómé and how he had a holy mission to reunite what the British put asunder so many years ago. History was the excuse, but oil of course was the object. And he kept waving his bombs around, and who knew what he would do with them? I always had to keep that in mind.

"Meanwhile, The Mouse and his corrupt gang of little princelings and princesses, so-called, were sitting atop all that oil, all of them worthless as they come. And there, I suddenly saw, was the chance to get rid of a tyrant and spread democracy a little further in a region that badly needs it.

"I know, I know," he said, holding up a hand as everyone stirred except the Vice President, who was listening with a rigidity that clearly indicated he didn't dare move for fear it might convey the wrong message to his formidable superior. "I *know* that wasn't the case, but I knew Mustafa's ouster could be made to appear that way to the world. And I knew it would appease Sidi and quite possibly tame him down for a while, maybe even"—he smiled wryly—"long enough so that I might complete another term and clear out of here before he decided to act up again. My successor could have his fun with him. I'd be out of it.

"You look shocked. But look at what we've got. We're getting rid of The Mouse. We're arranging for a free, democratic vote in Lesser Lolómé"—again he held up a hand at their stirring of protest—"we're providing that a sizable portion of the oil revenues will go to better the conditions of the people of Lesser Lolómé, always a worthwhile objective in the eyes of America's bleeding hearts who think I'm so wonderful and I wouldn't want for one minute to disillusion them—we're providing that American companies could have a crack at getting in there—and we're providing that in two years' time there should be a referendum of all the peoples of Lolómé to determine their own government in a free and democratic manner, also a devoutly beloved cause of America's most earnest and idealistic souls.

"Now, I am *not* saying, you understand—and you in this room do understand it very well, I know—that *this is what we are going to get.* This is what we are *providing.* These are the possibilities we are putting on paper; and the public reaction to them, which I think will be quite gullible and quite predictable, will give me enough turn-around room to get out of this and emerge free and clear, the heroic figure"—his voice became touched with irony—"who has brought freedom and democracy to a troubled corner of the world.

"You and I know, as you rightly say, Ray, what the chances are of any of it coming true. Virtually nil. But the public won't think about that because the public doesn't want to think about it. The public doesn't want reality. The public wants dreams. It can always be sold on dreams.

"We know, in this room, and they will know in the clever rooms of the media where my triumph will be given its final polish, that I haven't achieved much of anything, really. Actually it's a big defeat, which I will never admit outside this room, or again to anyone. The media will know this, but aside from a few expected and predictable critics, they'll never tell. They know how important it is to maintain the pretendings of the world. They know how much society and stability depend upon illusion. It's the foundation of their business. They'll never tell.

"This is what we have on paper. It doesn't seem much, really; its chances of ever being carried out in good faith are one in ten thousand. But it is something I can take to the American public and the world—I will hold it in my hand—they will see it. And hopefully this will calm them down and hopefully it will calm Sidi down for a while and permit me to get back to all the domestic things that keep piling up for me and never stop. A President doesn't exist in a vacuum, which many people forget, in which he can pick up one issue and consider it serenely for a while and then put it aside and take up another and consider that for a while. He is juggling a whole fistful of pins, at the same time, all the time. I have obligations to the country so far beyond little Mr. Sidi that he couldn't possibly imagine. He's one interest among many. We've given him much too much prominence in these past few weeks. It's time to put him back in the world's box of horrors and close the lid. We've got to get on with it. We've got better things to do.

"I'm not dealing here in this episode, and the ever-hopeful country and the world are not dealing here, with what *is*. That's reality and it's too frightening for them to face. I'm dealing with the promise of *what could be*. That's all they want—that's all they need to keep them happy. That's what I'm going to give them."

He paused, took a sip of water.

Ray Stanley shifted in his chair, started to speak, hesitated. The President deferred, waved him on. Ray spoke as if it pained him, which it did.

"There is a cynicism and a corruption here," he said slowly, "so far beyond the corruptions of money and sex and oil and the other petty

Washington nonsense the media always makes so much of and the public gets so riled up about, that it isn't even in the same ballpark . . . a corruption of morals and ethics and integrity so great that it almost can't be
grasped . . . so profound and deep-seated that it's almost as though it
weren't there."

"Pretend it isn't," the President suggested. "You'll feel so much better."

"Let's remember what's happened here," the Secretary said, sounding almost dazed, although he had been around politics for a long, long
time. "You were threatening Sidi, not Mustafa. Now you've turned on
Mustafa to avoid having to make good on your threats to Sidi. You're
using Mustafa as a stand-in for Sidi, and in the process you're giving
Sidi everything he wants. Mustafa pays for Sidi's transgressions because
you don't dare punish Sidi. You've done great damage to yourself, your
office, and the country, but you plan to come out of it smelling like a
rose. And you probably will. It's upside down. It's crazy."

"But how many will realize that?" the President inquired. "You're
right, a few will think—ponder—analyze—realize—cause a little rumpus and raise a little hell. But perhaps the major thing one learns in politics is that the American people have no memory; figuratively speaking,
everything lasts ten minutes and then it's gone. Collectively they have
the attention span of a two-year-old child. Modern-day communication
has destroyed their capacity to remember even as it has made it impossible for them to think. They are bombarded with information and opinions incessantly. It is just too much.

"If you can coddle them past that first ten minutes, you're home free.
All you need is a good, stirring, upbeat rationalization, and they'll forget
all about what really happened. They're sunny souls at heart; put a rosy
gloss on it, and you've got it made. Such is what I intend to do. It's what
I've done all my political life. It's always worked, and it will work now.
You'll see. The public and the media are champing at the bit to cut loose
and declare me a hero. I'm going to tell them why they should. . . .

"Incidentally," he said, tone changing, becoming warmer, more intimate, that of the likable seducer at work, "why don't you and Eulie stay
around awhile longer? I'm not so bad. I have to pilot this ship. I don't
always like myself for what I have to do, but there it is. It goes with the
territory." He gave them his most charming smile. "Stick around. I
might need you."

And with a cheerful nod to the others he stood up, said, "Thank you for coming, ladies and gentlemen, it's been an interesting morning, and I think we've accomplished quite a lot"—gave them all a friendly wave—blew a kiss to his wife, who did not respond—and strode out.

They moved slowly out of the room, not really talking—because what was there to say, their heads were whirling with too many things, filled with anger and resentment toward their clever host yet curiously, almost helplessly, sympathetic toward him too, on whom so much depended.

The Secretary and Eulie found themselves walking along the hall with Helen.

"And Sidi still has his bombs and his missiles," Ray said gloomily. "He's still a world menace, and he's still a loose cannon, out of control, free to do whatever he chooses."

"Yes," Eulie agreed. "And the President hasn't really achieved a thing."

"Oh, yes, he has," his wife remarked. "He's saved his own neck. And that," she said with an irony not so gentle, "is an achievement beyond price."

She gave them a sudden shrewd look.

"Are you going to resign?"

Again they looked at each other as they had in their talk with their colleagues in the department. This time there was no laughter.

"I really don't know," the Secretary said slowly.

"Nor I," the Deputy Secretary said. She sighed. "It's a terrible decision to have to make, at my age and with all my years in the Foreign Service."

"Yes," Ray agreed soberly. "It isn't easy."

"Think about it," Helen suggested.

The Secretary smiled, rather grimly.

"We are."

"He came as close to begging just now as he'll ever come," she said. "He wasn't kidding. He does need you. And he does have terrible responsibilities. Can you justify leaving him now?"

"He'd find someone," Eulie said.

Helen smiled briefly at the uncertainty implied in the conditional tense.

"Well, he would," Eulie repeated, smiling a little herself. "A cast of thousands waits in the wings."

"Well," Helen said, "you think about it. It doesn't have to be done today, does it?"

"If it isn't," the Secretary said with a rueful humor, "we may lose our flying speed."

"Give it a day or two," she suggested. "Give him that much courtesy. Then if you want to, go ahead."

"You're very persuasive," Eulie said.

The First Lady gave her a wry smile.

"He's habit with me," she said. "And I feel sorry for him. Which he would absolutely hate if he knew." Again the wry smile. "Don't tell him. And don't do something this serious on impulse. It wouldn't become either one of you." She paused as she started to turn away. "Why don't you give me a call when you've made up your minds? I'd like to know."

"We'll call you," Ray agreed.

"We appreciate your interest," Eulie said.

They watched the First Lady, always perfectly turned out, stylish and self-possessed, as she turned and walked down the corridor toward the elevator that would take her up to the family quarters.

"What must it be like to be married to someone that completely cynical?" Eulie mused. "Do you suppose she ever challenges him on it as you did? Incidentally, I thought you were great."

"You weren't so bad yourself," the Secretary said. "I couldn't help it. His approach to this thing is so completely cynical, so completely devoid of ethics and integrity—"

"He doesn't seem to think so," she said. "It's all a matter of practical politics, with him."

"And the damnable thing is that he's probably right about the public reaction," Ray said gloomily. "He's going to get away with it. Wait and see."

"I wish you were wrong," she said as they got into the waiting limousine that would take them back to State. "I wish he was wrong. But I'm very much afraid that he's completely and absolutely right."

4

And of course, a little later when all was said and done and settled down, he was.

"The President knows his country," Senator Wilson remarked to the Secretary two days later as they sat in Ray's office and read the digests of media comment that were coming in from all over the country and the world.

Aside from a few little glitches that might occur along the way to the strangest bit of presidential image-making ever to take place on the south lawn of the White House, it was already apparent that things were going to fall into place just about as the President had predicted.

There were those, like James Van Rensselaer Burden, Able Montague, Sally Holliwell, and Tim Bates, who expressed alarmed disapproval in columns, television shows, and general commentary. Nor were they alone. Quite a few members of the media were equally skeptical, equally insistent in reminding the country of how this had all begun, what the original issue was, how willfully and arrogantly the President had attempted to bluff Sidi into retreat, and how ignominious and demeaning to America was his own retreat, the blatant appeasement of Sidi, the ruthless sacrifice of Mustafa.

The country didn't pay much attention. The threat of war was removed, the bogeyman was gone back into his distant citadel, the President was seen to be, as the capital's most egregious newspaper summed it up for the great majority, "the strong and effective leader of democracy whom his admirers have always known would emerge triumphant from this little contest of wills with President Sidi.

"Few things in recent years," the paper assured its readers, "have represented such a victory for democracy as the President's removal of the corrupt Sheikh Mustafa from Lesser Lolómé. Few things carry greater hope for the future than the pledge he has secured from President Sidi to hold free and democratic elections in the soon-to-be reunited country of Great Lolómé."

The problem of the A-bombs and missiles was handled in the way certain elements of the media always handle subjects embarrassing to their pet beliefs and fiercely cherished biases. Nine-tenths of the time it wasn't even mentioned.

And when it was—

"It is true that Sidi's continued possession of atomic bombs and long-range missiles must raise some legitimate questions in many sincerely troubled citizens' minds. It must be acknowledged that these concerns are shared by the International Atomic Energy Agency and by many concerned scientists. Yet surely these concerns can be addressed—and settled—at some convenient future time in friendly discussions with President Sidi, now that cordial and cooperative relations have been reestablished between him and the United States.

"The possibilities for a peaceful, swift, and mutually satisfactory solution of this bothersome problem are everywhere apparent. We look with confidence to the President to secure an early, friendly, and constructive outcome."

"Do you really?" Willie Wilson murmured gently. "Well, well . . . Ray," he said abruptly, "are you and Eulie going to quit? If you do, I'm going to have you up before the Foreign Relations Committee in public session and give you a chance to spill your guts about the miracle-worker in the White House."

The Secretary smiled but shook his head.

"I don't know that I want to make a circus out of it."

"Are you referring to my distinguished committee as a circus?" Willie demanded with humorous indignation. "We'll show *you*. Anyway, don't duck my question. Are you?"

"I don't know yet," Ray said slowly. "What I want to do—" he paused and gave Willie a thoughtful look. "I tell you what. Eulie and I haven't had a chance to talk in the last couple of days, we've been so bombarded by media for comment on the general Lolómé situation. Why don't you come over for dinner tonight? We'll have Eulie, and maybe Jaime. I got the feeling in the NSC that he's getting very doubtful too." He gave a sudden wry smile. "Wouldn't that be something, if his three top foreign policy people all left at the same time?"

"It would embarrass him a bit," Willie said, "but it wouldn't hurt him much. He's riding high now. What time?"

"Come over about six, we'll have drinks and an early dinner and thrash it out."

"It would serve him right, at that," Willie said thoughtfully. "He shouldn't be allowed to get away scot-free with something as barefaced as this."

"He and his White House crew of diapered wonders will put the spin on it," Ray said. "But at least we'll have our own integrity where we can put our hands on it . . . if," he added as the Senator smiled, "we do quit. There's something to be said for staying in place and trying to influence events from inside."

"Haven't influenced much in this case, have you?" Willie noted dryly as he rose to go.

"No," the Secretary conceded with a rather bleak smile. "Thanks for coming by to see these news digests. I thought you'd be interested. See you at six."

"Wild horses couldn't keep me away," Willie said with a grin.

After he left to return to the Hill, the Secretary called Mary and told her they were having company, and why.

"Good," she said. "You've been so silent about it these last couple of days that I was beginning to wonder. It's been all I could do to keep my mouth shut."

He chuckled.

"I've regarded it as a sort of character test for you. You've passed with flying colors."

"Do you want me to invite Mrs. Jaime?"

"No, no. She doesn't speak very good English, for one thing, and I don't think he'd want her there, for another."

"Do you think he's going to stay?"

"I'm not so sure," he said. "I'm beginning to think Jaime has a few more surprises in him than we thought. I'm sure his wife will support whatever he decides, without question. As you will, of course," he added humorously.

"I *will* not!" she exclaimed. "If you resign on a matter of principle, I'll beam proudly. If you decide to stay with that—that"—her tone turned acrid—"that *clever* soul, you'll never hear the last of it, Raymond Cass Stanley, leader of world diplomacy."

"That's an inducement," he said with a chuckle. "Something light for dinner."

"To go with heavy thinking," she said. "Rosella and I will whip up something."

"And bring your own bright thoughts to the table, too," he suggested. "We need all the help we can get."

"Mine are very simple," she said. "*Go!*"

When he called Eulie a few minutes later, she was delighted.

"I think that's a marvelous idea," she said. "I've been stewing and stewing ever since the meeting. I want to go, but should I? Will it be fair to him? Will it really hurt him with his other responsibilities, as Helen suggests? How will it look to the country and the world?"

"Willie Wilson says it would embarrass him a bit but it wouldn't hurt him much. He's riding high, Willie says."

"Willie's right," she said. "But maybe that's a reason for staying. If it doesn't hurt him and make him think about what he's done, then what good would it do? Except shut us out of things and destroy whatever slight influence we may still have with him."

"He must think we have some," Ray said. "He wants us to stay. Helen wants us to stay . . . See you at six. We'll confabulate, as my dear mother used to say."

And so they did, until almost midnight, after relaxing drinks and an excellent dinner put together in some haste by the Stanleys' longtime Filipina cook, Rosella. Ray led them into the study shortly after eight, Mary, Eulie, Jaime, Willie, and closed the door with a solemn air. The discussion ran earnest and thorough for more than three hours.

During the course of it, they ranged over the whole diplomatic scene, reviewed the sorry course of The Matter of Lolómé, excoriated again what they all saw as the President's inept, wishful, and willful handling of it, and balanced as much as possible the arguments for and against resignation.

Willie acted as informal moderator and devil's advocate, though it was obvious from the first what he wanted them to do.

"Not that my opinion matters in such a momentous decision," he said, "but my basic rule has always been that if you really have principles, and if something really affronts them, which it obviously does here, then by all means, go. He hasn't taken your advice throughout this episode, what makes you think he would take it any more if you remained in office? Whereas, if you go, the public and political shock could be so great that it might jolt him into being more realistic and more cautious about things in the future. *Might.* I'm not saying it would."

"On the other hand," Ray remarked, "if he's heading for the kind of universal congratulations we think he is, neither our going or staying would have much effect on him, right? And it wouldn't damage him much politically, if at all, right? So—"

"So it comes down to what we feel about it," Eulie said, "and how strong our principles are and how much it means to us to act in accordance with them."

"Yes," Jaime agreed, speaking up after a long period of silence. "That is the question. Me, I did not like to be the messenger boy for this errand. I did not like to give old Mouse the ax. He ees not a lovely character and no doubt deserves everything he is goin' to get, but even so, I don' like to be a bully of somebody helpless. It is not a nice feeling."

"No," the Secretary agreed.

"But of course," Senator Wilson said, "there are a thousand and one other issues of foreign policy on which you have agreed with him in the past and presumably would continue to agree with him in the future. Would those outweigh the one matter of the Lolómés, which will very soon be forgotten as the world goes on to something else?"

"Yes," the Secretary agreed dryly. "He laid that all out for us in the NSC. He said it would be forgotten in ten minutes, figuratively speaking. He said the American people have no memory and the attention span of a two-year-old child. That was quite an interesting little lecture, wasn't it, friends?"

"You won't find its like in textbooks on democratic government," Eulie remarked, "but it was truer than most people like to think, I'm afraid."

"Realistic," Jaime Serrano agreed. "Not nice. But realistic."

"So, looked at realistically—?" Willie suggested.

"Looked at realistically," Ray Stanley said, "I think for the sake of my own self-respect, and to underwrite and reconfirm the general rules of ethical conduct which I have attempted to live by for forty years in the Foreign Service—I will resign."

"I think I will do the same," Eulie said gravely.

"Good for you both," Mary said.

"It's a long way from Riyadh," Eulie said, and again tears came into her eyes, "but here we are, the three musketeers, still together."

"Yes," Mary said, her own eyes filling sympathetically at the thought of so many years, such old friendship. "Still together."

Jaime cleared his throat.

"I do not have this sentiment about it," he said, "but I too have some principles. I do not quite know why the President chose me to be his national security adviser, except maybe a big campaign contribution—"

"Maybe," Willie agreed. "And to help him carry Miami and Florida next time."

"—but I have tried to do my best for him. But I don' have to stay if I don' want to. I don' have to stay if good friends whom I admire say they can't remain. I don' think I can either."

"That's nice, Jaime," the Secretary said, touched, "but don't get carried away. Don't let us influence you. You may still be able to contribute much to what he does."

"I doubt it," Jaime said, and added with a surprising bitterness, "I am jus' his trained monkey. It is maybe time for me to move on with my silly chatter."

"Not silly at all," the Secretary objected. "But—whatever you think best."

"I think bes'," Jaime said.

"Do you want to call Helen?" Mary asked. "Didn't she ask you to, Ray?"

"She did," the Secretary said. "Thank you for reminding me."

He got up, went to his desk, dialed the White House.

"This is Secretary Stanley," he said. "Has the First Lady retired? . . . Oh, good. Can you put me through, please. . . . Helen, this is Ray Stanley. I'm here at the apartment with Eulie and Jaime"—Willie lifted a warning hand—"and Mary, and we've been discussing the subject we discussed with you after the NSC meeting."

"Yes?" she said, quite impersonally, though he knew she was deeply interested and possibly a little tense; but it wouldn't be like her to show it. "And—?"

"I think the answer of all three of us is yes."

There was silence for a moment.

"It will be a blow to him," she said finally. "And, for a little while, a great political scandal. He will be very sorry."

"But he will survive," Ray suggested.

"Oh, yes," she agreed. "He will survive. You really think you must?"

"I'm afraid we do," he said. "I'm sorry."

"I'm sorry, too, Ray," she said. "I really am. Please tell Eulie and Jaime I said so . . . I think he's reading, I don't think he's gone to sleep yet. Do you want me to tell him, or do you want to wait and talk to him tomorrow from the department?"

"We'll do that," he said. "But you might prepare him now, yes."

"Perhaps you'll change your minds by tomorrow. I know he will be hoping that."

"He's always the confident optimist," the Secretary said, not knowing whether to be amused or sad. "But I don't think we will."

"One never knows, in this world," she said. "One never knows about anything. Thank you for calling me, Ray. All the best to you and the others. You have my friendship, no matter what."

"Thank you, Helen," he said gravely. He hung up and recapped the conversation briefly for them. They looked at one another with a sudden relief, a sudden release of tension, a surge of feeling good about themselves and their decision.

"*I* think," Willie Wilson said, "that everybody should have another drink."

As promised, they called the President in the morning. He expressed deep regrets, accepted their decision matter-of-factly since he had no other choice in the face of their obvious determination, and asked one favor: that they withhold public announcement until after the signing ceremony on the White House lawn and his own speech, which would conclude the hallowed ritual established by his recent predecessors, in which benign Chief Executives preside over the diplomatic achievements of others while cameras roll and thousands cheer.

This they agreed to, although as Willie remarked when Ray told him about it later in the day, "He's got you blocked there. Before his speech, you would have been a big sensation. After it, you'll be just a footnote—quite a big footnote, but still a footnote."

"Can't be helped," the Secretary said. "He had a right to ask and we had to agree."

"Oh, of course," Senator Wilson said. "But it's a shame. You can still come before the committee, though, if you'd like. That's a promise."

"We may do just that," Ray Stanley said thoughtfully. "We'll have to see what he has to say, and how things develop."

After that, events seemed to accelerate rapidly as they approached the great day at the White House. Inevitably, although they all did their best to keep it quiet, the impression got out, encouraged by much media speculation, that their resignations might be imminent.

The British ambassador called.

"I say, Ray," Tony Marsden said, "are you going to bite the bullet and pull out of that mess over there?"

"Not a mess on my watch," the Secretary said. "At least," he added wryly, "not until lately."

"But you're going to do it," Tony pressed. "It's all over but the shouting?"

"Stand by," Ray Stanley said. "Don't do anything until you hear the shouting."

"Good for you," Tony said. "I heartily approve."

The former Secretary of State called.

"Ray!" cried Reginald Pennebaker Sims. "Heartiest congratulations! I hear you're going to tell that wavering wishy-washy wimp where to head in!"

"I wouldn't say that, Penny," the Secretary said mildly. "I'm not prepared to say yet—to anyone—what I'm going to do."

"Not even to me, one of your oldest and closest friends in the Foreign Service?" Penny demanded. "And one of the most discreet, too," he added, so defensively that the Secretary could not help laughing.

"Penny," he said, "you're the absolute soul of discretion. Nobody could possibly be more famous throughout the service for it."

"Well, thank you," Penny Sims said, a trifle huffily. "I hope you're going to give him absolute hell when you all go public. When will that be, after the big show on the White House lawn?"

"Yes," Ray said before thinking, then caught himself hastily as Penny uttered a triumphant crow. "If we do such a thing," he amended, "that is when it would be. But I'm not saying—"

"Of course you're not," Penny agreed with a chuckle. "And Eulie's going to join you, eh? What a story that will be. Why don't you do it right away, before his speech? He'll blanket you right out."

"Penny," the Secretary said, "I am counting on your discretion. He asked us to wait and we made him a promise. So we're stuck."

"What a pity," Reginald Pennebaker Sims said. "You could have wiped the floor with him. Timing is all. You know that."

"I do," Ray said, "but he caught me before I had time to think."

"Pity," Penny said again. "Well, I'll keep quiet. But I hope the media come to me for comment afterwards. I think he's an absolute disgrace to his office. And a real detriment to the United States. I'll say so, too."

"Thank you, Penny," the Secretary said. "We appreciate your support. Mum's the word for now."

"I guess so," Penny Sims said, sounding disgruntled. "It is a pity, though."

Jimmy Van, Able Montague, and Sally Holliwell called him on a conference line a little later.

"Ray," Jimmy said abruptly, "is it true that you and Eulie and Jaime Serrano—?"

"Speculation, speculation, speculation!" he interrupted. "What became of the days of hard news that I grew up in?"

"Frightfully dull," Jimmy said.

"You must admit it's more fun now," Able suggested.

"Not necessarily," he said. "Not—necessarily. I have no comment to make about anything."

"We want you three to be on Able's show with us on Saturday," Sally said. "How about it?"

"Where did you guys get this idea, anyway?" he demanded.

"Oh," Able said airily, "that's just how things go in Washington."

"You know how it is," Jimmy said.

"Yes," Sally agreed. "Somebody hears—somebody sees—somebody guesses—somebody knows—somebody talks. The great sieve of the universe."

"If," he said carefully, "there were anything to your speculation, I expect that Eulie and I—and probably Jaime, though I can't speak for him—would be happy to be on your show, because some things need to be said. But I expect it would have to be after his speech at the White House signing, if at all. Anyway, I can't really speak for them."

"They'll do it if you will," Sally said confidently. "Can you give us a conditional acceptance?"

"Conditional on what?"

"Conditional on your doing what we all know you're going to do," she said with a cheerful laugh in which he joined.

"Don't call us," he said. "We'll call you."

"That's a promise?" Jimmy Van inquired.

"That's a promise."

"We admire you all greatly," Jimmy said.

"And agree with you entirely," Able said.

"And applaud what you're doing with all our hearts," Sally said—all of them more solemn and serious than he had ever heard them.

"Well, thanks very much," he said, touched. "You'll hear from us."

Two other calls touched him particularly in the next couple of days. Dolly Munson reached him next morning, his daughter soon after.

"Ray," Dolly said, voice old and slow ("because I *am* old and slow," she often said with a chuckle) but as warm and full of life as ever, "what's this I hear about you and Eulie checking out over there? And Jaime Serrano at the White House?"

"Dolly, darling," he said, "now, where did you hear a thing like that?" She chuckled.

"Right here in my living room," she said, "which is where one hears almost everything of any importance in Washington, isn't that right?"

"That's right," he said. "Well, just between us, because I know I can rely on your discretion—"

"Deep as a well."

"—it's true, but I trust you not to tell anyone until we make it official."

"It's all over town," she said, and inquired, with her famous relish for a good political scrap, "Are you going to let him have it? He's such a pathetic man—so mixed up, so out of his depth, so—*immature*, somehow. Such a disaster for the country."

"Well, you've seen 'em come and seen 'em go," he said. "You ought to know."

"One of the worst," she said. "Although sure to be reelected, I'm afraid."

"And with this as one of his triumphs to point to," he said regretfully.

"Shameful," she said. "Absolutely shameful. Well . . ." She seemed to be drifting for a moment, came back strong. "Well"—briskly—"why don't you and Eulie and Bets and the Jaimes come for dinner next week after it's all over? We'll have a little consolation party. Maybe I'll invite Willie Wilson, too, and Jimmy Van and Able Montague and Sally Holliwell, they've become such an inseparable trio since they went to Greater Lolómé and did that show with that dreadful man. Very small and intimate, just us." She chuckled suddenly. "We'll burn the President in effigy and chant vile things over his ashes. Will that make you feel better?"

"It would make us all feel marvelous," he said with a hearty laugh. "You've cheered me up immensely already, dear Dolly. I'll tell Mary and Eulie you'll be calling."

"It's a date," she said. "Good cheer, dear Ray, good cheer!"

Bets called a little later. Her voice was still heavy with grief, shock and sorrow for Samir still in full flood. But she was a good daughter, sophisticated in the world of diplomacy and of Washington, and family solidarity was more than ever important to her now.

"Daddy," she said, "Mom just called and told me about your decision to resign. I just want you to know I'm for it one hundred percent. I'm proud of you."

He felt a rush of feeling, tried not to let it show too much in his voice.

"Thank you, dear," he said gravely. "Bless your heart. Your support means a lot."

"You never dreamed you'd have it."

He was pleased to note a trace of the old humor returning. He ventured a laugh, not too hearty.

"Never . . . How are things going? How are you doing?"

"Oh," she said, voice turning somber. "Not too bad . . . I guess. The kids are still having a rough time, but they'll be all right. And I'm managing." Her voice became suddenly bitter. "I wish now I'd raised more hell about those nights out with Boo and his friends. If he hadn't been with them that night—"

"I know," he said grimly, thinking that he knew, or could guess, considerably more than she could. "But there was no way you could stop him. And it all seemed innocent enough."

"Wasn't it?" she asked sharply, and he realized again, as he had many times before, that she was as intuitive as her mother.

"As far as I know," he said flatly.

But she was not to be deflected.

"You never did tell me what Hugo Mallerbie found out," she said. "Did he discover what it was all about?"

"No," he said, thinking: this lie is necessary, and anyway, Hugo and the others haven't found out anything specific. At least, not yet. "Apparently just what Boo said it was, a gathering of friends who like to talk."

"Boo's still going," she said. "Joanie told me it's become more frequent in the last few days, almost every night, now. I still think it's odd. But of course," she said, bitterness deepening, "that won't bring Samir back, so why should I care? I have enough on my mind as it is."

"That's right," he agreed quickly. "Best not to worry about that, it's in the past now as far as you're concerned. Boo assured me it was all a tragic happenstance, it had nothing to do with his group. Samir just decided to walk home on his own and . . . it happened." (*And you at least knew it was going to,* he told Boo silently in his mind. *If you didn't know even more.*)

"Boo's been a comfort," she said gratefully. "He's called several times and offered to take the kids to the movies. They're not quite ready for that, but it was thoughtful of him. He's a nice man."

"Yes," he said, trying to keep suspicion and judgment out of his voice and apparently succeeding, for she dropped the subject and moved to end the conversation.

"Anyway, I just wanted you to know that I think you're doing the right thing. I've always admired your integrity and I admire it even more now. I'm proud of my father. I've always been proud of him. I wanted you to know that."

"Thank you, my dear daughter," he said quietly. "That fortifies me immensely. . . . Dolly Munson is going to have us all over to dinner after I leave, she'll be calling you. Meantime, your mother and I will be in touch."

"Not the biggest of families," she said, repeating a comfortable old inside family joke, "but a mighty solid one."

"Thicker than thieves," he agreed more lightly. "Take care."

"You, too, Daddy."

Brought back to various unhappy realities by their talk, he decided to put in calls for Hugo Mallerbie and Eldridge Barnes. He had not had time to check with them privately since the day of the NSC meeting.

Hugo had nothing new to report. As Bets had said, Boo's little group was still meeting, on a somewhat stepped-up schedule whose signifi-cance still could not be discovered. Apparently with Samir's death they had removed the only potential informer from their ranks. Nothing spe-cific was emerging.

"We'll keep on it," Hugo promised. "Joanie's still very annoyed with me for being suspicious and defends him like the tiger she is. He knows we're after them, but he's quite confident we're not going to find any-thing. He came in to see her yesterday and made a point of stopping by to chat with me for a while. All very smooth, you know Boo. He let me see he got a kick out of visiting me; we understand each other. That's where it rests, for the moment."

"Keep digging," the Secretary said.

"We will," Hugo Mallerbie promised grimly. "Be sure of that."

"Ray!" Eldridge Barnes said. "Are you resigning?"

"I'm not saying," he responded. "Do you think I should?"

"After that performance we saw in the NSC?" El said. "Yes, I think you should. If you have any self-respect at all. And I know you have plenty."

"I do."

"So—?"

"You'll be among the first to know," Ray said with a chuckle. He became serious.

"What about our little toy boat 'way out there on the great big Atlantic?"

"Still chugging along," El said. "Not breaking any speed records, but it's not that kind of ship. Plain old tramp steamer, battered and worn—at least that's the official description we're supposed to accept. Landfall in New York in about ten days, I'd estimate. We're still tracking."

"Good," Ray Stanley said. "Don't let up, even if I do go."

"No, indeed," El said. "I have a hunch about this one. We're going to stay with it."

"Good," the Secretary said again. "Good luck."

There was a knock on his door as he hung up. Basil Rifkin came in with another sheaf of media digests, which he placed on the desk with a sardonic expression.

"It's building into a landslide," he said wryly. "Can't keep a good man down."

"I know," Ray Stanley said with equal wryness. "Isn't it a shame?"

5   It was obvious, a handful of hot and steamy days later, that far from keeping a good man down, the whole machinery of White House promotion and worldwide media support was going into high gear to guarantee him the place in history which he obviously intended should be his.

From the White House press office came a glowing announcement of the forthcoming signing ceremony on the south lawn between the representatives of the two Lolómés. It was followed one day later by three thousand engraved invitations that went out to all members of Congress, the Supreme Court, the top echelons of the military, the entire diplomatic corps, and such notable private citizens as Ms. Bonnie Terhuitt of Concerned Citizens Against and Dr. Random Cruikshank and Dr. Feemahle Jackson-Washington of We Protest. Invited also were the editors and columnists of the nation's leading newspapers and magazines, a major scattering of prominent academics, and a dazzling array of right-thinking Hollywood luminaries (at this late date in the twentieth century, most of the wrong-thinking ones were already at rest in Forest Lawn). Though all major members of the working media would be there anyway in line of duty, the President had suggested to the White House social office that they also be sent engraved invitations. He knew this would flatter them.

It promised to be a great day. And this time, he congratulated himself, it would not be a ceremony in which disputants who had settled their differences without U.S. help in some venue thousands of miles away would be hauled into the world spotlight on the White House lawn so that some beaming President could receive a credit he had not earned and did not deserve. This time, he told himself, it would damned well be deserved.

Around the world the vast communications network of the media had already swung into line behind him. The approving chorus, moderate when the "Declaration of Understanding" was first announced, had swelled now to full, roaring spate. He was praised for his courage and statesmanship in being willing to abandon his previous adamant position against Sidi and participate in the solution of the crisis of the two Lolómés. His integrity was hailed, his farseeing vision given ecstatic due.

He was the hero of the hour, and all those misgivings, complaints, worries, fears, biting criticisms, and furious savagings of his course in recent weeks were suddenly gone and forgotten. A figurative memory of ten minutes, he had said—the collective attention span of a two-year-old child. And of course he was entirely right.

It was already being said, in Washington, New York, London, and indeed wherever television tube glowed and printer's ink touched page, that he would very likely emerge as one of the truly great statesmen of millennium's end.

After so much of this, Mary Stanley cried out in a humorous wail that combined anger, dismay, helpless amusement, and sheer exasperated frustration, "But he isn't! He just *isn't!*"

In this opinion, as she acknowledged ruefully to the Secretary, she was much in the minority. For every skeptical voice such as hers (and that of Big Bill Bullock, who had resigned from the diplomatic service and was now back home in Texas regaling friends and neighbors with his scathing opinions of "that shifty coward in the White House"), ten thousand voices sang hosanna for the President. Columns, editorials, news broadcasts, commentaries, eagerly supportive statements from campus and soundstage, flooded in upon 1600 Pennsylvania Avenue.

Rarely had the sounds of tensions relaxing and fears subsiding been so thunderous. Rarely had there been such acclaim for a President. Rarely had statesmanship such as his received such universal recognition.

So it was that all was festive, bright, and exhilarating as he and Helen looked down upon the happy scene from behind the curtains of her second-floor bedroom.

"I did this," he said with a satisfaction he made no attempt to conceal. "I deserve this."

"I know," she said. "I'm sure Sidi will be happy to give your helpful efforts their due. This may not be true," she added dryly, "of poor old Mustafa."

"He isn't coming," the President said with a certain triumph in his voice. "You remember he and his immediate family got out with Arthur Burton and the embassy staff. They're in London, staying at Claridge's and no doubt, as Jaime Serrano says, cooking cheeken on the hotel-room floor. I had Jaime call and invite him to take part, but he simply cursed me and hung up."

"I can't think why," she said, and he had the grace to laugh. "So who will represent Lesser Lolómé? An empty chair?"

"No, not quite," he said. "One of his sons called back and said the oldest brother, who is probably seventy by now, will stand in for him."

Below, the colorful, gossiping, restless crowd, cooking in the stifling July heat, was beginning to settle. On the podium the flags of the United States, Greater Lolómé, and Lesser Lolómé stirred idly side by side in the suffocating summer air. The Marine band was tuning up off to one side, preparing to play, when suitable, the presidential honors, "The Star-Spangled Banner," the "We Fearless Desert Men" of Greater Lolómé, and the "Sons of the Prophet, Ride with Us" of Lesser Lolómé.

"We'd better go down and get in place behind the south doors," the President said. "I think they're getting ready to whoop in the principals."

He and Helen reached the lower hall and took up their positions behind the doors. The band struck up "Sons of the Prophet, Ride with Us," and the ambassador of Iraq, who had volunteered for the duty, led to the podium the tiny, bent, scrawny, scraggle-bearded figure of Prince Salim ibn Mustafa al Bandra, oldest son of Sheikh Mustafa, dressed in a Western business suit that may well have cost three thousand dollars in Bond Street but did nothing for his shriveled little body. Peering and blinking about, expression angry, gaze hostile, he did not acknowledge the audience as he was taken to a chair to the left of the lectern.

The band finished "Sons of the Prophet, Ride with Us" and swung immediately into "We Fearless Desert Men."

Clad in his most gorgeous white and gold robes and gold turban, ornately carved silver scimitar hanging from his belt, back ramrod straight, gaze cold, arrogant, and commanding, Sidi bin Sidi bin Sidi entered on the arm of the ambassador of Iran, whose embassy was handling Greater Lolómé's affairs with the United States during the temporary break in relations. (To be resumed, Sidi had already been told privately by the President, with the appointment of a new ambassador tomorrow morning.) Sidi was led to the chair to the right of the lectern and stood at rigid attention until the band completed "We Fearless Desert Men."

Mary Stanley, seated between the Secretary and the Deputy Secretary in the first row directly in front of the President's position, whispered, "This is insane. It is absolutely insane. I have to laugh so I won't cry."

The band struck up "Ruffles and Flourishes," then swung with practiced ease into "Hail to the Chief" as the President and Helen advanced to the podium. The President handed her to a chair slightly behind and to his left. The band played "The Star-Spangled Banner." An elderly member of the diplomatic corps fainted somewhere off to the left in the dripping heat, nothing serious, but a small flurry while he was being swiftly taken away to a hospital, and succor. The President waited patiently for the disturbance to subside, then stepped forward to the bank of microphones.

"Please be seated, ladies and gentlemen," he said. "The one thing we can never control in Washington is the weather. Please remove any and all items of clothing that will make you comfortable."

There was a ripple of laughter, a rustle and bustle as they sat down.

"Unfortunately there are a lot of you here in the heat. But in a way that is fortunate, too, because it means that you place an emphasis and importance upon the ceremony we are about to witness which matches my own.

"You obviously agree with me that this is a great day for democracy in a part of the world where democracy needs all the help it can get. I am proud that I and my administration are able to contribute to it greatly here today."

There was a round of applause, hearty and enthusiastic.

"You have all been aware for some time, I am sure," he went on, easily and comfortably as he always did before an audience, "that all has not been well in that difficult area of the world known as the two Lolómés— Greater Lolómé, represented here today by President Sidi bin Sidi bin Sidi, and Lesser Lolómé, here today in the person of the eldest son of His Majesty Sheikh Mustafa, Prince Salim ibn Mustafa al Bandra."

Sidi bowed gravely in response to the applause, Prince Salim shifted impatiently in his chair but made no concession to the audience.

"It has been a long and sometimes difficult road," the President said, "but I can report to you today that we have reached a successful turning—a turning which will set the two Lolómés on the path toward the historic unity from which they were sundered so unfeelingly by former colonial rulers many long years ago. I am proud that I have been able to assist in this."

Again applause for him, warm and admiring.

"In this 'Declaration of Understanding' which is about to be signed by President Sidi and Prince Salim, it is set forth that His Majesty Sheikh Mustafa and his family, who have graciously recognized the overwhelming desire of their people for freedom and democracy, shall receive a suitable stipend for their long years of service to Lesser Lolómé.

"It is also set forth that a regency council will be set up which will both protect their legitimate interests and at the same time prepare for a referendum two years from now in which the people of Lesser Lolómé will choose, in a free and democratic election, what their future form of government will be.

"It is also provided that if the people of Lesser Lolómé and the peoples of Greater Lolómé wish to reunify into a revived, historic Great Lolómé, a free and democratic referendum will be held, in two years' time, to determine the form of government of their united country.

"It also provides that the government of Greater Lolómé will open its oil fields to free and fair international development, with the added proviso that a major portion of its oil revenues shall be used to benefit the people of Lesser Lolómé and, upon reunification, all the peoples of Great Lolómé. U.S. and UN guarantees of these provisos are also included.

"President Sidi," he concluded solemnly, "will you come forward and sign for Greater Lolómé, please?"

And he turned and bowed gravely to Sidi, who bowed gravely back, stepped forward, sat down at the small table below and in front of the lectern, took up quill pen, and with a flourish signed the large parchment document before him. He then stepped back but did not return to his seat.

"And Prince Salim?" the President inquired politely.

The prince looked about him moodily. A sudden tension gripped the audience. A silence fell in which only the busy *whackety-whack, whackety-whack* of an official helicopter flying over with two pool photographers could be heard against the muted sounds of the city outside.

"Your Royal Highness?" the President inquired, politeness noticeably more firm.

The prince got up abruptly, stepped forward, plumped down in the chair with an almost audible thud, seized the pen in a savage grasp, scrawled his name in huge letters, stood up, and started to return to his seat.

"Would Your Royal Highness shake hands to seal the bargain?" the President suggested, voice still bland but brooking no argument.

Sidi stepped forward and waited impassively, not, for the moment, offering his hand. Prince Salim stood for a long moment staring at him, hatred palpable. Then without stepping forward he shot out his hand. Sidi instantly responded with his, also not stepping forward. They leaned toward one another as far as they could go without toppling over—virtually on tiptoe, arms extended full-length—touched fingertips in the briefest, most tenuous way—instantly straightened up, whirled, and returned to their seats without giving each other another glance.

A mixture of amusement and applause swept the audience. The President, looking straight ahead so that neither Sidi nor the prince could see, permitted an instant's wry amusement to cross his face. A renewed surge of laughter responded. Then all became solemn again.

"Thus," he said gravely, "do these two old enemies embark together on a new course that promises great things for their troubled part of the world. We have witnessed this day the start of a new age in the Lolómes, of increased freedom and democracy where heretofore they have only sparked and sputtered. Now their pure flame is about to shine on all the peoples of the Lolómes. I am proud to have been a part of this. It makes me feel, and through me, I know, the people of the United States, that we have not labored in vain.

"Once again the beacon of liberty has touched a foreign land and brought to it the bountiful promise of a new day."

"Oh, *brother*," Mary whispered to Eulie, who smiled a trifle grimly. Their shared amusement turned to concern as the President, apparently not finished, held up his hand to silence the applause that welled up. A sudden premonition tightened the Secretary's chest and brought a sudden grim alertness to the face of Jaime Serrano, sitting directly behind him.

"One other, more personal note," the President said, voice dropping to its most casual, chatty level. "One other note that is logically part of this auspicious day. . . .

"For some time now," he said, ignoring them as they sat tensely just below him in the first row, looking over and beyond them to the abruptly quiet, fascinated audience, "it has been obvious to me that my Secretary of State, my Deputy Secretary of State, and my national security adviser, while discharging their duties with admirable skill and implementing my policies with steadfast loyalty, have not been entirely in sympathy with events as they have proceeded in the matter of the two Lolómes.

"They have had deep and earnest convictions about this issue which I am sure they will present to you at some future time when the occasion arises. But it has become increasingly clear to me that a fundamental difference of opinion has arisen between us. It is obvious to me, I am sorry to say, that the difference is unbridgeable.

"Therefore I have this morning requested their resignations—"

"You have?" Ray Stanley cried out, so shocked that he made no attempt to keep his voice down. It rang clearly over the crowd, provoking startled and uneasy laughter, a sudden excitement among the media.

The President ignored it and went calmly on.

"—requested their resignations, which I now accept with great regret, but with the recognition that without complete trust and empathy between us, the foreign policy of the United States will inevitably suffer.

"Their services to this country have been outstanding. I have decided this day to confer upon all three the Medal of Freedom, which as you know is the highest civilian decoration in the power of the President to give. A special White House ceremony will be held in the near future to confer upon them this high and justified recognition of their long and honorable service to the United States."

"Tell him to send yours Federal Express," Mary said to her husband in a loud half-whisper she made no attempt to conceal. "That two-faced son of a bitch!" she added, anger growing. "What can you possibly do to recover? He's taken it right out from under you!"

"So he has," Eulie Montgomery agreed, sounding dazed but keeping her voice down.

"What do we do now?" Jaime Serrano inquired, leaning forward to nudge the Secretary's arm.

"What can we do?" the Secretary responded in a grimly impatient whisper. "We smile and take it. All right?"

"He ees not," Jaime said thoughtfully, "a nice man."

"That's right," Ray Stanley said. "But a very successful one, as he judges success."

"And now," the President concluded, aware of their tense little flurry of conversation but ignoring it with a blandly impervious expression, "I want to say thank you all again for coming to witness this historic occasion. It marks, as I say, a new day for freedom and democracy in the two Lolómés. It marks one more success for the United States in its historic mission to promote freedom and democracy wherever in the world its influence can be helpful.

"Let us now pay respects to the flag and anthem of the new state whose hopeful birth we have been privileged to attend today—the flag and anthem of Great Lolómé!"

And he led them all in standing solemnly at attention while the Marine band tackled "Our Caravans Are Many and Triumphant" and the checkerboard red and green flag of Great Lolómé broke suddenly from the railing of the Truman balcony and waved beneficently over them all.

He turned and started back into the White House; was puzzled for a moment when he gestured to Helen and she shook her head; listened while she spoke briefly but firmly; shrugged with a rather grim expression, and turned away.

She left the podium, accompanied by four Secret Service men, and came down into the slowly moving crowd to where Ray, Mary, Eulie, and Jaime were trying to make headway through a clamoring group of media stars to whose shouted questions they were steadfastly refusing answers.

"Stand back!" the Secret Service's finest shouted angrily. "God damn it, stand back!"

And after a moment, with considerable grumbling and angry complaints to the Secret Service, all of whom they knew and were friendly with in a constant running-battle sort of way, the media reluctantly obeyed.

"Get us out of this," Helen ordered, and with the Secret Service leading, their little group was hustled through the west gate of the White House to their waiting limousine. Jaime, who had only to walk across the street to the Executive Office Building, stayed with them to the car.

Helen shook hands with Ray and Jaime, silently but with an extra pressure, and kissed Mary and Eulie on both cheeks with an extra warmth. She was not one to be overcome with emotion, but it was obvious she was genuinely moved this day.

"I'm sorry," she said simply. "I am sorry . . ." She smiled a sad little smile. "I still underestimate, sometimes . . . after all these years."

They all nodded, too overcome themselves for the moment to say anything in response. The departing crowd made way for the State Department limousine as they were driven off. There were looks of pity, calls of support. They acknowledged them gravely, with little waves.

Within the hour they each received a call from the Oval Office. Its occupant sounded as though he had been relieved of a big burden. Characteristically, he defended his action with a blithe, self-confident disregard for what he might have done to their feelings and their reputations.

"After all," he told Ray, "it isn't as though I'm doing you any harm, right? You and Eulie have ample pensions after all your years in the service, and Jaime has his own millions plus his wife's. You'll all be OK, isn't that right?"

For a moment, confronted by such serene gall, the Secretary literally did not know what to say. Then he decided to create a little uneasiness, if he could.

"Willie Wilson has invited us all to testify before Foreign Relations," he said. "We may feel we must accept."

It didn't work, of course.

"By all means!" the President exclaimed heartily. "By *all* means! I don't think it will do you much good, though. People aren't going to be very interested. You won't have to vacate for two weeks, but I have the new team all ready to go, and I'm going to announce them tomorrow. The focus from then on will be on them, as you know."

"Mr. President," Ray said dryly, "you take my breath away. You do think of everything."

"Not everything," the President said cheerfully. "But all the necessaries."

Next morning, page 1:

President Fires Top Foreign Policy Team. Stanley, Montgomery Out at State, Serrano Gets Boot at NSC

And the same day, page 1:

President Hails Democracy Birth In Lolómé as Two Sides Bury Hatchet, Sign Peace Agreement

And the morning after, page 1:

President Names Chase Bank Biggie To Head State Department, Picks Feemahle Washington for Deputy. Basil Rifkin Named to NSC Post.

And three days after that, almost blanketed out of the news in the swirl of excitement and comment about the new foreign policy team, plus new crises—or extensions of the endless old ones—in several of the many lands where crises never end, in this case North Korea, Bosnia, Cuba, and Haiti—there appeared quietly on page 9 (or thereabouts):

Lolómé Council Drops Referendum, Declares Two Countries United. Sidi Accepts Call to Head New Government as "King Sidi III." Says Great Lolómé Will "Never" Bow to International A-Check

And in the same editions—only this one where it had to be, on page 1:

Poll Shows 57 Percent Favor Reelection of President. His Diplomacy in Lolómé Cited As Major Reason for Approval

"You see?" Senator Wilson remarked dryly. "You can't win."

"And nobody remembers," the Secretary of State agreed glumly.

"Hell," Willie Wilson said. "Nobody remembers and *nobody cares.* That's the frightening thing. Nobody cares."

Out on the restless Atlantic, the "tramp steamer" chugged on. In the heavily fortified, fortress-like basement of the willing embassy that had housed Boo Bourassa and his friends from the beginning, they continued to meet. In the State Department, Raymond Cass Stanley and Eula Lee Montgomery gathered, sorted, discarded, or filed the official papers and memories of forty years.

Five days before the end of his tenure, the Secretary was informed by Eldridge Barnes of the CIA that "our little toy boat" had reached dock in New York and was tied up there.

———

"It appears to be waiting for who knows what," El said. "We're still watching."

He added incidentally that neither he nor Hugo Mallerbie could report any progress on Boo's chummy gatherings.

"He'll be missing them for the next few days," the Secretary said. "He and Joanie left yesterday to go out west to Jackson Hole for a brief vacation. He wanted Mary and me and Bets and the kids to go with them, but it's really impossible at this particular moment. But that would seem to indicate that he isn't involved in anything pressing that demands his presence here."

"Perhaps not," Eldridge Barnes said thoughtfully. "Perhaps not. I'm a suspicious old son of a bitch, though. I wonder why he wants to be out of Washington at this particular time. I wonder why he didn't want to go to New York."

"I couldn't say," Ray Stanley said. "Don't brood about it. See you at our farewell party here in the department, I trust."

"I'll be there," El said. "I still wonder why Boo and Joanie won't."

But that, the Secretary thought, was just part of being CIA. It was your job to be suspicious of everybody and everything. El was very good at it.

Four days before the end of his tenure and three before the big send-off his colleagues in the department were planning for him and Eulie, he decided on a sudden impulse to call the embassy that El and Hugo had determined to be the meeting place of Boo and his friends. The country was one of the leading players in the difficult part of the world where "King Sidi III" now held a commanding position as head of the reunited state of Great Lolóme. (Still complete with A-bombs and missiles, the Secretary thought bleakly. Still looking for trouble. Nothing settled, nothing achieved. All that effort, all that sweat and strain and struggle, and . . . nothing.) It wouldn't hurt to mend a few fences and massage a few egos in a country that might conceivably give Sidi some trouble someday.

He found the ambassador much friendlier than he had anticipated, cordial and talkative, in fact, downright chatty, as he rattled on about how things were very chaotic in the embassy right now, they'd called in the decorators to do over all the rooms and in consequence most of the top embassy people were leaving tomorrow for a two-week stay at home. Lower-level staff would remain to handle business.

"Have a good vacation," Ray Stanley said, more out of courtesy than any real goodwill, so difficult was this erratic country for America to deal with. "Have a good vacation."

"We will, Mr. Secretary," the ambassador said, with a curious lightness of tone that Ray could not quite define. "We will."

And with a formality that seemed a little forced, added, "Thank you for calling," and rang off.

The Secretary of State looked thoughtful.

Forty years in diplomacy had made him conscious of tones and inflections and significant emphases.

The ambassador had sounded a little odd, not quite normal, perhaps even a bit nervous and excited, under the voluble flow.

Did it mean anything?

One never knew, these days.

Better safe than sorry.

He decided he would tell El and Hugo about it if he could remember to do so in the next two hectic, final days of closing out the office.

One didn't want to become as suspicious as they were.

But, still—

JULY 1993–SEPTEMBER 1994